THE GHOST

OF BIG TOM

THE
GHOST
OF BIG TOM
A Saga of an American Family

L. Wayne Daye

authorHOUSE®

AuthorHouse™
1663 Liberty Drive
Bloomington, IN 47403
www.authorhouse.com
Phone: 1-800-839-8640

Published by AuthorHouse   07/06/2012

ISBN: 978-1-4772-0392-7 (sc)
ISBN: 978-1-4772-0391-0 (e)

ACKNOWLEDGMENTS

I would be remised, if I did not acknowledge some of the people who helped make this book a reality. I wish to thank my sisters, Doris, Josephine and Janette who served as my legs, ears, and best critics for their invaluable input.

My sincere appreciation goes to Felicia Farrar my editor for her consult, observations, and literary support in this project.

I am particularly grateful to Kenny Jeffers, Terry Johnson, Michael Williams, and others in my group of readers who kept me going when I had burned all my energy.

And my deepest gratitude goes to Yasmin Fozard for her unflagging faith in me in all that I do.

Thanks
L. Wayne Daye

In 1821, Kali a young nineteen year old slave girl on the Hatley plantation in Monroe County, Louisiana gave birth to a male baby who she named Tom. The Monroe County plantation was separated from Jackson Mississippi by the great Mississippi River.

At age fourteen Tom was auctioned and sold for $500.00 to a slaver from Murfreesboro, North Carolina named General George Newsome who would use Tom as a breeder supplying slaves to be sold and to work plantations and farms across the south.

Tom in later years grew to be over six foot eight inches tall, weighing two hundred and sixty pounds and known through-out eastern North Carolina and Southern Virginia as "Big Tom" the breeder. Big Tom's legendary life as the breeder would be a ghost that would haunt his descendents for generations to come.

BOOK I

THE LEGACY

Monday, November 15, 1997

The morning was chilled—the kind of chill that warned all who hit the streets to keep their coats close by. The chilled air, autumn leaves and bright sun was characteristic of Durham for November for the last three or four years. There hadn't been but two heavy frosts and snow wasn't thought of. Many local citizens felt Durham and North Carolina in recent years had evolved into an area affected by some type of global warming trend, not typical of the cold weather of years gone by.

It was ten days before Thanksgiving and Durham could not be described as anything other than a cocktail of chilled mornings and warm evenings. The temperatures lurked in the low thirties in the early mornings and the high sixties by mid afternoon.

Cedric Newsome was home after a day's work at Computech. He worked as an accountant with the micro-computer firm for five years, since graduating from Virginia Union University. He'd played linebacker on the football team for his four years at Union. He was elected President of the student body his senior year, graduated with honors and recognized amongst "Who's Who" of graduating seniors nationally for the school year of 1992.

On this evening Cedric was taking advantage of the two hours of down-time before driving over to the Chapel Hill Street YMCA to play with Computech's basketball team in a city league game. As he lay motionless on the couch, he contemplated how he'd spend the week off during the up-coming holidays in Miami with Angela. He and Angela had been college sweethearts for their last three years at Union. With Angela on his mind, he didn't feel motivated to play in the tonight's game but knew the Computech team which was filled with computer geeks who could barely walk and dribble the ball simultaneously needed him. He knew his teammates would be severely handicapped without his six foot five inch body of muscles and athleticism. To his team's advantage, the chocolate skin covering his massive body seemingly held the other team's players, in awe which was another advantage for Computech. As Cedric lay still on the big blue couch, he rationalized and motivated himself thinking, "The game and workout will be good for me, plus, it'll help me to further my company politics. Boy, who'd ever thought my athletic career would have come to city league basketball and that I would be motivated by career aspiration and company politics." His mind drifted back to the upcoming Thanksgiving vacation in Miami with Angela. He and Angela grew apart in the five years since graduation, the distance between Durham and Charlotte where Angela worked and lived hadn't helped. Their relationship had been an off and on affair. The rift in their relationship arose out of Cedric's inability to commit and to cease playing the field. Cedric's inability to commit in the relationship was anchored in his concept of manhood. Manhood to Cedric meant bedding every woman who made herself available. The Miami vacation would be used by Cedric in an attempt to reconcile his differences with Angela, and to finally commit to the relationship totally.

Cedric was snapped out of his day dream of renewing his love for Angela by his grandmother's voice, "Pooh, what in the world are you doing? You are as quite as a church mouse. You better come on and get yourself some supper before it gets cold." Cedric smiled saying "I'll eat after my ball game, granny." Clara replied, "You know you don't like cold food. Well suit yourself but you needs to eat. Your Aunt Ida came by and left you a copy of some kinda manuscript, she's writing on Granddaddy Tom. She's trying to get it finished by family reunion time, in the early summer. Ida said to tell you to take time and read over and let her know what you think." Cedric looked at his grandmother whose smile brightened his day, as it had since he was a child of three on the first day she and his granddad had taken him into their home on Riverview Road in the Old Farms subdivision. They'd rescued him after his mother and dad had virtually deserted him in a rundown apartment in the Few Gardens Projects. His grandma Clara, as she was called by family and friends was a soft spoken, kind-hearted woman of medium height and a full body. A body earned from sampling her, own cooking. Her head of silver hair complemented her round tan face. Grandma Clara's face still revealed the obvious signs of the beauty she had in her younger years. The years had brought with them, character lines of age and wisdom.

Cedric began to browse through Aunt Ida's manuscript. Since childhood his Aunt Ida had been the family advocate and police for academic performance and success among he and his cousins. She had an easy going character but her academic expectation for Cedric and the others were clear and uncompromising. Aunt Ida's personality was that of the stereotypical teacher. She'd taught history at Durham's Hillside High School for over thirty years, she never married and lived in a modest brick home on Peko Street which neighbored North Carolina Central University.

Aunt Ida had seemingly dedicated her entire life to teaching, the church and her family. She was always neatly dressed in modest suits or dresses, with her hair freshly coifed. Her slim thin body and olive brown skin had held its youthful appearance over the years. Cedric had always admired Aunt Ida's lasting beauty and determination to cultivate the potential of the young minds of her students and family. At a young age Cedric felt Aunt Ida was too tough, pounding him each time his grades fail below her expectations. In later years as a student at Northern High School he grew to appreciate her care and demanding attitude in academics.

Cedric picked up the green binder which held the manuscript and began to flip the pages. He'd listened to the folklore and legend of this family's history as told by his granddad and others as far back as he could remember. Most of the stories were related to Granddaddy Tom, as he had been called by the family over the years. "Big Tom" was Cedric's ancestral grandfather of four generations past. Aunt Ida being an academic historian had begun to put the legendary tale in writing.

As Cedric read, it captivated him and he became lost in time. It was 1820 and Kimbo, a young Mende tribesman stood by his hut and farm, admiring the field he'd cleared to plant the year's rice crop. His young wife Kali worked by the door of the hut preparing corn meal to be used for their evening's meal. Kimbo looked forward and prayed for kindness in the weather, with soft rain and warm sun in measured amounts. If the locust and worms didn't arrive he thought, he would have a great harvest. The images of life were bright and peaceful.

The following morning as planned Kimbo rose early to join his father and three other Mende tribesmen for an early morning hunt for deer. It was on the road which lead to his Mende village, a morning's walk away where he and the other tribesmen were approached by a band of men. The men were not Mende-men, Mandingo or men he'd ever seen before. Their skin looked almost pinkish white, they dressed in clothes which covered their bodies from shoulder to foot, carried knives and weapons like Kimbo had never seen before, guns. Although, they were not Mende or Mandingo, one of the men who had a tan skin with curled hair spoke the Mende language. The group of strange looking men shared the company of other African tribesmen in scant clothing who appeared to be serving as guides. Kimbo didn't recognize the other tribesmen by their tribal markings or language.

The tan skinned man asked Kimbo and the Mende-men for directions and the location to the nearest trading post. As they attempted to respond, the group of strange looking men encircled them as to listen to the directions. Kimbo was suspicious of the strangers and watched them carefully. When Kimbo's father finished giving the directions, the tan skinned man turned as if to leave. It was then that Kimbo and his tribesmen were attacked and taken captive by the strangers. As Kimbo and his tribesmen were being attacked, they put forth a furious fight where Kimbo's father and another tribesman were killed by the unusual weapon their attackers carried. It was the first time Kimbo and the other tribesmen had seen a gun and the results of its deadly force. Kimbo and his reminding tribesmen were marched several miles through the jungle and chained to a tree where they spent the night. The strangers with their yellow hair and using a foreign language set around the fire eating and drinking unfamiliar looking water from round brown bottles. Kimbo noticed the food and drink appeared to cause the men to become loud and angry. Finally, one of the men who appeared short and fat with a brownish mane, carrying a long weapon, the type which had blown a whole in his father's chest killing him, came over and placed a chained collar around Kimbo's neck. He then moved to Ubai and Sefu chaining their necks also. He then looped the chains around their wrist and connected another around their waist, leaving about ten foot of chain hanging. Then the strange pale man tied the three of them to the tree again. Throughout the early night the men stood over them drinking, pointing, speaking a foreign language and laughing. Once the men settled for the night Kimbo moved and put his weight against the chain. The collar around his neck tightened and choked him with each attempt he made against the chain. The next morning Kimbo, Sefu and Ubai were lead through the jungle like animals on a leash. Each time they resisted, their captors pulled at the chains, choking them almost breathless.

By mid-morning of the following day Kimbo, Sefu and Ubai and their captors arrived at a hollow clearing camaflouged by trees located one hundred or so yards from a river. The men marched Kimbo, Sefu and Ubai to the slave holding camp which was an assembly of huge pens filled with other captives. The captives in the cages came from different areas of Africa and spoke different languages. Many were ordinary villagers but some were warriors and from high rank among their African tribesmen. The giant cages were crudely built but strong and sturdy. The outer walls were made of wooden boards supported by large wooden post driven deep into the ground. The bars only allowed enough space for the captives to stick their fingers through. The roof of the cages was made of heavy planks and each one had a single door chained and padlocked. The campground was patrolled by the white men who carried large machetes and guns. Each time the white men came close to Kimbo he could taste their blood and thought of how easy it would be to kill each of them, if only he could free himself. His anger and contempt caused his blood to boil and pulse to throb.

As Kimbo looked around he counted close to three hundred men and boys in cages like himself. On the other side of the hollow clearing separated by several rows of trees, women were held in the same fashion. Each day, ten or fifteen more slave captives were caged. Each captive slave was feed a bowl of rice, a small fish or dried beef and defecated in a hole dug in the corner of the cage. The stench and cries of the captive slaves were overwhelming for Kimbo. It served to fuel his anger and determination to avenge his capture by taking the lives of his white captives at first chance.

On the second day, Kimbo realized that many of the men and boys in the cages were Mende and from his tribe and the white men had raided his entire village. Kimbo became concerned for the safety of the women and children of his village, not knowing that his young wife Kali and his unborn son that she carried inside her were caged across the hollow with many other women and young girls.

There were Mandingo, Mende, Yorubos, Iboe, Ashuntis and others from tribes that Kimbo hadn't seen or knew. As their stories circulated most had been surprised and taken in their villages or near, by areas by their white captors. The African captives were beaten, bound hand and feet like wild animals. Kimbo's prayer that a band of warriors from his village arriving, to save him finally vanished. All the young warriors from his village had been killed or captured. They hadn't stood a chance fighting against men with guns.

Almost every day at the campground, the white slavers and seamen came by peering into the cages and at times taking out certain tribesmen for a closer observation. Each time Kimbo was taken out for inspection his high spirited nature and warlike attitude lead to a struggle. The white men quickly subdued him by tightening the collar around his neck until he fell to the ground unconscious. The white men marched around Kimbo and the others captives feeling their arms, buttocks, and legs, and stopping to examine their teeth.

After sixty seven nights according to Kimbo's count, the white men and their African guides came with guns and clubs. They began taking the captives from the cages. The captives were lined up, bound by their ankles and hands with a chain running between each captive linking them together. They were beaten for the least amount resistance and lead to the river, heading for the Atlantic. Kimbo and the other tribesmen had never seen the ocean or any sea vessel. Each captive was branded with a hot iron on the breast, imprinting the mark of Portugal the country of origin of the captain and his crew. They were then loaded onto boats, twenty tribesmen to a boat, bound together. Four of their captors pulled the oars, while another stood holding a gun.

Kimbo and the other tribesmen knew the boat was carrying them to an unknown destination. As the tribesmen became fearful, excited and desperate to abandon the boat, one of their captors stood and whipped the entire crew of bound captives with his rawhide whip. Kimbo observed the tribesmen ahead and behind him yelling and rocking their boats also, but were silenced by the captors and their whips. Within an hour Kimbo and all the slave captives were loaded onto a huge ship with a British flag flying high called the Louisiana. The Louisiana was a sea vessel larger than Kimbo could have imagined.

Later Kimbo sat on the deck of the Louisiana while he ate a bowl of rice and drank water from a cup. Kimbo had struggle with the white men each time he was brought to the deck for his food and exercise rotation. The White men would become winded from exhaustion after their rumble with Kimbo.

On one warm and sunny morning after being at sea for six days and finishing his bowl of rice, Kimbo noticed the yellowed haired captain with a whip in hand observing him. The captain pointed and ordered "bring him to me." Two of the captains African crewmen came over to Kimbo and wrestled him to the deck into submission. They grabbed his arms and feet, dragging him across the deck in front of the captain. One of the African crewmen held his machete against Kimbo's throat to keep him under control. The yellow haired captain stood over Kimbo speaking loud enough to draw the attention of the other tribesmen. "I know you and the rest of you niggas don't understand what I'm saying but ya'lla understand this heh whip." Looking at Kimbo the captain then said, "yous a tough one, I like your spunk but I'm the boss on this heh rig." The captain drew back and swung his whip, striking Kimbo across his back. The whip slashed

Kimbo's skin as if he'd been cut with a knife. Another strike, then another until the captain had landed thirty lashes onto Kimbo's now bloody back. Kimbo withstood the entire whipping while only making moans and groans which had the sound of anger rather than pain. The captain held his whip and observed Kimbo's anguish while shaking his head in disbelief. He's a high spirited nigga, we gotta feed him well, dem qualities is highly marketable, he'll bring top dollar on auction day." One of the sailors was then instructed to wash the blood from Kimbo's back and cover it with a salve. Kimbo was then taken back into the belly of the ship and chained neck and leg between the decks with only eighteen inches of space, not enough to turn around, immovable alongside the other tribesmen. Until the next day Kimbo would lay in the dark unable to move while breathing the rancid air which circulated through the aisles.

The voyage across the Atlantic seemed to take forever. The captain and his crew smoked their pipes, drank rum, used their whips at will and satisfied their sexual desires through raping the female captives. The white men viewed their African captives as animals, ignorant godless creatures, a lower breed of human beings and closer to the monkeys in the trees than man. The white men failed to realize the tribesmen were humans who came from a great heritage and culture. Dehumanizing their captives justified the victimization of the African tribesmen and soothed their conscious.

The captain constantly warned his crew not to damage his human cargo. The ship's crew at time seemingly forgot the captives were merchandise which was to be sold to the highest buyer. Some of the crew if not controlled would whip the captives until the life had nearly vanished from their bodies. The captain being a businessman kept a watchful eye on his cargo, making sure no . . . one damaged his goods.

Meanwhile, Kali never knew what happened to Kimbo the morning of his hunt for deer. She had awakened that morning to find him gone to never return. During the middle of the afternoon while she worked in the small garden behind the hut she was astounded by unfamiliar loud cracking sounds. The sounds were almost like the cracking of thunder. Then she heard the screams and cries of the women and children. Kali and the others in the village were being attacked by the white men and their African troop. The entire village was raided, burned and ran-over by the assault. All the tribe's people who weren't killed or escaped to the brush were taken captive. Kali and the others were chained and marched through the jungle to the slave campground, just as Kimbo had been earlier. They were chained, caged, branded and loaded onto the Louisiana.

It was not until a week later that Kimbo got word that his wife Kali was also chained in the belly of the ship. The news of Kali's capture and kidnapping encouraged Kimbo to gain his freedom, so that he could rescue Kali. Kimbo thought of plan after plan as he laid the belly of the Louisiana. He attempted to discuss the idea of escaping with the other tribesmen. Kimbo found difficulty communicating with other tribesmen who spoke languages other than the Mende language. Beyond the language barrier, the tribesmen in general were confused, angry and afraid. Inside he knew escaping was impossible.

Kali was spared the humiliation and victimization of being raped, only because of her pregnancy. By the time the Louisiana sailed Kali showed the physical signs of carrying a child. The captain being ultimately motivated by profit ordered his crew of rapist not to lay a hand on any women who carried a child. The captain's care for the pregnant women wasn't out of concern for humanity or any reverence for the women's health but he realized the increased dollar value of any female slave carrying a child. The slave woman with child brought a higher price.

As Cedric read his Aunt Ida's narrative, the legend was told that after three months the Louisiana docked in a harbor in the Caribbean's on the Island of Jamaica.

The Louisiana with its human cargo had made it to a point of safety. The sky was blue, the water appeared crystal clear and the sun beamed over the sand. The small town annexing the harbor was alive with people moving throughout the marketplace. In the belly of the ship Kimbo and the others knew the ship had docked. All the captives below became anxious not knowing what was in store for them next. Jamaica was the location where in days the cargo would be sold to businessmen dealing in slave trading. They would buy in bulk, taking anywhere between twenty-five and fifty slaves at a time. Then each slaver would take his personal cargo by charter to settlements and towns across the Caribbean's where he would resale them for two or three times what he'd paid.

One day after the Lousianne docked the captain and his crew led their captives off the ship up the beach to a holding area of pens with bars. The cages were rectangular shaped with wooden bars that reached fifteen or so feet from the ground. The roofs were covered with a mesh wire supported by planks. Each pen held up to three to five hundred men at any given time. Kali and the other women and children captives were held in a smaller pen with as few as one hundred. In front of the pen was a single cage where the slaves were examined and observed. In front of the pen was a platform which served as an auction block.

Kimbo as well as the other men had been provided with burlap type pants only. They wore no shoes or shirts. The captives were mostly naked. They were still guarded by white men with clubs and guns.

Kimbo, Ubai and Sefu stood next to one another waiting for one day, then two with anticipation of their day on the auction block. As they ate their meal of a single yam, a fish and water they whispered a plan of escape. They had no idea where they were but knew the small harbor town had an outlaying jungle. Perhaps, the jungle would be a place of escape from the white men if only they could make it out of the pen. Kimbo knew Kali was being held in a different part of the campground with the other women. If he could escape he would return and rescue her. But for now he had no way out. Kimbo's body felt strong and his anger overwhelming. If only he could rip the shackles from his body and run free. Kimbo only shared his plan with Ubai and Sefu, there were no others he could communicate with or trust. He knew that he, Ubai and Sefu could only get out the pen through the door which was patrolled by the white men with guns.

One the third day in the pens Kimbo, Ubai, and Sefu noticed a man who appeared to be an African tribesmen who was working outside the pens, supposedly delivering water and supplies to the white men patrolling the pens. As the tribesmen bowed with submission at each of the white men demands, the tribesman made eye contact with men in the pens. The white men soon dismissed the tribesmen as being a harmless servant. As the tribesmen passed the pen filled with African captives he repeatedly murmured, "maroon, tonight." The tribesmen looked into Kimbo's eyes and with his finger motioned the cutting of the throat while softly saying "white men." Kimbo didn't understand the language of the tribesmen but felt a connection as he and the tribesmen's eyes locked. He knew in his soul that something was planned.

The tribesman who posed as a servant was a messenger sent by the maroons. The maroons were former African slaves who had escaped from the plantations and slave pens, who took refuge in the mountains of Jamaica. The word maroon derived from the Spanish word "Cimaroon" meaning untamable, wild, and unruly. The maroons who escaped to the wild mountain terrain of Jamaica were seen as maroons because they refused to submit to the life of a slave. The maroons had a commitment to liberty or death but not slavery. The mountain terrain provided the ideal refuge for the runaway slaves. The maroons had been scattered throughout the mountains and swamps for over a hundred years and their descendants remained committed to wrecking havoc on the plantations which held slaves. They were a well organized and disciplined fighting force of gorilla warriors. They'd raided the townships over the years with recurrent frequency.

The servant who visited Kimbo and the other tribesmen was a part of a carefully planned operation focused on an upcoming attack on the slave holding pens. The maroons would attack the site, free as many captives as possible, replenish their food, ammunition, supplies and kill as many white men as need be.

On that up-coming evening the maroons who were nested high in the mountains began to make their way down to the harbor. They were armed with antiquated weapons but their tactics, camouflaged bodies and gorilla warring style would compensate. Meanwhile, Kimbo and the other captive tribesmen rested in the holding pens awaiting their fate. Then right after mid-night fifty of the maroon warriors began to creep into the camp site and ambush the slave holders as they stood watch over the camp. The maroons were as silent as the night. The white men were killed, robbed of their weapons and keys to the pens. The maroons went to each pen unlocking the gates. They motioned for the caged tribesmen to exit the cages and to follow them. Many of the caged tribesmen had submitted to their capture and the consequence of being property commanded by the white men and refused to leave the pens. Their refusal was perhaps, out of fear of recapture, not knowing the maroons who came to rescue them and what the maroons had in store for them ahead. As the maroons came to Kimbo, Ubai, and Sefu's pen with the keys for the gate and shackles, all three of them sprang to their feet. Kimbo, Ubai, and Sefu along with a hundred or so of the other captives willingly vanished into the brushed jungle as though they had never been present. They were now soldiers in the maroon gorilla army.

The next strategized and silent attack took place in the harbor abroad the Louisiana and the St. Lucia the only other ship docked alongside the Louisiana. The maroons searched the ship for supplies. Kimbo, Ubai, and Sefu and other newly freed captives were ushered along the shore by the brush and expected to wait in silence as the maroons boarded the ship and carried out their mission. As the maroons moved onto the two ships in the harbor with fifty warriors boarding each ship, Kimbo's blood began to boil. His mind return to his capture in Mende-land, the murder of his father at the hands of the white men, the whippings he'd received by the captain and his wife Kali who was still held captive. Kimbo couldn't contain his rage and warring spirit. He spoke to Ubai telling him that he had to join the maroons on the ship. Ubai tried to discourage Kimbo but knew there was nothing that could stop him. Kimbo tasted the blood of revenge.

Kimbo made his way to the Louisiana and joined the maroons. The maroons were in position aboard both vessels. They'd boarded without being noticed by the crew of sailors who patrolled the ship and its supplies. The ship's crew had not received word of the escape at the holding pens. Some were relaxed, others intoxicated and others asleep without the thought of a surprise attack. The squad leader of the maroons named Cujo was off-set by Kimbo's surprised and unwarranted presence aboard the Louisiana. Cujo looked into Kimbo's eyes, and scanned his body from head to toe and without a word and passed Kimbo a stone spear while motioning him to join the others.

Kimbo headed directly to the belly of the ship to make sure his wife Kali and the others hadn't been left aboard the ship. Upon reaching the belly of the ship and finding it empty, Kimbo knew for sure that Kali was in one of the pens off shore with the women and children. He planned to return to the holding pens for her at the first opportunity. The darkness in the belly of the ship was complete. Kimbo moved with caution, he didn't want to make a sound as he crepe across the squeaking deck that would alert any of the ship's crew that hadn't already been overtaken by the maroons. He made it to the far side of the ship where the supplies were stored. He could smell the aroma of the salt, spices and dried meat. He came upon a huge wooden crate. He slide the lid open and found it filled with razor shape machetes with two foot blades. Kimbo armed himself with two of the machetes, leaving the spear Cujo had given him behind. He quickly searched and inventoried the supplies he'd found. The area was filled with cloth, food, machetes, spices, dried meat and rum.

Kimbo then began his walk to the deck of the ship. He could hear screams of pain coming from the sailors as the maroons seized their vessel and took their lives. As Kimbo climbed to the second tier of the ship, he could hear the sound of footsteps, coming in his direction, down the aisle. Kimbo could barely see the two men who were attempting to hide from the maroons. As he drew near he recognized the stench of the rum and the distinct odor of the yellow haired captain who was accompanied by one of his crewmen. At that moment a bright flash of lightening cracked and illuminated the sky. The flash of light penetrated the doorway of the second tier long enough for the captain and his crewmen to recognize the solemn face of Kimbo. The captain cried out, "Jesus Christ dat niggas loose." The captain armed with a machete and the crewmen with a pistol turned, positioning themselves for the ensuring battle with Kimbo. The crewmen reached for his pistol but the captain grabbed his hand warning "the shot will bring the other heathens, we want have a chance." The crewmen and the captain both drew their machetes.

Kimbo with a sarcastic smile drew both his razor sharp machetes and moved forward eyeing the two men. Kimbo let out a cry and dove at the crewmen, severing the lower portion of the crewmen's arm with the first blow. The crewmen let out a shrieking howl and fell to the side of the wall. The yellow haired captain ran, scrambling to get away. Kimbo drew his machete back and plunged it into the crewmen stomach. The crewmen fell to the deck, his blood streamed from his body. Kimbo then used a powerful blow and beheaded his onetime captor. The yellow haired captain now paralyzed with fear pleaded for his life forgetting he and Kimbo didn't speak a common language. The only communication between Kimbo and the captain was channeled through body language. The captain knew death was certain. Kimbo stood over the captain with the resolve of death on his face. Kimbo raised his machete and plunged it into the captain's belly and chest. He pulled the machete from the captain's stomach and swung down hard, cutting the captain's head from his body.

Kimbo returned to the deck of the ship to join the maroons, his new comrades. The maroons had completely over taken the vessel. The crewmen who hadn't been killed had abandoned the vessel, running for safety. The maroon warriors were looting the ship for its valuables and supplies. Kimbo found Ubai and Sefu had joined the maroons as they unloaded the valuables from the vessel. Kimbo spoke to Ubai disclosing what had occurred in the belly of the vessel. Kimbo had killed animals during his years of hunting with his father and other tribesmen but he'd never killed another man until that day. Kimbo had known he either kill or be killed. He was faced with men who had captured, kidnapped and whipped him as a show of control and on that night, in the belly of the ship, was ready to take his life. Kimbo felt no remorse!

Kimbo watched as the maroons robbed the ship. He could tell the moroons were well trained, experienced and rehearsed. Kimbo motioned to the maroon party leader, Cujo. Cujo was a tall muscular warrior in his mid-twenties had been captured five years earlier in the Congo. Cujo wore his hair in "locks" and was armed with a mighty sword and a pistol. Cujo approached Kimbo with an uncertainty. The two warriors faced each other able to communicate without one word being spoken. Their stories were written in their eyes and across their faces. Their souls and war-like spirits had bonded them. Both men chose death over slavery. Kimbo pulled both his razor sharp machetes and motioned to the belly of the ship. Kimbo then used his hands to act as if he was eating food while again pointing to the belly of the ship. Cujo signaled for the maroon warriors to enter the belly of the ship. The warriors found the bulk of the ship's supplies in the belly of the ship and quickly unloaded them into the forest where they would be hauled in the mountains.

Kimbo had scored points with Cujo. Cujo knew he had met another strong warrior with a great resolve to fight against the capture and enslavement of African people. Cujo, Kimbo and the other warriors disappeared into the forest. By the time the white men had recovered and organized themselves from the attack on the slave pens and the raid on the ships in the harbor, the maroons were far away.

As Kimbo, Ubai and Sefu traveled with the maroons into the blue mountainous jungle, they began to feel safe although they were in a new land amongst unfamiliar tribesmen from many African tribes. The closer Kimbo and the maroons came to the maroon's fortress, the more evident were the security look-outs, traps and warrior patrols. Once arriving at the fortress, Kimbo as well as Ubai, and Sefu were stunned. There in the high nested mountains were a well organized village with women, children, goats, chickens and life without an apparent threat. Behind the thatched roof living quarters were small gardens that were tended by the women and children. Kimbo felt a rush of emotions as he observed the goings and comings of the maroons in the village. He felt as if he was almost back in Mende-land.

It had taken almost a day and a half to reach the village from the harbor. The men unloaded the supplies from the crates, examined each weapon and stored all the food that wasn't distributed among the villagers. For the next several days the maroons in small groups traveled down the mountain for the remaining war booty. They traveled at night with extreme caution, knowing the white men would be on the lookout for their return.

Although, Kimbo didn't speak a common language with any of the maroons, he made it known through his actions that he intended to join them on their journey back down the mountain. Kimbo had one more battle he had to face. He had to rescue his wife, Kali. Armed with his two razor sharp machetes he traveled down the mountain toward the harbor. He had planned the rescue attempt with thoughtfulness. He didn't know what was ahead but knew there would be white men who patrolled the pens. He'd wait until early morning, sneak quietly into the camp of cages, overtake the patrolmen and free Kali. Once the maroons reached the edge of the brush by the port town and harbor, Kimbo began his walk to the campground of cages. As he approached he continued to veil himself in the dark shadow of the brush. He could see several white men on patrol. With a closer look, he counted three men by the pen which he thought held Kali. Kimbo crept closer and closer. He was now within yards of the pen. He could hear the chatter of the men talking, and smell the rum the white men passed among themselves as well as the stench from the waste inside the pen. Kimbo took deep breaths as he stalked and waited for the right opportunity for his attack. He wanted to catch the men in single form, one at a time. Finally, one of the men came toward the brush, the patrolman in an intoxicated state stopped to urinate by the edge of the brush. The others paid him no attention. At that moment, Kimbo approached the drunken patrolman from behind and slit his throat without a sound coming from the now dead patrolman mouth. Kimbo circled and moved around the edge of the camp. The two remaining patrolmen began to call for their missing comrades. One of the other patrolmen walked out of the camp in search of his missing friend, leaving the camp with only one half drunken patrolmen. Kimbo eased into the camp with weapons drawn and pounced upon the lone patrolmen, killing him with ease. Kimbo searched the fallen patrolmen for the key to the padlock which held the gate closed to the pens. As he found the keys and turned toward the pens the last patrolmen ran into the camp with his pistol drawn. Kimbo charged the patrolmen, unarming him of his pistol. Kimbo and the patrolman became engaged in a fierce fight of human will, strength and determination. Kimbo and his foe fought without weapons as the women in the pen watched. Kimbo's strength and youthfulness was too mighty for the patrolman to overcome. Kimbo found his powerful arms locked around the patrolman's neck and with at twist of his entire body broke his challenger's neck, killing him.

Kimbo calmed his spirit, knowing it was critical to think clearly. He noticed that only a fraction of the women that once filled the pen remained. Kimbo opened the heavy wooden door. He called out Kali's name. He saw women of all ages, sizes and from many tribes but Kali was nowhere to be found. Kimbo was approached by a young Mende girl who gave him the bad news. The young girl disclosed that Kali and twenty-five other women had been taken away on the great vessel by white men. The news of Kali being shipped away caused Kimbo's heart to sink. He felt helpless, a great loss, anger and a sense of undying revenge. Kimbo retreated to the mountainous brush taking fifteen of the women with him. He would live his life out in the blue mountains of Jamaica as a maroon warrior leading more than one hundred raids, freeing slaves.

It was now approaching eight months since the Mende village had been raided, a day Kali would never forget. The cries of the women, children and the murder of the tribesmen who fought with the white men were as fresh as the day it occurred. Kali was now aboard another great vessel named the Delaware, chained without mobility in route to America. Her days and nights were filled with the torment of existing in the belly of the vessel, hunger, uncertainty and extreme fear. Kali and the other women were members of tribes-people from across Africa, who would become slaves on southern plantations in America. Kali had never been outside her village until the day she was captured and kidnapped. As she lay in the belly of the vessel she could feel her unborn child growing inside her. She looked forward to being taken out each day for exercise and food. Although the bowl of rice and fish was usually rancid and foul, she forced all of it down with water each day, feeding herself and her unborn child. After an hour she'd be lead back into the belly of the vessel and chained until the next day. It took two months before her journey ended. Sometime in late September of 1822 Kali and the other tribes-people arrived in New Orleans.

On the second day after docking in New Orleans, Kali and the others were marched ashore. The men were shackled ankle and wrist and bound by a long heavy chain that ran down the center of the entire group. The huge bull chain held the men in single file. Kali and the women marched behind the men in similar fashion. The march to the market house was a daily occurrence until all the captives were auctioned off to slavers who'd come from across the south, looking for prime stock. The African tribes-people were auctioned and sold the same as other livestock. Each day the market house drew a great crowd of traders, buyers, and onlookers. Spectators walked by and peered into the pens which held the African tribes-people who were on display. The onlookers gawked, laughed and at times seemed amazed with the mostly naked Africans. The one time proud Africans were reduced to the status of animals by the slavers. Kali as well as the others had become merchandise in the Euro-American socio-economic system of slavery. Their enslavement would join them with other African slaves held hostage in America. The Slave system in America was not like any before it. The decision to invade Africa and capture, kidnap and enslave its citizens was based on skin color. All of mankind, formal religions and nations collectively moved against and supported the enslavement of African blacks. Meanwhile, the world was espousing the concepts of freedom, liberty and equality for all of mankind. The wealth produced by the slave trade drew in more and more nations.

Each day, until every captive was auctioned into slavery, Kali and the others were held in pens and booths. When the slavers were ready, they were brought out onto the large platform where buyers examined every part of every one of them. The men and women all stood together stark naked. Kali and the other women were valued least for their laboring qualities but mostly for the qualities which made them a "broad mare." The buyers circled each woman examining her breast, hips, robustness and potential to breed, the same as with horses and mules.

By the end of the third day Kali, three other women and six men had been auctioned and sold to a slaver name Sherman Hatley. Hatley owned a large tract of land in Monroe County Louisiana. His Monroe

County plantation was separated from Jackson, Mississippi by the great Mississippi River. Hatley was a man in his late forties, blond headed, with a thick mustache, medium height and pudgy. His face was red, from his daily use of whisky as a social lubricant and nerve enhancer. He examined the tribesmen slapping their butts, feeling their arm muscles, eying their teeth and genitals. When approaching the women he starred at each one with a sexual mischievousness. He walked over to Kali close enough for Kali to smell the rum on his breath and the tobacco in his pipe. Hatley looked into Kali's eyes, obviously noticing her beauty. His eyes then traced down to her breast and full stomach where she carried her unborn child inside. While examining her back and forth, Hatley talked of his possible use for Kali as a field hand or a breeder depending on how she faired after dropping her child. Hatley also knew he was purchasing two slaves for the price of one. By the end of the day Hatley had purchased Kali for five hundred dollars.

Kali and the other nine tribes-people Hatley purchased were chained and loaded onto a wagon. The wagon was drawn by two white horses which headed for a barge on the shoulders of the Mississippi River. The one time citizens of Africa and now slaves were walked onto the barge, chained and feed a bowl of rice and beans. Kali and the other slaves spent the night chained to the wall of the barge. Early the next morning the barge moved down the Mississippi. Once away from the site of New Orleans the slaves were unchained one at a time and allowed to walk free. Although, the chains were off, Hatley and the crewmen who carried whips and guns watched closely. By early afternoon the barge docked. Hatley summoned all his newly acquired stock off the boat. One by one the slaves unboarded the barge onto the ground. Under their feet was the dirt they were brought to till and would be thrown in their faces upon death. Hatley was greeted by a young slave who drove a wagon drawn by a team of fine horses. The slave who drove the wagon greeted Hatley with smiles and ran to complete each of Hatley's commands. Kali observed the slave addressed Hatley as "Massa Hatley" and Hatley called the slave Amos. Amos forcefully roped tied each of the women slaves and shoved them toward the wagon. Then he chained the men arm to waist to the wagon. Once the women were loaded and the men pulled along from behind, the wagon headed for the Hatley plantation. The plantation was more than a day's ride. The women aboard the wagon and the men pulled along the rough roads barefooted all traveled with fear in their hearts. Late in the night the wagon came to a halt. They camped and rested until early morning. Amos in Kali's eyes was the most strange and different looking black man she'd ever seen. Amos did not have the blackness of skin or the profound African physical traits of the tribesmen of the Mende or Mandingo. As she observed him build the campfire, she wondered how he'd become to have such an appearance. Amos under Hatley's command cooked beans and dried beef over the campfire. He served his master until he couldn't eat anymore and rationed Kali and the other slaves enough to satisfy their hunger.

By mid-morning the next day the wagon with the newly purchased slaves arrived on the outskirts of the Hatley plantation. As Kali sat in the wagon, she was intrigued with the large manicured fields of cotton, corn and peanuts. The fields were being tended by other blacks who appeared similar to the tribesmen from Africa. The men commanded teams of mules and horses as they tilled the fields. There were women and younger slaves in the fields walking and working behind the men with long handle hoes chopping grass. Kali noticed that some of the slaves were as black as the tribesmen of Africa but others were extremely lighter. As the wagon drew closer to the center of the plantation she saw a large painted house which faced the road. The surroundings were well kept and clean. Behind the big house was a row of cabins, some made of logs and others of planks. A wagon road ran from the back of the main house down in front of the row of cabins. As Kali looked about she saw small children, black and white playing in the huge backyard. To the back of the cabin were huge stables for the horses and mules. There were storage houses for the feed. Kali as well as the other new slaves were in awe of what they saw. Amos drove the wagon to the huge horse stable and stopped. The house slaves, the children and a number of field slaves came to observe the new arrivals. The Hatley's hadn't brought slaves in over twenty-five years. Kali and the others were looked upon as pure African stock. The other slaves owned by the Hatley's, had no direct experience with Africa or the voyage across the Atlantic. The Hatley slaves had been breed, born and raised in Louisiana on the Hatley plantation. They had never known freedom. Kali would come to realize there was a major difference between the Africans who had newly arrived and the plantation slaves.

Because Kali was carrying a child, her youthfulness and stunning beauty, Mrs. Hatley chose her to work in the main house, at least until she bore her child.

The Hatley's were considered by the slaves to be kind and had come to be loved for their semi-human treatment toward the slaves. Two mulatto women and Amos the driver had lived in close association with the Hatley's since birth. Massa Hatley was known to spare the whip, only using it in extreme cases. The slave children played with the Hatley children as they grew-up together. Young Missy Hatley had great affection for her childhood playmates and nanny.

Kali and the new arrivals were faced with the transition from being once free citizens of Africa to a person owned by another, with no rights and who worked without pay. The socio-economic slave system that held Kali wasn't based on a personal indebtness. The slave could not earn his freedom. It was a permanent status for the slave's entire life.

The other Hatley slaves along with the slave driver would teach Kali and the others how to become slaves. It would be achieved through a process of psychological stripping, retraining and physical intimidation. Kali and the other slaves didn't experience the customary stop-over in the West Indies at the slave breaking camps, camps where experts in prescriptive conditioning of slaves whipped, tormented and killed rebellious tribesmen in an effort to break their spirit into submission to a sub-human status. Kali and the other new slaves would be taught their place. Massa Hatley barely had to say a word. The slaves he'd owned from one generation to the next were well indoctrinated as slaves and most didn't consider life in any other fashion. The Hatley's and their slaves adjusted Kali's name to Callie and pronounced it in their extreme southern vernacular. The Hatley slaves like most other slaves knew the boundaries, acceptable behavior and consequences for non-conformance. Kali was mostly mentored, taught the English dialect and nurtured into becoming a slave by the two mulatto women house slaves. Kali was taught and learned to clean, cook, nurse the children and communicate with the Hatleys in the required submissive style in a short time. She was stripped of her name, language, religion and all other cultural identity. Kali struggled with her inferior status but through fear of the consequences of the whip, like others before her, she kept her anguish inside. The other Hatley slaves facilitated the process by advocating the truths of the world as seen from the eyes of the Hatleys. Kali's exposure to the intense psychological retraining combined with her helplessness caused her to become a totally dependent individual and a good slave. The slavers across America had created a socialization process which was built on fear, distrust and envy for control purposes. The slavers pitched the old against the young and the dark skin against the fair skinned. No matter how loyal the slaves were to their masters, a sense of distrust existed concerning the black slaves. The slaves were taught to only love, respect and trust whites.

In the third month after arriving on the Hatley plantation, Kali gave birth to the child she'd carried across the Atlantic. Missy Charlotte Hatley named the child Thomas. Little Thomas was robust and a healthy baby. Each time Kali looked at Thomas she saw an exact copy of his father Kimbo. Thomas unlike the majority of the slaves on the Hatley plantation was as black as the night and extremely larger than the other children. His presence caused Kali to grieve the lost of Kimbo and the simple life she'd known in Mend-land.

Thomas soon became known by the slaves and Hatleys as Big Tom. He acquired that name from Massa Hatley by the age of eight. By that time of around eight or nine years old Big Tom like the other boys had assigned chores. Each day he chopped wood, carried water from the well and collected eggs from the chicken houses. In his spare time he enjoyed playing with other boys on the plantation and fishing in the nearby river. He was taught to ride and handle horses by Massa Hatley. Massa Hatley had a special liking toward Tom. In time Tom rode horses with mastery. Massa Hatley owned fine horses. He attended local races and betted with the eagerness of a professional sportsmen. The local races were held on Saturdays on different plantations. Slavers would come from miles around with their prize horses and skilled riders. Amos whom Massa Hatley had a brotherly affection rode the Hatley horses with skill. He was the best rider across four countries. Massa Hatley's affection for Amos was by-way of Amos's mother, who nursed him as a child. Hatley often spoke of his fond memories and childhood when Miss Mammie nursed and cared for him. Uncle Mathew, as Hatley called him was Mammie's husband and Amos's father. Uncle Mathew was the man who'd taught Massa Hatley how to hunt big game, fish and ride horses. Hatley grew into manhood with a great affection for Amos's parents, at times greater than the affection for his own mother and father. On the day that Amos's mother died, Hatley buried her, with respect, alongside his own mother. Massa Hatley promised Miss

Mammie on her dying bed that he would look after Amos and provide him a home on the plantation for the duration of his life. He assured Miss Mammie that Amos would always be protected from being sold. Amos in turn guarded Hatley property and livestock as if it was his own.

In time Kali won the affection of Mrs. Hatley and Missy Hatley. They convinced Massa Hatley to provide Kali and Thomas a room in the main house so that she could be accessible to them. They passed on their unwanted and old clothing to Kali and on occasions brought her fineries from shops in New Orleans. Kali along with Tom ate the same food she prepared for the Hatleys. Kali and Tom were looked upon with deep affection by the Hatleys.

Meanwhile, Amos began to desire Kali's company and was trying to gain her attention and affection. At opportune times, he'd invite Kali and Tom to his cabin to share meals with him. Kali wasn't attracted to Amos. Being breed and as a slave he was completely different than Kimbo, the independent, free spirited warrior, Kali's only measure of a man. Amos and Kali's relationship became one where Amos felt love and Kali settled for the convenience of his company. The fact the Hatleys had chosen both Amos and Kali to be the benefactors of their affection threw them into one another's sphere.

After Amos had serenaded Kali for two years, to no avail, he spoke to Massa Hatley concerning his interest in Kali and his desire for her to become his wife. As was the custom and practice on many plantations across the antebellum south, Massa Hatley decided that Kali would become Amos's wife. Massa Hatley announced his decision to Kali and Amos, as if Amos didn't have any say so in the matter. Kali was praised and congratulated by the other slaves and the two Hatley women. Missy Hatley took it upon herself to coach Kali and to continuously tell her how lucky she was to receive Amos as a husband. Missy Hatley assumed the role of wedding planner. It would be a grand affair. Kali didn't love Amos with the passion of a wife. But, she accepted the situation and moved forward as had been planned. In her mind she knew marrying Amos would secure her and young Tom's lives on the plantation. Kali followed Missy Hatley's every detail as her wedding day approached.

On July 4th, 1826 Amos and Kali were married in the grand-room of the Hatley's main house. Every slave on the plantation along with the Hatley's attended and watched as Amos and Kali jumped the broom. The wedding was held in the Hatley's grand-room with the Episcopal rector of the white parish performing the ceremony. The Negro slaves were in total adoration. The guest, who were all slaves except for the Hatley's, were seated around the grand room in the mansion. The wedding cake had been baked, by the sister of Mrs. Hatley. During the ceremony, Massa Hatley stood by Amos and invariably laid his hand on his shoulder, as a show of love and support.

The wedding and its pomp was atypical of marriage ceremonies of slaves from far around. The marriage and wedding feasts of slaves usually synthesized African form. Ordinarily, the impoverished slaves performed their weddings among themselves with very little ceremony. The man usually made the bride a gift which upon her acceptance became his wife.

After the wedding, Kali with her son Tom moved into Amos's cabin. Weeks prior to the wedding Massa Hatley commissioned the slave craftsmen to remodel Amos's cabin. The two room cabin was turned into a five room house with a porch that was surrounded by flowers and a walk-way. Amos was happier than ever in his life and Kali was content with her situation.

By age twelve, Big Tom had two sisters and one brother. Big Tom and Amos had failed to develop a harmonious relationship. They were extremely estranged from one another. The atmosphere in the cabin was tense. Big Tom at this time was as large as the average man, being six foot tall and weighting nearly two hundred pounds. Big Tom, as he was now exclusively referred, was high spirited, head strong and could work alongside any man on the plantation. Being Kali's son and Amos's step-child allowed him privileges beyond the other boys, and most of his testy behaviors was excused.

Over the years Kali had relived the stories of the Mende people with Big Tom and spoke of his father Kimbo with high regard. Although, Big Tom's feet had never touched the soil of Africa, he appeared to have been possessed with the spirit of the Mende tribesmen. For some unknown reason Big Tom didn't succumb to the indoctrination of the status ascribed to the slave and carried himself with an air of pride and independent thought.

By age fourteen, Big Tom totally disregarded Amos as the man of the house. Big Tom challenged Amos at will and ignored all of Amos's attempts to father him. Big Tom was now over six foot five inches tall and well over two hundred pounds and high spirited. This caused Amos to feel threatened. Amos was physically intimidated and felt less than the man in his own home. Kali found herself caught between her son, the Mende-man, and her husband the submissive slave. She was becoming afraid that Massa Hatley would be called in to remedy the problem. Kali attempted to talk Big Tom's spirit down, warn him of his actions as well as assured Amos that he'd settle down. But inside she knew Big Tom identified himself with the stories of the Mende warriors of Africa. She prayed for Allah to protect his life.

Amos decided that solving the problem with Big Tom and recapturing his rightful position in his home was a must. Amos had his fill of Big Tom and the unrest which came with him. He knew that Kali would never agree to Tom being housed on slave row or any suggestion which would alienate him from the family. Amos felt resentful toward Kali for showing what he saw as favoritism when it came to Tom and the other children. It was like Big Tom represented Kali's first love, Kimbo. The idea of Kali re-living her love for Kimbo through her son caused Amos to become vengeful. Amos began to plot and scheme on how to get rid of Big Tom once and for good.

Shortly thereafter, Amos accompanied Massa Hatley on a weeklong trip to New Orleans. Massa Hatley made the same trip each summer to buy special gifts and fineries for Mrs. Hatley and Missy. He also used the trip as a time to stay abreast of the business surrounding the cotton industry, slave trading and the political opposition which southern planters faced worldwide.

During the weeklong stay Massa Hatley with Amos trailing one step behind enjoyed the taverns, restaurants and spent money in the brothels. New Orleans was overrun with fancy girls of the night. One could find any type women desired. Southern planters thought nothing of using the special market to sell their beautiful slave girls into a life of prostitution. Other planters farmed out girls to the bordellos or permitted them to roam the streets and bring in the proceeds. Once Massa Hatley had his fill, he and Amos would start their journey back to the plantation. Mrs. Hatley and the plantation slaves were all aware that Massa Hatley's business trip included the pleasures of the New Orleans night life. Each time Massa Hatley and Amos returned, the plantation buzzed with gossip of their exploits.

On the last day as Amos packed the wagon with the boxes and gifts for Mrs. Hatley and Missy, he noticed ahead of him down the street stood a slave market. The market was surrounded with men in fine suits with walking canes and cigars stuffed in the corners of their mouth. The men talked, laughed and mingled with one another. In front on center stage slaves were marched up to the auction block. The prospective buyers examined each slave and offered bids as the auctioneer sang in a rhythmic cadence.

Amos realized he'd just witnessed the answer to his problem with Big Tom. He secured the wagon and walked close enough to observe the buying and selling of the slaves. He studied the auctioneer and slaves as they were sized, sold and distributed among the buyers. Amos puffed on his cigar and smiled cynically as he entertained the idea of Big Tom being sold and out of his life. He knew first a plan had to be concocted to convince Massa Hatley to get rid of Big Tom.

Once back on the plantation Amos tried his best to act as if all was well. Amos's showed no concern for Big Tom. This was only to deceive Kali and others away from his true plan. Behind the scenes Amos began to plant his seeds of deceit. He made negative comments here and there concerning Big Tom to Massa Hatley. He spoke of Big Tom's rebellious nature, mean strick and accused him of being lazy. Amos in time saw that he'd began to turn Massa Hatley against Big Tom. Massa Hatley became short fused and intolerant for the least of Big Tom's boyish behavior. As a result, Big Tom was assigned to work in the fields with the men and expected to do his equal share each day. Big Tom's magnetic personality soon won the affection of the field slaves and he seemed to be faring well among them. Amos realized at that point the he must engage the second part of his plan. Amos then informed Massa Hatley that Big Tom was causing trouble among the field slaves, trouble resulting from Big Tom telling stories of the Mende, Mandingo and Ilbo warriors of Africa. Amos told that Big Tom was attempting to teach the slaves about freedom and how the white men had invaded parts of Africa killing, kidnapping and enslaving its people. Amos suggested that Big Tom's stories were causing the slaves to become hostile and unwilling to work as usual. Amos presented his stories in secrecy and as if he was afraid for himself if the others found out. Amos swore Massa Hatley to silence and suggested that Big Tom had to be stopped.

In days to come Amos went to Massa Hatley with tears in his eyes and with the only solution he felt available. As he cried for the pain Kali would experience he laid out to Massa Hatley a plan that consisted of selling Big Tom at the New Orleans slave auction. Amos warned that to quell the brewing unrest and work stoppage created by Big Tom's stories and influence, selling Big Tom was the only way to secure the safety of the plantation. As terrible as it would be for Kali and his siblings, Big Tom must go. In a short while Massa Hatley came to agree with Amos's plan. Therefore, Big Tom would be sold. He'd be the first slave auctioned off by the Hatley's in over thirty years. Amos was relieved and smiled on the inside.

Then Massa Hatley and Amos contrived a plan to remove Big Tom from the plantation without Kali and the others knowing his future. Massa Hatley arranged for Big Tom to be auctioned and sold. The plan was to allow Big Tom to travel with them to New Orleans on their next trip and once there, they would take him to the slave market. At the slave market he'd be surprised, chained, caged and sold.

In July of the following year Amos and Massa Hatley executed their plan with preciseness. Big Tom traveled with Amos and Massa Hatley to New Orleans to never return to the Hatley plantation. He was sold along with the other slaves who had been bought up for sale in the auction on their second day in New Orleans. Big Tom was surprised, chained and caged by the local sheriff at Massa Hatley's request. Big Tom never saw Amos or Massa Hatley again after his surprised capture. The auctioneer sang the bids and Big Tom was sold for one thousand dollars to a planter from Murfreesboro in Hertford County North Carolina. Big Tom was only fourteen years old but his statue made him a high priced commodity.

Big Tom's new owner and Massa was named Cyrus Newsome. Massa Newsome's interest in Big Tom was motivated by his interest and involvement in slave breeding. After the official end of the international slave trade in 1807, planters such as Cyrus Newsome became a part of breeding slaves for profit. Slave breeding help satisfy the demand for slaves in the slave holding states. Fertile female slaves were prized breeders and male slaves were valued according to their stock and breeding abilities. Massa Newsome brought Big Tom with plans to use him as a field hand and breeder on his plantation in North Carolina. He'd examined Big Tom from head to toe and was impressed with his physicality. Massa Newsome believed Big Tom could sire a prodigy of off-spring of high value in the lucrative slave market.

On the very next morning Massa Newsome started his trip, heading back to North Carolina. He traveled with his overseer Cecil and with Big Tom who was laced with chains around his wrist and ankles. The three men was said to have ferried their way back to Norfolk Virginia and from there boarded a horse drawn wagon. Massa Newsome was proud of his latest purchase and made sure Big Tom had plenty of food and water. He bragged and showed Big Tom off to others along the way just as was the practice with the purchase of a prized bull or stallion.

During the entire trip from New Orleans to Norfolk, Big Tom experienced a range of emotions. He felt fear, anger and a desire for his mother's protection. At times he was blinded with the tears of a child, knowing he'd never see his mother and siblings again.

On the second day abroad the wagon, the horses were spooked by a brown bear while traveling through the dismal swamps between Suffolk, Virginia and Hertford County North Carolina. The horses ran out of control, leaving the wagon road causing the wagon to overturn landing on top on Massa Newsome. Cecil the overseer and Big Tom were both thrown from the wagon but unhurt. Cecil gained control of the horses and with Big Tom's help the wagon was removed from on top of Massa Newsome. Massa Newsome suffered a broken arm, head wounds and bruises. Cecil and Big Tom had saved their Massa's life. Massa Newsome was thankful and would never forget their services to him.

After three years on the Newsome plantation Big Tom had become head driver at the young age of eighteen. There wasn't a man around Murfreesboro and surrounding counties who matched Big Tom in statue. He was a sight to see and a delight in the eyes of women, the Negro and white women alike. Big Tom had captured the favor of the slaves on the Newsome's plantation through-out manning the other men in work, strength and charisma. Massa Newsome being observant and a businessman put Big Tom in charge as head driver which benefited him in maintaining control over the other slaves through Big Tom. With Big Tom as a part of the controlling force among the other slaves, Massa Newsome could sleep more peaceful at night. Big Tom benefited by-way of the privilege which came along with being the head driver. His job was to see that the work was completed but not to complete it himself. Big Tom rode the fields and around the plantation on a tall white horse, up and down the rows as the other slaves worked the crops.

The Newsome's main house stood in colonial splendor, on the side of a hill which overlooked the fields fleeced with cotton or lined with tobacco, corn and peanuts. Near the back of the house huddled rows of log cabins, corn cribs, pack houses with the stables and pig pens a hundred or so yards away. The big house was at the center of the Newsome's plantation. The field and gardens with wagon trails leading the way all radiated from the main house. Massa Newsome owned one of the largest plantations between Maryland and South Carolina. There were more than four hundred slaves on the Newsome's plantation, a combination factory, and village and police precinct. It ran with a well ordered regimentation. Big Tom drove the slaves in the field and maintained order in the quarters. Feared and respected by most slaves, he was an integral part of the plantation command structure, holding a position roughly comparable to master sergeant under a lieutenant who was the overseer who worked under a captain slaveholder. The most important slave on the plantation was the head driver who was not required to work like the other slaves and Big Tom held that position with pride. Big Tom was treated with more respect than any of the other slaves by Massa Newsome, the overseer and the other slaves. He was required to maintain discipline at all times, to see that no slave idled or performed substandard work in the field and to punish with discretion.

Come daybreak the rooster made his call. The morning air was filled with the smell of sowbelly frying down in the cabins on the slave row to go with the hoecake and buttermilk. Tom being without a wife or family prepared his morning meal and was always the first man on the yard.

Soon after he'd rang the ole bell, with the wind on the rise it could be heard on some other plantations a mile or two away. Then if you listen closely you'd hear more bells at other places all ringing. Then the overseer would toot the ram horn with a long toot and then some shorter toots.

Big Tom would go down slave roe hollering right and left while picking the ham out his teeth with a long broom straw.

The horn and bell sound about five in the morning. One hour later the field slaves were to be out of their cabins and in the fields already working. You'd see the stragglers and late comers scurrying to make it to the field to avoid Big Tom's whip. The overseer and drivers were armed with whips, drove the workforce. The overseer sometimes carried a pistol and was accompanied by a vicious dog that trotted alongside the horse. The slaves on the Newsome plantation not like the Hatley slaves of Big Tom's boyhood days, worked from can see to can't see, their days never ended. After the field work the slaves had chores around the plantation such as feeding the mules, pigs and chopping wood. Finally when they reached their cabins they had to prepare a meal, and eat before Big Tom marched down slave row making sure every slave was inside their cabin. The life of the Newsome slaves consisted of hard work, tough words, a little hoecake, bacon and field scratching from sun up to sun down. The day of rest came on Sunday. The only other time that work was suspended was on Christmas. The slaves enjoyed themselves on those days with parties in the barns, open fields or in the slave cabins. This type of life style crushed the lives and souls of the slaves from one generation to the next.

By age twenty-five, Big Tom had become the joy of many young slave girls on the plantation. His prestigious position as the head-driver, charm and being without a wife set the stage for his notoriety for bedding many women. He'd already fathered several children on the Newsome plantation by this time, aiding Massa Newsome in his slave breeding. Marketing and slave selling venture. The demand for slaves in the slave holding states such as Maryland, Virginia, North Carolina and South Carolina provided a demand for slaves from the breeder's market. Massa Newsome and the other slave breeders built wealth in raising slaves from infancy to an age that commanded a higher price. Slave breeding was one of the surest means for planter's to acquire wealth. The value of the planters slave stock was measured the same as his wealth in terms of livestock. The slaves were raised for use and for market. Massa Newsome and other slave breeders commanded both young girls and women to have children. A breeding woman was worth up to one fourth more than one that did not breed. Big Tom provided Massa Newsome with good stock and in time a flow of children from the women on the plantation.

Big Tom like other men who were slaves, were in a condition that transformed them into boys, existing in the body of men. He was trained to think that his worth was valued through his ability to perform hard work and sire children. Big Tom's complete identity was determined by his anatomical characteristics and genitals. His mentality was guided by sexual appetite and physical status. His actions were driven by his feelings and instinct. He functioned in the mental and social capacity of a boy, although he resembled a man in outward appearance. Big Tom functioned with reason, discipline and order. The plantation and society around him were predictable and he marched to the beat of the drum.

Big Tom's identity was through his sexual and physical qualities which projected a larger than life myth. These type of myths and tales of Big Tom and other slave men played havoc on the psychic of white men and black men alike. White men became intimidated by the reported sexual powers of the black male slave and feared them gaining access to white women. By creating sexual fictions about black males, white slaves owners caused the Negro slave to be more attractive to white women. The Negro male slave being powerless with no authority or ownership of property in society, viewed less than human with no rights and few protections according to the law measured his manhood through the siring of children and the ability to bed women. That particular definition of manhood would become endemic and would haunt Big Tom and his ancestors for generations ahead.

Big Tom sired at least a dozen children each year on the Newsome plantation between the age of twenty-five and sixty-five years old. It is said that he even stood by while many of his off-spring were sold by Massa Newsome in the slave market. Big Tom's attitude of indifference was not of fear but through being indoctrinated in the views of his master, seeing slaves as livestock and part of the life of the slave. Big Tom knew his ability to produce children made him an asset to Massa Newsome. It was as if they had a partnership of convenience which included profit and pleasure.

Big Tom not only fathered children on the plantation among the Negro slave women. It was said that he fathered more than one child with

Massa Newsome's niece. He also was to have fathered children with white women around the Murfreesboro and Ahoskie, North Carolina area.

Massa Newsome, to make money on off times, charged other planters for using Big Tom to stud their slave women. According to family folk-tale, Big Tom was the most virile male slave in eastern North Carolina and the Southern Virginia area. Legend has it that once Massa Newsome rented Big Tom out to a white planter in North Hampton County, North Carolina, the planter supposed to have locked Big Tom in a barn with fifteen or so female slaves on a Friday afternoon. Big Tom who rode his white stallion on those stud-for-hire trips, left the barn on Monday morning and returned to Newsome plantation. The next year thirteen black babies were born on the North Hampton County plantation.

Big Tom was given free range to travel off the Newsome plantation to provide stud service, to buy supplies and haul crops to the market in Suffolk and Chesapeake to the north and to Greenville and New Bern to the south. During his trips he passed through dozens of small towns and settlements along the way. During his travels Big Tom helped coin the expression "there's a nigga in the wood pile." The expression spoke to the sexual liaisons across racial lines. Although, white men had say so over the law, the plantation and the slaves, white women exercised nominal control over their homes along with their lives and sexual activities. White women very well knew of the white male's sexual desires and pleasantries, whether with prostitutes or black mistresses. Those practices by white men was accepted and seldom discussed. But, on occasions white women would turn the tables on white men by sexually consorting with slave men. On occasions such as when Big Tom traveled to the market he'd offer to chop wood for food or shelter overnight. It was a practice for slave men while traveling on trips sanctioned by their masters to stop at different white homes and offers to chop for a meal. After watching the black slave male strip off his shirt and chop, white women would entice or order them into the bedroom for a sexual liaison. In those situations Big Tom and other slaves had little choice. Obey and risk being caught. Refuse and risk being charged with rape. Most often the slaves obeyed and moved on.

The white men made the association when returning home and finding freshly cut wood. White housewives told the story of a wandering slave who chopped the wood for a meal. Nine months later when a dark skin or black baby arrived in the family, the white man of the house would know the slave performed more duties than chopping wood. Big Tom's seed was spread throughout Hertford, North Hampton, Bertie, Currituck, Wayne and Green counties in North Carolina as well as southern Virginia. Much of the amalgamation in that part of the state came by way of Big Tom and his legendary sexual exploits. Eastern North Carolina with its large cotton and peanut plantation was known as the black belt. A label arriving because of the number of slaves living on plantations before and after the emancipation of slaves, it's also an area with large pockets of mulattos stemming from race mixing.

Big Tom over the years married on four different occasions. His wives bore a total of thirty-six children combined. His last wife who buried him at age eighty-six in 1907 was name Molly and was the grandmother of Cedric's grand-dad and aunt Ida.

As Cedric read, he realized he was from the seed of Big Tom, and the Newsome family had spread across the eastern United States. Big Tom's progeny now worked in various professional capacities in every income category and were continuing to bear children and the bloodline into the future.

Cedric glanced at his watch and headed for the door. If he didn't hurry he'd be late for his basketball game at the Chapel Hill Street YMCA. While in route to the gym he continued to think of the story he was reading of grand-daddy Tom. Aunt Ida's manuscript got his attention, and told a great story of the life of their ancestral grand-dad who'd laid the foundation for the Newsome family. The entire Newsome clan had sprung from the loins of Big Tom. He'd set the stage for the men and women for generations to come.

April 10, 1969

Eighteen year old Paula Newsome was a senior at Northern High School and in the sixth month of pregnancy. Each morning she had the task of selecting clothing to hide the fullness of her stomach. She prayed for the day she'd graduate so she could stop hiding herself behind over-sized clothing. Being pregnant as a teenager wasn't the most honorable position to be in among students and society in 1969. In the past year school hadn't been important or anything she's looked forward to. Paula's life had been consumed by a teenage love affair with Derrick Scales. Derrick and Paula played hooky at every opportunity, sneaking into cheap hotels to smoke pot and enjoy the sexual interludes that followed. Paula was once a prize student. But, by ninth grade she had loss interest in school and spent her energy fighting the binding rules in her home. Paula had grown to view her parents as old fashioned, controlling and insensitive to her desire to have a social life like other teenagers. Jack and Clara Newsome had planned for Paula to graduate high school and continue her schooling at some college or university. Paula only wanted to party with Derrick, smoke pot and didn't bother to concern herself with life beyond each day. Paula's life priority was chasing the pleasures of life and Derrick Scales.

After graduation in June, Paula and Derrick's son was born. Jack and Clara Newsome offered to support Paula and her son Cedric. They offered to afford her a college education on the condition that she discontinued her relationship with Derrick. Jack and Clara saw that Derrick was headed nowhere fast and carrying Paula with him. Derrick was street wise, a pot head and moving toward a life of crime.

In three months Paula moved into Few Gardens, a Section Eight Housing Projects. She signed up for AFDC, WIC, Food Stamps and all other services available for a single mother at eighteen years old. Paula chose a life with Derrick in the toughest housing projects in Durham. Paula's appeared to have accomplished her goal in life. She had a male partner and a child which signified her arrival of womanhood.

Paula and Derrick's life became one of drinking, drugging and waiting for the first of the month "mother's day," when the AFDC check, food stamps and other social benefits they felt entitled became available. Derrick stayed on alert to exit the premises in case the social worker came around. The rules governing Section Eight Housing prohibited Paula from allowing Derrick to live with her and young Cedric. That condition provided Derrick with the opportunity to consort with other women and the excuse to steal time with them. He was in and out of Paula's apartment at will. Paula didn't have any basic complaints that concerned her. Life was fine. Derrick came over with alcohol or other drugs, provided her sex and his absence allowed her free range to play men for money and dope. All was well!!!

Paula and Derrick's drug use grew from opportunity using on the first of the month or when the chance presented itself, to daily use. Their daily use put them on the street looking for means to make money and buy drugs.

Derrick had grown up in a black section of Durham called the "bottom". His father had come to Durham from Charleston, South Carolina in the early 1940's. He worked at American Tobacco factory and sold black market lottery tickets. He was a tough man of few words who offered very little affection to his four sons. He provided them a roof over their heads and used his fist if they got out of line. Derrick's mother stayed in the home and followed the words of her husband, John Lee Scales. The "bottom" was a neighborhood that was a rock's throw from Forest Hill, one of the most prestigious white sections in the entire city. The streets of Forest Hills were laced with large two and three story mansions with manicured lawns. The lawns and mansions were attended by maids, butlers and gardeners. Durham's high priced doctors, lawyers, politicians and businessmen lived in Forest Hills. The Forest Hill Park and the streets were off limits to blacks with the consequences of arrest for trespass.

The "bottom" which was in striking distance represented one of Durham's most impoverished areas. The "bottom" was known for fights, killings, gambling, numbers joints, and shot houses. The majority of the duplexes and single dwellings were shotgun type houses heated with coal. There were two stores, one on the corner of South Street and another on the corner of Fargo and Enterprise Streets. The residents of the "bottom" lived hard and fast. The weekends were filled with drinking, parties and trying to dodge trouble. Sunday mornings the church bell rang at St. Joseph's and the doors swung open for worship. The same Saturday night patrons of the shot houses and gambling joints filled the pews. Monday morning started another week of hard labor in the mills, tobacco factories, construction sites or in one of the Forest Hill mansions. Five days of hard work and then came the week-end, two days fun filled and care free.

Derrick, his brothers and friends were a noticeable part of the cosmetic make-up of the "bottom" since age twelve and thirteen. They hung out in front of the store fronts with the comradeship of a wolf pack. At a young age the "bottom boys" patrolled their neighborhood looking for the opportunity to prey on any intoxicated patron from the shot houses or victimizing anyone vulnerable. The young treacherous "bottom boys" watched for the opportunity to make a dollar. Derrick and his brothers Ray and Otha Lee soon became known for their toughness, quickness to use a knife, pistol or their fist to obtain desired results. Other youngsters were not allowed to come in the "bottom" without consequence. By age sixteen Derrick and his crew were leaving the "bottom" to invade upon other similar neighborhoods in north and east Durham. The "bottom boys" were tough and well respected on the streets. By the time Derrick met Paula he'd traveled back and forth between Durham and Newark hustling drugs, counterfeit money and robbing other hustlers. He was a true and dangerous predator.

Now that Derrick and Paula were in love with dope, Derrick became even more dangerous and uncertain. He had grown into a man of enormous statue, handsome looks, with street savvy and an intimidating body language. He dressed slick, was smooth and at all times sized up those around him looking for any weakness to be exploited. Derrick taught Paula to shoplift from expensive stores while he watched, turn her out to tricking with men at the Biltmore Hotel on Pettigrew Street and took her with him to Newark and Harlem periodically. Tricking came easy for Paula, due to being tall, good looking and over-run with alluring game. She'd acquired the nerves of steel through her association with Derrick. She had more grit than most men.

During this time young Cedric was being left with his grandparents Jack and Clara Newsome for days and weeks at a time. Clara realized that her grandchild was being neglected. She helped out whenever Paula asked. Paula called for money to buy food, pampers and to pay utilities. Paula's parents soon got word that young Cedric was being left unattended for hours as Paula and Derrick went out to the streets to hustle and buy drugs. One night Jack and Clara responded to a call and drove over to Few Gardens at ten o'clock. The call had come from a concerned neighbor. They arrived to find young Cedric alone and crying. They rescued their grandson and decided to never return him to Paula. Paula appeared relieved and offered no resistance.

Young Cedric was moved from Few Gardens to the home of his grandparents in River Forest. In a short time he began to flourish into a happy little boy. He became the apple of his grand-dad's eye. Jack Newsome rode Cedric with him in his big Buick to the barber shop while he played his regular Saturday checker games, brought him tokens of love home from the Quik-Stop and rocked him to sleep in his recliner each night. Grand-daddy Jack became Cedric's hero and friend. Cedric's Grandma Clara bathed him, nurtured and helped him with his school work. Cedric soon forget about Paula and Derrick, only thinking of them during the times of their impromptu visits or phone calls. Jack and Clara Newsome provided Cedric with structure, stability and love. Cedric knew dinner was served at six thirty each night, he knew who prepared the meal, who helped him with school work, who rocked him to sleep each night and that Sunday morning meant going to church. Cedric was blessed to have his grandparents and an environment where he could develop and prosper into a healthy young man.

By early high school Cedric had grown to be a promising athlete and a good student. His Aunt Ida tutored, argued and poised him into the ownership of high academic values where he connected the dots between high school performance and a successful life as an adult.

Over the years Cedric came to realize although his grand-dad loved his grandmother and cared for her every need, he also had a string of other women. At first Cedric felt angry and disappointed, because of the idea he had of his grandfather and grandmother's commitment to one another. But, in time he came to know that his grandma knew more about his grand-dads other women than he'd ever assumed. Cedric found that all the Newsome men, uncle Cleve, Uncle Will, Uncle John and the entire stock of Newsome men prided themselves in having a string of women. It was the way of the Newsomes. Cedric at times rode with his grand-dad when he visited other women. His grand-dad would introduce him with pride saying "this heh is my grand boy, he's about to become a man." Jack Newsome's introduction usually brought a smile and an under-current of sexual lust from the women.

By ninth grade at age fifteen Cedric thought nothing of his grand-dad and the other women. He'd accepted the idea that men were supposed to have an assortment of women. He now viewed it as part of being a man.

On July 10th, 1985 a Friday night Cedric celebrated his sixteenth birthday. His grandparents threw him a party-cookout in their back yard. Cedric invited his friends who were mostly athletes, cheerleaders and students from Northern High School. They grilled hamburgers, hotdogs and music blasted from the Wolf and Tweeters. Cars lined the street in front of the Newsome's home for the most of the evening and night. During the party Jack Newsome asked for the music to be stopped so he could say a few words. His speech was short and direct. He spoke of his and Clara's love for Cedric, how proud they were of him and surprised him with the keys to a new Honda Accord. Cedric was knocked off his feet and speechless. All he could do was to hug his grandparents and thank them for the car and of course the party.

On the following Saturday Cedric's grand-dad asked him to drive for him as he visited a few friends. They drove by Crystal Barber Shop on Fayetteville Street where Jack played a few games of checkers with the men at the shop. Crystal Barber Shop was the local site for the toughest checker players in Durham. The barber shop was usually filled with retired men who sat around the table and talked shit to one another, lying about the exploits of younger days. Some of the old guys could whip an amateur player in ten moves or less.

From the barber shop Cedric drove his grand-dad to a couple of shot houses and ball ticket joints. Jack Newsome was known for playing ball tickets and being very lucky when it came to hitting for the money. Cedric admired the comradere between his grand-dad and his cronies. He knew his grand-dad enjoyed that side of his life a great deal.

Their last stop was Mrs. Genieve's, who everybody called Genie. Mrs. Genie had worked with Jack Newsome at Leggett & Myers tobacco factory for some twenty years. After work she ran the biggest after hour spot in Durham on South Roxboro Street. Her busiest nights were on the week-ends, Friday through Sunday. Her big white two story house would be packed with niggas from top to bottom. It was the last stop after the Stallion Club, Brown Derby and Club 55. Mrs. Genie sold fish sandwiches, chicken sandwiches, chittlings, pork chop, liquor by the drink and had hook-ups for anything else you'd want. On this particular evening Cedric and his grand-dad had beat the late crowd, no one was around but Mrs. Genie and her niece Desiree. Desiree was visiting from New York and was introduced as such. Desiree was twenty-six years old, sexy and the best looking women Cedric had ever seen. She was pecan tan, with the prettiest set of legs and rear-end a women could possess. Her waist line was trim and her breast appeared as if they wanted to jump out of her tank top. To make matters worse for young Cedric or maybe better, her face belonged on the front of a magazine. Mrs. Genie called Desiree over telling her that Jack was her long time special friend who they'd discussed earlier. Mrs. Genie pointed at Cedric saying "that's his grand boy, who just turned sixteen, ain't he a cutie." Looking at Jack while winking her eye, Mrs. Genie then said, "Ced, Desiree got a birthday present for you." Cedric was surprised, embarrassed and didn't know what she was referring to. Desiree came over and rubbed the back of Cedric's neck while looking at him as if he was a sirloin steak. Desiree put her arm around Cedric's shoulders as she stood beside him, as he sat at the kitchen table. Desiree's presence, touch and the stroking of the nap of his neck with her nails caused him to get an uncontrollable erection. As he sat in the chair at the table, Desiree looked Cedric up and down, before saying "his awfully big to be only sixteen and good looking too." Mrs. Genie laughing replied, "He's, like his grand-daddy." With that Mrs. Genie gave Jack an affectionate slap on the shoulder. Desiree looked at Cedric in the eyes and commanded, "Come with me," at the same time she'd took, Cedric by the hand leading him to one of the upstairs bedrooms. Desiree a high class New York hooker had been paid by Jack Newsome to usher his grandson into manhood. In Jack Newsome's mind the rites of passage to manhood was through the sexual canal of a woman. For Cedric to be a man he must be a stud, a womanizer, defined by his ability to consort with women. Desiree earned one hundred dollars, a price well below her New York rate. She'd opted to perform her service as a favor to Jack and the chance to have a young boy. Desiree shared a quadric of sexual acts with Cedric he'd never imagined. She offered the warmth of her mouth, swallowing his entire male anatomical part. Then she gave him insane pleasure in every conventional and unconventional sexual fashion possible for a man and woman. In twenty or so minutes she released him to return to his grandfather. Cedric was almost too embarrassed to enter the room where his grand-dad and Mrs. Genie waited. To ease his embarrassment, Mrs. Genie sent him to the ice box for a soft drink. After returning with the soft drink he found his grand-dad on the phone. Cedric could now relax, feeling that the focus was off him. Once off the phone, Desiree and Mrs. Genie escorted Cedric and his grand-dad to the door. Desiree winked at Cedric saying, "I think I'd like to see you again before I leave for New York." Cedric smiled in a down caste manner and exited the door. Once in the black Buick, Jack Newsome looked at Cedric and proudly proclaimed, "You're a real man, now!" Cedric smiled and drove the big Buick down South Roxboro Street.

The next two years passed smoothly and fast for Cedric. He was successful in both academics and sports. He had been fortunate to have played at Northern High because it had one of the top high school football programs in the state for over twenty years. His senior year the team finished with a record of 15-2 and as state runner-ups in the play offs. Cedric was selected All-Conference, All-State and invited to play in the Shrine Bowl. Cedric was seen as a top notch linebacker amongst the coaches across the state. Because of his dedication and hard work he graduated in the top twenty out of five hundred seniors. In June of 1987, Cedric Newsome marched across the stage, received his high school diploma and cast a wink at Jack and Clara Newsome. In two months he headed for Richmond, Virginia on a scholarship to Virginia Union University.

November 23, 1997

Michael Wiles and Kevin Trapp sat in the shadows nervously waiting as customers withdrew money from the Tyvola Road Mall ATM banking machine. Michael and Kevin watched for the opportunity to victimize and rob the first customer who was alone and when the area was free of witnesses. They'd been on a crime spree for over a month breaking into homes, stores and stealing anything that wasn't nailed down. Both Michael and Kevin were strung out on drugs, using everything from crank, pcp, meth, and alcohol as a chaser. Michael had spent five years at Pope Youth Center after raping his first cousin at age fourteen. At age eighteen he was shipped from Pope to North Carolina's Central Prison for another eight years before completing his twenty year sentence. Now at age thirty he was on the streets in Charlotte where he'd grown up, living from one day to the next and from crime to crime. He was a tall wiry man, with a shaven head signifying his claim as a member of the skin heads. His nose and ears were studded with ear rings and hoops. He appeared not to have had a bath in a month. While in prison he'd joined up with the skin heads for protection and his attraction to the idea of hate and blame against minorities as an excuse for this failed life. The skin head philosophy gave him a reason to feel a rung higher on the ladder than others, based on his so-called Arian bloodline. Since being released from prison he'd vacated all the ideas of the Arian brotherhood, only holding onto the concept of blame and hate toward minorities.

Unbeknown to Kevin, Michael had not only robbed and stole at every opportunity but had committed more than five murders in the last eighteen months. Kevin, a small man of twenty years with a scruffy head of black curly hair was a tag along. His motivation to team up with Michael was because of his love for drugs. Kevin had a sociopathic attitude which predicated most of his opinions and behavior. But he hadn't bargained for what was in store for him as Michael's crime partner. He was almost ten years younger than Michael. He'd been raised in a middle class white family in North East Charlotte, not far from UNC-Charlotte. Kevin who rebelled against his parent's rules smoked pot and used some type of speed almost daily since age fourteen. Kevin dropped out of school as a freshman at South Mecklenburg High School and took to the streets, finding his way to biker clubs frequented by the Outlaws and Hell's Angle's. He'd met Michael at one of those bars and had stayed around Michael ever since. Prior to his crime spree with Michael, Kevin hadn't been involved in any crime to speak of. He was mostly a small time pot head who'd strayed from the upbringing and life style of his parents. Kevin was living in hotels and at times he'd go to his parent's home for a day or two before fleeing from the discord as it erupted between his dad and himself. His dad loved him but could not accept the way Kevin lived so carefree, irresponsibly and apparently with no plans to better his life.

On the other hand, Michael Wiles was a child raised by his grandmother in a home with three other cousins, all dropped in Nancy Wiles lap by her son and daughter. She provided as best she could for her grand children on a tract of land that had been in the Wiles family for fifty years. The five room white clapboard house was tucked in the woods a quarter mile off Interstate 77 between Charlotte and Mooresville.

Nancy's two oldest sons Tommy and Billy ran a junk yard and auto repair shop some fifty yards in the back of the Wiles house. The junk yard and auto repair shop was left to them by their father who died an untimely death in an automobile crash on I-77. he was driving drunk and died one mile from his drive-way. This junk yard and auto repair shop earned enough money to provide for the upkeep of their mother and the Wiles children.

Sylvester Wiles, Nancy's late husband was an ole tobacco chewing country boy and the best mechanic around. He drank his whisky daily, rebuilt engines, transmissions and fixed anything on a car his customers complained of. He started training his sons Tommy and Billy at the age of ten. After his death the Wiles brothers continued on with what he'd taught them and worked the business he'd left behind.

All of Nancy Wiles' grandchildren fared well in school and behaved as expected, except Michael. From the time he was a young boy Michael was noticeably withdrawn, slow in school and exemplified outburst of rage and anger. By age six he was found to be killing small animals. He'd kill and bury kittens, puppies and birds. He was also becoming unpredictably violent and couldn't be trusted to play with the other children.

In school Michael kept to himself much of the time. In the fourth grade he threw a dart into the eye of another boy unprovoked. From that time forward Michael began to drift in and out of school on suspensions until quitting by the sixth grade. He then moved to Charlotte for a couple of years with his mother, Velma. Soon after he returned to his grandmother's at age fourteen, after his mother had her fill of him. Three months after returning Michael raped, sodomized and physically beat his cousin Susan. Susan was a sophomore at East Mecklenburg High School, a good and well respected student. The entire student body and community were stunned by Michael's attack on Susan. Michael was subsequently arrested, convicted and sent away to prison.

Years later after his release from prison, Michael graduated from killing small animals to killing people. He moved through the city of Charlotte committing crimes to support his drug habit and laying in wait for unsuspecting victims to satisfy his thirst to kill. Michael was a psychotic opportunity serial killer. He only needed to find his victims alone to carry out his next kill. His victims were not connected to him, one another or didn't have to anger him. Killing gave Michael an emotional filled rush. It was a similitude to a sexual climax. He was a madman!

The decision to commit the next robbery at the Tyvola Road Mall ATM banking machine was impulsive and with a simple plan. The plan was to wait for the opportunity and victimize the first lone customer, taking all the money and valuables available.

Angela Slade worked for the Charlotte-Mecklenburg School System as a food service coordinator. She'd accepted the position almost two years earlier after earning a Master's degree in Food and Nutrition from the University of North Carolina in Greensboro.

Angela was tall and athletic with a well toned body. Angela had continued to weight train and run three or four times each week since she'd graduated from Virginia Union. Her workout routine was a carryover from her days as quarter miler.

Today, Angela was all smiles as she thought of the upcoming Thanksgiving holidays and her plan to spend them with Cedric in Miami. As she moved around she thought back on her days at Union where she had met Cedric. She had loved Virginia

Union and its free spirited atmosphere, close knitted student body and friendly approachable professors. Her father had graduated from Union and was a dedicated alumnus. Her mother being a Hampton University alumnus created a family campaign on which school she should attend. The campaign between Joe and Claudette Slade didn't leave her in much of a position to consider other schools.

Claudette Slade had warned her daughter "don't waste your time dating any of the athletes, find some professional minded young man and concentrate on your studies." For a month or two Angela made a half-hearted attempt to comply, being ever conscious of her mother's advice. But then she'd met Cedric Newsome and her mother's exhortations flew out the window.

Angela had grown up in Wilmington, North Carolina in a modest brick house on West Fourteenth Street. She was the only child of Joe and Claudette Slade. The Slades were a loving couple and reared Angela in a peaceful and nurturing environment. Joe a tall fair skinned, balding man and a home-body, worked his yard and flower garden. He played a little golf, drank his scotch and watched baseball on weekends. He wasn't a man with interest in other women and disdained men who consorted with women outside their marriage. Joe Slade was in love with his wife and daughter. Angela grew up with hugs, kisses and a great deal of pampering from her father.

Claudette Slade taught Home Economic at Williston High School and was Angela's mother and friend. Claudette was the "hen of the roast" in the Slade home. She was assertive where Joe was laid back, she called the shots. Claudette was active in the community; heading up food drives for hunger, participated in all the social functions of the Delta Sigma Theta Sorority and was a lady on the go. She'd taught Angela proper social edicts and shared her expectations for her in clear turns. She expected Angela to succeed in the classroom, to behave with decency in all matters and to select a young man with a promising future.

Angela had strayed from her mother's advice in her choice to date Cedric. Today, the very thought of Cedric the star football player, honor student and her heart throb was enough to warm her heart as she planned for their Thanksgiving holiday. Since speaking to Cedric a week earlier and his proposal to spend the holidays in Miami together, she'd thought of nothing else. He'd told her that he'd missed her and was finally ready to commit to her, if she'd have him. She could still remember how special she had felt after dating Cedric for three years and on Christmas day of their senior year, he presented her an engagement ring. It was the most romantic moment of her life. She thought back on when Cedric pulled the small black velvet box from his inside coat pocket. He had professed his love for her and eased the ring on her finger. She knew how blessed she was to have Cedric's love and admiration, despite her mother's advice. Cedric was everything she wanted and ever hoped to find in a man. From his quick mind and handsome face to his short cropped hair, warm black eyes, soft lips and well chiseled athletic body.

Cedric had said. "We'll spend Thanksgiving together and I'd like to share an important decision I've come to with you. I'll see you in Charlotte and from there we'll fly to Miami".

"Two days and counting", Angela thought with anticipation. But still she couldn't forget the disappointment of times passed, when she'd drawn the line and returned Cedric the engagement ring to Cedric because of his infidelity. Angela had demanded that Cedric cease his habit of jumping from co-ed to co-ed and to work on his out of control habit of bedding women. Cedric promised to refrain from his old ways and verbally committed to a monogamous relationship. In time Angela found that Cedric still had other girlfriends in a lesser capacity but had continued with his womanizing. Angela confronted Cedric and allowed him to explain himself. With patience she listened as he reclaimed his desire to be monogamous, he'd understood the value of fidelity in relationships but in some way he felt that manhood depended on his relationship with more than one woman. It was like a part of who he was as a man. The thought of confining himself to one woman, in his mind reduced him to something less than a man. A man less than all of the other Newsome men, and the man his grand-dad had taught him to be. Cedric spilled his heart to Angela. She consoled him and understood his struggle. But, she also realized that because of the difference in how they viewed manhood, relationships and the importance of fidelity, that Cedric wasn't ready to be her husband. With all the strength inside her, Angela, in tears, drew the line and called the engagement and relationship to a halt.

After three years of a off and on relationship with Angela, Cedric finally came to his senses. He knew he loved Angela and that she possessed all the assets of a good wife. He prayed she would reconsider and accept the engagement again. Cedric decided that before completely losing all chances with Angela, he'd commit to her, terminating all other women from his life.

Cedric discussed his proposed plan to commit to Angela with his granddad and Uncle Cleve. He explained. "Our fallout was my fault, I couldn't commit and Angela refused to put up with my freewheeling habit of chasing women. She returned the engagement ring and called the relationship off. Not because of lost love but because of principal. She refused to accept my infidelity." As Cedric, his granddad and Uncle Cleve stood around the counter in Uncle Cleve's Buy Quik discussing his decision, both the older Newsome men scornfully warned against marrying any women who'd expect a Newsome man to settle for one woman. Uncle Cleve who was tall, six foot four or five, very black, street wise, dressed sharply and with one gold tooth in the front of his mouth and who had children spread all over Durham and other cities, always had the last word. Cleve said, "As many whores as it is in the world why would you want to tie yourself down with one with a foolish notion like that?" Cedric knew there was no use in trying to argue or persuade Uncle Cleve or his granddad's opinion on the issue; he only wanted to inform them of his plan out of respect. His granddad and Uncle Cleve both were important to him and without a doubt loved him dearly. The older Newsome men viewed manhood as being closely tied to one's ability to seduce and bed a variety of women. They laughed with jester saying, "All us Newsome's are studs, boy, it's in our blood, that just how it is. We's been studs starting way back, as far as everybody knows. Now, you gonna get married and be a house husband, tied to your wife's skirt tail. We'll see how long that last. Boy a women's got to give a Newsome man free range to run, and as long as he pays the bills and treats her good, that's bout all she'll get." Cedric offered no opposing view on the topic of marriage, he wasn't sure he could be satisfied with only Angela but he knew he'd be miserable without her. Cedric nodded and accepted the admonishments from the older men and asked for their blessings.

Cedric drove across the city in route to home. He became preoccupied with the story Aunt Ida had written on the history of his ancestral grandfather "Big Tom." He was struck with awe and pride when considering the history of his family dating back to Kimbo, Kali and the Mende people. Aunt Ida's manuscript was informative and had left him with a sense of an emerging new identity and self image. Cedric, overnight, felt connected to a people, a land and a world outside the boundaries of the United States. Inside he felt a sense of greater power and human worthiness. He still hadn't realized that "Big Tom's Ghost" and life as the breeder had affected the psychic of the Newsome men and women in the present day.

Being on the north side of Durham, Cedric decided to drive through the block. It had been awhile since he'd drove past the corner. Guys from North Durham hustled drugs on that particular corner twenty-four seven. He was sure Fat Ralph and Goofiend would be out. As he drew closer to the block he thought, "Damn, I haven't seen either of them in almost a year." He'd heard they had hooked up with some Detroit dope boys and had locks on the corner with heroin and cocaine. For that reason he'd purposely stayed clear of both Fat Ralph and Goo. As he turned off Angie Avenue onto Elizabeth Street he could see young men on every corner flagging cars trying to market their drugs. As he topped the hill on Elizabeth approaching Dowd he could see Fat Ralph's huge image a hundred yards away. He was sitting in a chair on the corner across from Jones's Funeral Home watching his stash across the street. Fat Ralph was clad in a UNC warm up suit and hat. If you didn't know better, you'd think he was a member of the UNC football team, "defensive lineman." Cedric thought "boy is that a waste or what." Fat Ralph coming out of high school was the biggest, and most sought after lineman in the state. Fat Ralph chose hustling over college. His choice was encouraged by the poverty of his single parent upbringing and a set of values that disregarded education as a means of breaking the cycle of poverty. Although he'd become a ruthless and tough hustler, Fat Ralph's basic nature was kind and gentle. As Cedric stopped and parked, Fat Ralph sprang from his chair, "Damn, wass up Ced, wass going on, it's been awhile man. What brings you through?" I was over by Uncle Cleve's store and while I was on this side I decided to drive throw." Cedric replied.

"How's the family, Ms. Clara and your granddad?" Ralph asked.

All's well!" Cedric recanted.

Cedric turned as Goo jumped out of a Mercedes and headed his way. Goo was all smiles, and still thin as a rail, dress liked the hustler of the year and appeared to be zooted on heroin. Ralph and Goofiend, both had begun to use the product they sold. It came with the turf, a part of the life of a dope dealer, for most. Off-times dealers became their own best customers. Cedric stood around kicking it with Fat Ralph and Goo for ten or fifteen minutes and prepared to take off. Before he could step-off Fat Ralph tuned serious informing him they needed to talk for a few minutes. Fat Ralph with a whisper disclosed "KiKi your little cousin been coming through buying dope." KiKi was only fifteen years old. She was the second daughter of Cedric's great aunt Helen, Jack Newsome's youngest sister. Cedric didn't know KiKi very well. She was only a child as far as he was concerned. Cedric had no response and didn't know what to say or think at that moment. He accepted the information with an "Oh yeah!" and a "thanks for the tip."

As Cedric drove away, the idea of his young cousin using dope ragged at him. In frustration he pounded the steering wheel with both hands.

On the way home he stopped by Fines Restaurant on Roxboro Road to grab a fish dinner. Fines' was run by Josh and Berma Dockery. The Dockery's had been friends of his grandparents for as long as he could remember. They attended Greater Saint Paul Baptist Church along with his grandparents. The restaurant had been in the same location five or so for years. Once inside the restaurant he was welcomed by Mrs. Berma as always and surprised to see the Dockery's daughter Wendy behind the counter. The last he remembered she was in D.C. married, he thought, after leaving Hampton University. To see her working in her parent's restaurant was new. Mrs. Berma took his order, asked of his grandparents and busied herself with preparing his take-out.

Wendy had graduated three years ahead of Cedric and her brother Johnny at Northern High. Johnny and Cedric had been close friends and playmates since elementary. Wendy was older, and always seemed more mature than he and Johnny. She was a majorette and home-coming queen. While in high school, Cedric thought she was the best looking girl in the world. Wendy was nice and chocolate with hazel eyes, five foot eight inches tall, a voluptuous body and an enticing sexual presence and strut. Cedric had always had a crush on Wendy since childhood but was intimidated by her older age and good looks. Strangely, he still felt the same shyness in his gut. He wondered what had brought her home.

It was always said that she was the exact image of her mother in younger days. Jokingly or maybe not so jokingly, the story was that Fines Restaurant's main attraction in the early days was Mrs. Berma, not the food. Mrs. Berma was still a beautiful woman at her age with a great smile and teeth. Wendy greeted Cedric with an open friendliness. Now, she appeared to be more on his level of maturity. Cedric couldn't help but notice her sexy and curvaceous body as they talked. Wendy, as he perceived it, gave him indications of being interested in him or maybe it was just her sexual aura. Mrs. Berma brought Cedric his food. He paid Wendy, said his good-byes, waved at Josh Dockery who sat at the table by the window as always and headed out. Driving home he thought of Wendy and how fine she looked. He said to aloud, "Damn she's bad."

Angela looked at her watch, it showed 10 o'clock, the night was dark and the air chilled at around thirty five degrees. She left her apartment in "The Parks" on the corner of South Tryon and Tyvola Road to drive to Food Lion. She wore a blue and white adidas jogging suit, white running shoes and a Charlotte Hornets baseball cap. She'd planned each day since receiving Cedric's call. Tonight she would grocery shop. She had planned to stock her refrigerator and empty shelves with enough food to carry her and Cedric for a day or two, if need be. They'd planned to leave Charlotte the day of Cedric's arrival but anything could delay them. If so, she'd have enough food to cook their meals at home and steal every available second with Cedric. But, first she had to stop by the ATM to withdraw cash. She ran out the door cross the parking lot to her 1996 Toyota Camry. She started the engine, turned the heat on full blast and exited on Tyvola Road headed to the ATM. The ATM was in the same Mall location as Food Lion. Angela pulled up in front of the ATM banking machine. No other customers were there. As she opened her car door to exit, Michael Wiles nudged Kevin and put his cigarette out with the toe of his boot, twisting and grinding the cigarette into the asphalt.

Angela walked up facing the banking machine and began to enter the series of account numbers. Without her noticing, Michael had moved up behind her, standing about six feet away as if he was a customer waiting to use the ATM. Kevin was still in the shadows of the trees which lead to the wooded area behind the bank. As Angela turned while putting her cash withdrawal in her purse, Michael slapped her across the face with such a force that she fell backwards against a clump of brambly brushes. She screamed "what are you doing, who are you?" She started crying after realizing that she was being attacked, "take the money, please, don't hurt me anymore." Michael laughed harshly and demanded, "I'm going to give you exactly what you need, you black bitch." Angela scrambled to her feet, "You're crazy," she shouted as she attempted to turn to look for help. Michael reached out and grabbed her by the back of the neck, yanking her so hard that she lost her balance and fell against him. Then he pulled her left arm behind her back, twisting it until she felt excruciating pain, she heard her arm snap. He forced her into the wooded area behind the bank. "Crazy! You think I'm crazy?" He shouted in her ear. "Well, I'll show you what crazy really is." Spinning her around, he knocked her to the pavement with a hard punch to the side of the face. Angela lay where she was, dazed, unable to get up, as disbelief turned to fear. As she wondered what would come next, she felt the toe of Michael's boot slam into her rib cage. She heard another man's voice, Kevin saying, "You're going to kill her, let's just take the cash and get out of here." Michael shouted, "Shut the fuck up and get out of my way." When Angela tried to crawl away, Michael caught her by the hair, and when she tried to wiggle loose, he choked her, cutting off her breath. Wherever she turned, Michael's thick Dingo boots were waiting for her, thumping into her body, again and again. "Please", Angela begged.

Wiles shouted. "That's right, beg you bitch, beg for your goddamn life."

Michael mounted her, ripping off her jacket and then started to claw at her jogging pants. He reached at her bra, yanking it off with one snatch. He ripped her panties away, tearing them into two pieces.

Angela could feel the callused hands sliding down her body, over her breast, along her thighs, between her legs . . . . places only Cedric had explored. She could feel him force her legs apart and then he drove himself deep inside the most private part of her body.

Angela screamed. She had never felt pain so intense before. It was as though she was being torn apart, the pain started in her thighs and shot up to her abdomen. Michael put one of his hands over her mouth and the other hand was now occupied with a huge hunting knife. He continued to jump up and down inside her. Angela couldn't move, she couldn't even say a word. She could only lie there and take whatever he issued. Tears rolled down her face and blood began to trickle down from where he pressed the big knife against her neck. Angela then knew she was going to die, that he would not let her live, she prayed it would be quick.

Michael removed himself from inside her and in one motion slit her throat. He stabbed her again and again. She only made one initial moan.

Kevin stood by in shock as he watched the entire blood-quenching scene. He started to move away "Where do you think you're going?" Michael smeared. "We're not through with her yet. Go search her car, while I put this worthless bitch in the trunk. We have to take her with us, and get rid of her." Michael drug Angela's now dead body to his red 1980 Impala and threw her in the truck. With a change of mind, he ordered Kevin to take her car and follow him.

Michael cruised down South Boulevard as if nothing had happened with Kevin nervously following in Angela's Toyota Camry. They turned right on Old Pineville Road and then onto Neal Road. They drove on Neal Road pass the old Jim Lyons place. There Michael drove off the road to an old abandoned farm house with an old well in the back. Michael summoned Kevin out of Angela's car to help him unload Angela's body from the trunk and dropped her head first into the well.

Michael instructed Kevin to stay calm saying, "This is no big deal, just do as I say." He informed Kevin it was now time to get rid of the car. Kevin followed Michael back to Pineville off Highway 521 which passed the James K. Polk memorial and crossed Sugar Creek. They turned right onto Meets Road and drove by an old landfill which hadn't been used for thirty years. The area had now grown to woods and thicket. Michael drove Kevin down a unused road which led to a rock quarry. The rock quarry was filled with deep dark water. Michael and Kevin pushed the Toyota into the hole of the rock quarry. Michael slapped Kevin on the shoulder as he gave him a cynical smile saying "Let's go get high."

November 24, 1997

One day before Thanksgiving. Claudette Slade was up early and pacing back and forth with the phone in her hand. She'd spent the entire night before trying to locate her daughter. Angela had left a message on the Slade's answering machine informing her parents she'd call after returning from the grocery store. She had sounded upbeat and told her mother about Cedric and her upcoming holiday vacation. Claudette had called over a dozen times without an answer. In her gut she knew something was wrong. Angela had never gone away or stayed out without leaving word of how to be reached. Plus, she'd left the message, promising to call after returning from shopping. As Claudette paced the floor, Joe Slade attempted to calm her down, "Honey she'll call, it will be okay." Claudette couldn't sit still. She called Bridgette Moore, Angela's girlfriend and co-worker. Bridgette had spoken with Angela two days earlier and suggested that Claudette call Cedric. When speaking with Angela last, they'd spoke of Cedric and their upcoming trip to Miami, where Angela detailed the plans for the holidays with him.

Cedric had been home for several hours. On his way he'd stopped by the Exxon on Roxboro Road across from the entrance of River Forest to buy gas. He'd surprisingly run into Warren Hill and his family. He and Warren had graduated from Northern High together almost ten years earlier. Cedric met Warren with an outreached hand and smile. He noticed Warren wore a full beard and kufee. Warren presented the same laid back, easy going style, as he always had. After high school Warren had left Durham to attend college at Winston-Salem State University. Cedric and Warren exchanged phone numbers and talked for a few minutes. Warren informed Cedric that he was now called Khalil Mujihad and was a Sunni Muslim. Khalil introduced Cedric to his wife, who was dressed in the traditional Ijab (dress for Muslim women) and was very beautiful. Khalil's two children were quiet and disciplined. Khalil presented Cedric with a book entitled, "Life of Muhammad" as a gift. He invited Cedric to Ju'mah prayer service on any Friday at his convenience. They parted and promised to stay in touch. As Cedric drove the four blocks to his home and grandparent's house, he thought of the people he'd seen that day and how their lives had evolved since high school. Fat Ralph the best linemen in the State was now a drug dealer. Goofiend the quiet mouse of a guy who'd followed the athletes around was now a player . . . . drug dealer and Warren Hill the quiet, smart kid from a Baptist family was a Sunni Muslim.

At home Cedric discussed Aunt Ida's family manuscript with his grandma saying "I think the manuscripts so far is well written granny and I am amazed at the history of the Newsome family. I now know where the Newsome men and women thing started." Cedric laughed, "Boy granddaddy Tom . . . . Big Tom had all the ladies, Uh? He must have fathered over a hundred children. Where are all our cousins now? Does anyone know? Boy, we must have blood relatives all over Eastern North Carolina and Southern Virginia. Aunt Ida is doing a good job, writing about granddaddy Tom." His grandma Clara nodded her head and replied "I see that paper got you all stirred up."

At exactly 9:15 the phone rang, it was Claudette Slade. With only a casual hello to Clara Newsome, she asked "May I speak with Cedric?" Clara Newsome could feel the seriousness in Claudette's voice. Without a word she'd passed the phone to Cedric. Cedric reached for the phone with a frown on his face as he said, "Hi, this is Cedric, how are you?" Claudette said, "Hi son," as she asked, "Tell me you've heard for Angela today," praying for him to say yes, Claudette held her breath. "No, Mrs. Slade I spoke with her last night around seven." Claudette informed Cedric that Angela was missing; she'd not answered her calls, nor had she been home since late last night. It had been over twenty-four hours since anyone had heard from her or seen her. They both agreed that wasn't like Angela. Cedric promised to call a friend who'd played football with him at Union, who now worked as a policeman in Charlotte and ask him to run by Angela's apartment.

Henry "Hank" Brown had just started his day when the phone buzzed. It had been over a year since he'd spoke with Cedric. "Ced, boy this is a surprise. We haven't talked since the homecoming football game." Hank Stated.

Cedric replied. "I've been okay. Listen, I need a favor."

"Sure, Ced anything." Hank replied.

Hank knew right off Cedric's call was serious. He could sense it in his voice.

"Angela may be missing or in some sort of danger. I'd like you to run by her place and check it out." Cedric laid out what he knew. Hank promised he'd get on top of the situation and call as soon as he sorted it all out. As soon as Hank left the police department on Fourth and McDowell Streets, he headed directly to Angela's apartment on Tyvola. When he arrived, he went to the door, knocked but no one answered. Hank looked through the window and could see the lights and television on but there was no movement inside. He then searched for Angela's car as described by Cedric. The car wasn't there.

Hank used his cell phone to call Cedric, "Ced there's no sign of Angie. I knocked on the door but no one answered. The lights and television was on, I could see them through the window."

Cedric gasped, and asked, "What about her car?"

Hank replied, "No sign of her car in the lot. I don't know Ced. It doesn't seem right." Cedric paused, he'd become more concerned.

Hank asked. "Do you want to file a missing person report? I think it would be a good idea."

After his phone call with Hank, Cedric called the Slades in Wilmington. Joe Slade answered after only one ring.

"Hello, Slade's residence." Joe Slade said.

"Hi, Mr. Slade this is Cedric. This is what I've done in an attempt to locate Angie. I have a friend who's a policeman in Charlotte, I asked him go by her place. He called and there was no sign of Angie. He looked around, the lights and the television was on as if she had run out, for a minute. Her car wasn't in the parking lot. So, we don't know. Hank thinks maybe it's time to report her missing. I plan to drive down to Charlotte to take a look around tomorrow. I think you may have to be the one to report her missing."

"I guess." Joe Slade replied.

"I'll meet you at the apartment at 10:00 A.M." Cedric replied.

Lisa Mueller was up at seven o'clock, dressed and out. She had a week's vacation from her job as a loan officer for the Bank of America on Tyvola Road. She was taking advantage of the time off to spend the holidays with her family in Boone, North Carolina. She wanted to give Tippy, her frisky golden retriever, a good run in Freedom Park before regulating him to the cramped back seat of her Honda Accord for the two hour ride to Boone.

As Lisa ran through Freedom Park, she spoke to Tippy saying, "If traffic's not too bad, we'll be in Boone in time for lunch."

It was too early for most Charlotteans to be up and about. Lisa and Tippy had the park to themselves. In thirty five minutes, Lisa and Tippy headed up the path around the little lake back to the car, it had been a good run. Lisa checked her watch it was 7:45, with Tippy into the back seat and headed for Tyvola Road. Lisa always used the bank at Tyvola by habit. For some reason working at the bank made it sensible to do business there. Lisa pulled in front of the bank at 8:04. None of the bank's employee's had arrived. That was perfect, because she didn't want to run into any of her co-workers on her time off. As Lisa opened the car door, Tippy leaped out the back seat. Lisa finished her transaction and then called for Tippy. "Tippy?" She called, "come on boy. We don't have all day." There was no response. Lisa frowned, peering around the corner of the bank. The three year old retriever was well trained, usually responding to her voice commands instantly. Lisa walked around the corner of the bank to find Tippy sniffing around the leaves in the small wooded area. She looked as she called Tippy, "get over here." Then she noticed what appeared to be semi-dried blood and a cell phone on the ground in the area. She quickly commanded Tippy to come to her and led him to the car. Lisa was perplexed. She decided to call the police.

The police arrived, interviewed Lisa, took possession of the cell phone and roped off the area behind the bank with yellow tape. It was now a crime scene.

In an hour the crime scene investigators had arrived. One of the officers found a gold chain and necklace with a heart locket inscribed with the names "Cedric and Angie Forever." The investigator collected samples of blood evidence and along with the cell phone and necklace then headed for their crime lab downtown.

Office Henry Brown had left notice to be contacted at the first sign of any break in the case.

Detective Sergeant John "Red" Williams was less than one year from retirement. He had put in thirty tough years with the Charlotte Police force, playing it straight and clean, right down the line which was a tough thing to do. His living room wall was covered with medals, and his gold watch was waiting for his retirement party.

From one side of Charlotte to the other he knew the hustlers, whores, drug dealers and killers. He'd seen his share of gunshot wounds, stabbings, beatings and murders, but in his thirty years he hadn't yet become immune to it. Every crime scene had affected him. "Red" had been raised in Cabarrus County on a farm and had moved to Charlotte in the mid fifties. He was taught to respect the law and people, although the law wasn't always just. His two sons had been taught the same. He was known throughout Charlotte as a fair man but tough once you'd crossed the line with him. There was no doubt in his mind the crime scene at the Tyvola Road bank was a place where a murder had occurred. "Red" called Officer Brown saying, "I'm out here at the Tyvola Road crime scene, brace yourself Hank it looks bad." "We got blood and a few articles." Hank asked "What type of articles?" "We found a necklace with the name Angela and Cedric inscribed on it and the woman who called 911 found a cell phone in the leaves. The crime lab people will run the number and test what we have."

Officer Brown replied, "Sergeant Williams, I appreciate your call and please keep me posted."

At 10:00 A.M. the next morning Officer Hank Brown met Cedric and the Slades at the Park Apartment Complex where Angela lived. With a sad face Officer Brown informed them of what the police had found. Struggling with the obvious shock and pain of the news Cedric asked, "Is there still a chance she will show up and be okay?" Officer Brown replied. "Yes, until we find her there's an outside chance she's okay."

Joe Slade asked, "What's the police doing in an effort to locate her?"

Brown disclosed, "We are checking with all the hospitals in the area and the forensic guys are processing the articles found for finger prints and DNA, that could help lead to the person who apparently attacked Angie. Whoever's involved could be holding her." Cedric asked, What about her car?"

Officer Brown listened and shook his head saying. "The car hasn't been located yet."

By 1:00 p.m. the Wednesday before Thanksgiving the crime scene investigator's forensic lab was able to match the finger prints from the cell phone to prints in the State's crime bank with Michael Wiles. The Charlotte Police Department Homicide Division issued an all points bulletin (APB) for Wiles. They had no recent address but his family's address out off Interstate 77 between Charlotte and Mooresville came up as the last known address. Detective Sergeant "Red" Williams drove out to the junk yard and was welcomed by Tommy Wiles, Michael's uncle. Detective Williams parked his black Ford cruiser, exited the vehicle and made his way to the door of the auto repair shop, dodging puddles of mud as he carefully placed his feet. Tommy Wiles stood by the raised garage door, wearing a pair of oiled coveralls, a Levi Garret ball cap and looking like he hadn't been close to any water in a month. As Detective Williams approached,

Tommy with a nervous body language spoke, "Good morning."

Detective Williams while chewing on his cigar replied, "Morning".

Tommy then inquired, "Can I help you, sir?"

Detective Brown hesitated then responded, "Well I hope so. I'm trying to locate Michael Wiles. Have you seen him around?"

Tommy stepped forward appearing to be more at ease now saying, "Michael haven't been around but once or twice since being released from prison a couple years ago. And we don't welcome him coming back. He's bad news and a lunatic. I don't want no parts of Michael. What's he done now?"

Detective Williams replied, "I'm not sure whether he's done anything or not, I'd like to talk with him and ask him a few questions. If he shows up or calls contact me immediately." Detective Williams reached inside his jacket pocket and handed Tommy a card with his name and phone number on it. Then he asked can we keep this little visit between us? But if you hear from him, make the call."

Tommy Wiles nodded his head in agreement and put the card in his pocket. Detective Williams thanked him and made his way back to the cruiser, started the engine, noted the area as he turned on to highway 21 and headed for I-77.

By Friday after Thanksgiving, Cedric and the Slades had set up a Web Site W.W.W. find Angie.com. In addition, the police department had promised that a missing person's flier would be out by Monday of the upcoming week. Over the weekend a crowd of about five hundred people spent two fruitless days searching for Angela. The Charlotte-Mecklenburg School staff had last seen her when she left work on Tuesday, November 22, 1997. Searchers walked hundreds of city blocks looking in abandoned houses, wooded areas, ditches and creeks a ten mile radius off the Tyvola Road Mall. They came bundled for the cold, the temperature was in the 30's, everybody tried to be optimistic. But, Angela was nowhere to be found. On Sunday evening, Joe Slade and Cedric spoke to the media and vowed that family and friends weren't giving up on finding here.

Tuesday, November 30th, 1997

Sergeant John Williams was in route to Wilmington, North Carolina to interview Joe and Claudette Slade. The Slades were the last to be questioned in a week of questioning co-workers, neighbors, friends and Cedric. He was accompanied by a thin man with a pinched face, thick coke bottom glasses and dressed in a dark brown suit. In previous days, Sergeant Williams and his partner had cruised by the local biker bars trying to lay eyes on Michael Wiles. The local news papers had ran stories daily on Angela's disappearance and suspected murder. Charlotte's WBT-TV had carried the story for almost a week, questioning co-workers, friends and the Slades. The Charlotte Police Department was squirming as a result of the media coverage and community pressure. Angela Slade was a young woman with an unblemished past and who had lived her life in a socially acceptable fashion. She was a high school and college athlete and honor student, an only child hailing from Wilmington with parents who were both school teachers and pillars of the community. Angela was the classic victim!

There was no sign of the only suspect in the case, Michael Wiles. He was probably on the run and hiding out somewhere in the drug and biker sub-culture in Charlotte. Sergeant Williams knew that it was only a matter of time before Wiles would surface and be caught. Meanwhile, as a formality and to cover all the bases and his ass he needed to interview the Slades. He'd learned a long time ago not t overlook anyone in cases of murder and missing persons. Not that the police considered either of Angela's parents as a suspect but he had to make his rounds.

During the drive to Wilmington down Highway 74, which carried them through Monroe and Fayetteville, Williams enjoyed the change of scenery. He and his partner discussed how the media had latched onto the case, Williams said, "You know the media guys give me the impression they'd like the case to go unsolved for as long as possible." Colin Madlin looked over the top of his coke bottom glasses out the corner of his eye at Williams as he replied, "Those guys make a living off other peoples miseries. The longer the case draws attention the better it is for them." Williams gasped while adding, "We need to solve it as soon as possible." The pressure was on.

Sergeant Williams exited off Highway 74 onto Highway 86 to Wooster Street which led them directly to 710 West 14th Street where the Slades were waiting. The Slade's home was a modest brick ranch-style with a well kept lawn surrounded by assorted colorful flowers and green shrubbery. Sergeant Williams exited the cruiser and lead the way to the front door. He rang the door bell, took a step backwards and waited for someone to answer the door. In two or three minutes Joe Slade opened the door dressed in khakis, a red and black checked flannel shirt with a pipe in his mouth which gave the aroma of Prince Albert's cherry blend tobacco. He greeted the Sergeant and his partner, "Good evening gentlemen, come in, we've been expecting you." Williams and Madlin were escorted into the den and seated on a burgundy couch in front of a fireplace filled with burning oak. As Sergeant Williams observed the surroundings he noticed the fine furniture, the plush carpeting and decorative wallpapering. In the den was a cherry wood case filled with trophies Angela had won throughout the years in track and field. Pictures from early childhood to her graduation day from Virginia Union University were scattered over the walls. In a few minutes Claudette joined her husband on the love seat. She took his hand as she seated. Claudette Slade's head ached from the jumbled, confused events of her life, since Angela's disappearance. The magical times for her and her only child had vanished overnight, forever. The pain and the realization that people killed one another had become a reality. It made her extremely nervous and from the first day of Angela being reported missing, she'd kept a weak stomach. At night she'd woke with nightmares, dreaming that Angela was crying with out reached arms, but no matter how hard she tried, she couldn't grasp Angela and pull her to safety.

"I was assigned to the case when your daughter was officially declared missing. Officer Henry Brown, who is a friend of Cedric's filled me in on his short meeting with you guys on the morning of the November 25th at Angela's apartment." Joe and Claudette both nodded, acknowledging what Sergeant Williams was saying. The burly detective had small brown eyes, a prominent round nose, mixed gray hair and a weathered face. The navy blue blazer he wore appeared a little tight across his girth.

The other man cleared his throat. "I'm Colin Medlin," he said, "investigator for the district attorney's office."

The Slade's shifted their attention. Almost skeletally thin, the investigator's dark brown suit hung poorly on him, appearing as if it was on a scarecrow. His crisp starched white shirt was at least two sizes too big and his hands and wrist were as small as a woman. His thick coke bottom glasses kept sliding down the bridge of his nose and every few seconds he'd reach up with his left pinky finger and push then back.

"I'd like to ask a few questions for our records." He spoke in a brisk impersonal voice. He reeled off questions, "When was the last time either of you spoke to your daughter? Did Angela have any enemies you know of? Had she mentioned any problems with anyone lately? Do you know if she knew anyone name Michael Wiles?" The Slades answered each question to investigator's Medlin's satisfaction. Nothing had changed from their earlier disclosure to Officer Henry Brown. Angela had called and left a message two days before Thanksgiving, telling her parents she'd call after returning from shopping. The Slades didn't know of any enemies, threats or problems Angela had with anyone. The name Michael Wiles didn't mean anything to them. With the mention of Michael Wiles, Claudette looked at investigator Medlin with dismay. She asked, "Who is Michael Wiles?" Sergeant Williams replied. "His prints were found on Angela's cell phone which was recovered at the crime scene. We're trying to locate Mr. Wiles for questioning." "I'm afraid." Claudette replied.

Medlin fishing a pen from his pocket to make another note said, "You see, the way it works is, Sergeant Williams files his report and then my office investigates. Try to think positive and stay hopeful." Investigator Medlin stated.

"I see." Joe Slade conceded.

The two officers exchanged glances and rose to their feet.

Claudette asked, "You think this Wiles person took her life, don't you? Why did he do such a thing? Why?"

Sergeant Williams sighed, "There doesn't always have to be a reason for some of these guys until something sets them off."

"I can't promise that we'll get this guy." Medlin said, returning his pad and pen to his pocket. "These type cases are difficult at best, and we don't have very much to work with. But don't you worry about that right now, we'll stay on it." Medlin was already halfway to the front door, Joe and Claudette Slade clutched one another's hands as the officers left. The

Slades felt terrible and powerless. Maybe, it was because the officers had probed for every tiny detail of Angela's life since her high school days, going over and over the same ground coldly, creating the crime time after time.

"Don't you think you were a little impersonal with them" Williams asked as he walked with Medlin down the sidewalk to the cruiser.

"It's how you get the truth." Medlin said with a shrug.

"So, what do you think?" Sergeant Williams asked.

"I think Wiles is our man. Investigator Medlin recanted.

"Do you think you can find him?" Investigator Medlin asked.

"Oh, I'll probably find him, if I look hard enough. He's probably peeping from under some rock back in Charlotte. Sergeant Williams responded.

"He shouldn't get away with what his done to this girl and her parents. My gut tells me she's dead." Investigator Madlin said.

Medlin continued, "Sergeant you know these cases are tough enough to solve even with a ton of physical evidence, and we're dealing with only one or two pieces of evidence that leads to Wiles. Wiles' fingerprints on the cell phone is all we got."

"We'll get more," Williams insisted.

"Maybe so," Medlin agreed, pushing his glasses up his nose as he crawled into the passenger's side of the cruiser. The two officers started their three hour drive back to Charlotte.

June 10, 1997

Cedric and his mother Paula Newsome drove down Duke University Road. They were on their way to Duke Hospital to visit Derrick Scales, Cedric's father. Derrick had been hospitalized two weeks earlier with pneumonia. The pneumonia was his latest bout with illnesses resulting from AIDS.

Paula had spoken with Cedric concerning his father and his illness in May. They'd found themselves in an open and honest dialogue concerning Paula and Derrick's life and failure as parents. Paula offered no excuses or justifications. She candidly told the truth of how she and Derrick had been thinking and living. She explained, "Ced, our lives were of drugs, recklessness, immaturity and one of failure in responsibility. You were caught in the middle, until mama and daddy took you." Cedric listened attentively as his mother struggled with her disclosure and her attempt to set the record straight. He was filled with hurt as he looked into his mother's tear flowing eyes. Inside he knew she was doing her best to start the healing between them. He wiped the tears from her eyes and placed his finger over her lips saying, "All that's in the past, I understand and I forgive you." He could see his mother was evolving into a different woman and he was thankful for her change. Paula raised her head as she dried her tears and continued to speak. "Your father was a mean and treacherous man, who lived a dangerous life. Nothing or nobody stood in his way. He robbed, killed or conned for what he wanted. Throughout his life what he wanted mostly was money and drugs." Cedric listened carefully. "In the last years because of his growing addiction to heroin, what he wanted was drugs." Cedric with a great concern asked, "What caused Dad to start using drugs and living that type of life?" Paula hesitated and replied, "I guess a variety of things pushed Derrick to the streets. I guess the greatest reason was the environment he grew up in and his attempt to survive life in the hood. Derrick's street and hustling life caused him to serve ten years in New York's Elmira Penitentiary. While at Elmira he continued to be a tough guy, he ran the block in prison. I was told he controlled the card games, the drugs and other contrabands. Five years later he caught a fifteen year sentence out of Newark for a robbery and was sent to Trenton State Penitentiary." Cedric was shocked and amazed. "Momma I never knew he'd served so much time." Cedric said. Paula sighed, "He done time in D.C.'s Lorton and North Carolina's Caldonia Farm." Paula shared with Cedric how his father had controlled her and other women through fear, intimidation and a strange kind of love. She said, "I remember clearly the night he sliced my face with a straight razor. It happened while he was in a jealous outrage and from my insolent mouth." He was a treacherous man. Any woman or men who stood in his way have battle scares to show. He never had or took the time to be your father. Paula said. "I believe he loved you in his crazy kinda way. At times he'd speak of you with passion, especially when he was zooted on dope . . . . saying "We gonna get a house and be a family and all. He didn't know how to be a father." Paula explained as best she could. Derrick's behavior was what he believed proved his manhood. He'd been taught by his father, who had been taught by his father. Derrick used and relived what had been passed down to him. You see Cedric, in his view a man had to be tough, uncaring and ready to die for what he wanted and not willing to back down from anyone or anything. He'd been raised with a crazy view of manhood." Cedric was blown away.

Cedric recanted.

"Mom it's a wonder if he didn't end up dead."

Paula agreed. "Yeah, you're right and me too. It took me years before I realized that love shouldn't hurt, and I didn't have to accept abuse and mistreatment for the sake of something that looked like love or just to be with a man. I finally realized my womanhood is not measured by any man or being attached to one. I have realized that I can be okay alone."

As Cedric listened to his mother, he felt sorrow, anger and forgiveness. He knew at times life's circumstances influences decisions and that decisions caused particular outcome. His mother and his father as young adults had made bad choices which affected each of them. Paula had released all the words held inside her over the years. As the words gushed out of her mouth, so did much of the guilt. Cedric remembered his mother saying that in fleeting moments his father could be kind. There was a heart inside Derrick Scales.

A week earlier Derrick's sister Ester had called Paula informing her that he was severely ill and had asked for her. Paula was stunned by his request. Paula had later called Cedric informing him that his father's condition had worsened. She wanted to visit with him before it was too late. Paula hadn't seen Derrick in over two years. She felt that she at least owed him one last show of kindness. Paula asked Cedric to accompany her. She advised, "It could be a chance for the both of you to find some closure with one another." She added, "At least you will have a chance to stand before your father face to face as a man."

Cedric never thought the day would come when he'd see his father again. His heart pounded at the thought. "First, I'm rejected and practically thrown away by a father I've never known and almost overnight he's back in my life." The child inside him longed for a father's love. But he didn't try to fashion the hospital visit into something it wasn't. It wasn't a father celebrating a reunion with a long lost son. It was a man, a stranger on his death bed. Cedric had thought about fatherhood a great deal over the years. His definition of fatherhood had changed from the biological donor of sperm to the man who'd cared for him. Jack Newsome had made sure he had food to eat, clothes to wear and had loved him unconditionally. Derrick Scales had allowed him to enter the world but hadn't helped him to live in it. But, still amidst all the conflicting thoughts and conversations with his grandparents, he agreed to accompany his mother on the hospital visit.

Cedric parked on the third level of the hospital parking garage on Duke University Road. He and his mother skirted across the street and made their way into the hospital's main lobby. The ride up the elevator to the fourth floor intensive care unit was done in silence. Once the elevator stopped for the fourth floor, the sterile antiseptic smell met them head on. The shinny hallways were buzzing with nurses in white uniforms with trays of medicine. The clerk at the nurse's station was an older looking white woman with a pointed nose, wire rim glasses and with bluish grey hair. She was busy on the telephone as he and his mother waited. The clerk's eyes peered over her glasses at Cedric as she finished her phone chat. "Can I help you?"

Cedric replied "We're here to see Mr. Derrick Scales." The clerk replied. "He's in room 408."

It was obvious to Cedric once in the room, he was with a dying man. Paula burst into tears when she saw Derrick. He had contracted HIV through his risky life-style of sharing needles, impulsive sexual behavior or maybe engaging in male to male sex in prison. No one knew for sure. He'd continued to use drugs and engage in high risk behavior until he began to suffer from the complications of AIDS a year earlier. He'd called his sister Ester from New York trying to hide his condition, only disclosing that he was sick. By the tone of his voice and how it was said, caused Ester to suspect the he had HIV/AIDS. She drove to New York to find him to sick to walk. He was exasperated from trying to be the brave, tough man he'd been nurtured to be. He was alone, sleeping on a mattress in a shooting gallery. In the last year, Ester had nursed him through bouts of illnesses.

At the hospital, a week earlier the doctors had told him he had a collapsed lung. Shortly after his arrival the other lung collapsed. His diagnosis was pneumonia caused from the complications of AIDS. The tough, treacherous man who once had a sculptured muscular body was now bones with skin stretched taut across it. In his frail face, his eyes and mouth looked monstrously large. Derrick was asleep with tubes running from his nose and hooked up to a breathing apparatus. Paula and Cedric sat quietly in the room in silence.

Their silence was broken when a young, Middle Eastern doctor entered the room. He appeared with a high spirited presence. "I'm doctor Hakim Ibn Rahman." Cedric stood to shake the doctor's hand. "I'm Cedric Newsome, Mr. Scales is my father. The words felt strange coming from his mouth. He'd never publicly acknowledged Derrick as his father before. "This is my mother." The doctor advised, "Your father must have some surgery if he's to ever have a chance of getting out of that bed and living a somewhat normal life again. We must repair his lungs so he can be detached from the breathing apparatus and breath on his own."

Paula's life was more stable and calm than it ever been in her adult life. But the stability and calmness didn't preclude her from hurting. A part of her still felt love and compassion for Derrick. If there was any type salve for her pain, it was seeing Cedric and his father together with the opportunity to find closure after so many years. Paula and Cedric concluded they would visit Derrick daily until he got better. Paula only visited a couple of hours each day but Cedric stayed throughout the day and night, only leaving enough to eat and change clothes.

Looking at the condition of Derrick, Paula wondered why God had spared her. Why she hadn't become infected with HIV when she'd shot heroin and sometimes shared needles with Derrick and others. Like Derrick, she had been promiscuous during her younger and drug using years. The fear of AIDS pushed her to be tested twice. She thought, "No way, the test could be correct, how could I missed being infected? It's got to be the work of GOD." It was easy for her to imagine herself in the same condition as Derrick. She knew if not for the grace of GOD, she would have been infected and sick as well.

Cedric's life for the time at hand had come to sitting beside the bed of his dying father. He and his father spent much of the time combing through his father's past. They discussed the difficult relationship Derrick had as a boy with his father, his tough upbringing and life as a ruthless criminal. Cedric was convinced that part of the reason God had him by his father's side was to lead him back to the love he had for his father as a young child. Every chance he got, he assured his father he'd forgiven him and understood his life. Each day Cedric realized he was watching his father die. One afternoon after waking from a long medicated hours sleep, Derrick took Cedric's hand as he begin to speak in a low weakened voice, "You know I loved your mother since we were teenagers, she was such a pretty girl." And with a weak laugh he continued. "I couldn't resist her, I had to have her. When you were born I was a proud young father, strutting like a peacock. I didn't know how to take charge of my life. I thought it was about being a gangster. That's what we all thought back then. Because of my twisted ideas of life and manhood I missed out on you. Now, I realized more than ever that none of the so-called good times and fast living was worth it. In my last days like most men, I know what's important, is family, if you got one."

The candid dialogue between Cedric and his father was the by-product of dying slowly. Derrick had time and the courage to empty his soul to his son. He wasn't concerned with being tough and carefree anymore. He captured the chance to be honest with himself and with Cedric.

In the last days Derrick's hospital room was a parade of traffic, people he'd not seen in years came by to visit. The room on any given day was filled with old friends from the "bottom", old school-mates, family and street hustlers. They all came to show their love for a dying man. During those days Cedric was beside his father's bed waiting on his every need. Derrick could feel his son's love around him. Cedric's love brought him peace and made dying easy.

People seem to die the way they live. But, in the end like Derrick, they all want the same thing: to be understood, comforted and to feel loved. On the eighth day after being hospitalized, at 3:09 P.M., Derrick passed from a peaceful sleep into death. Cedric was there by his side.

Derrick funeral was held four days later at Mt. Vernon Baptist Church on Roxboro Street, in the "bottom" two blocks from where he'd started his life. In the midday sun in the month of June a congregation of family and friends marched inside the red brick church. Derrick being a street hustler had no insurance coverage for funeral or the hospital bill he'd left behind. His sister Ester paid for the funeral from her saving. Cedric came with a check for $3,500 dollars and offered it to his aunt Ester to help with expenses. She assured him that she had enough to cover the expenses. Cedric looked Ester in the face saying, "I had to ask you, it's my responsibility." Ester's reassurance of having enough money to cover took a load off Cedric because he wanted the best for his father.

At 2:30 P.M. a large crowd of people were seated and the long black limos were parked. The church was mixed with family, friends and street hustlers all dressed up in their finery, had turned out in masses to bid farewell to one of their own. Following the attendant down the aisle, Cedric and Paula were lead to the first bench in the church. Paula took the first seat, then Cedric, aunt Ester, brothers Ray and Otha Lee. The remaining family members and friends filed in behind. Even with all the church windows and the doors opened, the early summer afternoon had the church steaming hot. People fanned themselves franticly. The slow low playing of the organist was almost drowned out by the appraising "oohs" and "aahs" from the spectators as the casket was rolled down the aisle. The expensive maroon casket adorned with full length high polished stainless steel handles was beautiful. It was stylish, a befitting send off, symbolic of Derrick's flair for dress and style.

Reverend O.C. Brown positioned himself behind the pulpit, read a long verse from Isaiah and commented, "The Lord Giveth and the Lord Taketh Away. The Lord blessed Derrick Scales with forty-two years in His Kingdom and decided it was time to take him on home." The sound of the people sniffing and crying quietly could be heard. Cedric and Paula both were wiping tears that ran slowly down their cheeks. The choir was lead by the soloist, a short dark round balding man who sang, "I'm Gonna Build Me a Cabin in Glory."

Reverend Brown turned things over to the funeral director, who walked up front to escort the immediate family to the casket. Paula was first, lingering and wiping away tears. She was assisted back to her seat. Cedric chose not to move from his seat. Derrick looked skeletal. The collar of his starched white shirt was meticulously folded back over his navy blue suit collar. The way he'd liked it to be. After all the family had viewed the body, the hustlers marched by tossing dollar bills into the casket which was the way hustlers sent one of their own off to glory. The procession of people met at Beechwood Cemetary where Derrick Scales was laid to rest. Cedric was left to contend with his short-loved relationship with his father.

December 8, 1997

The hunt was on. Detective "Red" Williams had a daily obsession with tracking down Michael Wiles. Wiles, was the only suspect in Angela's disappearance and was implicated by street sources in other robberies and assaults across Charlotte. Detective Williams was using all his resources on the streets to find Wiles. He pressured informants, prostitutes, and defendants awaiting trial for any information and leads to Wiles. Detective Williams periodically drove out to the Wiles family home. At times detective Williams hid in the woods by the Wiles' home place to see if Kevin visited his family. He'd cruise Wilkerson Boulevard talking to the prostitutes on the stroll each night after 9 P.M., asking questions and showing Wiles' picture. He visited the Doll House and Silver Dollar Lounge each night offering money and asking questions of anyone who'd listen, hoping to get a lead. The lounge managers were uncomfortable but knew he'd keep coming until he got his man. All eyes were on the lookout for Wiles. Detective Williams was a driven and determined man. He hadn't felt such an obsession with a case in years, since his earlier days on the force. He went days without a sound night's rest, almost every moment, everywhere he went he looked for Michael Wiles. He'd created a file on Wiles' life starting from his childhood. He had notes from teachers, old friends, family, the police, prison officials and a variety of pictures.

Michael Wiles was a man on the run. He could feel eyes on him everywhere he went. The Charlotte News and Observer had listed him as the suspect in Angela's disappearance while laying out his life in chronological order. The news story listed his past criminal history and displayed three different photographs pulled from police files. Since the night of November 24th when Angela was raped and murdered, Wiles and Kevin hadn't missed a day without being "jacked" on methamphetamines or crack. The day after day use had Wiles even more paranoid and delusional. He hadn't let Kevin out of his sight. Inside Wiles knew Kevin would break if pressured and tell of the murder, robberies and burglaries. He knew Kevin was weak and afraid of being locked away. Inside, Michael had a thirst for blood, brewing like a volcano. Combined with his psychological dependence for a daily dose of meth and crack, suffering from sleep deprivation and the psychosis induced by the drugs, he had become crazier than ever.

Michael and Kevin's days were spent hiding out in an old abandon farm house on the Brandon place. The Brandon farm was adjacent to the Wiles place. No one had lived on the Will Brandon farm in more than ten years. Old Mr. Brandon who was widowed had died in 1985. Both his sons Seth and Belton who attended the University of Tennessee had chosen to stay in Tennessee after finishing college. They never returned, leaving the farm unattended. The old farm house had no water, lights, or bathroom and only scattered pieces of furniture inside. Wiles and Kevin camped out on the floor each night on blankets, used candles for light and the fireplace for heat. They ate beans and sardines out of cans by the burning fireplace. They ventured out only for drugs and food. Everywhere they went people told them the police had been looking for Wiles and asking questions.

Kevin was living in fear. He was nervous and afraid of Wiles. He knew Wiles was unpredictable and violent. His addiction and love for drugs caused him to remain with Wiles, in spite of his fear. Kevin became a puppet around Wiles, obeying each command and not challenging any decisions as long as he got drugs.

Meanwhile, Wiles was looking for the opportunity to prepare for Kevin's murder. He needed a chance to dig a grave. The opportunity came when Kevin disclosed he'd like to visit his mom while his father was out of town on business. Wiles agreed to the visit on the condition that Kevin promised not to discuss any of their crimes and where they'd been hiding out.

Later that night around nine, Wiles and Kevin eased the red Impala from behind the old farm house and drove down Interstate 77 to Interstate 85 North and exited onto North Tryon Street. North Tryon carried them pass UNC-Charlotte. Wiles turned the red Impala left on Brandenberry Drive, an exclusive upper middle class neighborhood. Wiles sucked on a cigarette as he peered out the window of the car observing the houses. He looked at Kevin saying, "Boy your folks live around the riches. You didn't tell me about your neighborhood, I bet there's, all kinds of goodies in some of these houses." Kevin pointed and told Wiles to stop in front of a two story red brick colonial style house. Before Kevin could open the door of the car Wiles togged on his coat sleeve instructing, "Don't forget! Don't say a word about our business and where we're camped out." Kevin with a sheepish facial expression and with down cast eyes replied, "I won't." Michael instructed," I'll pick you up at 8 P.M. tomorrow night." Kevin jumped out of the car and dash for the front door.

Michael drove back to the old farm house. Once inside he threw a log on the dying fire in the fireplace. He stirred the fire with the poker sending sparkles of fire up the chimney. The fire began to roar and he warmed his hands and then got "jacked" from the remaining meth left from earlier. Wiles then put his old navy pea coat on, buttoned it up, tied a scarf around his neck, found his work gloves and headed to the old barn in the back to find a shovel. In the barn he found a square blade shovel. He walked a mile or so in the woods behind the old Brandon house to his graveyard. The area was familiar; he'd dug graves and buried his victims in shallow graves in the wooded area before. Michael dug Kevin's grave as he drank a beer he'd brought along. After fifteen minutes of digging he stopped to light a joint. He finished the four foot deep grave in an hour.

The stage was set Kevin would die at the first opportunity. Michael felt an emotional rush as he thought of murdering Kevin. It gave him the same anticipatory feeling as he felt when he waited for his next blast of meth. He had it all planned out. He'd use the ten pound sledge hammer he'd found in the barn as his weapon. He'd placed it in the old farm house days ago without Kevin noticing. He knew if Kevin noticed the hammer, he'd explain it was there to drive a wedge while splitting wood for the fireplace.

The following night on December 9, 1997, Michael Wiles sounded the horn of the old red Impala exactly at 8 P.M. as promised. Kevin ran out the house immediately and jumped into the car with Michael. He was on edge. He hadn't had any drugs in over twenty-four hours. All he could think of was his next blast. Michael greeted Kevin with a cynical smile as he slammed the door in a low tone, "What's up man?" Kevin ran his mouth non-stop, explaining he'd enjoyed his visit with his mom, had a bath, some decent food and that his mom had given him one hundred and fifty dollars. He anxiously requested, "Let's go find some meth." As he spoke he handed Michael the cash. Kevin felt as if he was walking on egg shells with Michael. He was always trying to gain Michael's trust, friendship and approval.

Michael reached for the money and smiled, cramming the money in his shirt pocket as he headed south on I-85 south to I-77. He exited off onto Wilkerson Boulevard, drove to the "red light" district and parked two blocks away from the Silver Dollar Lounge. He ordered Kevin to stay in the car. He didn't want anyone to see Kevin with him. Michael opened the door of the Impala, stepped out onto the street, pulled his hat down on his head, looked from side to side and walked toward the Silver Dollar. He spotted his connect, Big Jake a six foot six inch, long bearded man outside leaning against his 4x4 Chevy truck. "Well, if it ain't the most popular man in town." Big Jake said. Michael looked at Big Jake as he gritted saying, "Let me get a quarter." And without another word, Big Jake took the money and passed Michael the small package of meth. Jake warned, "Hey man take it easy be safe."

Michael made his way back to the Impala where Kevin was anxiously waiting. Michael entered the car without a word and headed down Wilkerson Boulevard to I-77 North toward Mooresville and exit onto

Highway 21 for the old farm house. Michael stopped at the country store as he turned left from Highway 21 onto Horn Road. There he brought beer and a few can goods to quench his hunger on the following morning.

Michael drove the Impala down the overgrown and weeded driveway to the old house. He parked the car behind the house out of sight. He and Kevin dashed into the cold house. Inside Michael stooped in front of the fireplace with matches and kindling to start a fire in the fireplace. While working to start the fire, Michael began to pick and probe Kevin, "So how did your mom like your little visit?" Kevin rubbing his hands together trying to warm himself replied, "She was glad to see me as always and tried to get me to stay." Michael stirred the fire asking, "Did she ask you why you were in such a rush to go when you left?" Kevin pacing back and forth behind Michael as he knelt in front of the fire retorted, "No she thinks I'm shacked up with some stripper. I told her we were staying in her hotel room. The idea of me staying with a stripper called for a ten minute sermon. Man I had to get out of there. I was glad to see you when you drove up." Michael was uncertain of whether Kevin hadn't dropped any useful information to his mother. He knew that Kevin off-times ran his mouth not stopping to think what he was saying.

In fifteen minutes the fire in the fireplace had begun to take the chill out the room. Kevin was anxiously waiting for Michael to settle down so they could smoke the meth they'd purchased. He didn't dare ask for the dope before Michael was ready. Once the fire was burning strongly, Michael turned with a smile and sprang to his feet saying, "Let's try the dope and see if it's any good." Kevin walked over to the corner where he slept and picked up the glass pipe. Michael filled the pipe, lit it and motioned for Kevin to hit it first. In minutes Kevin was zooted, talking out of control and feeling like his heart was about to jump out his chest. The meth had his heart and mind racing. Kevin paid Michael's demeanor and penetrating stare no mind. He was enjoying the chemical affect of the meth as it attacked his brain and nervous system.

While Kevin sat at the old wooden table sucking on the pipe, Michael eased behind him. Michael picked up the sledge hammer and with a powerful blow, slammed the hammer down onto Kevin's head, crushing his skull. Blood splashed and splattered over the entire room. Kevin made only one sound when the hammer made its initial contact, he gave a semi-scream. He was dead almost instantly. Michael let out a blood chilling laugh as he stood over Kevin's trembling body with the hammer in his hand, legs spread apart and a cigarette dangling from his lips, ready for the next assault if need be. Kevin's body trembled and trembled as the life it once held faded away.

Michael placed the hammer back in the corner of the fireplace. He calmly set at the table and finished smoking from the pipe Kevin had been using minutes before. He smoked the remaining meth he'd brought with Kevin's money. When the meth was all gone he put on his navy pea coat, gloves and hat. He went out to the shed and got a wheel barrel. He loaded Kevin's body in the wheel barrel and pushed it down into the woods and dumped the body into the open grave. Michael filled the grave with dirt, debris and covered it with leaves. He then pissed on the grave and journeyed back to the farm house for a night of rest.

December 14, 1997

It was cold and the ground was covered with a thin coat of ice which came from the rain of the night. Basil Keane was up as usual at 5:30 a.m., going through this morning dumb-bell workout. Over the years his six foot frame had carried the same one hundred and ninety pounds. He looked excellent for a man of fifty-two. As he looked out the front window of his multi-level home on Wendover Road, he noticed the two cars in his driveway had a thin coat of ice and frost causing the windows to look as if they'd been sprayed with a thin layer of white paint. After finishing his workout, he turned on the coffee pot to brew his morning start up fuel. He'd drunk a cup of coffee each morning by six o'clock for over twenty-five years, as a habit. While the coffee brewed he went outside to inhale the fresh morning air and fetched the newspaper from the driveway.

Each morning he prepared breakfast for his wife Martha and himself. By 6:45 the table was set with steaming hot coffee, scrambled eggs, toast or bagels. On some mornings he'd be creative by making a soufflé. Basil started the breakfast routine back when his two children were in elementary school almost twenty years earlier. He and Martha found that teamwork in preparing the kids for school made it easy for the both of them and created a sense of family sharing on a daily basis. After the children Darrah, and Bobby, left for college at UNC-Chapel Hill, Basil continued his breakfast routine.

Basil and Martha Keane had been married for over thirty years. They'd met in high school in Union, South Carolina as sophomores in geometry class. Basil's family owned a small farm and had always made a living selling tobacco, wheat, corn and vegetables. He was a good student and complied with his parent's rules.

Martha was reared by parents who ran an all purpose country store. By age ten Martha had been trained to help out in the store. She stocked the shelves, ran the register and assisted customers. She was smart, attractive and wanted to be a nurse.

After high school Martha enrolled in the nursing program at Central Piedmont Community College in Charlotte. After being away for one year in the big city of Charlotte, Basil decided to ask for her hand in marriage. He wasn't willing to risk losing her to some city slicker. In Basil's eyesight Charlotte was the big city, comparable to New York where one's morals and principals could be eroded just by breathing the air. Martha accepted his hand in marriage and in 1969 they were married in their hometown of Union, South Carolina on a Saturday afternoon in June.

Basil moved to Charlotte with Martha and it had been blissful ever since. Martha was out of the door each morning by 7 a.m., in route for Charlotte Memorial Hospital where she worked as the head nurse on the intensive care unit. She had worked on the same job for the last fifteen years. Her first job offer after college was for a doctor in private practice starting right out of college. The doctor, in time, lost focus on why she was there. He became impossible to work for. His desire for Martha as a woman compromised his ethics and ran her away. Charlotte Memorial allowed for a more open, non personal work environment.

Basil started to work for the Mecklenburg County Planning and Development a month after coming to Charlotte, in 1969. Over the years he'd worked up to being supervisor of the surveying crew. He supervised a crew of six men who worked from one side of the county to the other. His crew measured, marked and documented land space of properties.

On the morning at hand, Basil and his crew had been working in Pineville for the second day. They'd worked cutting away brushes and measuring property off Neal Road around the old Jim Miller property. At noon as usual the crew of men decided to take lunch by the old house place. The men were engaged in playful discussions of their plans for the

Christmas holidays. Basil described his anticipation of returning to Union for a few days of dove hunting. Being a country boy at heart, he drove to Union to hunt dove with a few old friends every chance he got. He'd been dove hunting since he was twelve years old. His father brought him a twenty gage double barrel shotgun at twelve and with old speck, their trained pointer, the best bird dog around, Basil killed his first set of dove. He'd been hooked every since. They'd parked the trucks by the old well in the back yard of the old house. As they settled into their lunch, they became distracted by an awful stench. The men folded their bag lunches and began to look around the area for the source of the odor. Bob Latham a fifty year old black man who'd worked with Basil for ten years realized the odor was from the well behind them. Bob with the other men around used his flash light to look into the well. In a few minutes they saw what appeared to be a human body floating in the well. Basil used his radio to call the planning office and reported what they'd found.

By mid-day, the old Jim Miller's home place was swarming with sheriff's deputies, CSI officers, investigators from the coroner's office and many others. Lights flashed everywhere, blue for cops and red for the ambulance. The yellow Mecklenburg County Sheriff's cars were parked all around the old house and backyard. The partially decomposed body would be that of Angela Slade. The body had not been removed from the well. One cop took pictures while others scribbled notes and looked around. Radios squawked, just like in the movies. People in uniforms were bumping into one another. Small white bags with unseen things in them were removed from the well.

The photographer stood by the well and at times looked into the well and flashed away. Finally, a stretcher emerged from the ambulance and was carried to the well. The CSI officers had bought Angela's body from the pit of the well. Two CSI officers grabbed Angela's feet and two others her arms and gently lowered on the stretcher.

Detective "Red" Williams arrived as the CSI officers were taking the body from the well. He could see the body was that of a young black female. He knew in his gut, they'd found Angela Slade. Within two hours the identity was confirmed. Angela's driver license was found in the zipped pocket of her jogging suit jacket which clung to her partially decomposed body. The confirmation that the person heisted from the well was officially Angela Slade caused Detective Williams' stomach to turn over. He hadn't been so affected by a case in years. Maybe it was because in some way

Angela represented the daughter he and his wife Emma had lost years prior to a hit and run driver. This is why the Slade case gripped him.

Detective Williams stared at Officer Henry Brown's telephone number pinned with two dozen other notes on the chalk board behind his desk. Officer Brown had asked to be called at the first sign of a development in the case. Detective Williams called Brown and caught him in the station house. His tone of voice alerted Brown, and he knew the news was bad. Williams said, "Brown this is Williams down in Homicide, how you doing?" Brown softly replied, "I'm doing."

"Listen, the girl Angela was found this morning out in Pineville in a well." Williams said. As he described the incident of how the body was discovered he choked up for a second and cleared his throat. Officer Brown was speechless for a second and couldn't find any words except, "Damn, damn, she didn't deserve that. She was a good person." Then Brown asked, "What do we do at this point?" Detective Williams in a slow methodical tone replied, "We have the task of informing her family, first. Tell you what, I'll call her parents and maybe you call the boyfriend. Look, I know there's no easy way to do this, do the best you can."

Cedric believed he'd prepared himself as best he could for the worst news. Realistically, he knew usually someone missing for weeks most likely had been killed. Although, logic told him Angela was dead, in his heart he prayed for a miracle. The possibility of Angela's death helped him put things in a different perspective. He became smarter than he normally was from the lessons he'd learned while not knowing Angela's fate. His relationships with other women had become of no importance as he waited in despair. Over the months before Angela's disappearance he'd realized she was his measurement of a woman; with all the women he'd consorted with since the breakup with Angela, none had treated him with the unconditional love and sincerity of Angela.

The phone rang at 4 p.m., as Cedric rearranged some files on his desk. For weeks he'd been virtually unproductive at work, merely showing up each day in a trance. His co-workers each compensated for his inability and offered any help they could. When he recognized Hanks voice, sorrow took over his soul. "Hey, Ced this is Hank. How's things." Cedric apprehensively replied, "I've been making it."

"Well, there's no easy way to say this. We found Angela this morning. She's dead. I'm so sorry Ced. I wish I could change things." Cedric felt as if his heart had been ripped from his chest. For a long moment he was speechless. Finally he asked, "where was she". Hank explained where they'd found Angela, and that the police was hunting the suspect whose finger prints were found on her cell phone. Hank then asked, "Do you want me to drive up to Durham to stay with you awhile."

Cedric tearing and choked up countered, "I'll be okay. I just need some time. I'll go home to my grandparents."

Hank replied, "I'll check in with you each day. Is anyone with you now?"

In between sobs Cedric reassured Hank that he was upset but would handle things.

After finishing the phone call with Hank, Cedric sat in his office until 6 P.M. in solitude. He cried and prayed for the strength to endure. He stared at the picture of Angela on his desk and cried some more. At 7:00 p.m. he gathered himself, waited to make sure the other staff had left for the day and exited from the Computech complex. Driving down Alexander Drive from the Research Triangle Park, he felt anger toward Angela's murderer and guilt for breaking up with her over what was now non-sense.

Once on Roxboro Road he was attacked by hunger pains. He hadn't had any food in two days. His senses were out of touch with the rest of his body, he hadn't thought of eating. For days he'd been forcing himself to function out of necessity. At the moment he decided on fish from Fine's Restaurant. He drove to Fines for some of Mrs. Berma's fish, macaroni and cheese and whatever else she suggested. As he parked, he could see Josh Dockery at his usual table by the window reading the newspaper. Once inside the aroma of the food and the smiling faces of Mrs. Berma and Wendy lifted his spirits to a degree. Josh summoned Cedric to join him. Josh, a strong and tough man, looked Cedric directly in the face asking, "Are you okay? I heard about your friend being missing down in Charlotte. I spoke to your grand-daddy on yesterday." Josh's inquiry was direct and masculine but laced with love. The care seen in Josh's eyes caused Cedric to choke up. Cedric replied, "Well, I don't know how I am right now. I received a call around 4 o'clock. and the police in Charlotte found Angela's body." Josh reached out and placed his hand on Cedric's shoulder. "I'm sorry son, is there anything I can do?" Then he called, "Wendy, Berma come over here!" Wendy and Mrs. Berma made their way over to Josh's window table. Mrs. Berma inquired, "What's going on over here?" Josh explained that Angela's body had been found. "Listen", said

Mrs. Berma. "I'm, we're all so sorry about Angela. Ced you know you're like one of my children. If there's anyone who don't deserve all this is you, and of course neither did Angela." Her voice cracked and she broke off. Wendy standing by her mother interjected, "No one deserves something like this; this is horrible." Wendy looked at Cedric and saw that his eyes were drowning in tears.

The Dockery's words were the first expressions of condolences that anyone had given Cedric since receiving the news of Angela's death. He was not prepared to deal with it. The dark cloud of sorrow imprisoned inside him for week's suddenly burst loose as he wept. Wendy knelt and embraced him where he sat. It was a sensitive and caring embrace. Wendy whispered "It'll get better." As she spoke she rubbed his back. Her presence and warm caring touch consoled him.

"It didn't have to be." Cedric said, "The suspect is a guy who'd raped before and was let out of prison. Plus, I shouldn't have been so stupid. Chasing women, and running Angela away. If not for the breakup, we would have been married, living in Durham. I feel terrible, it s my fault." Josh replied, "Son things happen the way they're designed and for a reason. We're here for you. Don't forget that. And don't blame yourself."

Cedric replied. "I know if I need you, I can count on it. But, I chased all the women who came my way for all the wrong reasons and that is why we broke-up. I'm twenty-eight years old and the only woman I've ever loved is dead. I had my head stuck up my ass and was concerned about stroking my ego, chasing a collection of skirt tails that meant nothing to me. I cared more about trying to prove my manhood, than about the woman who loved me."

Wendy who was walking away stopped and stared passionately at Cedric and said, "Ced, there's nothing you could have done." Cedric countered and said, "Maybe not but I can't see that right now." Wendy turned pulling napkin out her pocket, walked over and dried Cedric's eyes. She hugged him again. Her firm body, sweet perfume and tenderness created a reincarnated feeling of the comfort he'd felt in Angela's arms. Wendy scooted over to pick-up Cedric's food which her mother had waiting. She returned and sat, talking with Cedric concerning the investigation attentively as he forced down the food.

Cedric finished his meal, said his good-byes and headed for home in River Forest. He was happy to be living with his grandparents. He knew they would console and comfort him until he felt better. He'd thought of moving out many times but decided to wait out his plans to marry Angela and build their own home. They'd brought a five acre tract of land in Rougemont, where they'd planned to build their dream house. Their break-up had put everything on hold. But, tonight he was thankful for the company his grandparents would provide him.

Detective Williams didn't know exactly what he'd say. He thought, "How do you tell a father and mother their child have been found dead in a well and sheild them from the pain?" He knew that informing someone of a death was one of the acts of life where there's no rehearsal. He gasped a deep breath before picking up the phone. He slowly dialed the Slade's number. Part of him prayed no one would answer. The phone rang twice then Joe Slade's baritone voice was on the other end. "Hello, the Slade's residence."

Williams replied, "Mr. Slade good evening, this is John Williams, Charlotte Police Department." At the sound of Detective Williams' voice Joe Slade's hand trembled as he held the receiver. He noticed how the sun shining through the den window and, simultaneously knew his daughter had been found dead. Detective Williams paused before saying, "We found your daughter this morning around noon. She had been killed it appears. I'm sorry Mr. Slade." Joe Slade's voice cracked as he replied, "I see. Do you know what happened?" Williams replied. "Not for sure but we believe she was attacked at the ATM banking machine on Tyvola Road. Where she was possibly robbed, killed and taken to the location where we found her." Detective Williams hesitated thinking of how cold and heartless it had been for the killer to have thrown Angela in a forty foot well and now he had to be the one to give him the gory details to her parents. He finally replied, "She was pulled from an old well down in Pineville right outside Charlotte." As Detective Williams struggled to disclose the information to Joe Slade with as much care as possible, he could hear Claudette Slade in the background screaming cries that sounded like a wounded animal. Detective Williams again said, "Mr. Slade we need you to come to Charlotte to officially identify your daughter." Joe Slade paused before speaking, "I'll be there tomorrow."

John Williams hung the phone up and wiped the moist tears from his eyes and grumbled out loud, "I'm getting to old for this." He thought, "I know Michael Wiles is my man and that bastard's gonna do it again. I know it." He grounded out what was left of his cigar and reached for his jacket. He felt if he could just track down Wiles, nail the sonofabitch, a giant load would be lifted. He left out his office determined to find Wiles before another innocent person was victimized by the psychopathic madman.

The young attendant, directed Detective Williams, Joe Slade and Rev. Neal Davis to a room with refrigerated bins, and pointed to a wheeled stretcher where Angela's body lay covered with a sheet. "That's her" Joe said in a flat voice. "That's Angela," Rev. Davis repeated. He was the Slade's friend and Pastor and had come along with Joe on his sad journey to Charlotte. He placed his arm around Joe's shoulder. They both turned away. Detective Williams brought the sheet back over the corpse with one professional turn of his wrist. After hundreds of trips to the morgue I've learned how it's done he thought.

The Detective walked beside the two men under the naked glare of the florescent lights and corridors with the smell of antiseptic and embalming fluid. The hallway light was sickly white and silence as dead as a desert night.

"Are you guys alright?" Williams asked. Slade replied, "We're okay, these are tough times, I want you to know we appreciate your kindness and help." Joe Slade's words tugged at Williams' heart. Claudette and I will be looking to hear from you."

December 20, 1997

The long black limos and hearse with a procession of cars following eased down Fifth Street to the corner of Red Cross and parked in front of Saint Stevens Methodist Church. Saint Stevens a medium size red brick church was the oldest black church in Wilmington and had been the Slade's church since moving to Wilmington in the 1950's. Joe and Claudette Slade sat quietly in the limo as the crowd assembled by the door of the church. Claudette was draped in a satin black dress, gloves, black cashmere coat and with a scarf tied around her head. Joe Slade in a black suit and top coat had the look of a statesman. They'd painfully planned their daughter funeral not the wedding they'd dreamed of for many years.

If Joe Slade had his way, he would have disallowed all the public announcements of the funeral and limited it to just a few family and friends. He despised the fatuous performances funerals were frequently turned into by those officiating. However, he knew Claudette had always shared herself with others in public and private. She would have said, "If people care enough for Angela to want to pay their last respects, why not let them." Plus, Joe knew that was the tradition of funerals in the black community, where everyone's welcome.

Many hundreds of mourners filled the red brick church, most of whom had been a part of Angela's childhood through her work life.

Reverend Neal Davis, a small thin man on the late side of fifty, voice was sharp and impressive. He made direct eye contact with different individuals in the congregation as he spoke. "Angela was a beautiful and happy child in her early years. I can remember her vividly standing right here speaking of God as part of her Sunday school class with her pig tails, bright colored dresses and pan-leather shoes. She never left the church. As a teenager Angela stayed involved with the church when other young folk turned their backs on God and found their way to the streets. Each Sunday while she was in college she attended church and never missed a Sunday coming to Saint Stevens when she was home. Angela was a good child. God works in mysterious ways. God saw fit to call her on home. Our hearts aches and are heavy burdened this evening but God knows better than we do. I believe that we'll meet Angela again in heaven, those of us who make it. Angela has paid the price, she has completed her task. She's going on home to be with her Lord. Don't weep and worry about Angela, she now rests in Gods loving arms. What we must be concerned about is learning to live for the Lord ourselves. Finding the Lord for ourselves and making sure we are in that number. So that we can meet Angela in Heaven, where everyday will be Sunday and all our worries will be over. Hallelujah. Angela was raised in a home of love and where God was in charge. I know it's hard for us to understand but Jesus was ready for Angela to come on home. Goodness and mercy shall follow her . . . . and she will dwell in the house of the Lord forever. Angela was a beautiful and beloved girl and her soul has found its sweet, tender and final resting place."

The conservative Methodist congregation was mourning quietly throughout the eulogy until the soloist motioned to the pianist. The full sized and middle aged women with a voice akin to Mahalia Jackson offered her version of "Precious Load." Her beautiful voice and passionate tone tugged at the heart string of everyone in the church. Before she finished, the quiet cries and moans were audible and emotional. Hardly anyone in the church had a dry eye and could contain themselves.

A caravan of family and friends from Durham had joined Cedric on the trip to Wilmington. His mother Paula, grandparents Jack and Clara Newsome rode in the car with him. Other family and friends followed closely in a line of cars for the entire drive. As they circled through the streets of Wilmington, people stopped in their tracks, their mouths gaping open at the sight of the procession.

For Cedric the days since Angela's body was pulled from the well had been filled with grief and sorrow. The thoughts of Angela had been absolutely too much for him. At night while he slept he saw her again and again. She stood by his bed and at his window. Her slender body still girlish and fine toned. She came and caressed him where he lay and he felt the small miracle created by her touch. He heard her voice, heard certain expressions she used to echo through his brain, but when he woke she was not there. He then pressed his face into the pillow and cried himself back to sleep. In days past he'd become preoccupied with a building anger for Michael Wiles. His stomach was knotted and his chest felt like it would explode. He had fantasies of tracking down Wiles, confronting him and tearing him apart . . . . slowly, methodically inch by inch. Then he imagined throwing his broken body into a fire, watching it burn to a crisp. But, he knew that wouldn't bring Angela back. It wouldn't help. He had to allow Detective Williams to do his job. Today he knew he had to get through the funeral, one minute at a time.

After the burial, Joe and Claudette Slade invited the Newsomes over to their home. They chatted, looked at albums, laughed and cried as they looked at faded pictures of Angela. Cedric lounged on Angela's bed in her room that had been left the way it was when she went off to college. He opened the closet, the drawers, touched her things and breathed the ghost of her fragrance. Later he watched as the Slades and his grandparents sat on the front porch, recounting tales of Angela's life. As Cedric looked out the window he was dismayed by life's irony where both families were in Angela's home like she'd imagined so many times. But, today they were gathered without her being there. Inside he knew he'd never be the same.

December 22, 1997

It was two days since Angela's funeral and three days before Christmas. Cedric was severely depressed and overtaken with grief and quilt. He'd second guessed all his actions of the past. A great sense of lost had incapacitated him completely. Wendy Dockery had called earlier from the restaurant asking, "How are you doing? I figured you needed someone to check on you. I'm making sure you're okay." Cedric didn't have much to say but assured her that he was hanging on." Hearing her words of empathy and concern brought it own unique and positive reaction which was only temporary.

He was sluggish from tranquilizers and a night of broken sleep. The night of drugged sleep was broken as Angela came to visit him . . . . with her hair swaying across her shoulders, gentle smile, solemn eyes and her voice soft yet urgent. Cedric in the twilight of sleep reached out for her but she was gone.

Khalil read about Angela's disappearance and murder in the Durham Herald Sun newspaper. He'd also run into Fat Ralph over on Dowd Street and talked with him a day later. Fat Ralph informed him that Angela's funeral would be in Wilmington and he planned to attend with Goofiend. The entire thing stroke Khalil as being ironic, not seeing Cedric in almost ten years then running into him at the Roxboro Road Exxon, on the same night the news broke of Angela's murder. Khalil hadn't been inside a church since converting to traditional Islam nearly ten years earlier. Khalil the same as all other Sunni Muslims had to protect his monotheistic belief in one GOD by staying away from any gathering where partners, equals or intercessors were associated with GOD. He very well realized that if he attended Angela's funeral, at some point those officiating would violate that principal with calling on Jesus as their Lord. Therefore, attending Angela's funeral was impossible.

Khalil felt a close connection to Cedric's pain. He'd genuinely liked Cedric while in high school at Northern High. Cedric had been a popular athlete, student and an everyday kinda guy. He never had the big head. He associated and talked with everybody. Khalil also identified with the loss of a loved one through violence. His younger brother Larry who had taken to the streets and hustling had been gunned down in a drive by shooting on Corporation Street some eighteen months earlier. The Jamaicans who'd killed him over who'd sell dope on the block hadn't been arrested. The police seemingly had chalked it up to a trade related murder and written it off, case closed.

Khalil drove down Roxboro Road to River Forest in route to visit with Cedric. He'd offer his condolences and support. As he turned off Roxboro onto Whipperwill Drive he noticed the beauty of the day. It was a bright sunny wintery day and the colored leaves on the oaks and maples highlighted nature's splendor. The streets were quiet and the neighborhood offered a sense of peace and safety. Khalil leaned forward looking for the number 2408 Whipperwill Drive or the sight of Cedric's SUV. "Oh, there it is." He recognized the olive Toyota Land Cruiser. He slowed his speed and pulled his Maxima in behind the SUV. He didn't know exactly what to expect or what he'd say. He only knew he must reach out to Cedric as a friend. Reaching out to others in hard times was a form of charity which he was obligated to do and give as a Muslim. He observed the tailored lawn, neatly trimmed hedges and the Christmas decorations as he approached the door. He pushed the door bell and in a minute or two the door opened. Clara Newsome smiled as Khalil announced "I'm here to see Cedric. He's not expecting me but I'd very much like to visit with him. I went to Northern with him back in high school." Clara invited him inside replying, "Come in son, he's in the back, I'll go get him. I think I remember you, but all ya'll change so much after high school."

Khalil stood in the middle of the den until Clara returned. With a smile she announced, "He'll be out in a little bit. Have a seat make yourself at home." Khalil admired the clean, wholesome and comfortable room. There were pictures of Cedric, Angela and other family members scattered through the room. Most profound was a huge old looking framed picture of a tall big black man, who was dressed in work shoes, denim trousers, a brimmed hat and holding the reins of a white horse. As Mrs. Clara sat with Khalil waiting for Cedric, Khalil inquired, "Who's the strong looking man in the old picture." Clara smiled and replied "That's grand-daddy Tom. He's Cedric great-great grand daddy. He was a slave in Eastern North Carolina down in Murfreesboro. He was called Big Tom. All the Newsome men, including Cedric measure their manhood according to Big Tom's legacy. Good or bad." Khalil in admiration acknowledged, "He looks like he was a tough man."

Within ten minutes Cedric walked into the den. Khalil stood and reached out to hug him. Mrs. Clara excused herself and left the two men alone. At first appearance Khalil noticed Cedric's sad facial expression and life-less body language. He carried himself as if he barely had enough energy to move. He looked as if he hadn't shaved or combed his hair in days. As Cedric found a seat he gasped and said, "Hey Warren, excuse me Khalil."

Khalil smiled saying "I came by to check on you. You've been on my mind since I got the news and I had to come by. I hope I'm not intruding or anything."

Cedric lazily replied, "No man, you're more than welcome. And thanks for considering me."

Khalil asked, "How are you holding up?"

Cedric with a listless gesture replied, "I don't know man it is tough going." Khalil could see Cedric was in an emotional hole. He explained, "I'm here to offer my support. I believe I can somewhat identify with what you're experiencing. Eighteen months ago my younger brother Larry was gunned down over on Corporation Street in North Durham in a drive by shooting. You remember Larry, he was at Carrington Junior High our senior year at Northern."

Cedric nodded his head, "Yeah! He was breaking all the records in yards over there." Khalil continued, "Larry was my pride and joy, the ultimate kid brother. And I was his hero. The lost devastated me for a long while. Finally, I was able to put it into perspective. I finally was able to look at it from a religious point of view. I referred to Islamic thought and found that some of the wise people said, "Impatience over what is lost is a calamity or misfortune. And impatience over what is expected is foolish. When we question the events and misfortunes of life, we are showing signs of being annoyed with the decree of GOD the Almighty. You see Cedric, different from Christian thought, Islam teaches us to believe in GOD's decree of predetermination. We believe that GOD knows everything, creates everything and what GOD'S does not will, does not occur. And GOD in His knowing and creating is just and wise. No misfortune befall us but by the leave of GOD. And whosoever believes in GOD, He guides his heart and GOD is the knower of all things. Fatimah, the daughter of GOD's Messenger the Prophet Muhammad was once sent for, as her child was gasping for its life. But, the Prophet returned the Messenger and sent her good wishes saying, "Convey the salaams (greetings) to her and say, whatever GOD takes away or gives, belong to Him, and everything with Him has affixed term in the world. And so she should be patient and anticipate GOD'S reward in the Hereafter. Anyone who GOD intend good, He make him suffer some afflictions. So you see Cedric the preordainment of GOD will abide. His commandments are applicable to all of us and none can prevent them. Be it the patient or the impatient. Cedric the acceptance of GOD's preordainment helped me to overcome the loss of my brother."

Cedric listened attentively as Khalil explained his view of GOD's power over all things. Then he finally said "Khalil you make all the sense in the world. But, I feel so guilty, like it's somehow my fault. If I hadn't been such a foolish man, chasing every woman in sight maybe this wouldn't have happened."

Khalil smiled as he said, "Brother Cedric, it was GOD will that Angela left us. Don't blame yourself for that. That was to happen as it did. But what you can do is change the parts of your character you don't like anymore. Learn from what has happen and use it to improve on yourself in future relationships. There was nothing you could have done." Cedric replied, "Khalil it's all sickening. The suspect in this whole thing is a guy who has done stuff before. Like rape and was sent to prison for twenty years, then paroled after only four years. I just would never have believed this type thing could happen to someone so close to me."

Khalil nodded saying, "You or I have no way of knowing that some psychopathic nut was going to spot Angela at the ATM and victimize her." Cedric nodded in agreement. "Khalil your logic and wisdom is correct. It'll take time for me to get through this but I will."

Khalil asked, "So Cedric, when do you plan to pick yourself up and get back on a daily schedule and work?"

Cedric replied. "I'm not going back just yet, Khalil."

Khalil asked. "What do you mean by just yet? The only thing I'm sure of is that I can't just pick up my life where I left it before all this happened."

Khalil retorted. "I understand how you feel, but once you back on track, I'm sure you'll begin to feel better."

Cedric cut in, "It's more than being able to get back on track. I don't want to pick up my life where I left it. It's not just a question of Angela's death, healing my wounds, and getting on with things. Whatever I was before, I'll never be again. I don't want to be the same type of man. There had to be something fundamentally wrong with the man I've been. I got to take a close look at myself."

Khalil looked at his watch and said, "Man I've been here for almost two hours, I didn't mean to stay so long." With that he bounced to his feet. Cedric rose slowly from the chair he'd occupied with a look of relief and a half smile. He walked over and gave Khalil a manly hug saying "Man thanks a million for caring and coming by. You don't know how your visit has helped me." Khalil welcomed Cedric's remarks with a tug on the shoulder. Khalil promised to check in with him in a week. As Cedric and Khalil headed for the front door, Mrs. Clara shouted, "Ced, Wendy's on the phone for you." Khalil held up his hands to Cedric saying, "I'll see myself out."

BOOK II

"EVOLUTION"

July 20, 1952

It was 6:00 A.M., and Mammie Dockery a dark, overweight and stern women in her late thirties called out, "Josh you better get heh and eat. You know yo daddy and ol Mr. Whitefield is bout ready to go to the bacco field." Young Josh moved with a deliberate slowness making his way to the kitchen table for a breakfast of molasses, hoe cake and fried side meat. He took his time eating and headed down to the barn to meet his father and Herman Whitfield. He knew Junior Whitfield, who was seventeen the same as he, would already be there, standing around looking cynical making smart remarks. Once young Josh, a tall, strong and handsome young man made it to the barn, his father was waiting, "Josh you're late. Go harness up the horses so we can get to the field. We shoulda have picked a cart of bacco by now." Herdine Dockery pushed his son partly to impress Herman Whitfield whom he'd sharecropped with for five years and also because he knew they had to pick over thirty acres of tobacco before week's end. Josh hurried down to the horse stable, open the door and called for Old Mack, "Come heh boy," while simultaneously making a clicking sound, Josh bridled old Mack and in the ten minutes had dressed him out in the work harness. He moved to the next stall where Pete the white mule awaited. Pete was not as obedient as Old Mack and appeared to be not as intelligent. Josh knew he had to be more forceful with Pete to get the harness on. With Old Mack and Pete behind him, leading them with the leashes from their bridles, he headed for the tobacco carts. He hooked the animals to the cart using chains running from both sides of the harness to an iron singletree attaching them to the carts. Josh started his long day, beginning with the early morning dew from the tobacco drenching his clothes causing them to become soaking wet. By mid-morning the blistering sun beaming down had dried them as he stooped picking leaves from the stalks of tobacco. By noon the gum from the tobacco covered his hands, arms and clothes like glue. This was the first day of four more to come. By week's end they'd picked the entire thirty acres, plant by plant, leaf by leaf. Josh, his father, Herman Whitfield, Junior Whitfield and two hired hands Rufus and Percy had stayed in the fields each day from sun-up to sun down, every man caring his load except Junior. Junior being the son of Mr. Whitefield, the owner of the farm and the one calling the shots allowed Junior to drive the full carts of tobacco to the barn each time they were filled, where the women looped the tobacco onto sticks.

Each day Mammie Dockery rushed to finish preparing the mid-day meal and to get her two daughters Delores, Queenie and the youngest Dockery boy, Duffie, fed and to the barn. They'd loop the tobacco as Junior drove it to them from the field and emptied it onto the large table. Mrs. Martha Whitfield, Herman's wife would work only to mid-morning and come back mid-afternoon. The work distribution was unbalanced and so was the profit at season's end.

Queenie was one year younger than Josh and Delores on year under her. Little Duffie had come along seven years behind Delores. Queenie and Delores both were smart in school, obedient and had been trained to respect the authority of the Whitfields and other white folk, the way sharecroppers should. Their attitude of respecting whites was mostly because they were white. The respect was one that went unchallenged by most black sharecroppers. It was the way things were and had been for the longest.

Queenie, Delores and Josh all attended Person County Senior High School. The school was the only high school for blacks in the county. Queenie and Delores were both strikingly beautiful and the apple of Josh's eye. The boys in school all seemed to have fantasies when it came to the Dockery sisters. Queenie especially stood out. She was not only shapely with flowing silky hair but had a beautiful tan complexion and a face made for magazines. In addition she was as plain as day, friendly and outgoing. Junior Whitfield had his eye on Queenie as well, with his own plans.

Neither, Josh or his sisters had plans for their lives after high school, other than not carrying on the tradition of sharecropping. Josh a rising senior and good student was pressured by his father, who was pressured by Herman Whitfield to quit school. Herman Whitfield needed another full time man on the farm and Josh filled the order. Josh did not fold under their pressure and stayed in school. He didn't know what he wanted after graduation but knew whatever it was Herman would not be a part of it. Josh with a quick and sharp mind had long determined the means did justify the ends economically as a sharecropper. He had long notice that he and his family performed most of the work while the Whitfield's enjoyed the greater profit. He'd thought of joining the army but hadn't made a final decision. Joining the army was what many of the young black boys decided on after high school. Few considered college. The army, farming or a public job were their options, Josh knew he'd decide in due time.

Being born in 1945 in Person County to parents who were sharecroppers, Josh had never been fifty miles from his farm community of Shakragg, a small pocket community in the northern section of Rougemont in North Carolina just across the Durham County line into Person County. It was tucked away down miles of winding red dirt roads which sent one through a barrage of left and right turns before arriving. It was neighbored by Helena, another country community. Both Shakragg and Helena were populated by poor red neck farmers with attitudes that reflected their southern upbringing and disdain for blacks. The poor black sharecroppers were accustomed to the disdain of the whites and comfortable with their own inferior view of themselves. The farthest Josh had ever traveled outside of Shakragg was to Rougemont mostly, with its gas stations and all purpose stores. At times he pleasured his rides to Mariah, another crossroads section with a store and a gas station. Once as a little boy he remembered traveling once or twice with his father and Herman Whitfield to the tobacco market in Durham and Lynchburg, Virginia. In his seventeen years that was the extent of his travels outside Shakragg.

August 15, 1952

Queenie was taking care of her evening chores. She'd milked old Daisy, the Dockery's Jersey milk cow and carried the full two gallon bucket to the house and sat it on the table. Her mother Mammie was preparing supper, cooking mackerel patties, biscuits and fresh cabbage. As Queenie sat back for a breather her mother looked over saying, "Queen, honey, I need you to go to the hen house and see how many eggs you can find. It's getting late now, and I need the eggs to finish my mackerel. Now, run along girl." Queenie caught her breath as she replied, "Alright momma, I'm going." Queenie pushed her way out the kitchen screen door and strolled slowly toward the hen house. The hen house was fifty or so yards in the back of Dockery's house. With the sun going down she watched carefully with each step as she walked down the narrow path, being watchful for snakes in the path and in the weeds. Once she'd stepped on a six foot long chicken snake and had been petrified with the thought of snakes ever since. Lurking behind the brush by the hen house Junior Whitfield watched her. He'd spied and watched her for an hour before while she squatted exposing her thighs to milk old Daisy.

Once in the hen house, Queenie carefully looked over into the nest, making sure there were eggs in the nest before sticking her hand inside. She knew sometimes chicken snakes crawled into the nest and choked down the eggs. Queenie was doing fine. She'd collected over a dozen eggs which she held in the hem of her dress as she walked from nest to nest. Turning to leave she was startled by Junior Whitfield's presence. He looked at her with a lustful and mischievous smile. She could feel his eyes searching her exposed legs as she held the eggs in the hem of her loss fitting dress. Queenie gathered herself saying, "Junior, you scared me, what are you doing up here in our hen house?" Junior took a step forward and replied, "I'm doing a little hunting myself. I've been watching you each night when you come to milk old Daisy and gather the eggs."

Queenie feeling fear rising inside asked, "Watching me for what?" As he stepped closer she said, "Boy you better move out my way. What's wrong with you looking all crazy?" Junior whispered, "I heard about you black girls and how ya'll like to do it." Junior grabbed Queenie and knocked her to the ground into a semi-unconscious state. The world around her became dark and blurry. He was like a wild animal, ripping at her clothes. He tore her dress away, ripped her panties off and into shreds, and when her head started to clear he hit her with a crushing blow to the jaw knocking her unconscious again. When Queenie awoke she was laying on her mother's bed with a compress on her forehead. After staying away so long Josh had gone out to look for her. He'd found her unconscious, half nude and with bruises on her face. Josh awoke her and they slowly walked back to the house as tears rolled down her face. Josh angrily asked, "Queen who did this to you?" She murmured, "Junior attacked me and hurt me." After reaching the house and walking through the screen door of the kitchen she collapsed. Mammie startled let out a scream. She ran to Queenie and helped her from the floor into a twine bottom chair. Mammie with a mixture of confusion, surprise and anger on her face asked, "Baby what happened to you out there?" Queenie sobbing as her mother wiped her bruised face with a warm cloth replied, "Junior, momma, he, he attacked me."

"Did he hurt you girl? "Yes momma real bad." Mammie looked and saw the blood on Queenie's under garments while saying, "Come on honey, let's me clean you up. We'll see about Junior later." During the entire sequence of events Josh stood by in blinding anger not saying a word and then walked out the house into the backyard. He couldn't take anymore and needed to get away to himself.

One hour later Herdine Dockery came in from the fields. With his usual jovial spirit asking, "Honey you got supper ready, I'm as hungry as an old hound dog. I could smell the mackerels and cabbage before I made it to the house." There was no response from Mammie, and stillness was in the house. He knew something was out of order. He asked, "What's the matter round heh?" Mammie approached him from the bedroom with concern on her face wiping her hands on her apron. "Herdine there's a problem with Queenie." He looked around asking, "What you mean a problem with Queenie, what she go and do?" Mammie blew a breath of frustration as she said, "Herdine she ain't done nothing, that damn Junior Whitfield hurt her while she was out in the hen house." Herdine with bulging eyes of anger asked, "What 'n' the devil you mean he hurt her?" Mammie approaching warned," Calm down now, Junior attacked her and forced himself on her." Herdine in a rage ran for his shotgun in a rack over the door screaming, "I'll kill that white son-of-a-bitch, who the hell do he think he is?" Nobody harms a Dockery and get away wit it." Mammie ran and grabbed onto his arm pleading, "Calm down for a minute before you do something we're all be sorry for. Think, if you shoot and kill Junior you'll be hanged or in jail for the rest of your life. Then what'll happen to us?" Herdine calmed himself but replied, "Honey the son-of-a-bitch hurt my Queenie."

Josh had come into the house in the middle of all of the fuss. He heard his parent's entire conversation of what Junior had done. What stuck in Josh's mind most were his father's words. "Nobody harms a Dockery and gets away with it."

After the fuss in the house had quieted, Josh went to Queenie's bedside and held her hand. She cried covering her face. Josh spoke softly, "Queenie don't cover yo face, I still love you and none of this heah is any fault of yours." All this belongs to Junior."

Herdine went to Herman Whitfield about Junior's assault on Queenie saying, "Herman we got us a little problem, that boy of yoin forced his-self on my Queenie. And I don't like it a bit." Herman appeared unconcern and unmoved by Herdine's words and acted as if the rape committed by his son was okay. He finally said, "Herdine, you know boys will be boys, we all have sowed a few wild oats in our day." Junior and your Queenie just had a little misunderstanding they'll be alright just give em a little time. You know Queenie is awful pretty, I'm sure it's hard for a youngun like Junior to stay away from the likes of her." Herdine steaming angry only replied, "I guess you might be right." But in his heart felt anger, hate and shame.

In the months that followed Josh became increasingly angry with his father and mother for not addressing the violent rape which Queenie had suffered. He invariably mentioned his disagreement. He argued, "Momma you got to called the sheriff and make a report." He confronted his father while working in the fields on many days saying, "Pa we can't let Junior, get away wit hurting Queen like that. We got to do something. Call the sheriff or drive over to Roxboro and make a report or something." Neither parent would agree or bulge. Finally, in a rage his father said, "Josh leave it alone, I don't wanna hear another damn word about it. You're only tryin to start trouble. Things is the way they been always, leave it alone." At that moment Josh lost respect for his father as a man. He swore to himself he'd never grow up to be such a weak man.

After having his way with Queenie with no consequences, Junior strutted around like someone had pinned a medal on his chest. He made sly remarks. Looked at Queenie with lustful eyes and no one said a word. He began to flirt and make inappropriate comments to young Delores. Junior acted as if he had rights to both the Dockery girls.

Josh was filled with a storm of anger and contempt on the inside. Josh was planning his revenge. He'd be smart, savvy and patient. He knew he would exact retribution against Junior in time. But, for now he had to conceal his anger, hate and plan for vengeance. He'd acted as if everything was fine. Laughing at Junior's jokes; never mentioning another word of the rape to his parents; worked the fields each day as normal. Josh knew Junior's time would come.

January 8, 1998

Michael Wiles drove slowly down Brandenberry Drive. He hovered over the steering wheel of the old red Impala as if he was urging the car forward. This was the house 1624 but Kevin's father's SUV is missing. Michael thought, "He's on another one of his business trips, maybe." For days Michael had been pre-occupied with burglarizing the Trapp's home. Kevin had boasted of the fineries inside during one of his drug induced verbose tangents. Michael thought, "I'll ease inside once I know who's there, and take what I can. If the old man's not there it'll be like taking cake from a babe." He drove on by the house, circling the block once. He'd planned to wait and watch the house until Martha Trapp left. For the last ten days he'd stayed virtually off the streets day and nights. He knew since killing the girl at the ATM he was a wanted man. Although there wasn't much evidence to tie him to the crime, especially since Kevin was the only witness and was also dead and out the way. His face being splashed all over the papers and T.V. had destroyed his once reasonably normal human existence to that of a hunted animal, and all because one black girl had been killed. Kevin's death didn't matter. No one knew or realized he was gone. The hunt for him by the police, his hiding out in the old abandon house, the risky drives out to burglarize and buy drugs all were wryly and somehow appealing and an exciting game.

Michael sucked on the cigarette hanging from his lips. On impulse, suddenly feeling a fresh surge of blood pumping he pulled his car to the curb and cut the engine off. He eased his door opened, ground out the cigarette with the toe of his boot, flipped up the collar of his navy pea coat and preceded to the Trapp's house. He'd rung the door bell to make sure no one was home before jimmying the door. He'd watched the house and saw no movement. He thought, "Mrs. Trapp must be out." Once at the door he pushed the door bell. He waited and within two minutes the door swung open, Mrs. Trapp stood there with a black stare and asked, "Who . . . what do you want?" Then with fear written across her face she tried to close the door. Michael stuck his foot in the door keeping it open. It didn't come at once, but moment by moment, without any rules of time or planning. There was just the instance itself, Mrs. Trapp's face her fragrance, her loose fitting robe, it was taking place, which was how he preferred it, Michael's heart raced. When it neared its peak, when it seemed ready to explode he reached for his bowie knife and stabbed her repeatedly. Up close, the scent of heated fear mixed with the fragrance of her perfume and blood drove him senseless. Martha Trapp's screams and attempt to fight him off was short and futile. After twenty plunging strokes with his bowie knife her body was lifeless. Michael lifted himself off the lifeless body, looked down on his victim, brushed his hair out his eyes and surveyed the room. He then found the linen closet, grabbed several pillow cases and began to fill them with silverware, jewelry and anything of value as he circled through the house. He filled the pillow cases and deposited them in the backseat of the Impala. He returned to the house for guns out of the gun case, small T.V.'s and kitchen appliances. In forty-five minutes he was on I-77 headed to Mooresville to the old farm house. Mrs. Trapp's life and death meant nothing to him. He made the left on I-77 onto Highway 21 then onto the rutted dirt road leading to the farm house. As he exited the car the moon flicked among the tall oaks, and the air was piney and aromatic as if it had just rained. Michael with no regard for the life he'd taken went inside to evaluate his take.

Jim Hollis was up each morning by 6 A.M. for his morning run. He'd relocated to Charlotte from Fishkill, New York when IBM opened its manufacturing facility on Harris Boulevard. Jim had only ten more years before retirement. He'd worked himself up to area manager in the card and printed circuit board section. His wife Susan was also a career IBMer and worked in quality control. Their move to Charlotte had been good. The southern city was friendly, the housing affordable and the air clean. They'd found a lovely home only three miles from the IBM facility right off Highway 49. Things were good. As Jim stretched, loosening up from his run he noticed his neighbor's, the Trapp's front door half ajar. The Hollis house was directly in front of the Trapp's house which allowed him to have a clear view. He'd never seen the Trapp's up and out that early in his six years of being their neighbor. He didn't give it much thought. After completing his three mill run circling through the neighborhood, twenty-five minutes later, Jim noticed the Trapp's door still ajar and their small dog outside in the drive with his leash dragging from his neck. The dog made his way over where Jim stood going through his cool down stretches. The dog was whimpering, wagging his tail and behaving nervously. Jim looked down and noticed what appeared to be blood stains on the dog's small feet. He took the dog by the leash and decided to take him to the Trapp's door. Jim thought, "Maybe the dog was outside without anyone knowing so." He made his way to the landing which led to the front door. There he called, "Mr. Trapp, Pete this is Jim," he called several more times with no answer. He then walked to the half ajar door and knocked softly, "Hello, hello, Pete, Martha anybody home?" No one answered. Jim then pushed the door open and peeped inside. The sight horrified him. Martha Trapp was laid out on the floor in a puddle of blood. Her clothes were torn half off her body exposing her private parts. Jim's heart raced. He backed out the door, ran across the street into his house waking his wife Susan. He fumbled with the phone as he announced, "Sue something terrible has happened. Martha Trapp is on the floor in her house dead." Susan retorted, "What you mean she's dead?" Sue repeated, "Dead, Oh my God." Already half dressed Susan asked, "What are you talking about Jim?" Jim raised his hands signaling Susan to be quiet as the 911 dispatcher spoke with him. Jim nervously disclosed what he'd found to the dispatcher, "I think my neighbor is dead . . . looks like she've been murdered, 1624 Brandenberry, right off Highway 49. Thank you, my name? It's Jim Hollis." Susan asked, "Jim what happened?"

Jim replied. "I don't know but the door to the Trapp's was open when I went out to run. Then when I came back the dog was outside with blood on his feet. I went to the door, knocked, no one answered, I looked in and Martha was there on the floor."

"I can't believe this," Susan said. She stood there with a puzzled look on her face. Susan's world had been overturned. She couldn't believe her nice quiet neighborhood of houses that slept, neat and lifeless after dark could experience such violence. How safe she'd felt in her bed, behind locked doors. As though no notion had ever crossed her mind that anyone in America would dare take it into their minds to do harm to a soul around her.

By 9:00 A.M. Sergeant "Red" Williams watched as the falling rain created a small flood. The rain came in sheets as he drove down Highway 49 toward Brandenberry Park. The water had created a stream across the

highway at the bottom of the hill before reaching the university. The stream swelled and gurgled as the water poured down. He slowed his patrol car and splashed across; it was as if he'd crossed the Mississippi.

Williams remembered his shock as the news reporter on the T.V. blasted that Martha Trapp had been stabbed multiple times during what appeared to be a burglary. Then his phone rang. The investigator on the other end had said, "You might want to get over here, the scene has Michael Wiles written all over it."

Michael Wiles had robbed and murdered again. The rape and murder of Angela Slade was a tragedy and the two were doubly, so. Williams knew he had a real psycho on the loose. He wandered what would cause a person to be so deranged. He'd talked to the prison psychiatrist where Wiles had served time for the rape of his cousin at age sixteen. The doctor offered several explanations. The explanations were as the doctor said, "The lack of superego, that area of the brain that controls self criticism and enforces moral standards. Without it Wiles functions as a psychological child in an adult body . . . . who simply did what he wanted to do without caring about consequences." The doctor continued as Detective Williams listened to each word. "It could hedge on the concept of nature verses nurture. Wiles' condition perhaps was brought about by his environment . . . . his home life, rather than through his genetics." The doctor, an old and frail white man with long frizzled hair said, "I believe most psychopaths are created. The lack of bonding in infancy could cause certain nerves in the mind not to hook up."

Detective Williams slowed to make the right turn onto Brandenberry. He knew that Wiles was working on being labeled a serial killer. Williams wasn't aware that Wiles had long since crossed that bridge. Williams knew in his gut there was more to come. He also knew by the next day the news stories would be predictable, banner, front page headlines in the Charlotte Observer. He drove in front of the Trapp home. Police cars lined the street. Jim Hollis was introduced and asked for his story for the fourth or fifth time. Neighbors stood around whispering and peering toward the Trapp home. The coroner's office had officially announced Martha Trapp as demised and the attendant put her lowered body into the orange and white vehicle. Williams searched for witnesses but no one had seen anything or knew anything. Jim Hollis revealed that she had a husband, Pete who was a local businessman and a son named Kevin. Neither was anywhere to be found. Within hours of the tragedy, Pete Trapp was located and called in from his trip in Charleston, South Carolina. He was heart-broken and issued a statement decrying the senseless loss of his wife of thirty years. He called for authorities to find the vicious killer.

The next morning Detective Williams read with keen interest how the Charlotte News and Observer editorial section told of a rising tide of fear and anger among Charlotte residents.

He questioned people on the street, they felt their lives were becoming more and more vulnerable to random violence. Many believed it was caused by drug crazed addicts and in the case of Angela Slade and Martha Trapp a psychopath who needed to be caught.

January 10, 1998

Detective Williams called the SBI headquarters in Raleigh from his car. Moments later he was put through to Special Agent Rick Cates, Chief of the Scientific Analysis Section. "Rick, I've got to ask a big one."

Cates replied. "You can at least say hello and ask how I am first, you big, ugly joker." Hey Mr. Cates, how the hell are you today? Detective Williams recanted."

Cates Stated. "I could smell the shit through the phone. Red when you want something you got to learn to kiss a little first."

"Kissing ass, don't suite me." Williams replied.

"That's for sure." Cates laughed. "So what's up big guy?"

Williams said. "I've got a sicko running around in Charlotte. He's killed two women in a month it looks like. God knows what else. I got some evidence from the latest murder. I need you to give it the full treatment fast."

"How, fast you talking?" Cates asked.

"Like yesterday, Rick."

Williams insisted. "I'd like to drive up to Raleigh today."

Cates hollered. "Damn, give me a break Red. We're dealing with a thirty day backup. Charlotte's not the only city in the state screaming at us."

Williams stated. "I need this one, work with me, my ass is starting to itch, and you know what the means."

Cates replied. "Yeah, the sicko is about to get sicker." Williams offered no response. Cates swore, "All right, all right, bring the stuff up."

Williams hung up and drove straight to Raleigh. He arrived at 2 P.M. at the SBI Headquarters on West Salisbury Street downtown Raleigh. Cates met him at the escort desk near the underground parking garage and helped him pick up the required credentials and magnetically encoded tag. The place was clean with the cold sterility of a research lab. Leading Williams down a long light pastel green corridor, the SBI agent nodded at the box of evidence under his arm.

Cates asked. "That's it?"

Williams replied. "Yeah, It's not a lot but it's all we've got so far. It's from the murder on yesterday."

Cates asked, "You think this guy is still in Charlotte?"

Williams recanted. "I think so, he's a local guy. His family lives right outside Charlotte close to Mooresville. I think he's been floating around Charlotte since the first murder."

Cates looked at his old friend. They'd been friends since then police academy in the early days. Where Williams went straight from high school into the Charlotte Police Department, Cates traveled on to enroll in law school and then to SBI.

"So how does it feel to be working on what looks to be one of the hottest, most talked about cases in the state?" Cates asked. Williams didn't answer and walked down the long hallway looking straight ahead. He only shrugged his shoulders and gave a grunt.

Cates said in a low tone. "Red, come on it's a big one. It'll make you the cop of the year in the entire state."

Williams agreed and stated. "You might be right but it don't look like we'll catch the guy, if we don't hurry. I know he'll kill again, but first we must be sure we're hunting the right guy. That's where you and your guys can help us out down in Charlotte. This evidence will hopefully give us what we need."

Cates slowed at the unmarked door, slipped his magnetically encoded tag in the slot, and led Detective Williams into the scientific lab. Then he went to find the required help. Detective Williams stood in the lab watching, looking around, fascinated in disbelief at the sophistication of his surroundings. He thought, "I see why they are successful up here." He could see how the huge open room was sectioned off. The hair and fiber section was to the right of him with cases of evidence from police departments across the state. There were bloodied and bullet torn articles of clothing, sheets, towels and ropes that had been used to strangle people. The cold storage section had newly arrived body parts packed in dry ice. The room was an assortment of the proof that people were violent and acted with finality in their anger.

Agent Cates returned to the room and shouted, "Let's go, I got my group briefed and ready in another room next door."

There were two women and a man. Cates introduced Williams to the group, Bill Waltz of latent prints; Madge Stoval from the hair and fiber and Melanie Hobgood from documents.

In a matter of minutes, using white surgical gloves and tweezers, Madge was sifting through the boxes of evidence and spreading it on a lit examining table. "Is this everything?" she asked.

Detective Williams replied, "The cart and carbodle."

Madged asked. "Whose prints do you think we'll find besides the victim and her husband?"

Williams stated. "Well, I'd suspect you will find prints belonging to one Michael Wiles." There were only two people living in the Trapp house, the victim and her husband. Their son Kevin, I was told was in and out."

Madge asked. "What makes you think it's the Wiles guy we're looking at?"

Williams studied for a moment the responed, "We found his prints at the crime scene of another murder victim a couple of months ago where he's the number one suspect, and she too was killed with a large knife after she was robbed and raped. Also, my gut and years of working murders tells me its Wiles in both these murders." The talking and questioning ceased as Cates buttoned his white lab coat. He looked around saying, "Let's see what we can find."

The forensic scientist all walked in different directions to separate work areas. Detective Williams found a seat and a magazine. Occasionally, he watched the scientist as they worked. He felt like an expectant father in the maternity ward waiting for the birth of a child. The knowledge of the scientist, methods and technology was all high tech and mind boggling. He prayed they'd find what he needed.

Detective Williams watched Waltz operating the helium-cadmium laser as he searched out fingerprints from the victim's broken eye glasses and made the prints fluoresce. From articles collected as evidence smudges began to glow and appear. Some were only oil stains, but others were clearly exposed prints. Waltz examined each article through a powerful glass then photographed each one under high magnification.

Madge Stoval was gathering hair and fiber samples from the bloodied clothes the victim had worn and patches of carpet cut from the crime scene. She showed Williams stains which were probably particles of food bedded in the carpet overtime. With her powerful magnification and photo enlarging she found small gravel which was perhaps transported into the house by the assailant. She peered through her magnifying glass at a foot print that was found and lifted from the kitchen floor tile.

Melanie Hobgood was in the documents section examining the victim's check book which was found outside the house by the door. She made the Carolina blue paper appear to glow under the assortment of lights. She put a different filter on a small but powerful television camera and focused it on the paper. Then she dimmed the lights, leaving only the muted glow of an infared bulb and the pale green light of the television monitor screen. The screen showed colorless impressions on the paper that slowly took the form of writing. The deep pressure points of written words revealed themselves. Melanie whispered, "In a little bit we'll know the last check that was written."

Detective Williams felt welcome and found each agent in the section warm, helpful and professional. Each one was eager to explain what they were doing. He could tell they loved their work.

In awhile he was ready to go. He'd had enough of the sterile lab, the home of the dead; the missing and the forgotten. He was ready to return to Charlotte and find Michael Wiles. The latent prints found on the Martha Trapp's glasses belonged to Wiles. For Detective Williams that was enough. But, he still had to figure out why Wiles chose the Trapp's house to burglarize and where was the Trapp's son Kevin?

June, 15, 1953

Saturday afternoon, Junior Whitfield was on his way to the fish pond. His head was buried inside a broad brim straw hat to protect his face from the blistering sun. He wore bib overalls, a white tee shirt and a pair of brown work boots. His thin young body swayed from side to side as he lazily followed the path to the pond. His face revealed a cynical child-like expression which was a true reflection of his personality. In his hands he carried his favorite bamboo fishing pole, a can of worms and a half filled Mason jar of moonshine. He'd gained permission to drink moonshine since the age of fifteen. The permission came by way of his refusal to follow his father's direct orders prohibiting his drinking but as with all the other of his wishes, his father gave way. For two years since that time Junior drank whenever he liked. You could be sure to find him sampling his father's moonshine each Saturday afternoon.

Herman Whitfield kept a personal stash of moonshine as long as could be remembered. He'd drunk on every occasion he could find an excuse too. He'd carried Junior with him out of the deep woods of Shakragg down Red Mountain Road to Copley's Corner while he drank and bought moonshine since Junior was big enough to walk. By age twelve Junior had a keen interest in drinking and by fifteen, he'd decided drinking was one of the rights of passage to manhood.

The store at Copley's Corner set at the intersection of four fork in the road. It was a white clap board building with two gasoline pumps, a mechanic's shop and store all in one. In the back of the store was a pasture with horses and cows. In the distance were tobacco fields, a big white planter's home and scattered small houses for the sharecroppers. The store was a gathering place and red neck stop-over where white men wearing gummy bib overalls, brogan work boots, Red Man ball caps with unshaven faces with tobacco stained teeth drank and raised hell. No decent man with middle class or upper class values would fit in or be found amongst the group. Blacks who happened to stop by for gas, merchandise or soliciting help from the half drunken mechanic was watched with peering eyes, ignored as much as possible and only given cursory assistance when there were a few dollars to be made.

On this hot Saturday afternoon young Josh Dockery followed Junior Whitfield to the fish pond, making sure he stayed out of Junior's sight. Over the past year Josh had learned all of Junior's daily patterns as if they were his own. He'd stalked, watched, studied and took mental notes of Junior's habits, likes and dislikes almost minute by minute. Josh had suppressed his anger for a complete year while at night planning his revenge. From the day Junior had raped his sister Queenie, Josh had decided Junior would pay the ultimate price for thinking he could violate Queenie or lay his hand on any Dockery without consequences. Junior hadn't realized on that day in the hen house, he'd crossed the line of no return.

Since Junior's assault on Queenie, Josh had planned his upcoming year. First he had to graduate from high school in June. Then he'd enlist in the Marines months before graduation in time to be scheduled to leave for Paris Island basic training after graduation. But, before he left he had to take care of Junior. The last year of living on Herman Whitfield's property and working beside Junior had been a mental challenge. Each day he'd looked in the eyes of the man he'd vowed in his heart to kill. During that long year he'd behaved as if his heart was free of malice and hatred. At times he'd gone out of his way to show kindness to Junior while others watched. He'd laughed at Junior's jokes and sided with him on issues when he'd totally disagreed, to cover his anger and plans. He'd become a master of deception.

As Josh lay in wait looking through the weeds, he knew this was his day to complete his plan. Herman and Della Whitfield had driven to Roxboro as they'd done this time of the month for food, household and farming supplies. His father Herdine had left for his weekly drive to Rougemont to buy a few items and as normal would spend time watching the Saturday evening baseball game on Red Mountain Road by Jones's Junk Yard. Queenie and Delores wouldn't venture more than twenty-five yard from the house. They'd be busy cleaning, watching American Bandstand and other favorite programs on the black and white T.V.

His mother Mammie would be busy also, and fussing like a mother hen over his sisters, cleaning, cooking and training them how to care for the house.

Josh had been in the thick weeds amongst the honey sucker vines for almost two hours. Laying and waiting for Junior to become intoxicated and defenseless on the bank of the pond. He watched Junior as he drank his moonshine, baited his hook, cast his line, relieved himself and hummed country tunes. Slowly it became obvious that Junior had drunk enough moonshine. The words he sang had become slurred and he could barely stand without weaving from side to side. Josh knew Junior wouldn't have a chance once he unleashed his attack. Josh was over six foot four inches tall and carried over two hundred pounds of muscles. He was one of a few men who could walk a plowed field with a two hundred pound sack of fertilizer under each arm. For country folk and farmers that was the measure of a real man's physical strength and Josh did it at a young age. He out manned all the boys around as well as the men on the farm including his father.

Josh carried no weapon. He was an excellent swimmer, who'd been swimming the fish pond all his life. When the time came he'd attack Junior and wrestle him into the pond, drowning him. He knew he must be careful not to leave any scars or bruises on Junior's face or body.

Josh slowly crept out the weeds. He came up behind Junior without being heard. He made special effort to surprise Junior in the same fashion he'd surprised Queenie in the hen house. Josh stood behind Junior within arms reach. Then he cleared his throat. Junior turned around startled with fear in his eyes. Junior in a slurred drunken voice said, "Boy you scared me, you wanna a drink of my moon?" Josh starring in Junior's red drunken face replied, "No, I pass."

"Oh, go on have some," Junior slurred. Josh what you doing down here anyway? You don't fish." Looking at Josh, slurring, red faced, eye lids blinking and without balance Junior announced. "Josh you know I like you, you and I are friends, I know, I had that little problem with Queenie, but we've still been friends." The mention of Queenie's name caused Josh's heart to race and his blood to pump. Josh looked around for one last time to make sure no one was in sight. Like a wild tiger he leaped on Junior with full force, wrapping his powerful arms around Junior's small and drunken body carrying him into the deepest part of the pond. Junior let out several muffled screams. As he hit the water he kicked as Josh carried him under. Junior struggled, wiggled and wiggled. Josh held him under the water until his body was lifeless.

Josh swam out the pond dripping wet, breathing hard and fast. He wiped the water from his face as he watched for Junior's body to surface. He waited ten minutes making sure Junior was dead and began his walk up the path in his wet muddy clothes covered with kuckerberries. He felt no remorse. He only felt a nervous sense of relief and a concern of whether he'd been seen. He made his way inside the Dockery's five room weather beaten clap board house as quickly as possible. He'd made sure not to run up the path, running would have possibly drawn unwanted attention. Once inside he filled the tin wash tub with water, sat it on the stove to heat and then gave himself a bath. He made sure he washed all the mud from his body and kuckerberries out his head. Once out the tub, Josh used the bath water to wash to mud from his shoes. As he sat on the side of his bed drying his hair the door of his room swung opened. Mammie Dockery stood in the doorway. He looked up at his mother with inquiring eyes.

She smiled, and asked, "Why in the world were you in such a hurry for your Saturday afternoon bath? Boy I can never figure you out. And how in the world did you get your clothes so wet and muddy?"

Josh forced a smile and spoke, "Ma you never stop with your questions. I was over by the Parrish place in the creek crabbing." Mammie turned to leave then said, "Be sure to clean up your mess."

Herman and Della Whitfield returned home right before 6 P.M. Josh who'd been uneasy all evening, recognized the sound of the 1950 Chevy pick-up when it slowed to turn into the Whitfield's driveway. The sound of the Whitfield's truck caused him to become more anxious but he didn't move from the chair under the magnolia tree in the back of the Dockery's house. He knew surviving the next twenty-four hours without giving any indication of his involvement with Junior's death was vital. He'd rehearsed this day a thousand times in his head. He knew he had to stay calm, thoughtful and act as surprised as the others when the time came.

The Whitfield's unpacked their truck, placing the farm supplies in the outside storage barn and the food in the house. Then Herman Whitfield settled back in his favorite chair in front of the black and white T.V. to enjoy a Pabst Blue Ribbon beer as he watched the Saturday afternoon Championship Wrestling. Della was busy in the kitchen cooking pork chops, rice and gravy. In a short while Herman stepped outside and called, "Junior, come here boy, it is time to do your chores." It was time to feed the horses, pigs and milk old Betsy. In ten minutes he called again, "Junior you better get started fo it gets dark." He yelled several times and returned to his beer and T.V. In a half hour at 7 P.M. Herman left his chair, buzzing from the beer he'd consumed and went out to search for Junior. He was a little irritated that he had to search for Junior. He thought, "That boy is getting more hard headed each day. I'll have to teach him a thing or two." As he walked outside toward the barn he yelled, "Junior, answer me boy. Where are you? Get here." There was not a sight or sound of Junior. Herman figured, "He must be down by the pond with that damn fishing pole." He walked the path down by the horse stable toward the pond, with each step he cursed and talked to himself. He was steaming mad. He swore Junior was impossible to deal with, "I'll straighten him out once and for all, just you wait."

When Herman finally made it to the pond; he saw Junior's lifeless body floating the water. He screamed, "Oh my God, no." Herman dove into the pond in an attempt to rescue his son. He then ran up the path to his house screaming and hollering. He stormed through the door reaching for the phone. His nervous fingers finally dialed the correct number, connecting with the Person County Sheriff's Office. In a half drunken and terrified tone he summoned the sheriff to his farm. In a half hour the Whitfield's farm house was swarming with three brown and beige sheriff's cars, an orange and white ambulance, uniform officers and a few neighbors who'd followed the ambulance to the Whitfield's. Herman led the officers down the path to the pond. Junior's blotted body still floated on top of the water. On the bank of the pond was the almost empty jar of moonshine, the can of worms he'd used for bait and the bamboo fishing pole was in the pond. Herman cried, "Oh Junior why you go and drown yourself?" The rescue squad pulled Junior from the water. Junior's body still ranked with the smell of moonshine. Junior was placed on a stretcher, covered from head to toe and carried away.

By the time Herman Whitfield and the sheriff's deputies made it from the pond, Mammie Dockery was at the Whitfield's house. Mammie held Della Whitfield in her arms, patted her back and rocked her as she wept. Mammie whispered over and over, "Honey, I know it hurts, God will see you through." She held her and rocked her. Mammie escorted Della inside the Whitfield's home where two white women who lived down the road took over consoling Della.

Sheriff Rance Blalock a silver haired stocky man with sun bleached skin called Mammie over to ask a few questions. Not that he thought she knew anything or saw Junior when he drowned. Sheriff Blalock's questions were only for his official report. Mammie spoke with the sheriff and assured him that she hadn't seen Junior all day. There hadn't been any sign of Junior around the farm since the day before when she'd seen him on the tractor by the tobacco barn. Mammie with a straight face informed the sheriff that since around 12 P.M., she and the Dockery children were all at home and hadn't seen or heard a thing. Sheriff Blalock scribbled notes on a yellow pad as Mammie spoke. After five minutes with Mammie, the sheriff had enough and threw the yellow pad into his cruiser joining the rescue crew who were preparing to leave.

As the sheriff's deputies, rescue team and coroner started the engines of their vehicles, Mammie hurried home. She walked to the backyard and placed wood around the old black wash pot. She called for Josh to come and fill the pot with water from the well. She started the fire around the pot to heat the water. Once the wash pot was filled with water; she added shreds of lye soap into the water. Mammie filled the wash pot with Josh's wet muddy clothes and clean clothes she'd washed on Wednesday. Mammie stood by the wash pot as the water steamed, punching the clothes with a stick while she sang, "Amazing Grace."

Mammie had been washing for twenty minutes when Herdine Dockery pulled his old black Ford truck into the dirt driveway. He parked his truck under the magnolia tree as always and walked over to Mammie by the wash pot. Mammie knew her husband well and at first sight she knew he'd had a drink or two of Melvin Jones' homebrew while at the ball game. Herdine looked at Mammie with a big smile on his face that highlighting the gold crown in his mouth. He asked, "Hon, what made you wash clothes on a Saturday evening? You should be getting some rest."

Mammie smiled graciously and replied, "I'd missed a few things on Wednesday and didn't want them to pile up." Herdine stood with Mammie chatting about his trip to Rougemont when Mammie interrupted him saying, "Herdine they found Junior drowned in the fish pond about an hour or so ago." Herdine seem to sober up instantly. His face was struck with shock and sorrow. Mammie disclosed the events of the afternoon while expressing her empathy for the Whitfield's. Herdine took his cap off his head, brushed his hair back with his hand, replaced his cap and said, "Hon, I'm gonna walk over to the Whitfield's to let them know we's sorry bout Junior." Mammie looked at Herdine straight faced saying, "Don't stay but a minute. They need their privacy now." As Herdine turned toward the Dockery house Mammie said, "Tell Josh to come here for a minute." Mammie continued to wash her clothes as Herdine walked away shaking his head in disbelief. In a minute or two Josh joined his mother by the old black wash pot. Mammie reached out and took her son's hand saying, "Come here honey." Mammie rubbed Josh's head of thick wooly hair, examining it closely, she then hugged him tightly. As she embraced him she said, "Everything's okay, now you go and wash your hair again. There's kuckerberries in your hair, go on now. Momma gotta finish her washing." Mammie cast a cynical smile as Josh walked away and continued to stir her pot of boiling clothes.

One week after Josh had drowned Junior in the fish pond, he was in route to Paris Island, South Carolina and Junior was on his way to the cemetery. Josh had boarded a bus in Raleigh with other young recruits at 6 A.M. on Friday morning of that week. As the bus traveled down unfamiliar highways, Josh knew he was leaving everything he'd ever known and cared about. There was no turning back, the dye had been cast. He'd enlisted three months before graduation and had exacted his revenge against Junior. As he observed the view from his window, he thought of how his mother, sisters and father all had hugged him as he boarded to Greyhound Bus with tears in their eyes. Josh's most intense felt emotion came from leaving the warmth and security of his family. He'd been raised around a family with a strong sense of family and kinship. He'd been a child with many relatives and a large extended family. Josh had no sense of nationalism, patriotism or any particular political ideology. He'd never given such things any thought. His only allegiance was to his family and kin.

Josh finally arrived at Paris Island Marine Base after ten hours on the bus. They'd stopped only once between Raleigh and Paris Island for their last civilian meal. On base the new recruits unloaded on a strip like parking lot with foot prints drawn onto the concrete, each at a forty five degree angle. The recruits were ordered to take positions in a set of the foot prints. Their next order was to go single file into the receiving area. The entire night was taken with filling out forms, being fitted for military clothing and settling into the barracks.

Josh spent the next twelve weeks in basic training. He and the other recruits were put through physical conditioning routines and general order classes. Each morning at 8:30 A.M. after breakfast they'd run for three miles and complete a routine of physical exercises. Then they'd attend general order class and fundamental Marine protocol. By 10:30 A.M., they'd be dressed out in their uniforms marching. Josh and the other recruits finally finished stage one (I) of their training. Stage two (II) carried them into Elliott's Beach. At Elliott's Beach they were taught to swim and float while wearing their uniforms, carrying back packs and weapons. Josh found the routine challenging but easy for a country boy who'd worked hard all his life and swam the fish ponds since a child.

By the end of the twelve weeks of basic, Josh and Jack Newsome a recruit from Murfreesboro, North Carolina had emerged as the top recruits. Josh and Jack Newsome liked one another instantly. They were drawn by their common background, being two of ten blacks out of two hundred and twenty-five recruits and their toughness.

They became the best of friends. It was very seldom you'd see one without the other. In eight weeks Josh and the two hundred and twenty-five other recruits graduated from basic training as proud Marines.

A month later, Josh and Jack were at Camp Lejune for FSTU training. They'd scored well enough to be sent to special weapons, tanks, AM tracks and RE-Con Ranger School. They spent their time training at Camp Gagle which was right outside of Jacksonville, North Carolina. On the weekends they hung out downtown Jacksonville on the strip. They visited the bars and topless joints on Kerr and Court Streets. On soldiers pay day like any other military town, Kerr and Court Streets the "Red Light District" would be overrun with prostitutes, traveling hustlers, con men and men peddling marijuana. Josh and his pal Jack kept their money in their pockets. They'd learned quickly that the best way to return to the barracks with their money was to keep a safe distance from the hustlers. In no time the two-some were wise enough to look for ways to make money. Jack began to bank roll the card games on post and Josh sold pints of whisky to his fellow Marines on credit until pay day at an increased interest rate. Josh Dockery and his partner Jack Newsome had grown into men with savvy, financial creatively and toughness. The young country boys from the farms of North Carolina were gone forever.

February 20, 1998

Old Mr. Mangum Barnhill owned and ran a country store off I-77 on Highway 21 between Mooresville and Charlotte. He'd known the Wiles clan for newly thirty years. Zeb Wiles had been raised on the Wiles farm as a boy by his father and mother in the 1930's. Mangum and Zeb had played with one another as children.

Zeb Wiles worked the farm as a Youngman, married his first and only girlfriend who bore him five children. Mangum Barnhill knew the Wiles family well. He knew the Wiles men liked their whiskey, guns and all of them had a mean streak. Mangum had watched Zeb's grandson Michael grow up since he was a lap baby. In Mangum's estimation Michael was the worst of the lot. He'd caught Michael a dozen times as a young boy pocketing candy and other merchandise from his store. Each time Michael would be defiant and refused to return the merchandise. Mangum would run him from the store and let his grandmother Nancy Wiles know of the latest theft. She'd pay for the goods while swearing that young Michael was the worst boy ever.

Mangum Barnhill like others around Charlotte had been blasted by the papers and T.V. concerning the murder of Angela Slade and Martha Trapp. He'd watched the evening news in awe and shock as the reporters warned the public to be on the look-out for Michael Wiles, the number one suspect in both murders. Mangum was old and set in his ways. Mangum and country folk in his day minded their own business and didn't get involved with law. The law was seen as an adversary, dating as far back as he could remember.

As far as he was concerned, the law only came around to harass people who were trying to make a living. He didn't concern himself with all the going on of city folk and the law. It wasn't any of his business. He only wanted to be left alone.

Mangum in the last month had become a little worried about his own safety. The fact he'd seen Michael Wiles almost twice weekly nagged him. Michael stopped by his store usually late at night for beer and small items of food. Each time Mangum's heart raced with fear as Michael took his time collecting items before bringing them to the register. Mangum noted the glassy look in Michael's eyes and the way he seemed to stare at him. Afterward Michael had driven away in his old Red Chevy Impala.

One Saturday morning, a week prior, Mangum woke up at 6 A.M. to do a little squirrel hunting. He'd walked the woods with his 22 rifle and squirrel dog he affectionately called Pup. After two hours and three or four miles in the woods nearing the Wiles place he'd come by the old Will Brandon house place. The weeds had grown up around the old house, the power lines were down and the place looked about ready to collapse. He wondered why neither of Will Brandon's sons had taken an interest in the place. As he looked closer he noticed Michael Wiles' old Red Chevy Impala parked in back of the house. Mangum stood at a distance making sure he stayed out of sight. He looked and studied. Mangum realized he'd found Michael Wiles' hiding place. The man every policeman in Charlotte was hunting. Mangum slowly backed away. He took care not to make any noise. He wanted no part of Michael Wiles. He never doubted that Michael was the right man. He'd seen it in his eyes each time Michael had stopped by his store. Mangum made his way back to his truck and headed on home.

The thought of the two murdered women and their families pleading for help from the public haunted Mangum. Since stumbling onto Michael's car behind the abandon house he'd been unable to rest. If he didn't call 911, another person could die. He thought that Michael might even choose him as his next victim. He knew exactly why Michael had chosen the old Brandon place as his hideout. The house set almost a half mile in the woods and it would take a stroke of luck for the police to find it. It was a good hide-out.

Mangum had watched all kinds of rescue shows on T.V. and knew for certain every 911 call was recorded. He didn't want to be recorded. He'd never tell anyone, not even his wife Ruth of forty years what he'd found.

The next day right after 4 P.M., Mangum starred at the phone on the counter by the cash register. He thought of the two innocent women and their butchered bodies. Mangum picked up the phone. He punched 911 and cleared his throat. He tried to disguise his voice. "Yeah, I think I can tell you where that guy Michael Wiles is hiding out." He spoke in the deepest voice possible and knew from the first syllable that it was a pitiful attempt at a disguise. He breathed hard and his heart pounded. "Who's calling please?" It was a women's voice sounding almost like a robot. Mangum replied, "Never mind my name. I tell you he's hiding out at the old Brandon place. A weed covered drive leads to the old house. It's next to the Wiles place outside Mooresville." Mangum slammed the phone onto the receiver. In his mind he'd done his duty. The rest was up to the police.

Word came to Detective "Red" Williams of the anonymous 911 call. At first he considered it to be another one of a thousand prank calls coming in. But, the fact the caller refused to leave his name, abruptly hung up and the location reported as Wiles' hide-out caught Detective Williams attention. Williams knew he had to follow-up on the call. Detective Williams called his Captain and told him about the call. He requested three men to assist as back-up to accompany him on the drive out to Mooresville. It was 8 PM by the time he was joined by the other officers. Detective Jorge Garcia rode with Williams as they headed up I-77 toward Mooresville with the other two officers behind them. They slowed and exited on Highway 21. Shortly Detective Williams saw what appeared to be an old washed out dirt road as described by the caller, leading into the woods. With a closer look it was apparent that there had been traffic in and out the weeded overgrown drive-way. Detective Williams drove pass the drive looking for a place to park the cruisers out of sight. A mile down Highway 21 he found a road that lead into the woods which appeared to be used by logging trucks. He pulled off the paved road onto the dirt logging road. Now, he and the other officers had to make their way through the woods to the overgrown drive-way and hope it would lead to the old farm house and Wiles. In twenty minutes Detective Williams and the other officers sat perched on a fallen tree watching the back of the old farm house and shivering in the darkness of the cold night air. About twenty yards to his left one of the back-up officers huddled in some brush, no doubt wishing he'd gone into another line of work. On the other side of the old house along the edge of the woods the other officer sat, watched and waited.

Detective Williams was wearing a wool blazer and crew neck sweater that the cool February air penetrated with ease. The patch of woods where he sat was located about fifty yards behind the old house, Williams was able to see the house was dark on the inside. There wasn't a light anywhere. But in his gut he felt it was the right place. He could see where someone had thrown trash into an old rusted out metal barrel and where wood had been chopped. There was a sense of invisible life, of people unseen yet still present.

Williams watched the clear sky and stars. He loved this time of the year, with the crisp air and long nights. With his leg growing stiff, still reminding him of an old football injury, he shifted to a standing position. He could see clearer now. There was an old chair on the back porch, a old wooden table in the backyard and a kerosene can by the back door. Then for the second time in the past hour he took out his service revolver, checked the chambers and slid the gun back into the holster. His gut told him Wiles would show up. He only needed to be patient.

At 11:40 Wiles drove down the weeded overgrown drive-way to the once abandoned house. He'd made his rounds, buying a quarter ounce of crystal meth and stopping at Mangum Barnhill's store for beer and sardines. Wiles parked the red Impala, exited the car, looked around and rushed inside the old house.

Moments later Detective Williams signaled to his men in the brush, who left the wooded brush and approached the backyard behind the house. One man was sent to the front exit while Williams and the other two positioned themselves around the back door. Williams stepped on the back porch slowly, trying not to make a sound. His men stayed on either side of the door. He drew his revolver and stood in front of the door, looked around and listened. Other than the sound of footsteps in the front room, the house was silent. Then with his gun extended in front of him, he crashed through the door.

Suddenly, the bright light beaming from the flashlight split the darkness in the house. "Police!" shouted a voice. Don't move!" Michael Wiles stood in his tracks and almost stopped breathing as the door crashed open.

"Hands over your head; slowly, nice and easy." Williams said. The other policemen came in behind him. The beam of light waved. Wiles didn't move, he stared at the four policemen who held him at bay. Wiles appeared to think for a minute and after taking a deep breath he raised his hands. Detective Williams walked up to Wiles carefully. He took Wiles hands down one at a time placing them behind him, cuffing him. Michael Wiles the suspected murderer had been arrested without incident.

Williams hauled Wiles downtown to Charlotte's Central Jail. On the way Wiles seemed unconcerned with being captured. He rode in the middle of the back seat and never said a word. Detective Williams knew the entire next year would be a legal circus, with squads of opposing lawyers and psychiatrist having a joy ride. Wiles would probably cop out to an insanity plea and come up for re-evaluation in a year's time after sentencing.

The Charlotte Police Department Homicide Division was totally unlike the noisy detective squad rooms seen on T.V, with their easy in and out access and chaotic atmosphere. Located on the fourth floor of Charlotte's fortress like hi-tech central jail, homicide could only be reached by elevator from the main lobby. The fourth floor doors would open only with a special key card. No one but homicide detectives and other homicide staff, and a short list of senior officers had key cards. All others needed advance approval and the company of a key card holder to enter.

Prisoners and suspects brought to homicide arrived via a guarded basement entrance and a secure elevator running directly up to the homicide office. The area was a quiet and controlled environment.

By 8 A.M. the next morning, Officer Henry Johnson and Captain Bill Timmons peered through the one-way glass as Detective Williams seated himself in front of Michael Wiles. "I hope the guy confesses," Johnson said,

"Leave it to Red," Timmons replied. "He'll work on him."

Normally a team of detectives would interview a murder suspect together, but Williams' previous successes supported his request to interview Wiles alone. Williams began; Timmons and Johnson watched and listened through the observation window. Wiles looked unmoved and worry free. He was thin unshaven, pale and appeared much older than his thirty years. He wore stained, torn jeans and a dirty sweat shirt. Timmons thought, "He looks pretty weird." Wiles seemed hard as he sat handcuffed to the metal chair. When Williams appeared he'd yanked on the cuffs, clanging them against the chair and shouted, "Why the fuck do I have to be chained?"

Williams stared at Wiles without saying a word, stood up and moved easily taking the cuffs off. Williams smiled asking, "How ya doin Michael? I'm Detective Williams; we met last night when you were arrested. Would you like some coffee or a cigarette?" Michael rubbed his wrist and muttered something about milk in his coffee. He seemed a shade more nervous than before. A tough guy, Timmons thought.

As a practice Detective Williams had brought a thermos, styrofoam cups and cigarettes. He poured coffee for the both of them, talking as he poured. "So you smoke Newport's, top brand, number one selling cigarette on the market. Sorry, I have no cream, you're have to drink you coffee black, hey, mind if I call you Michael. I'm John, everybody call me Red. See I want to help you out, if I can. In fact, I'd like to untangle this mess. Right now you're in a mess and I'd like to clear it all up."

Timmons stood behind the one-way glass, wringing his hands slowly and easily. "Get the Miranda over with Red," he thought nervously, knowing that Williams couldn't move forward until he advised Wiles of his rights, including the right to an attorney. Detective Williams wanted to present the Miranda with caution and in such a way that the answer came back, "No." Williams' skill in obtaining that answer was well known. Despite the low-key approach, Michael still appeared disinterested in the entire process. Williams let the pre-interview run on. He still hadn't mentioned the crimes being investigated.

Williams set directly across the table from Wiles. With some suspects he'd occasionally touched their arm or hand but not Wiles. Wiles had immediately set the physical boundaries between himself and Williams by folding his arms across his chest and with an emotionless facial expression. Williams knew he had to move beyond the pre-interview. He asked, "Is there anyone you'd like me to contact for you Michael?" Michael only stared at Williams. "Well if you change your mind, be sure to tell me."

Williams continued, "There's more we need to talk about, but I have to ask you this first. Are you willing to keep talking with me, just the two of us, like we're doing now without an attorney present?" Williams knew he was taking a risk with that question, though still within legal bounds. Michael looked straight into Williams' eyes and nodded.

Williams continued, "Good, cause I'd like for us to keep talking too. But, because of regulations I have to inform you of something. To get it out the way, you know about regulations. So, I have to tell you for the record, you have the right to remain silent, you need not talk to me or answer any questions, should you talk to me, anything you say can be used as evidence against you, you have the right to an attorney at any time, if you cannot afford an attorney one will be supplied free of charge."

Timmons felt relieve. Although police interview rooms were mostly soundproof, the voices penetrated the one-way glass in front of him, if need be later he could testify that Wiles was Mirandized. No matter how laid back Williams were, the words were given, though Wiles seemed not to care.

Williams looked Wiles in the face. "Now, we can keep talking or I can go back to work and you want see me again without an attorney." Williams slid the official release form across the table. Wiles with a cigarette hanging from his lip, while squinching his right eye from the cigarette smoke, signed the release form. He'd chosen to talk to Williams without a lawyer present. Williams was in the clear. Timmons was already convinced Wiles was guilty. He believed a confession was forth coming.

"So are you ready to tell me about Angela Slade and Martha Trapp? If you are, you'll be helping yourself. Okay, let's begin with Angela." Michael cleared his throat before speaking. Saying "I don't know her. I've seen her name in the papers but don't know her."

Williams looked at Wiles thinking, "This guy is going to deny everything." "Michael your prints were found on Angela Slade's cell phone by the ATM machine, the place where she was apparently attacked and murdered. How did that happen?"

Michael replied, "I was over by the ATM and found the phone earlier the day before it all hit the papers. I picked up the phone, started to keep it but decided not too."

Williams sipped his coffee and stared at Wiles. Wiles drank some of his. Williams finally spoke. "Something else Michael, when you were arrested earlier, you had credit cards, gas cards belonging to the Trapps and newspaper clippings of the Slade and Trapp murders on the wall in the old house."

Michael sucked hard on his cigarette and replied, "I love to read the papers, especially the crime section. Those cases interest me, just like everybody else in Charlotte. I bought the credit cards off some joker at the Dollhouse lounge on Wilkerson a day or so ago.

Timmons starring through the interogation window from the other side, knew Williams had trouble on his hands. "All right lets move on. Now your finger prints and fiber evidence were found all over the Trapp's house. How did it get there?" Williams asked.

Michael studied Williams before answering. "I visited the Trapps with their son Kevin before he left town."

Williams asked. "So where did he go?"

Wiles replied. "He met some stripper and headed out to Los Angeles with her about a month ago. Haven't heard from him since."

Williams looked into Wiles' eyes saying. "Michael I'm talking to you as a friend, you're in trouble. You're charged with two murders. That's big trouble and I think you know it, I'd like to help you but before I can you'll have to start telling the truth. Here have some more coffee. Think about it Michael, the truth will make everything easy, especially for you. When I get the truth, I can start advising you about what to do." With his head down and a smirkish smile, Michael twisted the cigarette out in the small black ash tray on the table in front of him. Then said. "I want to see a bail bondsman, I have nothing else to say."

Timmons still looking through the one-way glass cursed, "son-of-a-bitch." Then he pickup up the phone. He'd make sure that Wiles would be held without previledge of a bond.

It was early, 7 A.M. in the morning, and Cedric was at home with his grandmother Clara Newsome. "Cedric come fast." Her words were shouted. Cedric was in the shower but there was a seriousness in her voice that brought him out dripping, half blind, and groping for a towel. He dug the soap out of his eyes and stumbled into the den. Clara was setting on the couch with a cup of coffee in hand, staring at the T.V. Her eyes were glued to the screen. "I'm not sure," she said. "I just tuned in, but I think they've found Michael Wiles down in Charlotte."

Cedric was instantly beside her. His stomach was in his throat and water ran from his ears. He saw the familiar face of the WTVD ABC affiliate news anchor for the morning news, heard the professional smoothness of her voice, but could not make out only bits of what she was saying.

Then in the background, the camera was all over the place focusing on an old looking house surrounded by brush and weeds, patches of early morning mist, and a number of uniform and plainclothes policemen milling about. Finally, Cedric was able to discern that Michael Wiles had been arrested inside the old house the night before. The commentator informed her audience that he was the number one suspect in the Angela Slade abduction and murder, the Martha Trapp murder as well as other crimes in the area. She said Wiles was being held in the Mecklenburg County Jail.

Cedric's heart raced. Was it possible, Michael Wiles captured? He couldn't believe it. There was an insane rage tearing around inside him that said this wasn't how it should be. Not this way, Michael Wiles should've been killed on sight. He wished he could get to him. "I'm crazy! I'm losing it." He thought.

The commentator's voice broke through and he heard the facts of the arrest as they were known with the commentator describing the legal marathon which lay ahead.

As Detective Williams walked out the Charlotte Police Department at 9 A.M. the next day, he was like a rabbit on the run from a pack of hounds. Williams stood facing clusters of reporters, photographers, and minicam units. They made sharp, stabbing attacks, the strobe lights ripping the fog, their shouted questions flying, their faces greedy and with a false friendliness.

Hey Detective Williams," One reporter called "How did you finally find him?"

"A lot of routine pick and shovel work," said Williams. Williams walked through the crowd of reporters, raising both hands saying, "No more comments, please excuse me." He opened the door of his police cruiser and sped away. Cedric finished drying his hair and reached for the phone. He looked at the clock, it was 7:30 A.M. he dialed Angela's parent's telephone number in Wilmington. He had to give them bitter sweet news.

May 15, 1960

The rain fell as if the bottom of the sky had fallen out. It was the monsoon season. The temperature ranged all day around one hundred and fifteen degrees, the air was thick, humid and the landscape was a jungle of vines and swamp. Josh Dockery and Jack Newsome sat in their bunker amidst the military encampment in Plei Ku outside De Ning. The orderly row of canvass tents looked like a small shantytown. The continuous rain and bare earth had produced enough mud to stall a tank. The tents were located in a camp area built without proper drainage, and the day in and day out rain worsened the condition. The camp was like being in the middle of a river.

The camp ranked with the stench of men living in close quarters. Josh and Jack had been in Viet Nam for six months, with six months remaining to complete their tour of duty. "Do you think the rains gonna ever stop?" Soul asked from his cot.

"Damn if it looks like it." Jack answered as he peered out the tent. Soul whose name was James Stanley was a tall, slim dark man from Harlem. He'd teamed with Jack, Josh, Big Sam Brock and Roscoe Morrison forming a close-knit group.

Soul acquired his name because of his spirited nature, black revolutionary views and boldness in battle. Big Sam Brock came out of Greenville, South Carolina. He was the silent man in the group, the quiet storm. He'd only speak when he had a reason. He was courageous, dependable and a loyal friend to the other four. He stood barely six feet, weighted in at two hundred fifty pounds of mostly bulging muscle. Roscoe was fun loving and the life of the group. He sang all the Motown hits and forever ran his mouth about his plans upon returning back to the states and his home of Atlanta, Georgia. Jack turned and sat down, lit a cigarette and began cleaning his M-16,

"I love rain but I've had enough." Josh replied, "The farmers back in North Carolina would like to have some of this rain. They usually don't get enough for their crops on different years. I remember a time it didn't rain for two or three months, right in the middle of the time when the corn and tobacco needed it most."

"Josh when was the last time you cleaned your weapon?" Jack interrupted. He was in no mood for tales of Josh's life on the farm.

Josh looked around replying, "Damn if I know, why?"

Jack Warned. "These honkies might send us out anytime. The wet and moistness causes the M-16 to rust and jam awfully fast. I'd hate for you to jam-up out there in them rice patties. Especially, when my ass is in the sling with you and one them gooks are firing his weapon."

Josh got up off his cot and walked over to his M-16. "Yeah, this is my little friend. You right, I've gotta make sure its hitting on all cylinders."

In the back of the sixteen man tent, a group of six other Marines were smoking marijuana and shooting dice. Their loud laughter and the smell of the marijuana encompassed the entire tent. There seemed to be no concern of the rain or the war waiting for them outside in the jungles around Plei Ku. They took advantage of the down time to escape their surroundings through getting zooted on marijuana.

"You think they'll send us out again? We just came back from a week in the brush." Soul asked.

"We took some big hits out there, "Josh replied. "We lost fifteen men and six to injury, this damn war don't mean shit to me, I'm sick of it. We arrived here six months ago and damn near half the men who came with us is dead. The government is using us like bait and human shields. These damn people ain't done nothin to me. I need to be fighting dem red necks back in the states."

Jack intervened, "You're right one hundred per cent, they throwing our lives away. They don't care if we live or die. They'll send us out to soften up the target."

Josh stopped and looked at his friends saying, "That's why we gotta take care of each other best we can."

Big Sam finally spoke, "I'll tell you the only reason I keep on day after day is thinking about seeing home again, back in Greenville."

Josh continued cleaning his M-16, pushing a cleaning rod with a rag through the barrel. He looked at his companions as he spoke in a low tone, "As far as fighting for my country, I don't give a shit about that, especially when these honkies still treat us like dirt under their feet. The white boys over here in the brush with us act as if they love us, over here. It's only cause most of them is scared of dying. When we get back to the states they'll kick our ass again."

Roscoe added, "This war ain't done nothing to make me patriotic, hell like the rest of ya'll I don't know the real reason we's here."

Jack looked around with his eyes bulging, "We could always go AWOL and live in the hill with the Montagnard people and smoke opium and eat water buffalo."

"What?" Josh barked, "I rather be back on the farm kissing the boss's ass. That's all these crackers want is a reason to shoot us for treason or some shit. If I go down, I want to go down kicking ass and taking names."

Josh and Jack like many of the American soldiers were filled with an underlining of fear and outward resentment. The black soldiers especially were conflicted emotionally and politically. The root of their internal conflict resulted from fighting for the United States on the one hand and being disregarded as equal citizens back in the States on the other. Along with being at the bottom of the totem pole on the battle field when it came to rank, supplies and leave time, but first on the front lines and dangerous missions or latrine duty. The black soldiers didn't get first crack at ammunition and didn't get issued the new weapons. Josh Dockery, Jack Newsome and other black soldiers compensated with ingenuity and a close comradere. For most it wasn't about patriotism or winning the so-called war as it was about survival. The objective quickly became one of standing with one's own people and saving the lives of black men. The soldiers knew the government didn't care, so it was up to them. It didn't matter whether they knew each other. A brother was a brother. They were the same people. They had the same color skin or something close to it. They knew little about one another but had traveled a similar road in the States and in Nam. They were family to one another, the only family around, lying in the trenches fighting next to one another. The black Marines in the 1960's knew each day they went out in the jungle they were taking a gamblers chance with their lives and that things would be the same when they got home, a nigga would still be a nigga, and wasn't nothing gonna change. Uncle Sam wasn't their Uncle, he was just the same as Mr. Charlie, the patriotic red neck, keeping niggas in their places.

Josh as well as Jack changed substantially since their induction into the Marines. Their time on the front lines in the jungles of Viet Nam had the greatest affect on changing the both of them. Not only had they been trained to fight and kill efficiently, but Josh especially discovered he like it. He'd found a level of excitement in crawling through the jungles risking his life in the death games of war. Each day he woke with a sense of readiness to kill or be killed. Jack and the others in his group knew how he felt. He'd rather be out in the jungles, not that he wanted to risk the other men's lives. But, being in the jungles gave him a sense of control and he didn't have anyone ordering him around. In the jungles he used his own instincts to kill the enemy anyway he chose.

It was Tuesday, October 10, 1960 and according to Jack's watch the 1600 hour. His patrol squad had been penned down in a cross fire in the jungles outside Plei Ku for more than six hours in a fierce battle with the VC. The Marines had been answering the VC with blazing gunfire throughout the siege. The Marines had lost four of their own from fire which came out of the trees. The VC snipers tied in the trees had waited as they approached. The other VC's were camouflaged into the landscape as the Marines walked into the crossfire. Josh and four other Marines were in a fox hole thirty or so yards to Jacks left. Roscoe was barracked in a trench with one other Marine. The M-16's hummed and echoed as the Marines returned fire. Communications had been sent out for back-up but hadn't been able to reach their location. There were VCs all over the place. The Marines didn't see a way out. At 1600 hour back-up came and the VC began to scatter and disappear in the jungle. As the Marines began to submerge from the fox holes and trenches in cautious relief, Roscoe without noticing stepped on a mine hidden under the foliage. He raised his foot and the mine detonated with explosion that blew him twenty feet while taking off both legs with it. It happened so fast everyone was caught off guard. Jack, Josh and Big Sam rushed over to Roscoe. It was clear that an enemy's life or death meant nothing. The enemy was merely things to be killed.

Josh laid his rifle down and knelt beside Roscoe. The medic worked on Roscoe trying to stanch the flow of blood. Roscoe talked out of his head asking, "Where's my legs? I can't feel my legs."

Jack held his hand saying, "Its' gonna be okay, Bubba."

Roscoe in delirium asked, "Ya'll still my friends? We all gonna go home together like we talked about ain't we?"

Big Sam replied, "We's still your friends until the end of time, until the end of time." Roscoe looked up with dying eyes asking, "I need ya'll to promise me." A spasm racked his body, his voice noticeably growing weaker as he continued. "I need ya'll to promise me ya'll aw tell my family I died fighting like a true Marine." He looked from one to the other as he coughed and blood gurgled from his mouth. There was fear in his eyes. "I'm gon die." With that Roscoe was gone. Josh stood over Roscoe with tears in his eyes, and said nothing. He'd seen enough of the killing and thought the war had made him immune to the flotsam of violent death. He'd walked across ground red with blood and littered body parts. He realized that mankind was better at killing than understanding one another. He realized that history in part was written in the blood of those invisible men killed by their victors. Men behaved as if killing was the measure of a man. He thought of all the hypocrisy in the world. As a young boy he'd been taught that life was a gift from God and no human being had the right to terminate a life. But, as a young man he'd taken Junior Whitfield's life and as a Marine he'd learned that killing was fine when it suited the powers that be. Oh, how beautiful the theory. But, it rode on the convenience of the circumstance. Josh had enough of killing he was ready to go home.

In the seven years Josh and Jack were in the Marines, they involved themselves in the black market. They'd banked the card games on every base between Camp Lejune and Camp Pendleton. They'd loaned money at excessive rates of interest, sold liquor on credit and supplied marijuana as they moved from base to base. In Viet Nam they sold guns, ammunition, American cigarette, Zippo lighters, exchanged American currency for the VCs, and shipped heroin back to the States in cameras, pottery, dolls and stereo equipment. As a result they'd stock piled plenty of cash. Their last count was right at a half million each. They laughed and slapped hands saying, "Not bad for two ole country boys out of North Carolina."

In their last month in Nam after Roscoe's death they'd been extra cautious. The last days were mostly spent in the bunker gambling. Captain McDowell very well knew what was in Josh Dockery and Jack Newsome's records concerning gambling and suspicious of black marketing. Late on a Friday evening the silence inside the bunker was interrupted by a loud tapping on the tent pole outside. "Who is it?" Jack called out. "Captain McDowell!" a voice answered.

"Come on in Cap'n" Jack said, as they scrambled to their feet. Captain McDowell ducked under the canvas flap and returned the salute. He was offered a chair, but waved it off, "How you men doing?" Josh along with Jack nodded indicating all was well. "I came by to give a little warning advice." "You boys need to watch yourselves. You bout to go home in a little bit, the higher ups are getting complaints about all the gambling and hustling round here. You men's names surfaces at the top of the pile. Both of you been caught running games and God knows what else before coming to Nam, so the eyes are on you. I'd hate to see you leave with dishonorable discharges behind some bullshit. You men are good Marines, battle tested and second to none, so watch yourselves." Captain McDowell was one of the more respected officers because he was known to stand up for his men. It was not often that any officer at that rank took the time to talk to enlisted men in such a casual fashion. Josh and Jack appreciated his warning advice.

After the Cap'n left, Jack teased Josh, "I told you bout winning all the money wit dem crooked cards and dice like you been doin. You been trimming dem white boys of all they savings."

Josh smiled and replied, "Shit, a man shouldn't come to the table to play the game of chance unless he's prepared to lose, scared money need to be kept in your pocket.

"Yeah, and the way I hears it," Jack now laughing said, "You take big chances and is good wit the cheat too." Josh stopped in his tracks and looked.

"Jack hold on, you talk like I'm the master. Don't forget you taught me. If'n I won't yo man you'd have all my money in your pockets." They both had a long laugh at the expense of all the losers over the years. Jack said, "The major concern of the brass is white boys losing their pay in high-stakes card games to some slick ass nigga who'd leave them penniless each time. Head Quarters put out a bulletin on the matter and threaten harsh consequences on anyone caught. I saw the notice the other day. HQ got involved behind some of the losers running to the brass with empty pockets and telling." Josh then laughed, "Partner less just slow our roll and ease out of here. We've almost lived through our time in this war. Let's try to make it back to North Carolina in one piece." They gave each other a series of soulful handshakes to confirm the agreement.

By the spring of 1962 Josh Dockery and Jack Newsome were both civilians. They'd completed their tour of duty in Viet Nam and settled in Durham. They'd found a small house on Martha Street and were living as house-mates. Jack was drawn to Durham by his younger sister Ida who was a third year student at North Carolina College. He felt it was a good alternative to returning to Murfreesboro or settling in a larger city. Durham was small and southern but was a Mecca for black entrepreneurs. Jack welcomed the civilian life, enjoyed the availability of college girls introduced by Ida, frequented the Stallion Club on weekends and was in a comfort zone. Being an ex-service man with an honorable discharge, he soon landed a job with the American Tobacco Company. The pay was good and the work easy. On different weekends he'd drive down east to Murfreesboro to visit Clara Simmons who had been his girlfriend since age fourteen. Jack loved Clara despite his unsatiable desire for other women. Clara had bore a child with Jack at age fifteen. Paula their daughter was growing up fast and barely knew Jack as a father. Paula was thirteen years old by time Jack completed his tour of duty with the Marines. Two years later on October 10, 1962, Jack and Clara married. Clara and Paula moved to Durham. Jack found a small clapboard house on Berkley Street in Walltown and with a G.I. loan bought their first home. Although, he was married, loved his wife and child, he was unable to settle down with one woman. He ran the streets after women with an obsession. Granddaddy Tom's spirit seem to reincarnate itself inside Jack each time he saw a woman with a good looking face or rear-end.

Josh Dockery moved with a slower pace. He wasn't in a rush to be tied down to a whiteman's job. He declared he'd never work for another white man after leaving Shakragg and the sharecropping arrangnment with his family and the Whitfield's some ten years earlier. He wouldn't subjugate himself to that type of disrespect and be treated each day according to the whims of some white man. Such an imbalanced relationship had too many bad memories. He remembered how Herman Whitfield talked down to his father. Josh knew he'd have to answer to someone at some level but he knew it was a different and better way. He had taken care of his money, therefore, wasn't pressed to find a job. For the first year he floated about Durham looking for a business investment or for a niche to start a new one.

Josh spent a great amount of time in the home of Jack and Clara Newsome. He was at the Newsome's two or three times each week for dinner and on most Sundays joined them in worship at St. James Baptist Church. He was a handsome and well dressed church going man, who caught the eye of the eligible women and non-eligible alike each Sunday.

On those Sundays in church Josh paid attention to more than the sermon. He'd laid his sight on the most attractive young lady in the church. After noticing her for over six months he finally made his way to introduce himself. Her name was Berma Ramsey. The day he met Berma, St. James Baptist Church was filled to capacity for its annual Anniversary. Members and visitors who hadn't attended church since the year before crowded through the doors. The day started with Sunday school. After Sunday school at one o'clock the Anniversary program got under way. Reverend Wakefield Davis a bald, short, thick man with stocky arms from St. James Free Will Baptist Church of Fayetteville, North Carolina was the guest speaker. He ignited the congregation with his fire and brimstone sermon. He roared and snorted and used his white handkerchief to wipe the sweat from his face as he walked from side to side of the pulpit admonishing the congregation of their sin, hell bound and worldly ways. The other honored men of God who set in the chairs behind him in the pulpit encouraged his raging sermon at every opportunity with concerted amends. The women who sat on the front pews hollered. "Go head now. Preach." Then Reverend Davis worked his magic revealing, "God told me that, someone is having problems in their home, your marriage done lost its sparks. Your husband not treating you right, he's out all night chasing other women when you need him at home with you. Hallelujah. But God can bring that women chasing man back home. All you got to do is ask God to fix it sisters; ask God to defeat ole slufoot. The devil has no power over God. He will answer your prayers, but you must believe. Some-body's having problems on the job. The boss seems to be driven by the devil. Nothing you do suites him. Ask God to fix it. Burke the devil and ask God to fix it and set you free. Hallelujah, but God won't answer your prayers till you stop your sinful ways and follow God's law. God don't like ugliness and I don't either." About that time the church exploded. People shouted and praised the Lord.

After Reverend Davis finished his fire and brimstone sermon he sat in the center chair amongst the other preachers in the pulpit with his white handkerchief wiping sweat saying, "Thank you Jesus, Thank you Lord," Over and over again. For the next two hours the congregation was entertained with old time gospel music from a multitude of visiting choirs. The choirs took turns singing and ministering through their music. The day was as always concluded with the members and their guest sharing a meal under the large covered eating table in the back of the church.

Berma was impressed and taken aback with Josh. She'd seen him each Sunday in church setting with Jack and Clara Newsome and their teenage daughter, Paula. She never considered or expected that he would have an interest in her. Berma had believed Josh was too mature and worldly to have interest in a small town girl who'd been kept close to the nest like herself. She had grown up in a family with two other younger sisters, Della and Margie and a brother Jack. Her parents, Pervis and Emma Ramsey were plain folk who'd moved to Durham in the late 1940's from Caldwell. Caldwell a small community that was situated somewhere in the southern corner where Orange and Person Counties intersected. Pervis worked as a Janitor at Duke Hospital and Emma in Housekeeping at Watts Hospital. They provided their children a modest and Christian upbringing.

Pervis and Emma Ramsey noticed Josh as he attended St. James Church with the Newsome's. He hadn't given them a reason for any special interest until he approached their daughter, Berma. Once Josh's interest in Berma became known, the Ramsey's began to check into Josh's character, observed him closely and with caution allowed him to call on Berma after church. Although, Pervis had found no fault in Josh, he was concerned with Josh not having a job and that he spoke of working for himself. A young black man with a goal of entrepreneurship seemed impossible as far as the Ramsey's and most other blacks were concerned.

Josh and Berma were allowed to date only on Sundays after church in the beginning. Berma hadn't been allowed to take company as her parents called it until her eighteenth birthday. When Josh met Berma she was on the early side of eighteen only by three months. Starting that summer on each Sunday Josh was allowed to drive over and park his dark blue Eighty-Eight Oldsmobile in front of the Ramsey's house on Onslow Street and sat on the porch with Berma. He'd arrive around three o'clock and had to be gone by nine. By the fall they'd moved their Sunday afternoon courting to the Ramsey's living room but the rules hadn't changed. In several months Josh was allowed to take Berma to the movies and out for a burger or ice cream now and then. That restrictive dating was different for Josh who'd been across the world while in the Marines. But, he knew of such practices from his days in Shakragg. He'd also grown to have much affection for Berma, so the Ramsey's rules didn't sway him.

After two years of tightly chaperoned dating and a few passionate kisses, Josh asked for Berma's hand in marriage. Pervis and Emma Ramsey had grown to like and respect Josh greatly and without hesitation gave their permission and blessings.

On Saturday June 10 of 1964, Josh Dockery and Berma Ramsey were married at 3 P.M. at St. James Baptist Church. Their wedding was the biggest and most grand wedding ever held at St. James. The bride wore a long white satin laced wedding gown with a ten foot trail, a white pearl necklace and ear rings. Her long wavy hair was tucked under her veil and her facial make-up had been applied with perfection. Her eight bridesmaids wore pink satin dresses and shoes, with pink cosmetic pearls and ear rings. Berma was a stunning and beautiful bride.

The groom and his attendants were gray hickory stripped tuxedos, black satin comobums, white shirts and burgundy bow ties. Berthy's Funeral Services was hired to provide limousines for the groom, the bride, wedding party and immediate families.

The pews were filled to capacity with almost every active member of St. James Baptist Church, one hundred members of Josh's family from Shakragg and Roxboro. His parents were accompanied by his sister Queenie and Delores who now lived in Richmond. Another one hundred or so family members belonging to Pervis and Berman Ramsey from Caldwell filed in behind one another.

Pervis Ramsey dressed up like he belonged in Esquire Magazine in an expensive black suit with the tie and shoes to match. He proudly escorted his daughter down the aisle as the organist played the bridal march. Josh was accompanied by his long time friend and best man Jack Newsome.

The congregation of guest and witnesses were as quiet as church mice. During the exchange of vows between the groom and his bride Emma Ramsey, the bride's mother could be heard sniffing as the tears of joy rolled from her eyes.

At 4 P.M. sharp the newlyweds rushed from the church amongst cheers and falling rice to the long shinning grey Cadillac which waited. After the lavishly catered wedding reception at the Jack Tar Hotel, Josh and Berma were on their way to Niagara Falls for a week long honeymoon.

It was 6 A.M. as Josh looked out onto Pettigrew Street into an area known as Hayti. He'd parked his dark blue Oldsmobile in front of Fines Diner to unload the boxes of condiments from the truck. He'd opened his hotdog and hamburger joint and named it Fines Diner almost two years earlier. Pettigrew Street was lined with black owned businesses from one corner to the other. The Regal Theatre and Biltmore Hotel were on the corner of Pettigrew and Roxboro Streets. Josh's Diner, Pee Wee Shoe Shop, Elvira's Kitchen and the Green Candle take-out were all south of the hotel. Josh in the past two years had been able to do enough business to make ends meet and a little profit to boot. He figured he'd been able to save as much or more than most niggas who worked on some white man's job, plus he felt he had a degree of freedom as a bonus.

Now being a married man and with the responsibility of a wife, he knew his profit margin needed to expand. He had initially worked the Diner with only the help of Cecil. Cecil, a small wiry, clean shaven man with big bulging eyes and a Hershey chocolate skin was on the late side of forty. He spoke with a raspy voice and moved quickly. Cecil had no family, had been raised in the Oxford Orphanage until he was eighteen and at such time moved to Durham. Cecil and Josh first met the first day Josh started working to open Fines Diner. Cecil on that day as with every other day stood on the corner of Pettigrew and Henry Streets intoxicated off cheap wine begging for change. He'd approached Josh with his plea for a few nickels. Josh gave him the change from his pockets. From that day forward Josh refused to give Cecil a dime without him earning it. So, each day Josh found a chore for Cecil around the Diner. Cecil had to earn his wine money. After knowing Cecil for two months, one morning at 9

A.M. or so as Cecil staggered across Pettigrew Street severely intoxicated and taking his time crossing the street. He sung a melody not looking or being concerned with the traffic. He was struck by a pick-up truck. Cecil laid in the street, and no one moved with any urgency to call the police or an ambulance. Josh was in Fines cutting up onions and tomatoes saw the truck as it plowed into ole Cecil. Josh wiped his hands on his apron and ran out to the street. He scooped Cecil up in his arms, put him in the back seat of his Oldsmobile and rushed him to Lincoln Hospital about six blocks away on Fayetteville Street. Cecil suffered a broken arm, a few fractured ribs and a mild concussion. After being hospitalized one week, he was discharged. He came directly to Fines Diner and Josh. Josh cooked and served him several hotdogs with a Coke and had his first conversation with Cecil while sober with a clear mind. The near death experience was a life event which caused him to reach his bottom and never drank another drop of alcohol again. Cecil convinced Josh to hire him at Fines Diner and never missed a day of work since that time.

Initially, Fines Diner specialized in hotdogs, hamburgers, fries, soft drinks, chips and candy. For two years Fines had done well. After awhile Berma teamed with Josh and helped bring a new image and life to the Diner. Shortly afterwards, there was a constant flow of daily customers in and out the doors of Fines. Berma' voice could be heard shouting out orders to Josh and Cecil in the kitchen.

While many small businesses on Pettigrew Street in Hayti had come and gone, Fines Diner was picking up momentum despite the competition from the Green Candle and Elvira's down the block. Berma introduced chicken, pork chops, roast, veggies, pies and cakes to the menu. Fines offered ham, bacon and egg biscuits by 6 A.M. each morning. In less than a year their customers and close friends called daily ordering their meals ahead of time. Business at Fines was booming. The smell of fried chicken, pork chops and barbecue cooked in the huge smoke pit barrel out back filled the air a full block before entering the one story building. The tiny dining room was only large enough to accommodate ten tables and the kitchen was the size of a project bathroom. Despite its size, the surroundings were clean and immaculate, light hearted and each person was served and treated with care. The place stayed packed. Each of its ten tables was covered with a red and white checkered table cloth. A salt, pepper shaker and a bottle of vinegar set in the center. Cecil took pride in keeping the tile floor buffed and waxed. In front was a red formica counter with four stoles, a cash register, take-out window and Berma with her lovely smile. In the corner the Jukebox offered selections for a quarter. The juke box blasted sounds by B.B. King, Little Milton, Bobby Blue Bland, Percy Sledge, Marvin Gaye and Aretha Franklin as the customers enjoyed their food. There were two pay phones attached to the wall near the front door. At lunch the takeout line swung completely around the wall and ended at the cash register. The orders were taken from the price list above the take-out window. Josh, Berma and Cecil were barely able to get the customers in and out with efficiency.

There was no doubt concerning the food. It was among the best in the city. The constant flow of customers told the story.

Amidst all the work going on at Fines diner, in 1968, Berma gave birth to Wendy, their first child. Josh was a proud father and Berma a caring mother. A year later Berma gave birth to her second child a son, Randy. Josh and Berma's family life was prospering and the future looked bright.

Friday, June 10, 1987

Wendy Dockery was preparing for summer school at Hampton University in Hampton, Virginia. She'd finished her freshmen year at Hampton and had decided to attend the first session of summer school to get a head start on her sophomore year. She couldn't believe how quickly her freshmen year had passed. It seemed like only yesterday that she'd graduated from Northern High School in Durham, while her mother, father and brother looked on. On August 26, of 1986 her parents had driven her to Hampton University and said their tearful good-byes, realizing their little girl had grown up and their life with her would never be the same. Wendy was being turned lose in the world away from the protection of her powerful father and caring mother. She'd been spoiled, pampered and made to believe she was special to everyone in the world. Not knowing she was only special to her parents. In school at Northern High she'd been the head majorette, homecoming queen and the prize in the eyes of every boy who knew her. Her beauty was all overwhelming.

Wendy was stunning and sexually appealing to any man with any level of testosterone in his body, the old and young alike. For the first time in her life she was truly alone and on her on. She was exited as well as afraid.

Wendy's first year went well. She'd lived on campus in the freshmen dormitory and enjoyed the experience of dorm life. Her classroom performance had been excellent for both semesters allowing her to finish the year with a 3.75 G.P.A. She'd tried out and was selected as a majorette. While wearing the Hampton University white and blue she was admired by every man in the stadium at each football game. Later during the fall she was chosen as Miss Freshmen and was gaining recognition as the prize of the campus. During her freshman year she only dated on occasion and didn't involve herself with any special guy. She was aloof and was feeling her way around. No guy in particular had been able to hold her interest.

It was a hot sticky day. Wendy dressed in jean shorts, a Hampton t-shirt and sandals. Sweat poured down her back as she loaded her clothes in her new red Saab. Her father had surprised her with the car on her last visit home. She'd convinced her parents to afford her off-campus housing for the summer session and upcoming school year. She planned to move all her clothing and personal belongings by Saturday. On Saturday her parents were scheduled to be in Hampton to take her shopping for furniture.

Finally, with her car packed she drove down Sellers Landing Road heading for the Hampton Arms Apartments. She had fallen in love with Hampton. She loved the beach, the university, her friends and the attitude of the city. She looked forward to living alone but felt a little unsure of how it would be to manage her own life's goings and comings. Her parents had agreed to pay the bills. All she had to do was to study and continue to make the grades. Her mother had said, "I've taught you to be a lady. So, I expect the same from you in your own place."

College life was enjoyable. But it was drastically different from high school in ways the mattered. There were no bells. No one forced her to go to class or threaten to put her out if she didn't attend. She could do her home-work if she wanted to. Or she could fail. It was up to her. Not having rules or authority seemed to motivate her to do what was expected.

On Saturday her mother and father arrived as planned. They were in Hampton by 9 A.M. Her mother inspected the apartment, looking closely at the kitchen, bathroom, closets, the paint and carpet. Her dad stepped outside noticing the low volume of traffic and quiet atmosphere. He had always protected his Wendy and wanted no harm to come her way. He looked and thought, "I got to turn her loose. She'll be okay. I'll just have to keep up with her for awhile." Wendy approached her father from behind without him noticing. "Daddy what are you doing? Sizing up the area?" Josh turned and looked at Wendy with a smile and before he could speak she said, "I'll be okay, you and momma have taught me well." She hugged him tightly and announced, "We're going to the IHOP across from the university for a late breakfast before hitting the mall."

The day ended with Wendy purchasing every piece of furniture she liked. Her mom and dad spent the evening with Wendy having dinner at Captain John's Fish Camp, talking, laughing and catching Wendy up on the latest family gossip and tales of their family's past, stories she'd heard since a child.

One week later classes for the first summer session had begun. Wendy enrolled for two classes. Each class met each day for one hour with tons of readings and outside work. The idea was to cram a semester's worth of work into six weeks of class. The classes were fast paced and intense. Wendy enrolled in marketing and accounting class for the first session. Between the two, she had to stay focused and walk a chalk line.

Wendy had met Beverly Jackson her freshmen year as she tried out for the school's majorette squadron. Beverly was a sophomore from Washington, D.C., she was very attractive, both body and face. She was a voluptuous, tall young woman with smooth chocolate skin and ringlets of curly hair. She knew her way around campus and everyone on the yard. Beverly who everyone called "Bev" was a very good student and was also a party animal, a girl of the night. Beverly had grown up in a tough housing project in D.C. named Berry Farms, in South West. Berry Farms was typical of other drug infested and crime territory housing projects found in most cities. It was a section where tough young black men hung out and did their thing. The only whites coming through were tricks looking for a hooker, a junkie looking for dope or the white policeman trying to intimidate or enforce his law. The night life never ended, the young and old stayed up all night. Bev was introduced to the juke joints and private liquor houses at a young age. Places where card games lasted all night, liquor and drugs were sold from sun-up to sun-down . . . . small cozy, dimly lit places where people drank and danced until daybreak to forty-fives on the juke box. When they weren't dancing, they ate pickled pig feet, pickled eggs and fish sandwiches. Bev's mother had carried her in and out the juke joints as soon as she could walk. Beverly by way of a miracle was able to combat drugs, avoid pregnancy and graduate high school with honors and earn a scholarship to Hampton down in Virginia.

Wendy was taken by Beverly's light heartedness, candor and worldly experiences. Wendy and Beverly's lives and experiences were polar opposites. Wendy was amazed at Beverly's comfort with the streets. On given days Wendy and Bev rode in Wendy's red Saab, stopping by the stores where the young black men hung out. Places like Tiny Gaints, the IHOP across from Hampton campus or drove into North Pheobus Projects on Cameron Street behind Campus. Bev loved marijuana and would boldly approach the corner dealers purchasing whatever she needed while negotiating the price down. Her courage, street savvy and experience lured Wendy toward the streets.

By the middle of the summer Wendy with Bev's coaching could be found on Lady's Nite in the local night clubs around Hampton and Norfolk. By summer's end Bev and Wendy settled down to hanging out at the Showcase in Norfolk mostly or Second Bar and Grill and at times the lounge in the Radisson on Sailors Landing in Hampton. Wendy's parents had no idea of her night life and hadn't prepared her for what laid ahead.

At the end of August on a Friday night Wendy and Bev were perched at the bar in the Showcase over in Norfolk. As Bev sat with her back to the crowd looking as if she was from royalty and chatting with Wendy, she was tapped on the shoulder and surprised by Tyrone Beckwith. Bev in surprised turned, covered her mouth, eyes bulging and with joy, dismantled from the bar stool, hugging Tyrone as she screamed. "Oh my God Ty, I can't believe it you, I haven't seen you in years, what's, it's been six years? When, I was fifteen." Tyrone pushed Bev away and scanned her up and down with his hazel calculating eyes as he replied, "I see you're all grown up." His attention moved from Bev to Wendy. Bev stuttered saying, "I'm sorry, this is my girlfriend Wendy . . . Wendy this is Tyrone. Ty's my home boy, we've been knowing each other since I was ten or twelve years old. We grew up in the same projects in D.C. He was ahead of me along with my Brothers but we were always cool. Growing up, Ty was the boy who hypnotized the girls into doing whatever he wanted. He had a way with words each time he spoke." Tyrone smile and interjected, "Beverly stop blowing me up, that was a long time ago. Things aren't the same." Wendy noticed that Ty was tall, good looking with unusual hazel green eyes, something out of this world. Bev laughed remembering as she said, "Ty, you remember when the girls in the projects use to call you swami, because of your charm?"

Ty laughed, saying, "girl you need to cut it out." There wasn't a time Beverly could remember that he didn't have at least two or three girls coming around him. He was charming but had a mean side to as she remembered. He was cool, calculating and premeditating. Beverly remembered her brothers discussing him from years before. She'd seen him control the neighborhood as young man, years ago. His control was silent and with class.

Beverly was invited to the dance floor by one of the men who'd been trying to get her eye all night. Bev left Wendy alone with Ty. Wendy and Ty moved to a corner table and sipped Volka slowly, as they became acquainted. Their conversation turned intimate as if it was a first date. They laughed, danced and finally went outside to Ty's black Mercedes and smoked marijuana while listening to the O'Jays. They talked for so long the Beverly came out to look for them. When Ty spoke of what he wanted in life, he described children, his cars and everything down to the interior of each of the seven bedroom house he'd have. Wendy had never thought of her life beyond college but expected some day to have a good marriage, a country house and four children. But that was so far away.

Ty was a player, a man knowing what to say and with many faces. His voice was soft and gravely. He caused Wendy's mood to glow with lust and anticipation. On his later visits to Hampton he wined and dined Wendy in the evenings, smuggled up in the corner of the sofa and listened to jazz, Herbie Hancock, Al Jarreau and Chick Cores, while she fell asleep like a baby nested against her father's chest. For a woman who'd been spoiled and pampered, Ty quickly realized all the right buttons to push. Wendy found it easy to love a man who was so tender to her.

Wendy knew that Ty worked hard, doing whatever he did to keep money in his pockets and to maintain his expensive and luxurious life-style. After months of pampering, working on her mind and spirit, Wendy became clay in Ty's hands. He was able to shape her into any form he desired. She never questioned the long periods of his absence in D.C., how he afforded his life-style or detected the faintest possibility of Tyrone Beckwith's other life as a kingpin drug dealer and hustler. Wendy's naiveté had her blinded in the dark of the real world of Tyrone Beckwith.

By the end of her sophomore year, school became secondary to her relationship with Ty. Beverly had failed to convince her to keep her distance from Ty. Beverly knew Ty was a player, hustler and not the complete man Wendy had fallen in love with. Beverly was afraid for Wendy as she waited for Ty to turn the tables in his relationship with Wendy, a pretty naïve soon to be victim.

It was a Tuesday morning in late November. Wendy was still in D.C. on one of her long week-end trips with Ty. She'd been stored away in one of his luxurious apartments since Sunday night with no sign of him. She had called her answering service back in Hampton and listened to three messages from her parents. She felt nervous, wondering what she'd say to her dad when the time came. In the last six months her relationship with her parents had become strained. Her involvement with Ty had completely consumed her entire life. She'd lost interest in school and was failing in her classes. She felt as if her life was in a passage-way between two worlds.

August 25, 1989

It was just a week before Wendy was to enroll for the fall semester. She'd made a decision to drop from school and move to D.C. with Ty. The news of her decision went against Josh and Berma Dockery's wishes and advice. Wendy's rash decision caused a rift in her already strained relationship with her parents. When Wendy called to disclose her decision, she and her father had their first fight. Josh warned, "You're throwing your life away for some no good nigga. Who haven't been decent enough to come met your family." Wendy had no come back explanation other than that she was in love with Tyrone and wanted a life with him. From all indications Josh knew Ty was a hustler, no matter how modestly Wendy tried to describe him. Josh had known his kind, he'd seen dozens of them in his life. He knew no nigga could afford such luxury without a job or business to speak of. Josh also knew he hadn't nurtured, protected and planned for his daughter to end up with some high price thug. No matter how hard he tried, his warnings and admonishments didn't sway Wendy from her decision. Berma became irritated with Wendy and depressed over the entire situation. Josh cut off all money for living expense and with his son Randy drove to Hampton to pick up the furniture from Wendy's apartment. For the next several months the phone calls and other communication between Wendy and her family became non-existence.

In D.C with Tyrone, Wendy found a life of living in the fast lane. She was surrounded by hustlers and women lured by hustling men in an effort to live out their high maintenance life-styles. Wendy moved into a Brownstone in Georgetown on Wisconsin Avenue in North East with Tyrone. She was impressed with her surroundings but soon found herself alone in the spacious condo. Unbeknown to her, Tyrone had other condo's he also shared with other women. Wendy initially thought his absences were due to business trips, a business she knew nothing about. She knew of his real-estate investment and partnership in Upper Marlboro Maryland but didn't know it was mostly a front to disguise his illegal drug business.

Each time Tyrone came around he'd spend days dinning her in the best restaurants, shopping in Georgetown and pampering her with lots of love and attention. At night he'd entertain her at the Pelican Bay Lounge on Georgia Avenue, Sha La Rae in Crystal Virginia after dinner at the Esquire or the Double Tree Restaurant as it spun around the entire time they enjoyed their meals.

Wendy was completely in the dark. She had no idea of the real life Tyrone lived and the man she'd chosen. It soon became apparent through the street grapevine Wendy tapped into, that she was only one of a number of women in Tyrone's life. He had women working the bars and clubs with drugs. He had women who worked the malls as professional thieves. He had women who were professionals working in government offices. They were all his ladies. The only difference in Wendy's status was that she was his bottom lady for now and a private affair he'd chosen to keep outside the game.

November 20, 1991

Beverly was now a senior at Hampton and back in D.C. for the Thanksgiving holidays. She caught up with Wendy and invited her to meet for lunch at the Classic Restaurant out in Prince George County. Beverly hadn't seen or heard from Wendy in over six months and was concerned about her. As soon as Beverly laid eyes on Wendy she knew life wasn't good. Wendy couldn't hide her troubles from Beverly and didn't try. She complained, "I'm okay but Ty is never around. And I know he has all these other women. I love him but it bothers me knowing he's with other women when he's not with me. All I do is set at home waiting for him." Beverly listened with deep concern. She knew she had to come clean with Wendy. After Wendy finished her complaints and confessions of love for Ty, Beverly groped down her seltzer and said, "Listen Wendy there's something I must tell you. I should have said it a long time ago. But, I didn't think you and Ty would ever take your relationship this far. I thought it would be a fling for awhile and be over. This thing has been eating me up."

Wendy with a look of dismay replied, "What are you talking about?"

Beverly took a deep breath, gasped and continued, "Ty, well you know I've known him forever. He's not really into the real-estate thing, I know he has houses, apartment buildings and all but Ty has always made his money from drugs." Wendy was obviously stunned. Beverly continued, "I thought you would have known by now. He's like a kingpin in D.C., have been for a long time. My brother Terry and a couple of my cousins have been hooked up with him for years. I mean they control most of the dope in the projects. They got dope in the Montana Projects over in North East, Saratoga, and Potomac Gardens off Pennsylvania Avenue in South East. They got people all up and down Minnesota Avenue selling crack and whatever. Tyrone is nice but that's the side he wants you to see for now. Wendy I'm sorry for not telling you this earlier but I didn't know whether it was my business or not. Especially, after you started talking the love shit." Beverly reached over and placed her hand on Wendy's hand which was on the table shaking. Beverly continued, "Girlfriend, I love you and I'm ready to help you when you need me. I'm telling you this cause,

I love you. My advice is to walk away now, before he decides to use you in another way. You'll be replaced and he'll make you one of his workers. It's just a matter of time. I like Ty but I know him. If you decide to walk away, be cool, don't confront him or start a fight. Just wait until he's not around, pack and leave."

Wendy was in a state of shock and disbelief. She felt confused. But, in her gut she knew Beverly was telling the truth. All the signs had been there for months but it took Beverly's disclosure to break her denial. Everything she'd thought and wanted to believe fell apart in one sweeping conversation. In retrospect, she realized Tyrone never spent time with her as frequently as she wanted, when he was around his cell phone was always ringing, they went to dinner mostly in Maryland or Virginia, like they were sneaking around, usually to some up-scale night club or they'd stay at home listening to jazz. It was now apparent he'd kept her a healthy distance from his other life, standing back to see if and how he wanted the relationship to develop. He seldom carried her around anyone associated with him.

Beverly and Wendy finished their stressful and uncomfortable lunch. They hugged, kissed and promised to stay in touch until Wendy made a decision. Wendy returned home hoping to see things different. She thought, "Maybe Ty wasn't so bad. Maybe he's changed. I should at least, discuss my concerns with him."

That evening and throughout the night she called every number she knew trying to locate Ty. After more than five hours with no luck, she settled down in front of the T.V., depressed. She was wound so tight, her muscles ached. At 6 A.M the next morning the phone rang. She answered with a dry hello. It was Tyrone. In an authoritative and irritated voice he asked. "What's the emergency? Everywhere I've been you've left a message."

Wendy replied, "We need to talk."

Ty asked, "What about?"

Wendy replied, "You, and I guess me."

In a high pitched tone, Ty asked, "What the hell are you talking about Wendy?" He'd never spoke to her with such anger and coldness. Tyrone continued, "Tell me what's on your mind. I don't have time for no whimpering or bullshit."

Wendy took a deep breath. "You've been lying to me about everything. You have other women and I know what you do for a living. I'm just hurt that you've lied to me about everything."

Tyrone hesitated, and asked "Is that it?"

Yes, most of it" Wendy replied.

Wendy couldn't believe how he dismissed her concerns.

Tyrone then said, "Wendy I'll see you tonight."

Before she could respond he'd hung up." Wendy knew she'd bent too much and leaned to low simply to stay with Tyrone. She hadn't seen that Ty wasn't an honest man, a man like her father, who was a loyal, honorable husband and father. She didn't know yet that life was a series of lessons and that each person must study their mistakes to succeed.

Tyrone entered the door with a menacing look on his face. Wendy looked up from the couch as he sat directly in front of her with piercing eyes. In a demanding voice said, "Talk to me."

Wendy said, "I'm leaving you,"

Wendy blurted her words as she used her hand to brush her hair from her eyes. With a cold expressionless face Ty said, "You can't do that." Right then she knew it had been a bad idea to discuss her leaving with him. Beverly had been right.

"What are you saying?" Wendy asked. Tyrone rose from his chair and walked over to the phone and yanked it out the wall. He then threw the phone out into the hallway and double locked the front door. Wendy asked. "What the hell are you doing?" Tyrone walked to the closet and pulled out an extension cord.

"Tyrone!" She shouted.

He moved toward her gripping the cord around his hands.

What are you doing? She asked."

He coldly ordered, "Take off your clothes." His voice was demanding and cold.

Wendy asked in a fearful tone, "What's wrong with you?" She moved away from the couch, looking for a way to escape. Tyrone walked slowly toward her. Wendy pleaded using her most seductive voice, "Stop teasing me honey, Lets' talk okay." She replied.

Again, in a demanding voice Tyrone said, "Take off your clothes, Wendy." She nervously giggled and unzipped the front of her top and pulled it down. She then stepped out of her pants. He replied, "Everything off!"

She winced, saying, "Anything you say baby." Wendy tried playing the role of obedient whore as he examined her body from head to toe with piercing eyes. She stood before him nude waiting for him to make the next move.

"Turn around whore!" Her voice was dry and cold.

Wendy begged, "No Ty!" He shoved her around with one hand and she fell to the floor. He drew back the cord. The cord wrapped around his arms and hands, as she tried to protect herself.

"You're mine, whore." He shouted. "You'll do anything I say, you can't quit me bitch. You're mind as long as I want you." The cord lashed her legs and back. Her back burned as if it was on fire. She scrambled to stand and he kicked her in the ribs. He lashed her again and again the cord sank into her thighs as she screamed.

"You belong to me!" He hollered. Wendy finally was able to stand, jumping up and down, screaming. The cord stung her hips and cut gashes in her legs. Her body was on fire. She ran to the door, and shook the doorknob. Tyrone followed her talking to her in a low tone. "Bitch, you don't ask me bout my business. You hear me?" The cord dug into her flesh each time he unleashed it. "You're mine! You're mine! And don't forget it." Wendy fell to the floor semi-unconscious. He beat her until he was exhausted. She thought he'd killed her. Her body was numb. No more burning, No more stinging. No more pain. She felt outside herself, floating in an unconscious suspension. Ty scooped her up from the floor and throw her on the bed, placing her flat on her back. Tears rolled out the corners of her eyes and down her cheeks.

Tyrone spread her legs apart. He unzipped his pants. He climbed on her and shoved himself inside her. He thrust himself up and down inside her limp body. Wendy thought, "He's gonna kill me. What will my parents think? When I'm found beat to death."

Tyrone finished releasing himself inside her torn body. He walked to the bathroom and filled the bath tub with hot water. He looked in the medicine cabinet and got a bottle of rubbing alcohol. He poured the alcohol into the hot water. He returned to the bedroom and forced her to walk to the bathroom. Once inside he ordered her to get into the tub of hot alcohol water. The alcohol water made her scream. The alcohol burned her open wounds as if she was on fire. He refused to let her out the tub. While she cried, he sat on the side of the tub talking in a low soft caring voice. Saying, "You see what you made me do? You don't ask me about my business and you don't tell me when it is over." Then he sat and watched her in silence. He finally said, "I want you to finish your bath, don't call nobody and don't leave. I'll be back in a couple hours. Then we'll sat down and talk again."

The front door slammed and he was gone. Wendy used all her strength and crawled out the tub. She crawled on her hands and knees to the bedroom, dripping water along the way as she sobbed and cried. She pulled herself up by the handles of the dresser and found some clothes to cover her ripped body. Each time the soft pink underwear touched her skin, pain ran over he like electric currant. Finally, after being fully dressed she walked slowly to the couch, reached into her handbag for her cell phone. Each time she moved a muscle, excruciating pain ran over her body. She slowly dialed Beverly's mother's number and prayed Beverly answered. "Hello, Jackson resident."

Wendy in a weak voice, holding back her sobs and tears said, "Bev, I need you to . . . . Ty hurt me. I need for you to come get me."

Beverly shouted, "What happened?"

Wendy spoke as she sobbed, "I tried to talk to Ty about the lies and he lost it."

Beverly cut through Wendy's explanation saying, "Don't move I'll be there in fifteen minutes. Where's Ty?"

Wendy sobbed and replied, "He left said he'd be back in a couple of hours."

Beverly instructed, "Okay, pack your shit!"

The door bell rang. Wendy slowly opened the door. Beverly stepped through the door, and looked at Wendy, at that instant tears filled her eyes. She hugged Wendy and rocked her, in her embrace assuring her, "I'm here honey. I'm here it's gonna be alright." Beverly looked around the room from the doorway asking. "Did you pack your things? Pack all you can. You're not coming back here."

Wendy added yes, I packed." Beverly grabbed the two large suitcases and headed for the door with Wendy trailing. As they rode toward Beverly's mother's home on Michigan Avenue North East, Wendy like a zombie told Beverly of the beating as dispassionately as she could, as if it was a horror movie. Beverly slammed her hands against the steering wheel in anger shouting, "That motherfucker, he knows he's wrong for this shit. I swear, his ass needs to pay."

Wendy carefully undressed in the safe confines of Beverly's bedroom. Betty Jackson, Beverly's mother stood watching with a frown on her face. She worked as a nurse at Hadley Memorial Hospital and kept a supply of gauze, ointment and salves in her home.

After Wendy finished undressing, Beverly and her mother both began to apply the ointment on each wound. Wendy's body was so sensitive that she trembled with each gentle touch. Beverly finally blurted, "Wendy you're going to the police." She insisted. Mrs. Jackson interjected "But first she needs to go to the hospital." Wendy, thought, "Go to the police. What will she say? That Ty had raped and beat me. But I've lived with him for over a year."

Beverly and her mother were outraged over the horrific beating. "I can't believe he beat you like this." Beverly stated over and over again.

At Hadley Memorial Hospital, Wendy was a convincing victim of domestic violence. As the doctor examined her for broken bones and the nurse stood waiting to treat the superficial wounds, Wendy was neither sad nor angry. She described the events in a cool, detached manner. Before the nurse finished, Beverly walked through the door with two police officers. One was a tall dark athletic black man with a square chin. The other was a small framed forty something white woman. They stood for a moment in apparent dismay. Finally, the male officer spoke, "Please tell me what happened? Take your time."

Wendy walked through the beating for the third time in less than three hours. The female officer asked her partner to leave the room. Then she said, "I need to see your injuries." Wendy disrobed. The officer gasped, "My God, what an animal." She began taking pictures with a Polaroid. She took pictures of every inch of Wendy's body. She finally said, "You can get dressed, I'm so sorry." Wendy finished by giving the officers Tyrone's full name, address, hang-outs and tag number to his black Mercedes. The officers advised her to stay clear of him and to call the police if he came around. Wendy assured the officers she would do as advised.

"I'll find that animal. You must go to the police station and file an official complaint." The officer said. Wendy looked at Beverly with doubt in her eyes.

Mrs. Jackson insisted that Wendy stay at her house. She was afraid that when Tyrone found Wendy had left and about the arrest complaint he'd kill her. She'd known Tyrone since he was a child and knew he was bad news, just like his hoodlum father.

143

Wendy spent a restful night with Beverly by her side. The next morning she was awakened by the smell of bacon, eggs and toast. Mrs. Jackson served her breakfast in bed. Her body was more painful and in worst condition than the night before. She couldn't move without wincing.

Just prior to lunch Wendy's cell phone rang. It was Tyrone. "I'm gonna kill you bitch. They'll never find you or know who did it." He said. Wendy's hands shook so badly she could barely put the phone back into her handbag. Beverly noticed the fear on Wendy's face and asked, "Who was that? I know it was Ty. I'm calling the police. That bastard thinks he can do whatever he likes."

Beverly's brother Terry called saying that Ty wanted to make things right. Beverly refused to allow him to speak with Wendy saying "Bullshit, it's too late, Plus I don't believe you or Ty. I'm sorry! And please don't call here with messages from Ty." Beverly screamed. "Wendy is leaving here in a few minutes, and I'm not telling you where she's going." With that being said Beverly slammed the phone down.

Beverly hurriedly drove Wendy to the shelter for abused women off Euclid Street in North West Washington. She knew she had to stash Wendy in a safe location. It was an ancient looking two story house on a dead end street with security alarms on every door and infrared sensors throughout. It had taken two hours to be referred and secure the location. Beverly convinced Wendy to hide-out. She knew Tyrone would come looking or would wait to catch her on the street. Beverly wasn't concerned for her own safety or Tyrone feeling that she'd sided with Wendy. He knew not to touch her. Although, her brothers Terry and Ray were a part of Tyrone's drug ring, they'd go after anyone who threatened her, including Ty. It would be a nasty scene and Tyrone knew so. They'd proven their nonsense attitude concerning Beverly every since junior high.

Sheppard's Quarters was ran by a fifty year old white women, tall with long frizzled hair. She wore wire rimmed glasses and looked like a throw back from the 1960's peacenik flower child generation named, Sarah Caine. The house was occupied by seven other women. The abuse of the women was evident through their broken spirits, facial scars and splintered bodies. Sarah asked Wendy to unpack and relax for awhile. A couple hours later she called for Wendy to come into her office. Sarah spoke cautiously and with care. She took notes for records sake. She listened to Wendy's story, nodding and communicating mostly through facial expressions. She personally knew the difficulty of reliving the experience of abuse.

Finally, Wendy was out of words. Sarah reached over and offered a box of Kleenex for the tears that rolled down her face. With a voice of kindness and deliberate words Sarah begin to explain the recommended course of action. She warned Wendy of the danger to life and the number of women killed by estranged mates each year. Not trying to frighten but to help her to truly realize the seriousness of the situation. Sarah asked, "Can you leave the city? Do you have family who'll take you in?"

Wendy slowly replied, "My parents live in North Carolina. They sent me away to school to Hampton University, I quit school last year and it caused a big fight. I haven't been talking to them much since that time. The main problem was my moving to D.C. with Tyrone. It drove a wedge between us."

Sarah asked, "Why don't you call them. Sweetheart they're your parents and it sounds like they love you. Try calling them, I think you need them now." Wendy dropped her head as more tears filled her eyes. She was filled with embarrassment, shame, disappointment and ached with physical pain.

Tuesday, November 22, 1991

The bright sun filtered through the slats of the window blinds, laying out ribbons of sunlight onto the parka floor in Fines Restaurant. The noise and rumble of Berma chatting with Ester and Cecil as they unloaded supplies in the backroom captured Josh's attention away from tallying the receipts from the day before. It was almost 10 A.M., only an hour before the lunch crowd would began pouring in. Josh on the late side of fifty was still lean and fit. He'd worked hard at maintaining a high level of fitness over the years. He ran four days each week for three miles and went through his Marine Corps workout drill each morning. He moved from his favorite table and walked by the door looking out onto Roxboro Road. The traffic was steady. His mind drifted back to when he first arrived in the Bull City some thirty years earlier and how it had been good for his family. He wasn't completely satisfied with how his son Randy had turned out but knew it wasn't the fault of the City. He had a contemplative look on his face as he stared out at the winter weather.

He turned away from the street as his son Randy drove up and entered the drive-way leading to the back of the Restaurant. He noticed one of Jack Newsome's young nieces in the car with Randy. He remembered her being called Nikki; she couldn't be more than seventeen years old and already had turned to the streets as a way of life. Josh knew why Randy had come, so he decided to go back and take his seat at his favorite table by the window.

Randy entered through the back door, leaving Nikki in the car waiting. He rushed pass Cecil and Miss Ester without a word as if they didn't exist. His one time, well mannered and selfless young boy had become a man whose life was torn apart and controlled by his heroin addiction. He'd evolved into a stranger. A man Josh didn't recognize nor trust. Josh had seen it before in Vietnam in the 1960's where heroin, over ran a man's morals and sense of decency and turning them into unpredictable men driven by their monstrous thirst for dope. He knew he couldn't help his son until either he'd realized the dope was killing him and decided to stop or something greater than man brought him to a halt. In the meantime he'd decided to keep his distance as much as possible even if it hurt him to do so.

Randy was crying to his mother for money again. Josh watched Berma and Randy with a keen eye. He knew addicts sometimes become violent when sick for dope. He hoped Randy wouldn't cross that line with his momma. As he looked at his run down haggard son, he couldn't figure what would make someone stick a needle with heroin in it into their body. He thought, "Maybe the stage was set slowly, over, the years, long before he knew that drugs would help him cope with life. For some reason he was ready for heroin when the time came." As Josh studied his son he thought, "Maybe it was curiosity or his attempt to fit in with the world of hipsters."

Everyday or so, Randy came by to cipher money from his mother. Josh realized that Berma had set the stage with Randy when he was a boy, giving him almost everything he desired that she could. Now, she had painted herself into a corner and couldn't see a way out. She didn't know how to say no to Randy. For some reason she thought loving Randy meant permissiveness, giving and not holding him accountable for his actions. She'd shielded him behind her skirt-tail each time Josh had attempted to teach him to be a man. Requiring him to work for what he received, applying standards of discipline, responsibility, accountability and expectation of high performance. Each time Randy whinned, Berma had rescued him. She thought rescuing him was protecting him. But, she'd failed to realize that she was stunting his growth toward manhood.

As a high schooler, she'd brought him a new sports car, kept him in the latest styles in clothing and each time he'd fouled up it was the school's or teacher's fault. Now, he was a junkie and as far as Berma was concerned, it was the dealers or the worlds fault. No matter how many times he went to jail she'd gotten him out. She paid his drug debts and furnished him money for whatever the cause. She didn't know how to turn him a loose in the world.

Josh watched each day as his son deteriorated further and further. He'd decided that maybe a little jail time might save him. If not, he knew the dope or the life-style surely would kill him. As he watched without an answer for his concerns, the phone rang and Berma reaching for the phone shoveled a few folded bills into Randy's hand. Randy hurriedly exited through the back door making sure to avoid eye contact with his father.

Berma was caught off guard. She hadn't expected to hear Wendy's voice on the other end. Instantly, she noticed Wendy's subdued tone. Berma said, "This is a pleasant surprise. Your daddy and I were just talking about you two nights ago. You sound uh, are you okay?"

Wendy was slow to reply and was struggling to talk, holding back her tears as her voice cracked. "No ma, I'm not okay."

Excited Berma asked, "What you mean? What's wrong? What happened? Where are you?" Wendy was unable to speak. The words wouldn't come out, Wendy felt choked with emotions. Sarah who was close by took the phone from Wendy's trembling hands. Berma on the other end called out, "Wendy, honey!"

Sarah spoke into the phone saying, "Mrs. Dockery this is Sarah Caine from the Sheppard's House for Women."

Berma asked, "The Sheppard House? What is the Sheppard's House? What's Wendy doing there? I don't understand, what wrong with her? What happened?"

Sarah calmly replied, "Mrs. Dockery if you'll calm yourself, I'll try and explain the situation." Sarah was finally able to disclose the circumstance to Berma despite Berma's outburst of emotion and panic. Berma shouted, "Lord have mercy, you need to talk to my husband. Josh, Josh, please come to the phone. Hurry, it's some lady on the phone about Wendy, she's been hurt or something." Josh in a rush, marched toward the counter as Berma cried, "Lord ha mercy, what can happen next?" She walked in circles raising her hands over her head as she cried to the Lord.

With great concern Josh took the phone from his crying wife. "Josh Dockery here." He listened calmly and patiently as Sarah explained Wendy's situation. He didn't interrupt or ask a question until she finished. Berma could only hear him say, "I see, I see." He finally spoke, "Mrs. Caine, will she be safe there for a day or two until I can get there? Thank you. Please let me speak to my daughter." Josh remained calm. Wendy's solemn voice sounded through the phone. Josh could be heard saying, "Hi honey, stay where you are. I'll be to get you in a day or two, don't worry, just stay there." Josh eased the phone down, looked at Berma, reached for her hand, gave her a reassuring hug and stated in a dispassionate fashion, "I knew it would come to no good." As Berma cried and fidgeted, Josh looked at her saying, "Calm down honey, she's okay. That guy Tyrone beat up on her. I'll leave tonight for Washington."

Berma ringing her hands said, "I guess I need to go pack us some things."

Josh turned and faced Berma with an earnest tone saying, "Honey, I need to go alone." Berma knew from the look on his face not to argue the point.

Later that day Josh called his friend Frank Dowdy a twenty year veteran detective with the Durham Police Department. Frank and Josh had become friends over the years starting when Frank was still in blue. He and his partner, Patrolman Everette started dropping in at Fines' Diner back in the days when it was in Hayti. In time a friendship developed and had lasted over the years. Josh needed to find out who Tyrone was, what kinda man Wendy had fell prey to. He needed all the information which would lead him to Tyrone without inquiring on the streets of D.C. Josh told Frank, Wendy had gotten herself involved with some man in D.C. and he was concerned. He wanted to know something about him. He appears to be legitimate but has a slick edge about him. Frank agreed to look into Tyrone's life. Josh provided Frank with the personal information he had on Tyrone.

Frank made a call to a fellow detective he'd met who'd come to Durham two years prior tracking down a man from D.C for murder. Frank had spent days with Detective Walsh and they'd finally nailed the guy. Walsh owed Frank a small favor. Frank called Walsh in D.C. Walsh's office was in the back of the station. He'd chosen the back to move away from the constant noise and traffic in the station. His desk was covered with scattered paper, folders and a half filled cup of coffee. It was impossible for anyone other than him to figure out what was the priority. In his disorganized fashion he got the job done and was highly regarded by the other detectives in the District.

Walsh a lanky, middle aged man in his forties with graying hair of which had been jet black in years past. He wore steel-rimmed glasses and conservative expensive suites. He was surprised when he answered the phone and Frank Dowdy voice sounded, "Ivan, this Dowdy down in Durham, how you doing?"

Walsh still surprised replied. "I'm fine Frank. It's good to hear from you. What inspired you to dial my number after two years?" Without a direct response to Walsh's inquiry Frank replied, "I'd planned to call you before but these southern crooks have kept me going. I look up and its' been two years, how's things in the District?"

Walsh reclining is his swivel chair and in a light-hearted manner said, "Same old rat race, cops and robbers. I think the robbers are winning." They both gave a light-hearted laugh. Frank turning serious continue, "Ivan I need a little help."

Walsh listening said, "Shoot."

Detective Dowdy said, "A friend down here got a daughter in D.C. She's getting a little serious with some guy and he'd like to know more about this guy before the nuptials." Could you check around a little bit and see you can find out on this guy?" Ivan agreed to run Tyrone's name through the D.C. database which would include and list any arrest and convictions in Virginia and Maryland. Tyrone Beckwith came in for twenty lines. Walsh scanning the computer printout was dismayed, "Uh, bad dude." He'd been in and out of trouble since he was fourteen. He's been hit for assault on five occasions, two attempt murders, transporting drugs from New York, soliciting prostitution and God knows what else. With a further look into Tyrone's present life, Walsh found that he was said to be involved in a turf war in a few of the housing projects with the New York boys, young free lance drug dealers traveling south trying to establish themselves in the crack cocaine business. Bodies of the New York boys had been turning up in abandon houses and dumpsters as a result. Walsh found that Tyrone was suspected of being one of the major drug distributors in D.C. He also had prostitutes working the upscale bars and was hiding behind a real-estate partnership. Walsh shook his head thinking, "Not the kinda guy to take home to momma and daddy." In less than three hours Walsh called Frank back in Durham disclosing what he'd found. In addition he gave Frank Tyrone's car tag number, social security number, mother's address and the locations where he was known to circulate.

Frank hung up the phone and walked out the Durham Police Department and drove directly to Fine's Diner on Roxboro Road. He had to give Josh the information face to face. It appeared as if Josh's daughter was keeping bad company. Frank walked through the door of Fine's Diner and found Josh setting by the window reading the newspaper. As he approached Josh welcomed him, "Come on over here Frank, how's things?" Frank smiling but feeling official said, "I'm doing, good."

Josh looked around and asked Cecil to bring Frank some coffee. Frank didn't hesitate. This guy Wendy's seeing is a bad dude. His record is a mile long and he's been involved in everything from dope to suspected murder." Josh with a laid back outer expression responded, "Damn that don't sound good." Frank advised maybe you need to try and get Wendy away from this guy." Josh looked into Frank's face as he sipped from his cup of coffee, "Well me and her momma gotta try and see if we can talk her out of it. But you know Frank it's hard to tell these young folk anything these days. We'll do our best and pray no harm comes to her." Josh and Frank sat for awhile and talked of Durham's expanding growth, the influx of new businesses out in the Research Triangle and the job opportunities that had resulted. Josh purposely had diverted the conversation away from Wendy and her troubles with Tyrone. Frank checked his watch and stood saying, "I'd like to stay and talk longer, gotta run, suppose to be in court in fifteen minutes. Look, if you need any more help with this thing don't hesitate to call."

Josh thanked Dowdy saying "I'll see if I can get Wendy to stop seeing this guy. All I can do is talk and hope she comes to her senses, she's grown now and making her own decisions, again thank you. I'll see you soon." With that Frank was gone.

Tuesday, November 22, 1991

It was well pass 9 P.M. and a low fog stretched across the peaks and valleys of the piedmonts like a thick blanket. It brought a cold, wet sensation to the air. There were patches of pine trees, hillsides and knolls that peered through the blindness of the fog as Josh headed north on Interstate 85. His mind drifted to a time when he planned and sought revenge against Junior Whitfield. It had been over thirty years but it seemed fresh in his mind and heart. It suddenly seemed like only yesterday that he'd carried out his act of revenge on Junior for raping his sister Queenie. His blood still pumped and heart raced at the thought of his rage and memory of Junior's helpless struggle with him on that day on the bank of the fish pond. Tonight, that same anger and desire to make Tyrone pay for hurting his Wendy engulfed his entire being. He'd sworn years ago, no one would ever dishonor a Dockery while under his watch without due payment. He knew he wouldn't sleep until justice was served.

The sky was dark and the stars were twinkling as Josh entered suburban Alexandra Virginia. He'd been on the road just under four hours. In the early morning darkness, he could see that D.C was a City that never slept. Slowly as he entered the city, lights from the skyscrapers in the great Metropolis lit the sky like beams of daylight in the distance.

Josh didn't waste any time. He'd spent time in D.C. many years earlier and with the directions he'd gathered from Frank, navigated his way through the city with ease. He had to locate Tyrone Beckwith. At 2 A.M. his dark blue Brougham Cadillac turned the corner of the Potomac Gardens Projects in search for Tyrone's mother's residence. He'd read the number of the apartment on the paper the held in his hand. He stared! And with a cynical smile he thought as he spotted the number. "That's it. Good location if need be." He pulled his blue Caddy to the curb a block away and surveyed the area. There were a number of spots for a man to conceal himself and not be seen in full view of Minnie Beckwith's front door.

Josh fired up the engine of his Caddy and drove to the Pelican Bay Lounge on Georgia Avenue. Tyrone was said to frequent the Pelican

Bay each night before moving on to one of his ladies residences for the night. Josh circled the parking area in back, the front, the side and the adjacent streets. He finally was able to match the license tag on a black 500 Mercedes with the number he'd been given by his friend Frank. He realized Tyrone was a man of habit. That wasn't good for Tyrone but an advantage for him. He parked on Georgia Avenue and waited. At 3 A.M. Tyrone exited the lounge with two other men by his side. Josh watched attentively as the three men stood and talked for exactly four minutes. He recognized Tyrone from pictures he'd seen of him from Wendy. He couldn't be mistaken, tall, slim, red skinned with piercing green eyes and immaculately dressed. He thought, "Yeah, that's my man." Tyrone dashed to his car out of the cold. As he drove away, Josh eased his Caddy in gear in slow pursuit. Still a powerful and well fit man on the late side of fifty, Josh knew he could easily break Tyrone's neck. But, he wouldn't let his emotions over-rule his caution, logic and trained ability to take out an enemy at the exact time. He'd lay and wait. Timing and opportunity was the key. He followed Tyrone to the Potomac Garden Projects. He'd expected him to lead him to the Brownstone in Georgetown. He thought, "Maybe, he's staying away from Georgetown in an attempt to elude the police, who he thinks is looking for him for whipping Wendy." Josh watched as Tyrone parked, exited his car and then opened the trunk for an overnight and hygiene bag. Josh could tell he'd planned to camp out with his mother for a day or two.

Josh waited giving Tyrone time to go in and get settled. Then he drove out to Alexandra to find a hotel for the night. He thought to himself, "One more night should do it." Josh moved with caution and calculation. He was well experienced with the game of waiting for his prey. He knew how to be patient. He realized most men were caught and convicted because of their own carelessness. Most of them talked too much when they shouldn't. Many of them kept evidence around them without thought. Some even kept clothing with blood. Some left blood behind or other DNA.

Josh retired for the night in his hotel room. He slept through the night. At 8 A.M. he called Fines Diner. He spoke with Berma assuring her of his safe arrival and promised he'd be home in a day or so with Wendy. He showered and ordered room service. Josh enjoyed bacon, eggs, coffee and read the Washington Post while simultaneously watching T.V. In the back of his mind he was formulating his alibi. He wouldn't leave his hotel room all day. He had to stay out of sight as much as possible. He placed a call to the Sheppard's House and spoke with Wendy. He suggested to her that he was in the area but wanted to spend some time pricing restaurant equipment and maybe visit a few relatives. He told her to be ready to leave around mid-morning of the upcoming day. His demeanor was calm and level.

At 1:30 A.M. Josh was anxious to exact his justice. He was bored with the solitude of his room. He called room service and ordered warm milk to calm his ulcers and asked that it be delivered as soon as possible. When the milk arrived, he answered the door dressed in a woolen red and black checkered robe, house shoes, and his glasses on the bridge of his nose and with an expression of pain on his face. The young gawky white teenager acknowledged Josh's apparent discomfort and quietly set the tray of warm milk on the dresser. Josh tipped the youngster graciously and thanked him for his expedient service. It was all a game, Josh poured the milk into the toilet, flushed it and began to dress. He knew if asked the youngster would verify his presence in the hotel. By 2 A.M. Josh was dressed in all black. He wore a hooded sweat shirt, trousers, soft bottom shoes and was armed with one of his favorite pistols, a blue steel Colt.45 equipped with a silencer. He cautiously exited his hotel, taking the back stairway to the parking garage and his car. Without a sound other than the quiet singing of the engine of his Brougham, he was gone.

He drove to Potomac Garden Projects where he was sure Tyrone would end his night. He parked five blocks away and began to walk, blending in with the street's darkness, carrying the demeanor of a local. With a soda can in a small brown bag he made his way to the dumpsters that faced Minnie Beckwith's front door. Once at the dumpster he turned the can up as if to finish its contents. Looking around and disappearing behind the row of brown dumpsters. He stood and he waited. The stench from the decaying garbage filled his lungs. A block away a group of teenagers, three boys stood on the corner smoking pot, their long coats and oversized jeans causing them to look like throw-ways. A few porch lights were still on, yellow and white. There were cars parked on the street, not many, the neighborhood was slowing down as the early morning crept in. Several times someone came to the dumpsters to throw out trash. Josh's heart pumped. It looked right. He thought, "You're a dead man." Tyrone pulled in the parking space fifty feet to the left of the dumpsters where Josh waited. He exited his car taking his time without a worry in the world. Josh waited as Tyrone came closer. He slipped out from behind the dumpsters, with his .45 concealed by his leg. Josh gave the street one last glance. Checking to make sure there was no one in sight. Tyrone moved as to turn, meeting the force from Josh's Colt .45. He fired two shots to the torso and the one to the head, the mark of a trained killer. Tyrone was only able to give a weak sounding groan as he bounced to the pavement. Josh without hesitation calmly walked in an unhurried pace to his car.

In route to his hotel in Alexandra, he stopped by an all purpose Wal-Mart off I-95. He brought a bottle of anti-acid medication and kept the receipt with its hour and day stamped, crumbled it in a bag and carried it with him. Before he left the store's parking lot he searched and found a receipt that recorded a purchase time of 3:08 A.M. and the correct date. He exchanged the receipt for his own and placed the crumbled bag under his car seat, still creating his alibi.

Josh was up and out by 7 A.M. the next morning checking out the hotel. He carried his overnight bag to his car. In a hotel trash bag he carried the clothes of the night before. He loaded his car and drove to a Salvation Army drop box a block away discarding the unwanted clothing. He drove from Alexandra across the Potomac, tossing the Colt .45 in the rush of the winter water. He stopped at Denny's Restaurant after crossing the Potomac for breakfast. He breathed a sigh of relief. Satisfaction warmed his heart. He'd revenged the dishonor and debasement of his daughter. He held onto his principal of exacting his justice on anyone who laid a hand on a Dockery.

By 12'noon, Josh arrived at the Sheppard's House. Wendy heard his strong voice from the room where she'd spent a restless night. A sense of joy and safety encompassed her heart. With a degree of shyness and shame she walked out to meet her dad. Josh turned and without starring at the obvious bruises, hugged his child. He hugged and rocked her in his powerful arms. Tears ran from Wendy's eyes, she felt the choking sensation of her emotions. Josh finally released her saying, "Girl, get your things so we can go home." Wendy skirted off as quickly as her sore body would allow. Josh thanked Sarah Caine, offered and forced her to take the five one hundred dollar bills in his hand.

The plaintive blues notes of B.B. King's voice and guitar resonated as Josh headed down I-95 in route to North Carolina. Wendy reclined in her seat as the bright sun warmed her face through the window. Josh talked non-stop. He filled her in on family gossip, Randy's drug problem and the business of running Fine's Dinner. He spoke of the growth in Durham, but never mentioning a word of the incident with Tyrone.

The word spread like brush-fire. Back in D.C. in Potomac Gardens people speculated, creating many different scenarios for the obvious cold blooded murder of Tyrone Bechwith. The whispered stories on the streets and in the Projects ran from a hit squad of New York boys in the on-going turf wars on the street to control the crack cocaine market, to an Italian mob hit for an unpaid debt and finally the suggestion of a drug deal gone bad the night before. The truth was that nobody knew who or exactly why. Tyrone's death was the beginning for a story of a bigger than life legend of a player in the streets of D.C. The stories in time would grow to become such much greater and daring than the life he lived. But, as mankind would have it, that's how legends are created.

By 7 A.M. the entire parking lot where Tryone's body was found in a puddle of blood was encircled by yellow tape and labeled as a crime scene. People starred, whispered and appeared afraid to mention Tyrone's name as the investigators attempted to gather information. No one had seen or heard a thing. At least no one was talking. Tyrone's body had been found by a neighbor of Minnie Bechwith at 5 A.M. as he left home for the early morning shift with Amtrak. By that time Tyrone's body had grown almost cold and congealed blood covered his face and body. For the homicide and narcotics squads it was already being labeled as drug related and another end to a life of a man who'd lived fast and reckless, who reaped the reward of his deeds. Without any witnesses they were ready to classify it as a closed case and add it to the growing list of such cases in the neighborhood war zone.

Friday, August 20, 1998

Nicole Worsley lay in bed at Motel 6 with retching pain in her gut and feeling nauseous with the onset of the pain from withdrawal; a daily part of her life as a heroin addict. It was her body calling for another shot of heroin. She'd ended up at the cheap hotel out on Highway 98 on the East Side of Durham after tricking with some guy who said his name was Sam who'd paid with dope and money for the room. As her intestines stirred and twisted she wondered how she'd put an end to a life of shooting dope and tricking for money to buy more dope.

At age fifteen she'd entered the world of drugs and hustling. Two years later there she was lying in a cheap hotel sick and alone. In another place and time she might have been a junior in high school preparing for her senior year and eye-balling a list of universities she'd hope to attend. Today, right then her habit forced her to rise. She needed money and then dope. She had no idea how she'd accomplish either. First she had to hit the streets. Check out time was at noon. Lately Randy Dockery had been coming by on different days to give her a wake up blast and then take her out hustling in the malls and on East Main Street at night to turn tricks. But, last night they'd somehow missed each other, so she didn't know where he might be.

Nicole looked at the cheap Timex on her arm, it read 10 A.M. She had exactly two hours before check-out. Most of all she had to figure out who she'd work to get her morning blast. She'd used her good looks, sexy body and feminine ways with Randy Dockery and a list of other men, she couldn't remember. As she dressed her mind raced trying to think who and where she could get a favor. She thought of old man George but didn't feel like being bothered with his old ass. He always wanted to give her barely enough dope to get the monkey off her back and then wanted to screw half the day. She thought, "Maybe Fat Ralph or Goofiend over on Dowd Street, they both like me, always asking for some of my poo-nanny plus they good friends with my cousin Cedric. I might can work one of them." She finished dressing, squeezing into her jeans, pulling a burgundy and grey NCCU tee-shirt over her head, taking time to make up her face in case she had to hit the mall to do some boosting. She grabbed her black leather coat and called a cab with the last ten dollars she had in the world.

As the cab traveled down Elizabeth Street approaching Dowd she could see Fat Ralph on the corner setting on a milk crate talking to Randy Dockery. Nicole breathed a sigh of relief. She knew between Randy and Fat Ralph, the chances of getting her morning blast was pretty good. The cab stopped in front of Fat Ralph. She paid the driver and jumped out.

As bad as she felt, she approached Fat Ralph and Randy in as much as a flirtatious manner as possible. She'd learned since age thirteen to use her looks and sexual persuasion to get what she desired from men. As she approached she started her game, using her most seductive voice, "Ralph, hey baby. Hey Randy, what ya'll up to. Randy, I waited for you last night at my momma's house. I thought we were going to go make some money?" Randy absorbed her question and enjoyed the idea that she'd acknowledged her need for him in front of Fat Ralph. When Randy's face lit up, Nicole knew she had him.

Nicole continued, "Randy why don't you get me straight, then we can go make the money we missed last night." By that time Nicole had latched onto Randy like a puppy. She knew he was too weak for her to say no. She knew he had enough money for the both of them. She'd rode with him on different mornings as he hit his mom up for cash at the Diner. He'd always left her in the car and returned with no less than a hundred dollars which was a dream for a junkie. Nicole knew the Dockery's had money. The Diner and the real-estate the Dockery's owned made them one of the wealthiest families she knew. Josh Dockery and her uncle Jack Newsome were close friends and like family to one another. She used her Uncle Jack's relationship with Josh Dockery to manipulate Randy at times. She'd tease saying, "Randy you know me and you are family, you gotta treat me like family suppose to." With playing the family game and feeding him her young body, she worked Randy with ease.

After a day of getting blasted and sex with Randy, by 10 P.M. that night she was on East Main Street in a Blonde Wig around her young face, a white tee stretched over her bulging breast and a short black skirt that exposed her perfectly bowed legs and firm butt. She was in the mix, soliciting the pleasures seekers and their money. If anyone asked her age she'd tell them in an unflinching manner that, "I'm nineteen and old enough to do what you like." A lie she'd told many times before.

Nicole had been prostituting for less than a year since dropping out of the ninth grade. She left home citing her mother's demand for her to go to school, make good grades, refusal to allow her to go out and run the streets. Nicole ran away first for a day, then two and then for weeks at a time. Finally she left to live with her girlfriend and girlfriend's mom refusing to return home. She didn't see what was so bad about the streets. She seemed starved for attention especially from any male that offered it. In a year she'd slept with more men and young boys than she could count.

It didn't matter, she thought sex meant love. A love never offered by any man in her life. The free willing sex lead to drug use and anything else the men around suggested. She found herself roaming the seedy streets, in strip clubs, hotels and laying in the back seats of cars.

Her girlfriend Tiffany Moore, a young girl on the streets like herself introduced her to Kenny Baker at age sixteen. Kenny was good looking, well dressed, with a mouth full of gold. Although a small time pimp, not the draped in expensive clothes type but a casual dressed brother who'd figured out how to finesse a living off the backs of desperate and loss girls. Tiffany said, "Kenny can help you. He said he like you. He can help you make all kinds of money." Nicole met Kenny and felt he was special. He gave her the attention she never had. It didn't matter that he thought of himself as a pimp who took advantage of women with promises of love, protection and fancy things. Nicole found Kenny perfect for herself and she was perfect for him. Nicole was a girl whose world was upside down. Within a day she was performing fellatio and in two days intercourse for a fee. Although she was scared, the money, drugs and attention from Kenny kept her on the streets and ready to go. Within a period of six months Kenny went to jail for drug possession and she was on her own with a dope habit to feed. Nicole was in the middle of the waters of the street life without knowing how to return to the shores of the conventional world.

Cleveland Newsome was a stranger to Nicole. He'd supplied the sperm drop that impregnated Helen Worsley and not much else. Cleveland like the other Newsome men expressed his manhood through bedding women and fathering children. Cleveland like the other Newsome's, was tall, big and dark with a beaming personality much like his older brother Jack. He was a working man. He'd held down a job with the City of Durham's Sanitation Department since the early 1950's. He worked hard and lived fast. The blood of "Big Tom the breeder" was alive in his veins. Big Tom's character and notorious legend had been nurtured into his spirit and accepted as the standard by which men were placed above others. Cleveland had more children than he cared to know about. He'd selfishly sowed his oats leaving behind children as victims of his warped sense of manhood. He proudly advocated that the passage to manhood was through a long line of progeny springing from the male virility.

He'd never spent a day of his life with Nicole since her birth. At times he'd visited Helen when Nicole was a young child, not with interest in Nicole but in Helen. Once or twice he'd ran into Nicole on the street and through a sparkle of guilt acknowledge he and given her a few dollars. Big Tom's Ghost still continued to have far reaching consequences on his descendants. There was a confusion and misunderstanding of the true essence of manhood and womanhood that spread like a disease from one Newsome to the next.

By age fourteen Nicole had found other men to fill the void inside her that longed for the affection and love of her father. Nicole like many children who miss their fathers, found a replacement. She wasn't able to lavish her affection and adoration on her uncles, a grandfather or the male friends of her mother. Her Uncles barely knew her, both grandfathers were deceased and her mother shared her social life with men whose eyes and in later years hands searched her body.

Nicole grew up as the prototype girl in desperate need of her father. Cleveland Newsome never knew that fathers were just as important to girls as to boys. He'd failed in understanding either. Many young boys who miss their father turn angry at the world. Their rage festers into violence against women, society and even their brothers and sisters. Some seek out drug dealers and hustlers as father's and gangs as families. Nicole missed her father and tried to use sex to love her way into a man's heart. Nicole's insatiable sexual appetite had her labeled as promiscuous, but she was really lonely and searching to fill the void left by her fatherless existence. Nicole appeared to have grown into woman in many ways, but it was all an illusion. Inside was a little girl in a big girl's body, wanting and needing to be her father's princess. Nicole knew on the inside what she needed. But had to turn to the world in search of a father's love, a love Cleveland Newsome never offered. Nicole's soul cried out for a pure and basic love to judge the love of all other men. She carried a silent contemptible anger inside for her father, not a hostile, visible madness but a subtle, gnawing anger that never ceased. Her anger prohibited her evolution toward maturity and self analysis. Finally, she began to blame herself, carrying the burden of believing she was not worthy of her father's love. As she walked East Main Street soliciting the fun seekers, she trembled from the fear inside her.

Tuesday, September 10, 1998

Wendy Dockery hurried down Roxboro Road in her white Mercedes with her twin daughters Chyna and India in the back seat. Each morning for the past five years she'd dropped them at Weaver Street Pre-School and Nursery before rushing to meet the deliverymen at Fines Diner. The temperature and humidity registered in the lower nineties. She perspired freely beneath her white uniform.

She'd recovered from the brutal assault inflicted on her by Tyrone without a visible sign. Her skin glowed like rich sun teased caramel from a day in the summer sun, setting her hazel eyes off dramatically. Her black silky hair which grew well below her shoulders was pulled back at the nap of her neck. A shallow touch of lipstick and liner was her only make-up. Inside her, the horrific assault and deception she experienced while with Tyrone had caused her to fear even the idea of any relationship with men. The only treasured part of her relationship with Tyrone was her twins conceived on the morning Tyrone had beat and raped her.

The entire event surrounding her last days with Tyrone was nightmarish, from the cold brutal beating to the suspicious murder of Tyrone two days afterwards. Their relationship had turned sour over night. The specifics of it all, was still confusing and without clear answers and explanations.

If she chose, she could count the number of parties she'd attended since returning to Durham on one hand and have fingers left over. Her social life consisted mostly of a dinner out now and then, several movies, one or two concerts and on occasion a football game at North Carolina Central University when she could get away from the Diner. Those outings were usually in the company of Cedric. Cedric had become a good friend since the murder of his fiancé a year earlier. Her relationship with Cedric was of pure friendship. Not one of lust or sex, but of openness and genuine concern for another person. She had a ready excuse for every man who tried to date her. After awhile the excuses discouraged even the most persistent. If she found herself yearning for male companionship, her mind reflected back to her pain when involved with Tyrone. She believed that only a few men were interested in friendships, so kept men at an arm's length. She theorized that usually even casual dating led to an expectation of sex. She wasn't interested or ready to risk any emotional involvement at such a price.

Wendy had carried the entire responsibility of managing Fines Diner since her father's mild stroke eighteen months earlier. With her father's illness and partial paralysis, her mother stayed home to care for him. Her mother stayed close to home by Josh's side, only leaving long enough to shop or attend to the business of managing the Dockery's real-estate. Randy who continued to live from one shot of heroin to the next was not considered an option in helping out with the family business. He was more trouble than good. He was still in and out the Diner each day asking for cash.

Wendy along with Cecil and Mrs. Ester initially operated the Diner. Cedric hadn't returned to work and didn't know if he'd ever do so with Computech. Therefore, he helped Wendy at the diner. Helping the Dockery's at the diner gave him something to occupy his time, and a chance to give the Dockery's a hand in a time of need. It also, allowed him a chance to spend some time with Wendy, who had proven her friendship during tough times. She'd been his sounding board, and was willing to listen in the early days after Angela's disappearance and murder.

Fines Diner was Josh's brainchild and had lasted over thirty years. It had grown to be a landmark eatery and made him wealthy. When he became ill the business suffered. The first thing Wendy did after taking over was to look at remodeling and additions to the menu. She made a few changes to create an identity that represented new management. She approached Cedric who had shown his abilities in management and customer service, asking him to join her as a partner. She knew foods and food service but didn't know anything about running a business. As Cedric listened she explained her plan, "I want to offer a variety of rare foods in addition to the soul food, but with high quality. I would like it to be like an elegant home where customers feel comfortable as though they were calling on old friends. I see a setting with cushion chairs, candle lights, hardwood floors. I will offer morning breakfast and dinner. I want to add a little something to what daddy and momma have established." Cedric's eyes brightened with excitement, "I think it's a wonderful idea. I'd be glad to be your partner. I've realized that I'm not cut out for the corporate world anymore or not right now anyway. This will give me something to do with myself." The two of them shook hands in agreement. They knew what they wanted. Cedric brought into the Diner with money from his savings, stocks and 401K. It took six months before Fines was completely remodeled. After that it never looked the same and they never looked back. The result was an upscale eatery, part cafe' and part meeting room designed with expensive wallpaper, velvet cushion chairs, lace and ribbon table cloths, rich woods and flowers. It was bright and spacious and cozy and chic all at the same time. It was trendy and it caught on. A month after it was finished, there was a small write-up in the Durham Sun. After that, more than ever before. Josh and Berma as well as Jack and Clara Newsome were proud of Wendy and Cedric's partnership. It seemed such a natural fit.

Saturday, October 10, 1998

Wendy added a fine coat of lip gloss, flipped her hair, and stood back to consider herself in the full length mirror.

Labor Day had come and gone, fall was creeping in calling for darker clothes and shoes. Although it was early October, the mid-day temperature had climbed well into the seventies. But, as the night approached with its autumn air, it called for more sober attire.

It had taken two hours of trying on one outfit and then another before Wendy settled on a navy two piece suit that hugged her body in all the right places, a cream silk blouse, matching pumps and a string of off white pearls completing her vesture.

She turned, checking from every angle, looking for anything that was out of place. But everything was as it should be. With a satisfied sigh, she picked up her purse and headed for the front of the house where Chyna and India set on the couch in matching taupe dresses, black patent leather shoes, and white socks with neatly coifed hair. Wendy smiled as she said, "Girls lets hurry, we don't want to be late." With that Wendy with Chyna and India a step behind walked out into the fall night air.

It was a small get together for Jack and Clara Newsome's thirty-fifth anniversary as husband and wife. It was a family gathering. Cedric, his mother Paula, Jack's brother Cleveland, sister Ida, Clara's relatives from Murfreesboro and Josh and Berma Dockery were the core of the crowd. Wendy didn't question whether she belonged there or not. The Newsome's and Dockery's had been like family all her life. Since Jack and Josh returned from the Marines back in the early 1960's.

Wendy had been in and out of the Newsome's home all her life as if it were a second home. Cedric and her brother Randy were friends always. But, lately the dynamics in her relationship with the Newsome's was taking another turn. Cedric had become her business partner and best friend. A male friend that she cared for respected and trusted. She no doubt knew Cedric better than she knew her own brother, especially since Randy's run-away drug problem had changed him so dramatically.

Cedric answered the door. He was in a jovial mood, not often displayed since Angela's murder almost a year earlier. He'd been an absolute recluse since that horrible day, only attending church and working at the Diner with Wendy and the crew. Wendy was delighted to see Cedric's broad smile. He gave her a big hug and kissed each Chyna and India on the cheek. Wendy was becoming comfortable with Cedric's hugs and looked forward to receiving them.

Smiling Cedric said, "The women are in the kitchen, the kids are in the playroom and the men are in the den watching the Yankees and Pirates."

"Wendy recanted, "I'll try the kitchen first. Ma and Aunt Clara might need some help." As she headed for the kitchen she could hear her father's strong voice in debate with his old friend Jack Newsome. Two men cut from the same cloth. Josh loved the Yankees and hated whoever opposed them. His health was improving drastically. There were hardly any sign of the paralysis left, only a twitch of the mouth. Berma, with God's mercy had nursed him back to health.

The kitchen was in turmoil, which meant that Clara and Berma had everything under control. Although, it was Clara's anniversary, no one could keep her out of her kitchen. After a bare greeting, Clara shoved a platter of chicken into Wendy's hand. "Take it to the dining room." Wendy carried the platter and placed it on a table occupied with more food than she would have imagined. She trailed back to the kitchen where her mother presented her with a platter of assortment of ham rolls, stuffed celery and deviled eggs.

Cedric wore gray baggy slacks and a black crew neck sweater. Wendy noticed how handsome he looked. She though he had a nice face and great body. She quickly pushed the thoughts of Cedric from her mind. She'd never consciously looked at Cedric with any degree of lust before; the idea caused a sexual kinda nervousness inside.

"I'm not sure what all the excitement is about," he whispered as he helped himself to a ham roll and deviled eggs from the plate. "Grand-daddy know that uncle Josh have loved the Yankees since we were kids,"

Wendy laughing replied, "Ced you know they gonna argue through the whole game, they always do."

It was by plan, India and Chyna had ran straight to the playroom with the other children. Paula rushed to give Wendy a hug. The other Newsome's hung back, all except Uncle Cleveland. Even though he was old enough to be Wendy's father and some more, he examined her from head to toe with a broad smile of white teeth highlighted by the gold cap. He teased with a laugh saying, "Ced I see where you been spending yo time. Is dem yo two little girls? Is dem Newsome babies?"

Ced with a look of embarrassment replied, "No Uncle Cleve, those two little girls belong to Wendy, okay."

Josh looking and listening replied, "Yeah, dem's my grand babies." By the time Chyna and India peered out from behind Cedric. Chyna looked like a copy of Wendy and India a mixture of Wendy and Tyrone. India tucked her small hand inside Cedric's, leaned closed saying, "Cedic we can't make the game work right, fix it for Chyna and me please." Cedric scooped her up and headed for the game room.

Clara Newsome had stretched her cherry wood dining room table to its limited to accommodate the twenty adults and six children who crowded around it. She had planned to seat Cedric with his mother between Jack and herself, but Cedric insisted on setting beside Wendy with the twins on either side of them. "Well," Cedric smiled saying, "So much for your seating arrangement grandma."

The dinner was delightful. Paula and Berma did the serving, and refused to let Clara raise a hand. Berma repeatedly cried, "Clara this is your day honey, just sat there and let us cater to you and Jack."

The entire group made their way through the main course of chicken, ham, yams, macaroni cheese, asparagus and wild rice. Throughout the meal Cedric placed Chyna's small hands in the correct position on the knife and fork while Wendy directed India in the same fashion, while simultaneously casting admiration in Cedric's direction. In no time both girls were stuffed and still without food on their clothes. Their plates were so clean, they didn't have to be cleaned before washing, Berma was surprised and with her mouth hung open asked. "How did ya'll do that, those two young ladies never clean their plates."

Cedric replied, "Just a little persuasion of the right kind." It worked for today maybe not tomorrow." Wendy smiled as he spoke. Across the table Josh observed the happiness on his daughter's face.

Wendy sat in the back office of the Diner, in a baggy black sweat suit with a stack of invoices on the desk and a yellow steno pad in front of her, a ballpoint pen was clamped between her teeth.

She was contemplating the final details for a dinner party she'd committed to catering. The upcoming party was for a church member's wedding. Every detail seemed to be covered. Wendy spent thirty more minutes staring at the blank pad and menu, chewing on the end of the pen, trying to think, making sure she hadn't missed anything. Finally, she tossed the pen on the pad, stopped thinking and walked out into the dining area. She had a handle on things and felt an inner peace inside. Life was serving her well. She had a good business, great family, two lovely daughters and was being drawn to Cedric more each day. She kept her feelings for Cedric buried deep inside as far as she could stuff them and shared them with no one. For the first time in her adult life she felt safe and secure with a man outside her father. She was so engrossed in thought the door opening caused her to jump, "Hey," Cedric said as he stepped through the door.

"Hi," she replied, wondering why he was looking at her with questionable eyes. "Don't tell me I forgot something," she gasped, "What I forget?"

"No, no," he assured her hastily. "I just was thinking how happy you appear to be." "Okay, well I guess I am," she said. "I do feel blessed these days," Smiling and hesitating before continuing, "I was just going over the menu for Brenda Jones's party, I've covered everything, I think."

Cedric with a glow on his face replied, "Oh, okay, I thought I'd come in and go over the invoices and make a couple of calls. I have some billing questions for Byrd's Supply."

His presence felt familiar, and comfortable. When she sat down in the chair across from him, it was like being in a zone of comfort.

From the beginning, he'd put her at ease, teasing her like a sister, treating her like a valued friend and family member. It was hard to remember the Cedric of old, who'd played with her brother Randy through junior high and who dated together in high school. He had always seemed as too young to consider. As she looked at Cedric, she thought, "Boy, how people, and situations can change life. Who'd ever thought I'd be falling in love with Cedric." In a large part she supposed, the oddity was due to the closeness of the Dockery and Newsome families as well. Whatever the case, she knew a fire was beginning to burn inside her for the man who was now her friend and business partner. She couldn't help but to think whether he'd noticed the sparkle in her eyes or the sexual nervousness in her voice. He'd never attempted anything more than a quick peck on the cheek or a hand on an elbow to guide her across a street. She felt the connection, a flesh and blood connection between them.

Cedric looked forward to the new more frequent occasions when he saw Wendy outside the business. He found himself enjoying his time and involvement with India and Chyna as well.

In many ways, Wendy and the girls had come to symbolize the family he'd planned with Angela, the daughters Angela would never give him. He answered their questions, cheered their successes and basked in every smile and every giggle they chose to share with him. And always Wendy stood in the background in admiration. As time moved forward Cedric and Wendy were becoming more entwined into one another lives.

Wendy scooted out the office and returned with two glasses of fresh orange juice. They sipped in silence as Cedric focused his attention on the stack of invoices on the desk.

Wendy interrupted saying, "Chyna and India would like for you to come by the house tonight. They've learned a song for a school play and would like you to hear them perform, just for you." Cedric distracted from his work momentarily nodded his head agreeing, "Of course I will," with a smile.

Wendy nodded, "Great, I'll fix a meal. We can all eat before the premier."

The rain fell in sputtering rhythms, beating against the window panes with the sound of a snare drum in a marching band. Outside, the sky was over cast with dark rolling clouds. There wasn't a dry inch of earth anywhere in Durham. Cedric relaxed on the couch in the den of his grandparent's home watching the San Francisco 49ers and the Tampa Bay Buccaneers. As he looked out the large glass window leading to the deck he could see the force of the wind, pushing the rain and bending the trees, given credence to the awesome power of nature.

He'd finished eating a turkey club sandwich and was pouring soda into a glass of ice when the phone rang.

"Cedric!" It was Wendy. He recognized her immediately, but wondered why she'd called on Sunday afternoon the only day the Diner was closed.

"Yes?"

"This is Wendy. I hope I haven't called at a bad time."

"Not at all, how are you?" He replied.

"Just fine," There was a pause, "No, that's not true. I'm really not fine." She said, "Sometimes I answer based on my conditioned reflexes. As a matter of fact, I'd like for you to come over, would you happen to be free this evening?" she asked, "I'd really like to talk with you and don't want to talk on the phone."

Cedric though for a second, "Boy this sounds important. Where are you calling from?" he asked.

"I'm at home right now." She replied.

Cedric recanted, "I'll come over after the game goes off. That will be like an hour or so." They said their good-byes.

Cedric had been to Wendy's condo in Forest Hills on the Southside of Durham on a number of occasions over the past year. Each time he was surprised by how familiar it felt. The furnishing was relaxing, a big over stuffed love seat and couch, painting by Ernie Barnes, flowers, and dark mahogany tables.

He tapped on the door. Wendy appeared at the door in a red velour jogging suite, socks and a smile. She invited him in while holding her smile, "Hi, come in." There was a quietness in the air. Right off he knew Chyna and India were out. She escorted him to the couch. The room was pleasantly dark and the sounds of vintage jazz oozed from the wall sound system, making it impossible to believe that people under thirty had ever lived and loved.

She offered a glass of Don Perignon and the wine soon carried them past the initial uncertainties and polite ritual sparring. Cedric began to feel like a stranded traveler in the lull between two cities. The heavens had quieted, the rain had ceased and the calm was wonderful. Wendy had not gone into why she'd invited him over, he felt no need to press the issue.

Then as suddenly as that, she broke the spell as she spoke. "Cedric in the past year a friendship has grown between us in the nice slow way that lasting friendships always grow. I believe we have a lot in common and it's easy for us to talk to each other. We make each other laugh."

Cedric smiled warmly saying, "Speak more."

She continued, "We've known each other all our lives, but lately the energy between us seems to be changing. Maybe it's because we've been spending a great deal of time together with family and all. Chyna and India are growing more attached to you each day."

He smiled adding, "I'm glad they like me."

She hesitated momentarily before continuing. "You and I both had a bad experience some time back and we've never talked about either." For the first time in months he felt the emotions of his lost of Angela.

She asked, "How long are we gonna thrash about in darkness and live our lives surrounded by the business and family? I think both of us will have to move on with our lives at some point. There's something else I want you to know." She continued, "Since we've been working partners, I find myself depending on you more and thinking about you constantly. And do you know what I think mostly of how jealous you've made me." Cedric with raised eyebrows with an uncertainty on his face said, "Jealous, of what?"

Wendy quickly responded, "Of all you've lost, of the kind of feelings you and Angela must have had for each other." Cedric took some wine. He glanced at Wendy's eyes, but they showed more than he felt he had the right to see, and he studied his drink instead.

"I'm twenty-eight years old" she said "I've had only a couple of relationships, serious that is, and with Tyrone it was almost like being married. But I can't think of a man I've been involved with who cared for me and loved me the way you apparently loved Angela."

Cedric raised his eyes replying, "That's no great bargain either. Do you know what it is to live with the anger I have for Angela's murderer, Michael Wiles and take pleasure in nothing?" He paused, "I'll be honest with you, sometimes I wish we'd never had all that much. The hole it left might have been easier to fill."

Wendy's eyes flashed brightly. "Don't talk like that," she said. "You don't know what you're saying. At least you had it. All the love and joy was actually there."

Cedric responded, "But Wendy, I was foolish, I mean I was the reason we'd broke up, chasing other women that didn't mean a damn thing to me but a chance to prove my manhood in a twisted way."

Wendy advised, "Yeah, Ced but everything you felt and remember can't ever be taken away from you. The absolute worse is never to have had it all."

Wendy with legs tucked under her facing Cedric on the couch slowly circled the rim of the glass with the tip of a small finger. The act seemed to absorb her so totally that she might have been tracing her life. "You might as well know something else," she said, Along with all that happened between Ty and me, Chyna and India have been a blessing." Her eyes found Cedric's and grabbed hold. "I wouldn't trade them for nothing. You asked me if I know what it was to live with anger and take pleasure in nothing, well the answer is yes, I know. I was very angry, hurt and ashamed all because of Tyrone until a short time ago. I'm not angry or hurting anymore, but I still exclude myself from pleasure and the risk of men. But I still wouldn't give up even a piece of what I have today as a result. Chyna, India and you as a friend."

They sat there looking at each other, Cedric was almost afraid to move or speak. As if it might throw off a delicate part of the mood.

Wendy apparently had no such fear. She jumped from the couch heading for the bar for refills. As she walked Cedric was caught by her extraordinary figure, sexual swagger and good looks. Wendy looked back saying, "All in all Cedric, you deserve a life with more, you'll make some woman a good man. Just don't miss out on what could be for you." Cedric suddenly had a warm feeling inside. Then because he was neither a fool nor inexperience, he knew Wendy admired him as much as he admired her. She turned to him, "Thanks for coming over. I really needed to get that out." She looked at her watch, "I told momma I'd pick the girls up by eight." With that she escorted Cedric to the door, they parted with a hug.

At sunrise there was a low mist and fog stretched across the swampy low land off Hanson Road in Mooresville. It bought a cold, wet, tingling sensation as the air seeped through Burton Hogan's nostrils. Burton was a short burly fifty year old southern red neck who kept a wad of Redman Tobacco in his mouth and had lived in Mooresville since birth. He worked at Thurston Motor Lines in Charlotte driving a front end loader on the evening shift.

The mist created a wetness which allowed his hounds, Puny, Rex and Red Buck a sharpness in smell as they sniffed out the brush for rabbits. Burton had hunted the woods off Hanson Road since a boy along with the Wiles brothers, Ernest and Junior. In the last ten years he'd mostly hunted alone. Ernest left home to join the Army at age eighteen and never returned. He'd made a life in Augusta, Georgia with his wife and two children in the insurance business. He still occasionally hunted with Burton on his visits to Mooresville. Junior Wiles who still lived in Mooresville down the road from Burton and stayed nearly drunk everyday and hadn't shown an interest in hunting in years. For safety sake Burton was relieved he hadn't. Guns and whisky in the woods was a dangerous combination.

As the sun peeped through the fog, Burton heard ole Rex strike a tune and in a few minutes Red Buck and Puny chimed in as if they were singing a song. The sounds of the hounds were music to Burtons' ears. He knew they were hot on the trail of a rabbit or maybe a deer. Burton listened as his hounds begin to make a circle. He knew if the hounds ran out in a short circumference of a mile or so it was a swamp rabbit, Burton listened. The hounds were circling. He ran through the woods in an angle carrying his Remington automatic twelve gauge shotgun, filled with rabbit shot to cut the rabbit off as he circled. He finally stopped running. He was breathing hard, his chest heaving in and out. He could hear the hounds circling in his direction, straight to where he stood. In a matter of minutes they were less than one hundred yards away. Burton was alert as he waited and looked for the game they were chasing. There it was, a swamp rabbit. Burton waited until the hare was within twenty five yards and pulled the trigger. He'd stopped the rabbit in its tracks. He walked over, picked the rabbit up by its hind legs. Burton cupped his hands, making a cooing sound calling his hounds in. The hounds silenced their yaps and came straight to Burton wagging their tails and jumping around his feet. He spoke with them calling each one's name, "Good Puny, "Hear Rex", "Good boy Red

Buck." He showed the hounds the rabbit as he talked to them. He stuffed the rabbit inside the huge pocket of his light tan hunting jacket.

Burton checked his shotgun, clicked it back to safety and said, "Lets' go boys," while making a sucking sound with his lips. As he walked and kicked the brush he noticed Rex was sniffing and wagging his tail ferociously around an open area covered with leaves. Burton said, "Come on boy let's go" but ole Rex kept on sniffing and now scratching around the leaves. Burton walked over and kicked the leaves around. After removing the leaves, he saw a bone protruding from the ground. It appeared to be the bone of a deer's front leg at first sight. His heart seemed to jump from his chest to his throat. His heart pumped with fear, shock and wonderment. He stooped down to get a better look to be sure what he'd found. With a closer look, he was sure of the human hand. He stood up to settle himself. He looked around to pin point his location. He realized he was in the woods in the back of the old Will Brandon farm. The old Brandon house set approximately two hundred yards away. He knew no one had lived there in years; since Mr. Brandon's death years back. Burton summoned his hounds and headed out the woods to his green Chevy pickup truck. At the truck he put his hounds in the dog box on the back, took off his hunting jacket and put the Remington shotgun in the window rack. He felt anxious and nervous but he knew he had to report what he'd found.

Detective John "Red" Williams stood looking out the huge window in his office down on the Fourth Street as people made their way into the courthouse. The morning sky was finally clearing as the sun burnt off the early morning fog. The foggy haze that had been lying over Charlotte like a veil was being lifted and would be soon blown away by the stirring wind. Detective Williams turned, looked at his planner to be sure of the days priorities. As he flipped the black planner close, the phone rang. He picked the phone up on its second ring, "Detective Williams." It was Sheriff Bill Wilson. He'd known Sheriff Wilson for over twenty years and had a good personal and professional relationship with him. "Red, this is Bill down here in the Sheriff's Office? How are you?

Detective Williams answered slowly, "Bill, I'm okay chasing the bad guys."

Sheriff Wilson replied "Red, I thought I'd call you in on this thing out in Mooresville." With the mention of Mooresville Red's interest peak from zero to ten in a flash. He asked, "In Mooresville, what you got?"

Sheriff Wilson replied, "Got a call from a guy this morning out in Mooresville, says he found a human body buried out behind the old Brandon place. I remember you arrested the Wiles guy out there last year."

Detective Williams responded saying, "Right, that's the old house Michael Wiles was hiding out in when we found him."

Sheriff Wilson responded, "Why don't you meet us up there, so we can see what we got?" Detective Williams felt a nervous excitement as he scrambled for his jacket, knocking over a cup of coffee in a styrofoam cup. It had been over a year since Michael Wiles was arrested for Angela Slade's and Martha Trapp murder. Wiles, was being held in Raleigh's Central Prison for safe keeping and psychological testing. Detective Williams along with the Slades, Pete Trapp and Cedric Newsome who'd called each week were growing impatient with the delay in the trial.

Detective Williams had no answers for the Slades, Pete Trapp or Cedric. Everybody had to wait out the process.

Heading up I-77 North from Charlotte toward Mooresville, Williams' mind reflected back to Michael Wiles and how detached he'd been each time he'd questioned him concerning the Slade and Trapp murders. He showed no emotions, affect or sign of worry or what was ahead of him. The circumstantial evidence, the threat of capital punishment nor a deal for a lesser charge from the prosecutor hadn't been enough for Wiles to admit to the murders. His persona was cold and uncaring.

When Detective Williams arrived at the old abandon house he immediately saw Sheriff Bill Wilson and three plainclothesmen in coveralls standing beside an unmarked van. Williams parked his dark blue cruiser, opened the door, getting out without delay. He greeted the waiting men and breathed deeply. He looked at Sheriff Wilson while asking, "You think this'll be anything?"

Wilson enthusiastically replied, "Well the caller a Mr. Hogan seemed convinced that the remains were human, he is on his way to lead us to the sight. I just spoke to him by cell phone. I wouldn't be surprised if'n I ain't right".

"You might be right it could be a body left by Wiles." Williams said. "Wiles have a criminal history starting around age thirteen. Of course I don't know the exact specifics of his juvenile crimes; the juvenile records have been sealed, no record of anything before eighteen. But, I've talked to enough people who knew him including family and everybody says he's a nut case."

Williams and the other officers turned as Burton Hogan's green Chevy truck turned off Hanson Road onto the over-grown drive leading to the old farm house and the officers. Burton slowed his truck to a stop and bounced out the door with a nervous unsure demeanor. Sheriff Wilson took a couple of steps forward with his hand extended, "Mr. Hogan? Sheriff Wilson," looking around he said, "Detective Williams, Officers Haley and Brown." Burton nodded his head acknowledging each officer. Sheriff Wilson continued, "Thanks for the call, and meeting us out here."

Burton now red faced replied, "I didn't know what else to do."

Williams added, "You did the right thing." Sheriff Wilson with his eyes moving from one man to the next continued, "Well, we're ready, you lead the way."

Burton walking toward the brush behind the old house said, "Well we can cut right through this patch of woods and be right at the location." Officer Haley stopped while saying, "Hold on, let me get a pickaxe, a couple of shovels and rakes from the van."

Officer Haley and Brown brought over the pickaxes, shovels and rakes. Detective Williams looked around and spoke, "Hold on guys before we start digging, let me rake the leaves away from let's say a twenty-five feet circumference." Williams stripped off his jacket and began to rake. In ten minutes the area was clear of leaves and debris. Williams stood back breathing deeply. Sheriff Wilson and Officer Haley approached the area where the human forearm bone extended the ground. They began to dig. They went no deeper than two feet. Haley leaned into it, feeling the sweat break, welcoming the mindless physical effort. Detective Williams gave him a break and then carefully dug around the boundaries of the shallow grave. Each shovel full of earth trembled as he pitched it from the grave. The earth was hard, solid and complained as he dug it out. It moaned and grumbled as if trying to tell its story. The pickaxe hit something hard and solid. But it was only a rock. He carried his digging inward between the boundaries of the grave. Williams leaned on the shovel and starred at the ground. The other men watched in anticipation.

He squatted at the edge of the open grave, and could smell a scent of earthy odor, faintly unpleasant and soft with rot. The air from around the grave seemed curiously alive. For no reason that he knew, he reached down, grabbed a handful of dirt and kneeled there, staring at it, contemplating. It was almost as though the dirt was trying to send a message, trying to tell him what had happened.

Overcome with a sudden rush of madness, he gazed into the grave and saw it. It was the skeletal remains of a small man or maybe a woman. Meanwhile, Officer Brown who'd been busy digging around the area shouted, "Over here!" It came out in a low hoarse whisper, but instantly brought everyone around the earth he'd upturned.

Sheriff Wilson took immediate charge. Using the tips of his finger and a red handkerchief, he gently knocked the dirt aside enough to expose another human skull which had appeared to have been crushed. Wilson stood up and lit a cigarette. He looked at Haley ordering, "Go back to the van and call the chief. Tell him I need a forensic team out here right away. Quietly! No sirens and flashing lights, and no reporters or T.V. This must be kept quiet, that's important. I don't want a word of this getting out."

Detective Williams said nothing. He thought of the years he'd worked as a policemen and how he'd become immune to death until that moment. As the officers searched, they found two more graves. Williams walked to the last two sites and was met with the eyeless and faceless heads that peered out the holes. He felt the shallow grave yard was a central moment in his life as a person and a detective. He thought, "There are people who'll do anything imaginable. Life's not built on right, wrong or justice, no one deserves this. No, one."

When it was over, they'd uncovered four bodies. They left the remains in the shallow holes where they lay. Left for the forensics team and it's specialist to fully uncover. The bodies were mostly bones strung together by strings of rotted fabric and mummified, flesh. The earth had reclaimed its own.

Detective Williams' mind traveled to the loved ones of the four dead souls. He imagined the waiting, hoping and praying for a missing son, daughter or wife to one day return home, denying the logic and probability of their death. Then one day, answering the door for a cop and a set of dental x-rays. His soul wretched with pain, and his heart ached for the loss of life.

Detective Williams made his way up I-85 North in route to North Carolina Central Prison to where Michael Wiles was being held in safe-keeping. The four skeletal remains found a week earlier in the graveyard in Mooresville had been identified. The forensic specialist had concluded the remains were that of a twenty year old hooker from Gastonia name Pamela Little who'd been officially reported missing for eight months, another was that of Robin Marks, a twenty-six year old known to frequent the biker bars on Wilkerson Boulevard in Charlotte and who'd not been seen for over a year. When checking with Robin's parents they didn't seem to have concerned themselves with her whereabouts. They'd thought she'd left Charlotte with another biker boyfriend as that had been her pattern and usually returning home between escapades. There was also, the remains of a young male named Gary Newcomb from Patterson, New Jersey who'd lost contact with his family two years prior after affirming his homosexuality, resulting in a huge blow-out with his father. The skeletal remains with the crushed skull was Kevin Trapp who was believed to have left Charlotte a year of so earlier with a stripper in route to Los Angeles. Pete Trapp had felt his son's disappearance was suspicious and was sure Michael Wiles had been involved all along.

North Carolina's Central Prison appeared as a castle. The old prison was built sometime during the late 1800's. Central Prison was located in Raleigh on Wade Avenue right off the 401 Belt Line. It was North Carolina's State Prison that contained death row and housed the most vicious criminals in the State.

Looming ahead of Detective Williams was an immense succession of high grimly concrete structures a mile long punctuated by row after row of barrow and stoutly barred cellblock windows. A one story building extending forward, housed the prison administrative staff. On the Southside, three stories high were the prison workshops.

The heavy duty chain linked fences enclosed it all, each fence thirty feet high and topped with rolls of concertina barbed wire and a series of live electrical wires. At intervals along the fences, tall concrete towers were manned by guards armed with rifles, tear gas and search lights. From the towers they could view the entire complex. Driving through the parking lot, Detective Williams neared the main gate, a two lane entranceway with a uniformed figured standing guard. The guard, a tall, huge athletic looking black man in his thirties; wearing a gray uniform with sergeant strips on his white shirt, asked Williams for identification and questioned him concerning his business at the prison. Williams informed the guard he was there to serve additional murder warrants on Michael Wiles who was being held in safe-keeping. The guard entered the booth by the gateway and reached for the phone. In less than five minutes Williams was allowed to enter the city of men who lived in a world of their own. A world with its own set of laws and ways of life unlike the world which lay outside only a rock's throw away.

From the administrative building, where a forty something white woman clad in a pale blue dress, wearing bright red lipstick and horn rimmed glasses worked as if she had been programmed to show no human emotions. She officially cleared him, examining his identification and directing him to sign the necessary forms. He was similarly cleared through other checkpoints, taking ten minutes to reach the administrative building. Detective Williams was led by an armed guard walking quickly down brightly lit hallways. As Detective Williams observed, he noticed the linkages between the strict security outside and the tightly control check points on inside. The two paused briefly for clearance through two separate sets of electronically operated steel doors, opening to the main cellblock corridor, as wide as a two lane highway and running the length of a football field.

Detective Williams and the armed guard whose name tag spelled Sergeant Robinson stopped outside a secure control booth enclosed by steel and bullet proof glass. Inside were two female guards and a male lieutenant. The lieutenant approached the two men standing outside and slid a metal drawer outward. Williams inserted his Smith and Wesson 9mm automatic pistol, a fifteen round ammunition clip, and his police identification. The items were drawn inside the control room, where they would be placed in a safe until he'd finished his visit. No one had asked him about the recording device under his blue blazer, which he had strapped on prior to entering the prison. Williams didn't offer to mention the device.

"You'll be using one of the attorney visiting rooms to talk with Wiles and serve the papers." Robinson said, "We'll bring him to you there. You'll have about an hour with him, if you need it."

During Sergeant Robinson's absence, Williams checked his recorder concealed under his clothing. He hoped Wiles would confess to the murders of the people found in the shallow graves behind the old Brandon house and maybe implicated himself in the Angela Slade murder. The forensic specialist had enough evidence to connect him to Margaret Trapp's murder and the sledge hammer used to kill Kevin Trapp had been found in the old house. But, still there was not enough evidence to convict Wiles for Angela Slade and the others.

In ten minutes Robinson was back, accompanied by two prison guards who were leading and partially supporting Wiles on each side. Wiles' was clad in an orange jumpsuit and leg irons, with handcuffs secured to a tightly strapped chain waist belt.

It had been more than a year since Williams had seen Wiles; the last occasion had been in the interrogation room in the Charlotte Police Department. The time in safe-keeping, daily meals and the unavailability of drugs had caused Wiles to add a substantial amount of weight to his once narrow frame. He appeared to be twenty-five or thirty pounds heavier, he looked physically robust. His eyes still had the same piercing affect and his face the cynical expression.

Wiles' was seated at the metal table by the guards. He sat down in a relaxed fashion, tilting his head slightly to one side and starred into Detective Williams' eyes without speaking. Glancing down at the four murder warrants in the manila folder he carried, Williams spoke, "I'm here to serve four warrants for the murder of Pamela Little, Robin Marks, Gary Newcomb and Kevin Trapp." Williams read each of the murder warrants giving Wiles a copy after finishing each one. During the entire readings Wiles showed no emotion or concern with the whole affair. Detective Williams shook his head and asked "Would you like to make a statement or answer questions?" "But, first I must advise you that you can request the presence of an attorney and if you can't afford one, one will be appointed to you, and I remind you again that you are not required to make any statement or answer any questions." Wiles shifted in his chair, lowered his head for a split second, smiled cynically and asked, "Is that it policeman. I thought you'd found something big or maybe you were ready to release me." He turned to the guards saying, "I'm through wit this asshole, take me back to my palace." Detective Williams was dumb-founded but not surprised. Wiles hadn't given him anything on either of the prior occasions he'd tried to interrogate him. He was still the same icy and cold man without any concern of what faced him.

Sunday, June 16, 1999

The day of the Newsome family reunion was absolutely clear and the air was fresh from the rain of the night before. The temperature was expected to reach the upper eighties by mid-afternoon. Cedric set behind the wheel of a twelve passenger Dodge van filled with his grandparents Jack and Clara Newsome, Josh and Berma Dockery, Wendy and the twins and his mother Paula. The chatter and laughter between the passengers filled the air as Cedric navigated the van amongst the traffic down Highway 64 East. In two and one half hours, if all went well they'd be in Murfreesboro. The annual family reunion was held each year in Murfreesboro at the Newsome's home place. Although it was over one hundred years old, the old home was still standing. In years past there had been costly remodeling and repairs but the home that "Big Tom" the Newsome's ancestral grandfather had lived his last days in still stood. The house was a huge white colonial style structure with ten rooms, a manicured lawn, with the drive and walkway lined with white flint rocks, with rose brushes scattered throughout the backyard and a huge apple and pear orchard in an adjacent field. The home had been equipped with running water, in house bathrooms and central air during the last remodeling phases. The backyard was large and spacious where four long wooden tables had been especially set up for the reunion. The inside was furnished with Queen Anne tables, Duncan Fife chairs and other vintage furniture. Old faded pictures of "Big Tom" and his wives and prodigy lined the walls in the setting room. Jack Newsome's youngest aunt, Hattie from "Big Tom's" last wife Bulah lived in the home. She was a thin, brown skinned woman in her late eighties who wore her thick gray hair tied in a neat bun on top of her head. She was still frisky, high spirited at her age and had not been sick a day in her life, other than a common cold. She was the official host and took charge of the whole affair.

By the time Cedric turned off Highway 11 into the driveway of the Newsome's home place the yard was lined with cars and children running and playing over the green lawn. The cars showed license tags from almost every state between Florida and New York. Cedric found a parking spot by a huge magnolia tree on the side of the front yard. Before Jack Newsome could get out the van he was met by his cousin, Melvin Newsome's shouts, "Jack, I didn't think you was gonna make it, I thought maybe some woman had got the best of you in your old age." The entire time Melvin spoke he winked at Clara Newsome checking her attitude at the mention of another woman. Jack replied, "I wouldn't have missed it for the world. So, tell me about the no good yo've been up to and let me met the new woman of the year. I know you got a new one." Jack said. The two of them laughed, embraced one another and headed for the big oak tree in the back yard where the other Newsome men had gathered. Jack stopped and turned saying, "Come on Josh we're going under the oak over there. Be sure to roll your pant legs up. The shit gets mighty deep when the Newsome's get together."

Cedric took his time and helped everyone out of the van. He carried the large brown wicker basket of food to the house. Berma, Clara, Wendy, Paula and the twins followed close behind.

Once inside Clara, Berma, Wendy and Paula were assigned to squads of other women with various chores. Aunt Hattie had organized each chore. The squads of women cut-up fruit, squeezed lemons, assisted with the hot food, and organized food on the long tables out back while Cedric was sent to assist his great Uncle Cleve in making a wooden barrel of lemonade. The older men stood close by the lemonade barrel talking trash and chopping blocks of ice.

Three of the younger Newsome men, all carrying the sir names of their respective mothers stood in a circle in deep conversation. They were introduced as Terry Slack, Marcus Tolbert and Brandon Holmes. Cedric hadn't ever met either of them before but had heard whispers of them from conversations between his grandparents. Right off he recognized the similarity in physical traits. It was no doubt they were all from the blood line of "Big Tom." The three unfamiliar men were the illegitimate sons of George and Melvin Newsome. They'd made their way to the Newsome clan since becoming men. Neither of them had known their fathers but had searched them out as men in an attempt to connect with the missing DNA link in their lives. The three of them laughed in conversation as they placed charcoal in the grill's firebox and turned steaks over the flame. Cedric felt a desire to join them and planned to make his way over. He felt ambivalent and unsure of what to say. He found it odd to have cousins of his same age and generation that he had missed out on. He knew it wasn't any fault of his or theirs but resulted from the reckless search for manhood by uncles Melvin and George.

Around the entire yard men and women dialogued in the mist of laugher while focusing on a specific task with a sense of harmony, pride and belonging.

At 3 P.M., Aunt Hattie came out of the kitchen ringing a bell. Hattie's presence and bell ringing drew everyone's attention as they gathered with closed mouths.

Aunt Hattie cleared her throat, looked around at she faces drawn to her attention and with a smile that registered pride spoke, "Thank ya'll for coming. I'm glad to see every one of you. Ya'll faces is medicine for my sore eyes. I know grand-daddy Toms aw smiling from his grave over there by the orchard." Hattie slowly turned and pointed toward the field of apple and pear trees. Looking around at the children, Hattie continued, "We've still making babies both the men and the women and carrying on the Newsome name." Smiling, Hattie proudly announced, "Ya'll men and women got Big Tom all in your veins. I keeps seein all these younguns each year and new women too. I guess making babies and the men's loving women is in our blood." As Hattie spoke the Newsome men and women expressed a sense of pride and acknowledgment on their faces. "I wants us to enjoy ourselves, we got plenty some to eat and when we's finish go pay you respect to grand-daddy Tom down in the orchard."

Aunt Hattie then looked over to Bertha Vaughn saying, "Bert honey why don't you sang, us one of your songs?" Bertha was the oldest daughter of Cleveland Newsome and the sister of Nicole Worsley. Bertha had been born when Cleveland was barely sixteen years old, two years before he left Murfreesboro. Bertha's mother was Cleveland's first girlfriend ever and was his initial proof of his manhood, as viewed by the Newsome's. Cleveland the same as with Nicole, never took the time to get to know Bertha and was obvious uncomfortable each time she came near. Bertha's mother never had a relationship beyond their youthful lust affair. Cleveland joined the Army at age eighteen and hadn't looked back. Bertha a tall, fine women with shoulder length hair and heresy chocolate skin rocked the entire group singing Sam Cook's "A Change is Gonna Come." As she sang, mid-way through Nicole shouted, "Sing girl, alright now." Others looked about with whispers and smiles of joy. They knew they were being thoroughly entertained and that Bertha was a songbird. She finished her song with a joy that consumed her entire being, breathing deeply and wiping sweat from her forehead as she turned and said, "Cuttin Horace is gonna lead us in prayer." Horace Newsome was a tall elderly chocolate man, in his seventies, with a thinning frame on a man who was once strong and powerful. He was one of many grandsons of "Big Tom", he stepped forward using a cane for support. Horace closed his eyes and looked to the heavens saying, "Lord we's thankful for one more day. You didn't have to wake us dis morning Lord but you did. We could've been lyin on our cooling board right now, but we's blessed to still be a part of your Kingdom. I ask you Lord to forgive us of our sins and shortcomings. And help us Lord not to sin no more, help us to be a God fearing people and to be good husbands, wives and chulins for one another. Forgive us Lord caused we's done a lot of bad things, some without knowing any better. Guide us Lord out of our wrong doing and save our souls, Amen."

Cuttin Horace wipe the tears from his eyes as he returned to his straw bottom chair by the trunk of the old oak tree. Cedric finally broke himself from the trance brought on by Cuttin Horace's prayer. It almost seemed that Cuttin Horace carried the weight of sins for the entire Newsome family. He'd seemed over-burdened as he pleaded for the Lord's forgiveness. Cedric wondered had Cuttin Horace realized something in his years concerning the Newsome's that others had missed?

Right on time as if orchestrated, Aunt Hattie said, "You young folk line up behind the old so we can eat. Ya'll eat your fill now."

Cedric and Wendy seated the twins at a small table and lined up with the other adults who were mostly third and fourth generation ancestors of "Big Tom." They followed the others around the buffet of food. Without any planning Cedric and Wendy worked and operated as a couple, preparing plates for themselves and the twins. Jack, Josh, Clara and Berma all sat together amongst Aunt Hattie, cousin Bertha, Uncle Cleve, Great Uncle Horace and other older Newsome's, that Cedric couldn't name, enjoying themselves. The joy of one another's company, the chatter and food made the outside world appear non-existence. The concerns of business, politics, race relations and world peace had been shut out for that day. It was a time for family.

Throughout the day Wendy noticed how quiet, detached and uninvolved Cedric had been. His mind seemed lost in a distance, far away. As they sat engaged in one superficial conversation after another, assisting Chyna and India with the task of eating from paper plates, India brought him back to their world with a mouth full of food asking, "Cedric all these you cousins? You got a lot of cousins. Are they my cousins too?" Cedric glanced at Wendy with a smile then leaned closed to India replying, "Yes honey, they're your cousins to, okay." India appeared to be comforted by Cedric's answer and the new family membership. Wendy turned her attention toward Cedric. "So when are you going to tell me what's going on in that mind of yours? You've been in space all day." Cedric hesitated and looked at her with a stare. He'd realized his mind had been tracing back and forth between missing Angela terribly during particular moments and enjoying Wendy's presence during others. He finally offered, "I've been back tracking, thinking of Angela today for some reason and how life's not promised beyond the moment." Looking into Wendy's eyes with a sadness he continued, "We must learn to grab hold of life and love when it's available. You know Angie and I had all kinds of plans, but I basically blew it because of my womanizing, sniffing around like a dog at a fire hydrant. Unlike a dog, I wasn't too particular about who'd been there before me. Any old hydrant would do. I have so many regrets and so much guilt when it comes to Angie." Wendy wanted to comfort him. But her hands stayed balled at her sides, where they were ever since he'd started talking to her. Why was she suddenly afraid to reach out and touch him? She could feel her body aching to reach out and hold him. But, she couldn't move. As he looked into her face he thought of how she once seemed as a sister. Now, he was starting to see her in another light. His feelings for her didn't feel brotherly at that moment.

In an hour everyone was stuffed with the variety of soul food offered and the leftovers were put away. The whisky seemed to appear from nowhere. Jack, his brother Cleveland, cousins Melvin and Josh got involved in a game of bid wiz at a table under the oak tree. The combination of the card game, the whiskey and the soulful sounds blasting from a boom-box created a different atmosphere and mood instantly. It was like being at a outdoor juke joint. The young and the old alike became more relaxed and uninhibited. The men began to boast and brag of their exploits concerning women, proudly acknowledging their infidelities in marriage and relationships as though it was a proof and validation of their manhood. The validation of manhood through promiscuity wasn't admitted outright but came from the subtleties in conversation and dialogue. The men stroked their egos with such bragging and storytelling as the cards were dealt.

The women were not left unaffected by the "Ghost of Big Tom" and his legend of sexual prowess and virility. It was noticeable in many of the women through their flirtatious behavior and body language as well as their childbearing. It was quite clear that manhood, womanhood and adulthood in general amongst the Newsome's were affirmed through siring and bearing babies as well as through other sexual exploits.

As Cedric observed his family and contemplated his lifelong attitude concerning manhood, relationships and his breakup with Angela. A breakup caused by his infidelity, he began to realize the root of it all. He'd been taught the Newsome's definition of manhood by his grandfather directly. A grandfather who'd also called himself ushering him into manhood at the age of fifteen through a paid hooker. But the larger lesson concerning manhood had been nurtured into his psychic overtime by his grandfather and the like, formulating his overall attitude concerning women, relationships, himself and proof of manhood by-way of bedding women. That day in the backyard of the Newsome's home place, fifty of so yards from "Big Tom's" grave, it came clear to Cedric where it had all started. It grew from the slave, the breeder the family legend and icon "Big Tom." Cedric had a moment of clarification as he sat detached, listening and keenly observing his family, the ancestors of "Big Tom."

Cedric became conscious as never before, making the connection between the unequal numbers of unmarried relatives with children from estranged relationships, children born from different mothers and fathers. It was apparent that marriage and family stability had been severely affected by "Big Tom's Ghost." For the Newsome family, wives, husbands or parenting didn't matter. The family's passage into adulthood was through sexual lewdness which diametrically opposed the principal upon which marriages are stabilized and built; manhood and womanhood were established through being sexually promiscuous rather than being responsible for their prodigy. The Newsome family was connected by blood running from "Big Tom's" veins. However, their definition of what constituted adulthood had been miscalculated. Big Tom was the point of reference for the Newsome's rites of passage to adulthood. Cedric was convinced of his analysis and that the Newsome's were victims of the "The Ghost of Big Tom."

Meanwhile, on the front porch of the Newsome's home, a safe distance away from others, Nicole and Bertha were in deep dialogue. Wendy had taken Cedric's hand as they walked. She'd never held his hand before. It was an odd feeling for Cedric to feel the warmth of her hand clasped inside his. He didn't squeeze and tried not to send any signals by-way of the handholding. Her small hand was swallowed up inside his large hands that appeared like a baseball glove in comparison. As they strolled toward the back of the house where younger family members played a game of volleyball, Wendy snuggled a inch or two closer to Cedric looking up into his face, saying, "Ced, I'm sorry you're having a bad day but its gonna get better. Soon you will be able to live without all the regrets and guilt. I wanna help you get through this. I'm here for you, if you need me." Cedric looked down onto Wendy's beautiful face into her bright eyes, smelling her perfume and body aroma while casting his eyes on her incredible body, thinking, "Damn she turn me on." The conflict of missing Angela, attempting to suppress what he saw in Wendy's eyes and pushing down his attraction toward Wendy kept him on an emotional rollercoaster. He finally spoke, "Listen Wendy, I need to come clean, I do appreciate you in so many ways. I'm becoming more attracted to you each day. The brother, sister thing between us seems to be moving in another direction. I'm not trying to come on to you or anything but I'm feeling some different things. But memories of Angela keep me hurting."

Wendy came to a halt. "Ced, I'm relieved to hear that you're feeling some of the things I'm feeling. In time you'll be able to find closure and to forgive yourself. Until then let's just take a day at a time with our friendship and business partnership. It works, right?"

As Cedric and Wendy turned by the corner of the house, they were face to face with Nicole and Bertha. Nicole and Bertha were setting on the front porch, in the porch swing. They'd been there for over an hour. Nicole now a mother rocked her young child who was peacefully asleep, in her lap. The child was a love child, conceived as she'd turned a trick for money to feed her dope habit over a year ago. Her pregnancy had caused her to confront herself, the life-style she lived, and combined with drug treatment and therapy, she'd learned to love herself enough to leave the streets. Nicole was now a student at Durham Technical College studying computer Programming and Design. She was coming to terms with life and learning not to blame herself for her father's disregard for her during her life. She was finally beginning to be able to place the responsibility where it belonged without being resentful and had forgiven herself. She'd ceased to indict herself for her father's absence. Nicole and Bertha were sisters, daughters of Cleveland Newsome openly talking for the first time, bonding and making a pact with one another to share their lives. The mere fact of bonding and committing to share their lives filled a part of the void inside for the both of them. Before Cedric and Wendy appeared they'd shared their shame, loneness and feelings of guilt. They'd discussed how they'd sought love from men in an attempt to capture the love not offered by their father. They'd cried and hugged. Finally, they committed to caring and taking advantage of what each of them offered, which was a chance to be sisters. As Cedric approached, Bertha looked in his direction smiling as she said, "Ced, hey you sho have turned into a fine man."

Sheepishly Cedric replied "I've had to work at it."

Bertha continued, "I've seen your girlfriend here all day but haven't had a chance to really talk to her."

Cedric looked at Wendy with raised eyebrows asking, "Are you my girlfriend."

"Well, I guess it's safe to say so." Wendy replied with a smile as she said, "A special, sorta girlfriend."

Cedric lightly laughing said, "Bertha this is Wendy, she's Mr. Josh and Miss Berma's daughter. We've been around each other since we were children."

Bertha snapped her fingers, "That's right! I know I'd seen you before, Years ago at one of the reunions. You musta been ten or twelve years old."

Wendy smiling replied, "Yeah, we use to come all the time."

Bertha waved her hands, "Child you like family then."

Cedric turned his attention to Nicole saying, "Nikki, I'm glad you made it this year. How've you been?" Nicole with assurance on her face and in her voice replied, "Ced, I'm doing better than ever in my life." Looking at Bertha as Bertha held and patted her hand softly. "Daddy Cleveland called me, surprised me I'd have to say and asked me to ride down with him. He's been checking on me quite often since my baby came. He acts like he's a proud grandfather."

Cedric replied, "Well as granddaddy Jack says. It's a poor wind that never changes. Now, don't ask me what that means." The four of them laughed with questionable expressions on their faces. Bertha looked at Wendy asking, "Those twin girls belong to you? They're two little dolls."

Wendy graciously smiled and replied, "Those are my babies." The entire time Wendy never let go of Cedric's hand, her tight grip helped her to feel secure, so she held on.

Cedric nudged Wendy forward. They promised to stay in touch with Bertha and to check in on Nicole once back in Durham. Cedric cleared his throat, he then spoke. "Boy, this has to change."

Wendy turned in his direction asking, "What Ced?"

He thought before responding then said, "All these children outside of marriage, including me and all the rest. The idea of being a man or women, according to every Newsome appears to mean spreading ourselves around, and having babies. And fathering all these children without caring for them, I guess both the men and women need to look at themselves, closely."

Monday, August 20, 1999

Cedric sighed loudly and looked at the big pendulum clock that hung on the wall in the Mecklenburg County Courthouse. It was nearly 9 A.M. His stomach was in knots, he looked at each face as the elevator door opened, anticipating the arrival of Joe and Claudette Slade. He'd arrived at the court house at exactly 8:30 A.M. It was the first day of the Michael Wiles' murder trial. The prosecution had waited for two years since Wiles' arrest to have their day in court. Wiles had been through a battery of psychological tests to determine his competency for trial. Finally, in June of 1999 he'd been declared competent to stand trial. He knew right from wrong, so determined the psychiatrist at Central Prison.

But instead of a trial for each of the five murders Wiles' attorney had struck a deal with the prosecutor. After review of the evidence, Joe McKinnon, the State's Prosecutor, knew the cases against Wiles were all circumstantial and without one eye witness. Rather, than risk losing at trial at a huge expense to the taxpayers he opted for a plea. Wiles' attorney Bill Caviness was able to convince Wiles to accept the plea and not risk the death walk. Wiles agreed to plead to the murder of Martha Trapp, the case with the most evidence against him. Wiles would also admit to the murders of the other four including Angela Slade. He'd receive a natural life sentence without the possibility of parole.

The public followed the case's every changing event. The media including national newspapers and network T.V., gave prominence to the grisly crimes and concentrated on the fact that a serial killer had finally been locked away.

The expectation of the sensational murder trial of Michael Wiles prompted headlines in almost every newspaper in the country and was featured daily on network T.V. Outside of the Mecklenburg County Courthouse some pro-death penalty demonstrators paraded, their place cards urging death for Wiles. Journalist pushed and shoved, many unsuccessfully for the limited courthouse space allotted for the media. Charlotte's WSOC T.V camped outside with a live crew.

Consequent to the State Prosecutor's offer of a plea for only the Martha Trapp murder stunned and outraged the public. Wiles had marched in court, stood beside his attorney in the tense atmosphere of expectation and accepted the plea. The court was filled with whispers and the sputter of the on lookers. Presiding Judge, The Honorable Harold Watkins had to pound his gavel to settle the courtroom. In less than ten minutes Wiles with his cynical smile and demeanor and showing no remorse was lead away. He'd be officially sentenced within a month. As for the additional murders, the cases were officially closed.

Cedric who'd sat with Joe and Claudette Slade during the proceedings had a variety of feelings. He felt justice had been served but also that Angela had been cheated. Joe Slade could feel Cedric's confused emotions. Joe took Cedric hand as he spoke, "Son God's will be done. They have the guy who took Angela from us. He'll never be free to kill again, let it go." Joe Slade's words didn't register in Cedric's mind. He'd expected a full trial and a death sentence. It would take time for Cedric to digest the justice that was served.

The controversial guilty plea decision by the State Prosecutor Joe McKinnon produced an outcry from the families of the other victims, who desperately wanted to see justice in another fashion in the names of their loved ones who'd been lost. The proponents for the death penalty labeled the Wiles case as the proto-type for the death chamber. They declared that defense attorneys would use the Wiles case to wage a war to save the lives of other murders.

It had been one month since Michael Wiles' plead guilty to the Martha Trapp murder. Cedric had driven from Durham to hear the judge sentence Wiles to a natural life sentence. Cedric felt a need to witness the process play out. He was looking for closure so that he could move forward with his life. He held onto a small bible in an attempt to camouflage his anger. Other than Cedric, who sat in the third row on the right side of the gallery, the courthouse was empty. There were two reporters from the Charlotte News and Observer, a camera crew from WSOC T.V., the stenographer, Wiles' attorney, the State Prosecutor, the bailiff and a few other people scattered throughout the gallery that appeared to be Michael Wiles' family from Mooresville. From the corner of his eye Cedric could see an elderly woman among the Wiles' family crying, wiping tears with a white handkerchief and clutching a hand bag. Although, Cedric's heart was over-run with the desire for vengeance toward Wiles, a vengeance born from anger he'd carried since Angela's brutal murder, he felt sorrow for the crying woman.

Michael Wiles sat calmly, and unconcerned behind the defendants table facing the judge waiting. He appeared as if he was sating in the park on a bright sunny day without a worry in the world.

The spectators in the gallery sat in complete silence, motionless seemingly afraid to move, in expectation. The newspaper reporters and television crew buzzed amongst themselves. Everyone there waited nervously, on the scene waiting for the sentencing.

As the judge cleared his throat after more than five minutes of reading documents and shuffling papers, a sudden stillness fell over the entire courthouse as those with a vested interest strained to hear. "Will the defendant rise?" Michael Wiles glanced at his attorney as his attorney Bill Caviness nudged his elbow indicating for him to comply to the Judge's request to stand. Wiles stood to the left of his attorney behind the defendant's long polished oak table with his head titled upward starring at the Judge.

"Mr. Wiles, I'm going to ask you a series of questions. I would like you to respond to me with a simple yes or no. Do you understand?"

Wiles nodded his head with a whisper of yes.

The judge continued, "Do you understand the charge in which you are pleading guilty?" Wiles answered, "Yes."

"Do you understand that you've been charged and are pleading guilty to the first degree murder of Martha Trapp? Are you in fact guilty of first degree murder of Martha Trapp?" Wiles hesitated and then replied, "Yes."

The judge continued, "Do you understand that the penalty for first degree murder in the State of North Carolina carries a penalty from life in prison to a sentence of death?" Wiles answered, "Yes".

The judge asked, "Have anyone made you a promise, threaten or anyway coerced you to enter this plea?"

Wiles answered "No."

The judge asked, "Are you satisfied with the performance of your counsel, Mr. Caviness?"

Wiles answered, "Yes."

The judge asked, "Are you under the influence of any drugs or alcohol at this time?"

Wiles answered "No."

The judge finally said, "Thank you Mr. Wiles for answering the court's questions."

Judge Harold Watkins made sure he'd walked the fine line of neutrality and legal protocol. He was known as a by-the-book judge, and by-the-book he went.

"Mr. Wiles at this time would you like to address the court?"

Wiles answered "No sir."

The judge stated, "Michael Darnell Wiles based on your admission and plea of guilty to the murder of Martha Trapp the court accept your plea and therefore sentence you to a sentence of natural life. To be served under the authority of the North Carolina Department of Corrections to begin immediately at a location of their discretion."

Judge Watkins pounded his gravel and instructed, "Bailiff the prisoner is in your custody." He thanked the citizens for their orderly conduct and dismissed the court.

The silence in the courtroom was broken the wailing of the Wiles' mother, the women who'd wiped tears throughout the sentencing, and the chatter among the spectators in the gallery. The reporters scrambled to get out, everyone wanting to be the first to file the story. Michael Wiles stoned faced, oblivious to his attorney swaggered out the courtroom as the deputies lead the way.

Cedric felt a physical weakness and a sense of relief but also somewhat short-changed. Although Wiles was sentenced to a natural life sentence, the sentence somehow failed to directly attach itself to Angela. But, justice had been served. It was over.

Book III

Manhood In Perspective

Friday, November 10, 1999

I t was one of the best weekends of the fall season, with warm days
and chilled nights, near perfect weather for a Homecoming weekend.
The black Mercedes rolled quietly through Richmond's night traffic.
With the windows rolled up and the sounds of Frankie Beverly and Maze,
all the outside noise was muffled. Cedric, Carlos Butler a former wide
receiver on the Union Football team and Dean Stevens known as Chico
who was once the ultimate defensive linemen talked back and forth trying
to catch up with one another's lives; lives that had changed drastically
since their days as footballers and room-mates at Union. The three of
them hadn't seen one another in two years, the last time they'd met in
Richmond for Virginia Union's Homecoming weekend. Many changes
had occurred. Both Carlo and Dean were married and worst of all Angela
had been murdered. Carlo and Dean had both called Cedric once finding
out of Angela's death, to check on him and had continued to check in
on him periodically. But, tonight they intentionally stayed clear of that
horrific topic.

As they drove down Broad Street in route to Frankie's, one of
Richmond's most popular strip clubs, the street adjacent to the club was
meandering with men bursting with chatter and laugher rushing in the
satisfy their lustful eyes. Carlo a big man with a box shaped head and
broad shoulders guided the Mercedes on the busy street in search of a
parking spot. Once parked, the three of them who were in a light hearted
spirit lined with the others to enter the club. They'd planned to hit a few
clubs, and on Saturday, attend the game between Union and Hampton
University, and maybe swing by a few alumni parties on Saturday night.

Cedric had only decided to attend after receiving a call from Carlo,
who encouraged him to drive to Richmond for the game. But Cedric
didn't know Carlo had talked with his grandparents, who asked Carlo to
make the call. At first Cedric's thought going to the game was somehow
a betrayal to Angela. After a lengthy dialogue with his grandparents he
agreed to drive up to Richmond for the game. They knew his head was
screwed up with guilt when it came to Angela but they'd convinced him
he needed some downtime. Time to forget about the Diner, the daily
management concerns, and Durham. They convinced him, the weekend
could be a mini-vacation of sought.

As a line of men and sprinkle of women slowly made their way inside Frankie's, Cedric noticed that most were drinking or already drunk. Frankie's smelled of beer, cigarettes and sweat. The music blasted. The front room next to the street was empty except for two women who were droopy eyed and appeared stoned sitting across from each other in a burgundy leatherette booth. The bartender was wiping glasses and casually engaged in conversation with an attractive over made-up middle aged women.

The back room was jammed, thirty or forty men and a half dozen women in a cloud of cigarette smoke, clapping to the rock of the music that poured from the jukebox. There were two women with ten bodies and long hair pieces dancing on the stage. The women stripped down to their see threw bras and translucent panties. They were feeding on the crowd's enthusiasm. With another twist, grind and bump, both women popped their bras and slowly peeled them off, carefully cupping their firm breast. After a few more twist, grinds and bumps, they tossed the bras behind the bar and switched into a new dance, their exposed breast bobbling in the flashing ceiling lights. "Bottoms, bottoms, bottoms," the crowd was chanting, and the women both hooked their thumbs in the top of their panties and teasingly pulled them down inch by inch, turning, bending and rotating their hips, throwing their panties into the crowd.

Carlo raised an eyebrow as his eyes sparkled, and over the wolf whistles, Dean asked Cedric, "Are you okay?" At that moment one of the strippers chose to demonstrate her flexibility by doing a standing leg split along the length of the pole while she pointed right at Cedric as they sat in front of the stage. Carlo's lips twisted in amusement. The stripper came forward and stood in front of Cedric who had his eyes closed, her waist only inches from his face . . . . "Hey chocolate kiss, could I interest you in a private dance?" She asked. He opened his eyes, and they fell upon a small, mysterious navel surrounded by a sea of smooth caramel colored skin. A small triangle of gold medal connected to a chain encircled her waist. His eyes traveled upward and were immediately mesmerized by the slightly triangles that by design did not cover her D-cup breast. A slick covering of glitter spread from her cleavage to her face.

Almond shaped eyes smiled at him, as if they knew the secret of his lust, "So how about it chocolate?" The words flooded from rich plum-tinted lips with a strong northern accent. Then the stripper looked at her watch saying. "If you hang around til my last dance is over, you can take me home with you free of charge." She bent over, kissed Cedric on the face and strutted away. The stripper had the body, sexual presence and the good looks to entice any man whose body still produced any level of testosterone.

Carlo and Dean ordered another round of drinks, and playfully Carlo proceeded to tease Cedric saying, "Boy once you got it, you got it." Ced still knows how to catch the girls. What you do, lick out your tongue at her? What's up Ced? You gonna hit it or what? Man she got the hots for you, uh?"

Dean chirped in saying, "She don't know she's flirting with the man that holds the all time record at Union when it comes to fucking ho's." Carlo gave Dean some dap, with the old fist to fist knock. Cedric with a disinterested look replied, "She's fine alright and probably hot in the bed, but I'm not up for it."

Dean shouted, "What the fuck you mean, not up to it? That's the best looking ass you'll see all weekend. Damn man, you've lost your killer instinct or what?" As the music continued to blast and the strippers prepared to their last dance, Cedric's mind drifted back to Angela's death. For a moment he felt an overwhelming rush of guilt. He thought of his infidelity and womanizing that lead to his break-up with Angela. For some crazy, irrational and confused reason he still blamed himself for her death. No matter how much logic he reasoned with, the guilt still hung around, deep inside him. He hadn't been with any women since Angela's death. His guilt had towered over him like a dark cloud. He'd felt emotionally frozen most of the time and sexually afraid, afraid he'd hurt again. Sex which at one time was much like a sport was now so-sooo serious, risky and emotional. "Hey Cedric we're over here!" Dean called, "You were gone man, in another world, time and place."

Cedric snapped back to the present saying, "Yeah, I was gone man."

Cedric looked at his watch, "Hey guys can we get out of here! I've had enough of the bump and grind. Plus I'd like to be gone before Miss Hips finish her dance."

Carlo looked at Cedric as if he'd lost his mind. Cedric threw up his hands with pleading eyes saying, "I'm sorry guys, what can I say?"

Once back in his hotel room he turned the T.V. on. He flashed through several channels and finally pressed the off button. He sat on the edge of the bed and picked up the phone. He looked at his watch, 1:48 A.M He eased the phone back on the hook. In a matter of seconds he picked it up again and dialed Wendy. The phone rang once, twice, three times and finally in a low sultry voice Wendy spoke. "Hello,"

Cedric replied, "Hey, it's me Ced, I'm sorry, I know it's late, but I needed to call. You were on my mind."

Wendy responded. "It's okay, I wasn't really asleep. Are you okay?"

Cedric slowly said, "Yeah, I guess, I got a lot on my mind, have been for sometime but its starting to clear up now. I'm not going to keep you up. I just wanted to let you know, you're special to me, the best thing going is our relationship. Look go back to sleep, I'll talk to you on Sunday when I get in."

Right at that moment Cedric realized, it was clear how deeply involved he had become in Wendy's life and she in his. The Newsome's and Dockery's had always been close as if they were blood relatives but this thing with Wendy was different all together. A man and woman thing, respect, care, concern, compatibility, sexual attraction and enough differences to off-set the entire relationship in a challenging fashion. Cedric set with his chin in his hands on the edge of the bed at 2:30 in the morning realizing his love for Wendy. He suddenly jumped from the bed to his feet with a whisper, "Damn this is crazy but she turns me on in every respect." He thought, "let me go to bed, Wendy got me walking around in a hotel room at 3:00 in the morning talking to myself. I'll deal with this latter." He finally climbed in bed with a smile.

At 9:00 A.M. Dean and Carlo pounded on the door. "Alright, alright already hold your horses." Cedric moaned. As soon as he opened the door, Dean rushed him with a football tackle. "Yeah, I got your bad ass now." He slammed Cedric on the bed, shouting, "Yeah!"

Carlo hollered, "You ain't dressed yet? Man we been to the parade wit all the phat ass majorettes and shit. Stop dragging ass, we going down to IHOP for some pancakes, come on man."

Cedric replied, "Okay, okay give me a minute. Your ass need to stay away from pancakes, I see the extra pounds you caring."

Carlo shouted, "Ced oh boy, its married life. Good sex and good cooking."

Cedric peeped out from the bathroom saying, "Yeah, right! I wonder what the wife would say if she knew you were up here chasing pussy."

Carlo responded, "She knows I love her, and it's a man thing."

Cedric paused, "Yeah, that what's they say, uh."

By 5 P.M the clash between Virginia Union and Hampton was over. Union had won 13-10. Cedric, Dean and Carlo headed back to the downtown Radisson for some down time. The reminder of the night was filled with party after party, loud music, and the sexual sparring between men and women on the hunt for some strange and different tail.

Sunday by 2 P.M. Cedric was driving down I-85 headed back to Durham. The weekend was over. It had its highlights. Seeing Dean, Carlo and some of the other alumni had been great. The game was well played and Union had won. All was well.

In a short while Cedric's mind drifted. He recalled the conversation with Carlo concerning chasing pussy being a man thing. The idea carried him to his observation and analysis of the Newsome's during the summer while at the family reunion, where it became clear the legend of granddaddy Tom had predisposed the Newsome men and women to define their adulthood, self worth, and values through sexual expression and promiscuity. The incidence of out of marriage births, divorce rate, and failure in parenting were rooted in the Newsome's skewed family personality and socialization. A socialization concerning the definition of adulthood that indirectly and some cases directly was responsible for the pain, disappointments and the extreme level of dysfunction that had ran from one generation to the next. Cedric loved all the Newsome's, especially his granddaddy Jack. Jack Newsome had taken him in as a child and raised him to manhood. He felt proud of being from the blood of Big Tom but inside he knew Big Tom's Ghost and the definition which derived from Big Tom's life as a slave breeder had haunted his family for generations. Cedric contemplated the life of Big Tom. He knew Big Tom lived during a time and place of inhumane conditions. He had to survive in the world he'd been placed. As with all slaves, Big Tom had no power, money, citizenship or say so. In the eyes of the slave master Big Tom was no more than plantation livestock. He was brought and paid for to breed slave women to satisfy the market need for slaves, all over Eastern North Carolina and Southern Virginia the same as a prime stallion for breeding. Cedric could imagine how his ancestral grandfather had adapted and survived by way of the customs and role place upon him.

As Cedric cruised down I-85 he could feel, see and smell Big Tom's life. It was as if Cedric's mind was in another zone, time and place. It was clear the haunting Ghost of Big Tom had lived through the years in the lives of the Newsome men and women. It had been the only identifying mark of a man they'd ascribe too and possessed. The Newsome's held onto Big Tom's legend with pride. Cedric smiled scornfully thinking, "The same thing, that make you laugh will make you cry. Something has to change some way, and with someone!"

It was bright and clear on Monday morning. Cedric had made it to the Diner ahead of time. Cecil was in the kitchen rattling the pots and pans preparing vegetables for the lunch special. Cecil hardly noticed Cedric's arrival he was busy cutting and chopping carrots, squash, cabbage and singing Bobby Womack's tune, "Harry hippie." Cedric finally shouted, "Cecil you're in an awfully good mood and spirit today, you must have had a good day off?"

Cecil replied, "Hell, I'm just happy to be alive, most of my old buddies is gone, can't sing no mo. By the way how was your weekend up in Richmond? Who won the game?" Cedric shouted, "Union won 13-10. It was good to see some of the fellas. It was alright for a day or two but I'm glad it's over."

The front door of Fines popped open as Wendy and Ms. Ester came in talking and laughing lightheartedly. Ms. Ester headed for the kitchen with a smile to assist Cecil saying, "Lord let me go back heh and see what Cecil got going." Wendy stopped at the coffee pot for a cup of coffee. Once in the office she pulled up a blue cushioned chair across from Cedric and looked over the invoices he studied. Cedric's eyes met hers. She asked, "Well, so how are you sir? How did the trip go?" Cedric leaned back in his swivel chair, biting at the pencil in his hand and contemplated before speaking. Finally he spoke, "I dunno, something's different, I can't put my finger on it quite yet. But, it's good to be back. So, how are you?"

Wendy with bright eyes replied, "I'm fine, everything's great. Can I get you some coffee or something to drink?" She asked; suddenly remembering her manners.

"Yeah, a glass juice would be fine." He replied. She returned from the kitchen with a frosty glass of orange juice and a plate of donuts. "Looks good," He said.

They slipped orange juice and ate donuts in silence until Cedric sat his glass down on the desk top and stood up, walking to the copier and copied a hand full of invoices.

Wendy spoke, "Chyna and India would like for you to come to their school play tomorrow night. They also want to show you their costumes before the play."

Cedric nodded, "Oh good, I can't wait to see them all dressed-up. I'll come by tonight after we closed for the dress rehearsal."

In the past year since partnering up in business, Cedric and Wendy had spent most of their time together. Sundays after church for dinner either at the Dockery's or Newsome's, once or twice each week during evening hours, billing for the Diner, on Saturdays nights now and then going to movies. A friendship and attraction developed between them in the nice slow way.

They found a mutual respect, affinity and attraction for one another other. Conversation between them came easy and they made each other laugh. Cedric knew their attraction couldn't be ignored any longer. They both seemed to be waiting for the other to make the next move.

"By the way, I'm bearing another invitation." Wendy announced. Cedric stopped and looked, admiring her beauty. He heard her voice but his mind was in her pants. He could feel a rising in his crouch. He found his way back to his chair. Wendy continued, "It's only about two weeks before Thanksgiving, momma wants you, Uncle Jack and Aunt Clara to eat with us. She's making a turkey and all the trimmings. I would like very much to have your company as well as everyone else." Cedric mesmerized by Wendy's presence agreed to whatever she proposed without a thought. Wendy continued to chatter, "Thanksgiving is the one traditional holiday that ma takes serious. She has always called in friends and relatives from everywhere on Thanksgiving. My aunts Thelma and Gladys are coming with their children and Lord knows who else. Momma just takes for granted you're coming, last night she was saying something about you doing such and such. It's like we're both an automatic part of all the Dockery's and Newsome's plans, uh?"

Cedric grunted, "Yeah!" That's because our families have been friends forever, the business our new found." Cedric hesitated for a second looking up at Wendy, and continued, "Friendship and all. I'm glad they all feel that way. I mean, you know, comfortable with us." Wendy smiled. "So comfortable, I don't even mine them being a little leading and presumptuous at times." The two of them laughed lightly.

"Are we going to be open on Friday?" Wendy asked.

Cedric look at her saying, "Sure, it's one of our busiest days. We'll just make the best out of Thanksgiving Day, or why don't you take off and take a break for a couple of days." Cedric said, "You been here all month, or the last two or three months without a day off other than our scheduled closings."

"Are you sure Ced?" She asked.

"Yeah, Cecil, Ms. Ester and I can handle it on the Friday after Thanksgiving. We'll be okay. I think I'll call Nicole to see if she would like to help out, she's on break from school. I'm sure she could use the money. Plus, she asked me to give her some work if we could."

Wendy being pleased said, "Okay, it sounds like a good plan."

The Diner closed at 7 P.M. and by 8:30 the place was cleared, lights out and locked. Cedric, Wendy, Cecil and Ms. Ester all walked out together. Wendy offered Ms. Ester a ride home as she did on most nights. As Wendy opened the driver's side of the white Mercedes and popped the lock to let Ms. Ester in on the passenger's side she called out, "Don't forget the girls dress rehearsal."

Cedric replied, "I'll be over as soon as I run by my grandparents place." Wendy exited on Roxboro Road and was gone. Cecil looked over at Cedric with a smile saying, "Wendy's a mighty fine gal, and a hard worker."

"Yeah you're right," Cedric said. Cecil could see that Cedric cared for her.

By 9:30 Cedric had gone by his grandparent's home, showered, changed into a sweat suit and was watching attentively as Chyna and India modeled their costumes. He sat relaxed on the over-stuffed love seat in the den. Wendy was dressed in a white flowing terry cloth house-coat tied at the waist. The house-coat was opened exposing her long beautiful legs and thighs. Her hair was partially wet from the shower she'd taken and her body ranked with the smell of sweet perfume. She'd parked herself on the arm of the love seat just above where Cedric sat. As the twins walked and turned in their costumes, Chyna dressed as a ballerina in white and India in a pastel blue as an angle with a halo pranced and spun around. They were two proud and beautiful young ballerinas preparing for their first debut. After fifteen minutes of performing a similitude of their upcoming recital. Wendy rushed them off to bed.

Wendy returned from the twins' bedroom in a few minutes saying, "Ced, thanks for coming by. The girls really wanted you to see their costumes. I appreciate it also. Even though it's all a little much to ask of you, it's not like they're your kids."

Cedric said, "The girls are important to me, I guess in many ways I do think of them as my girls. So don't ever think that you or the girls as a bother, okay." She nodded. "Listen!" "Things here," pointing at himself, and at her, "have changed a great deal since we were kids growing up, where you were like a sister to me; the business, working together each day, laughing, talking and all." He paused, "Stop me if I cross the line." He said. "But, today, I'm not looking at you as a sister but a women, I'm attracted to. It's crazy and I never dreamed of this, I've been ignoring it for months the best I could. Last weekend in Richmond, in a strip joint with Carlo and Dean it hit me. I dunno, that's where I'm at." The entire time Cedric confessed his feelings, Wendy had starred him in the face. When he was out of words, she spoke, "Ced, for awhile now I've known I like you, and not as a brother. I've been afraid to say anything. I thought you'd think I was out of line, or something. I'd look at you and think; damn he's not the young boy I once knew. He's a man, good looking, responsible, and my best friend." They stood looking at each other. Cedric broke the silence, "Awkward or not, we feel what we feel."

"You're right." She answered. "Ced, you're a nice and good man."

"I'm trying to be." He said. "The man I was raised to be by my grand-dad, I don't like anymore. I'm finding I don't like. I mean grand-dad have been good to me. But, he like the other Newsome men have a view of manhood, I'm finding myself opposed too. He taught me to be a man, meant chasing women. That's been a problem for me in all my relationships and what caused Angela and I to break up. So, I'm beginning to see it all different these days. I don't want to be that type of man anymore." He suddenly looked at his watch and with a surprised look said, "Oh wow, it's almost 11 o'clock. I guess I better go."

Wendy nonchalantly replied, "If you say so." He took a chance and gave her a peck on the cheek and said good night.

She closed the door almost instantly. Three minutes later, he was right back at the door, ringing the bell. She opened the door almost instantly. "What did you forget to tell me?"

He blurted, "This whole thing is crazy. We should both be long past the point of playing these idiotic mating games."

She didn't blink or move. She glowed so brightly, he felt her warmth pass right through him. "Please", He said," May I come in?"

"Of course," She replied." He didn't even see the door. He saw nothing but her face. "How much time, how much ritual do you need?" he asked. Whatever it is, I'll try to give it to you. I know you went through some tough times also. You told me months ago you were afraid to get involved again, so I understand."

"You don't have to give me a thing, just being here, needing to come back, says it all. Just for us to get our feelings out in the open and stop dodging each other is enough." She said. Sudden doubts pressed him. "I want to be straight with you, no cheating this time around. Sometimes I feel so empty, like I don't deserve anyone and don't have much left to give. The guilt is bad sometimes."

"I'll be the judge of that," she said. She took a step toward him and stopped. "Look, I know you been hurting and I have too, you can't blame yourself forever. Nor can I blame myself for my blindness when it comes to Tyrone. All I care about is now, being happy again. We both can learn and benefit from our past and use it to help us. Sometimes, I think every word I've said, every move I've made in the last year was for no reason than to make you want me."

He suddenly found her cheek against his, her body wrapped in his arms and her scent arousing him. She pushed her tongue in his mouth. With his hands caressing her soft body, life came back to him from a long way off. The past two years had devastated him, left him all but dead. At times he'd felt no interest in women. It was a tough life and the breath had burned out of him. But, he was breathing again, taking air from her lungs into his, feeling separate parts of her body touching his own. The kisses finally ceased. He felt embarrassed, uneasy but excited. Wendy appeared more at ease, relaxed and assured. He spoke, "Well that's what on my mind. I guess I should leave now. She held his hand and kissed his lips. He backed away through the door and was gone in the night.

The moon stayed in sight all the way and Cedric's eyes barely left it as he drove to his grandparent's home. He drove in a daze. He couldn't believe what had transpired between Wendy and him. The time had come, after months of attempting to suppress what he'd felt for Wendy. He'd finally laid it on the table. He'd long imagined what he'd say. He'd at times had been sexually aroused and then punished himself for the fantasies that played in his head. He never thought the day would come when he'd have the nerve to talk frankly about how he felt. Never! Never was a concern with women before but for some reason Wendy was different. He thought, "What in the world will our folks say, grand-dad, grand-ma and the Dockery's?" He washed the thought from his mind. "We'll deal with it all somehow." Before he realized it, he was turning the key in the door at home. He could hear the T.V. playing in his grandparent's bedroom. He walked to their door, stuck his head in saying, "Hey, grand-ma, grand-dad," ya'll doing okay, I hadn't stopped to talk since coming back from Richmond, just wanted to check in."

Jack Newsome replied, "Well, we thought you'd slow down and find time to check in sooner or later. How was the trip?"

Cedric recanted, "It was okay. Union won the game. I saw some of the guys I went to school with, it haven't changed much at Union. Look, I'll talk to ya'll later, I'm going in the den and catch Sports Center. Just wanted to stick my head in and holler."

Cedric flipped from station to station trying to find something on the TV. Nothing could hold his attention. His mind kept floating back to Wendy. He felt excited and nervous at the same time. He couldn't identify the source of his feelings. He finally shut the TV off and went to bed. Throughout the night he lay awake, thinking of Angela and how he'd failed in that relationship. His thoughts moved to Wendy and he thought of the chance to be a different man. He felt afraid but sure he'd give their relationship his best. He'd never before been a one woman's man. It was time for a change.

Cedric woke at 6 A.M. He stared dimly at the white ceiling. Then he remembered he'd promised Cecil a ride to the Diner by 8 A.M. He jumped out of bed and quickly dressed in sweats and running shoes. He had enough time for a three mile run through Duke Forest before picking Cecil up. He was hoping it wasn't raining. He opened the blinds and stared out at the green lawn and clear sky. There was no rain and no visible threat of any. Somehow, it seemed a good sign for the day ahead.

In the forest on the trail, his heart pumped as he attacked the intervening hills. Within ten minutes he had broken into a mild sweat. The air was fresh and clean. He'd often found running offered time to think. His mind carried him to his conflicting ideas of manhood. As he ran he found himself in deep contemplative and analytical thought. The intervening hills he approached every two hundred yards became secondary to his thoughts. The concept of maleness and manhood laid on his mind. As his feet pounded the worn path, he critically thought of manhood according to the Newsome's compared to his new and emerging ideas. Big Tom's ideological ghost haunted his mind and spirit. Challenging Big Tom's Ghost was a new awareness and perspective and unheard of amongst the Newsome's. His mind traced back to what he'd been told over the years and what he imagined of Big Tom's legend, and his family's use of it. What he'd been taught over the years was becoming unglued. He was convinced that the Newsome's definition of manhood had out grown it s usefulness. As a slave grand-daddy Tom the slave was dependant, passive, unprotected by the law and totally waiting for someone else, the master to meet his biological needs. He delighted himself in being used as a stud and gained his personal value by his ability to produce children. Cedric thought," The slaveholders who implemented slave breeding and slave making understood some of the basic laws of human nature, and they understood that they could impede the process. The masters locked men like Big Tom into maleness so they would stay dependant, non-rebellious and essentially passive in areas of human expression and existence. Big Tom like other salves in his position protected his master and helped restrain the other slaves. Big Tom lived during a time and place that ordered his participation, a participation he assimilated into. Cedric was becoming aware that the male mentality from which grand-daddy Tom evolved still predominated the entire clan of Newsome men who had not been willing to take the responsibility of real manhood.

Cedric's thoughts and awareness was beginning to change his world. He could feel his mental awareness energizing him as he ran from one hill to the next and relaxing in between each crest. He thought of his lifelong attitude and belief that a man's measure was through his ability to seduce and bed women. That idea had been engrained and cemented around his entire identity. He never thought of manhood in any other manner. He'd accepted the Newsome's concept of manhood without thought. He was now developing the discipline to say no, "I will not and do not have to behave that way as a man. I refuse to be unaccountable, promiscuous and a womanizer. I can decide, I can transform into a different man." As he ran he drilled himself in positive self talk. A sense of sentiment and care for others occupied his mind. He'd hurt Angela, she'd been murdered; his selfish and misplaced idea of manhood had been a major part of their problem. His preoccupation and primarily purpose had been a concern of looking out for himself, and satisfying his warped sense of male affirmation. He ran and pondered his rising views of manhood as they were being crystallized. He was gaining a new level of power and reasoning. He questioned himself, "Did grand-daddy Jack teach me to be a man or live and function as a male or a boy? Is everything a game, a scheme and chance to get over or seen as fun? I've been merely rehearsing the part of a man. Life must have order and formality which takes precedence over my urges and desires." As he moved up the trail he felt a bounce and lightness of foot, fueled by his insights, producing an emotional liberation from "Big Tom's Ghost."

November 17, 1999

It was Wendy's birthday she'd turned thirty one years old. She'd taken the day off work upon the insistence of Cedric and Ms. Ester. Later she'd be accompanied by Chyna and India to her parent's home on Ole Cole Mill Road to be fussed over by her family. The house would be sparsely filled with a few friends, whom she barely knew anymore. Her mom would make one of her special double-chocolate birthday cakes and add the candles. Her father Josh Dockery would feed her ice cream the way he had since she was a child and tease her about joining the other maiden cousins and unmarried women.

But, tonight she scrutinized herself in the bathroom mirror and searched for signs of aging, she felt relieved no gray hair had mistakenly wandered into her head of flowing black hair and her skin appeared as young and wrinkle free as ever. She mixed herself a scotch thinking of the inexorable passing of time, and wondered what the next year of life would bring.

Luther Vandross concluded his upbeat song, "Having a Party" as she sipped the remaining scotch from the goblet when the doorbell rang. Not accustomed to drinking and feeling the resulting buzz, she opened the door. It was Nicole looking desperate asking, "Can I come in and talk with you?" As she walked through the door she looked around as if someone might be following her. "Sure!" Wendy replied.

Nicole didn't hesitate. She began to spill her story. "Me and Mike, my boyfriend of lately had a fight."

Wendy exited asked, "He didn't hit you did he?"

Nicole with a grit on her face replied, "I wish that punk would try some shit like that. Naw, girl he picked me up from the Diner and started up with me over some bullshit about this guy who likes me." Nicole groused, following Wendy into the den and dropping onto the couch. "I've never have seen him so angry, he scared me. I didn't want to go back into the Diner and tell Ced. You know how he can get when it comes to somebody pushing his female cousins around. So, I flagged a cab and came over here. I didn't want to go home, I thought he might follow me."

Nicole had changed completely. With close cropped hair, a modest fashionable style and was a student finishing her degree. She blinked her big brown eyes looking more like a school girl than a former hooker, addict and mother of a two year old.

"I'm having some scotch," Wendy offered.

"Girl you know I can't drink. I'm in recovery." Nicole recanted.

"I'm sorry Nikki, I forgot." Wendy replied with a look of embarrassment.

Nicole's eyes turned to the stack of cards on the glass top table in front of her.

"It's your birthday," She moaned. "I forgot it was your birthday."

"No, you didn't," Wendy reminded her, "You sent me an adorable card."

Nicole responded, "I mean, I forgot right now, you probably have big plans for tonight and I just barged right in."

Wendy shrugged, "I don't have anything important going on. Actually, I'm going to my mama's a little later but it's no rush."

Listening closely Nicole took advantage of the opening, "I need for you to take me back to the Diner to get my house key. When Mike came things happened so quickly, I walked out without my keys. When we started arguing, I told him to let me out the car. That's when I realized I'd left my keys. I was so upset and afraid I just stopped a Pine Street cab that was passing by, as soon as I got out of Mike's car. You know Turk? He was driving the cab. Anyway, he gave me a ride."

Wendy with glass in hand replied, "Girl you need to get rid of that Mike person. Give me a few minutes to finish getting dressed." Wendy walked back to her bedroom. Nicole shouted to Wendy from the den, "Can we stop by the mall?" I wanna buy you something."

"Well, I don't know" Wendy began.

"Please!" Nicole urged. "I'd like to, you and Ced have been good to me. I want to do this, Please."

"Okay," Wendy gave in.

"Great!" Nicole shouted, pushing her way toward the bedroom. "Can I freshen up my makeup?"

"Sure, come on in here. You can use some of my makeup if you like." Wendy replied. "Okay, let me see if the color matches me." Nicole said. Nicole joined Wendy as she dressed.

Wendy wore black silk pants and blouse with a string of white pearls and matching earrings and black pumps. She reached in her closet and grabbed her black leather trench coat, saying, "Okay, girl let's get out of here."

It was 8:30 by the time they arrived at Fines Diner on Roxboro Road. The lights were out and the parking lot was empty. Wendy parked directly vertical of the entranceway of the front door. Both women exited the car, Wendy searching for the front door key grumbled, "I don't like coming here at night after closing . . . oh here it is." Nicole mildly replied, "I'm sorry, I really am." Wendy stepped through the door fishing for the light switch as she entered with Nicole on her heels. With the lights on, the Diner came to life. As they proceeded forward, the swinging doors leading to the kitchen and office swung open. A small crowd of invited guess came out shouting happy birthday. From the left and right side of the dining room other guest emerged from behind tables, and some more came out of the rest rooms. Wendy stood with her hands over her mouth in surprise. The restaurant was filled with her friends and family. Josh Dockery and her mother Berma came forward offering hugs and kisses. Chyna and India in matching jeans outfits hugged her around the waist saying, "Happy Birthday Mommie!" As she looked around Cedric was carrying a huge birthday cake to a center section of tables. Nicole instantly began to place white candles on top. Cecil and Miss Ester rolled out a small buffet of steak, shrimp, garden salads, bottles of Don Perignon and Hore d'oeuvres as the music started. As Wendy surveyed the crowd she saw faces of people she hadn't seen since high school. There were a few of her long time customers, church members, Jack and Clara Newsome, Cedric's mother Paula, Fat Ralph, Goofiend and many others who smiled and surrounded her.

Caught completely off guard, she tried to fine the words to respond while controlling her emotions of being at center stage. With moist eyes she asked, "Who's responsible for this?" Cedric stepped forward confessing, "Well, I think it all started with me and turned into a conspiracy. We're all responsible." He lurched forward giving her a long passionate hug ending it with a kiss on the lips. Wendy wiping a tear from beneath her eye with one finger while smiling with joy replied, "Nicole you worked me on this one." Nicole ran and over and hugged her saying, "I always wanted to be an actress."

It was a wonderful party. They laughed and ate and drank and ate and laughed and drank some more. Wendy was happy and life was good. Pain, success and the time hadn't killed all her joy. Looking back she knew that returning to Durham, developing a partnership with Cedric had not been only a geographical move but had helped her heal emotionally as well. She realized her blessings of good family, friends and being loved. Her family had been her anchor and continued to stand firm. They'd cleaved together through the good and the bad, never bending or turning away.

She turned to Cecil as he acted as busboy and servant while he popped the corks off the bottles of Don Perignon, filling a row of glasses on the table. He fussed mildly as he nudged the guest to gather around. After the guest had accepted a glass, Cedric rose to his feet saying, "Can I have your attention just for a minute? I know its Wendy's birthday," he said, "Which is lovely an all that, I just want to say happy birthday from all of us and that we love you." Nicole held up her glass of seltzer and tapped Big Ralph's glass.

"Do we drink now?" Big Ralph whispered.

"Not yet, after a word from the lady of the evening." Cedric replied, causing everyone to laugh.

"Will you tell me when?" Ralph asked in response causing more laughter.

"Yes!" Cedric whispered.

"Do you promise?" Big Ralph asked making everyone laugh even more.

Wendy nervously looked around choosing her words, "I don't know what to say." Then she spoke. "Thank you all, this is a great surprise. I had no idea this was going to happen. I'm happy. It's my best birthday ever. I feel lucky, blessed. Life is good because of you guys. As you all know, I've been home for two, no, three years and been managing this Diner almost since I came back." She continued, "Three wonderful successful years, I might add. But it couldn't have been possible without Cedric, Daddy, Momma and Cecil and Miss Ester. In the process I've found peace and developed great friendships. I'm looking forward to more of the same."

Cedric looked over at Big Ralph saying, "Hold on bro" causing everyone in the room to explode with laughter. All the guest and family applauded, "Hear, hear" everyone saluted. Wendy blushed. To Wendy everyone echoed, raising their glasses. Cedric turned to Fat Ralph saying "Now!" he prompted and they all drank.

The guest begin to mold around the room amongst one another amongst chatter and laughter. Wendy walked by Cedric's side, took his hand and planted a kiss on his lips and walked away. Fat Ralph with an inquisitive expression murmured, "I see who gets the lady of the evening." Cedric, Fat Ralph and Goofiend all teased and laughed at Ralph's truthful observation.

Cedric stood in intimate conversation with Fat Ralph and Goofiend for more than a half-hour. At conversations end, he was surprised and elated that both his long time friends had made life changes. Both were off the corner. The drug dealing and hustling were behind them. Fat Ralph lived with his kids and their mother and worked each day at Nortel out in Research Triangle Park. He talked of marriage and fathering his children. Goofiend, although not married nor committed in a relationship worked at Duke Hospital in the operating room as a technician trainee. Cedric was amazed, blown away and proud. He thought, "Who says people don't change. And you'll never know who."

Cedric's conscious awareness and emerging perspective of manhood was validated even more through what he saw happening in Fat Ralph and Goofiend's lives. He realized the movement in their lives was a move toward responsibility and manhood. They were once boys trapped in men's bodies, like many others including himself, boys evolving into men, through the games of life; thinking that playing games with the lives of others and their own was being a man. Desiring and working to acquire the toys of materialism, no accomplishments that move the world and empower oneself or a people; men possessing no real power, only possessing symbolic authority and the materialistic expressions of men with power. Like other boys in men roles, the toys of the world preoccupying their minds. Boys in men's bodies, driving flashy cars, equipped with the latest and loudest stereophonic equipment, buying CD's over books; misdirected priorities leading them to buy clothes and other faddish materials over stock, maintaining mistresses over wives. Such men according to Cedric's new view failed to engage in productive work or activity. Their days being filled with massaging their shallow egos through women, projecting the image of a player, telling jokes, espousing rehetorical philosophies and not having an impact toward world definition. Men operating as boys involved, and not committed to anything in a real sense. Not to his family, the people or himself. Rehearsing the part that real men live. Cedric's thoughts had taken him away from the others in the room as he reviewed his new wave of thinking.

In the moment of deep thinking, Cedric could feel himself escaping the Ghost of Big Tom, moving from being a male to a man, acquiring, the awareness, discipline and ability to exercise control over self. His budding consciousness, new reasoning and knowledge were the inspiration of his transformation.

With the joy of his perspective lifting his heart, he found his way to his grandfather Jack Newsome. Jack and Josh Dockery were in deep dialogue concerning street crime but paused as Cedric joined them. Cedric quickly acknowledged, "I'm just checking on you guys to make sure ya'll don't need anything. I'm on my way, just checking."

By 11 o'clock the party began to wind down. Being a Monday night, Tuesday morning around the corner and another work day lay ahead, Wendy was ushered out by Nicole as Cedric and Cecil began to put the party leftovers away. Before leaving, Wendy shared the card she'd received from her brother Randy with Cedric. Randy hadn't been around for over two years. The birthday card came as a complete surprise. He'd sent the card from the Step One Impatient Drug Treatment Center in Winston-Salem where he was finally trying to face himself and his heroin addiction, Randy had remembered Wendy's birthday and promised to call soon.

Wendy sat cross-legged in the middle of her living room floor, in a baggie black sweat suit, surrounded by an assortment of Christmas cards. There was a yellow pad on the floor beside her, a ballpoint pen was clamped between her teeth. There was a smudge of ink on her chin.

She struggled with the task of deciding on which cards should go to whom on her list. She felt the words should be appropriate and capture her personal well wishes for each person.

An hour later, she had merely completed her list, so engrossed, she barely heard Chyna as she creped down beside her, dressed in pink pajamas. "Mommy, is Cedric coming tonight?" Chyna asked. Interrupting her thoughts, and yet not really interrupting them at all. Wendy stopped addressing the envelope she held in her hand and turned toward Chyna.

Chyna continued, "Is today Sunday?"

Wendy looked at Chyna and replied, "Yes, today is Sunday."

"Then Cedric's coming." Chyna asked again. I want to show him me and India's new Cinderella video."

"Good," Wendy replied. "As I recall he brought if for you guys."

"Yeah" Chyna answered with a smile.

"Listen, mommy!" Chyna cried, "I can sing the song just like Cinderella."

"I'm listening honey" Wendy replied.

The song was a short version but Wendy listened in admiration as her little angel did her best.

"Did you hear?" Chyna shouted jumping up and down, "Did you hear?"

Wendy smiling said, "I heard you and it was wonderful."

Then Chyna asked, "Will Cedric be here before it gets dark? I want to sing for him too?" Wendy replied, "I think so."

Chyna recanted, "Make sure mommy, will you, I want him to hear me sing and watch my video." Then Chyna turned serious asking, "Mommy can Cedric live with us and be me and India's daddy?" Wendy filled with amazement and wonder stopped stuffing Christmas cards in envelopes, looking at Chyna and asked, "Where did that idea come from?"

Chyna slowly replied, "Me and India was talking about it. He wouldn't have to keep coming over, he would be here."

In amazement Wendy inquired, "You mean every night?"

India asked as she walked down the steps from the upstairs joining her sister and mother. Wendy laughing asked, "What are you two doing, teaming up on me . . . or what?"

India shouted, "He would be here to tie my shoes for school."

"Yeah"! Chyna shouted, "And mornings and afternoons, too." Wendy sat still, amazed with the twins, not believing her ears. India turned to her mother, "Are you going to marry Cedric, mommy? Is he going to be our daddy?"

"Would you like that?" Wendy asked. Astonished at how simple the most complex things could become in the eyes of a child.

"Oh yes." Chyna breathed.

"Yeah mommy" India said. "Well girls, mommy don't know about all that, it's not so simple. Run on now, so mommy can finish her cards."

The days and weeks leading up to Christmas moved rapidly. It was one of the best Christmas's Wendy could remember. From the moment Cedric arrived barely past dawn to participate in the official opening of gifts with her and the twins, to the moment she departed with him near midnight, as he drove her and the twins home from her parent's home, where they'd had dinner.

Her mother had taken photographs of Wendy, the twins, Cedric and Wendy, Jack and Clare Newsome and of Josh. She made Wendy promise to frame them. Berma loved pictures and said as she snapped away, "Pictures will help us not to forget what we looked like when we're not here." Wendy with a smile of sentiment said, "Ma, I'll frame them all and I'll put one of the girls and Ced in the office at the Diner, since that's where I spend most of my time."

As Cedric drove from Hope Valley North in route to his grandparent's house and home in Old Farms, he'd toyed with the nervous anticipation of what was to come. He reached over to the glove compartment and picked up the small gift wrapped box. The small box contained the engagement ring he'd planned to present to Wendy. A part of him said, "She'll be overwhelmed with joy, another part didn't know." He couldn't determine the outcome but knew he wanted her as his wife. The past two years working with her, being her closest ally, soul mate and her, his, had convinced him she was the women he wanted to grow old with. He wasn't willing to lose out on love again. This time he'd move before it was too late. His relationship with Wendy had been different than any other. There'd been no sex, although he'd at times being filled to the brim with lust. They had built a solid friendship and respect for one another and fell in love as a result. He knew she was a loyal and responsible woman with a concrete set of principals and was fun to be with. Plus, she was gorgeous and sexy. This was his chance. No more womanizing, no more bouncing from one woman's bed to the next. He envisioned a new approach to manhood, relationships and life; it was time to act upon his new reasoning. They really hadn't dated in a true sense. He'd had no interest in dating or meeting women since Angela's death. The idea of dating for some reason seemed a betrayal to Angela. His guilt driven conscious had had him at an impasse'. For the most part he'd been quite content with his neat safe life of no involvement. He sometimes missed the kind of intimacy that could be found only with a woman. But, after the shock and pain of Angela's death, the meaning of love had changed. It had become more serious and emotional, rather than physical and sexual. Until the recent six months he'd felt dead with no attraction to women other than casual or business, women who'd circled around him at church, the Diner and on occasions when he went out. There wasn't one of them whom he felt the slightest desire to share anything intimate or sexual until Wendy. Life's circumstances had thrown them together. In times her presence began to stir in his soul. Against all the guilt ridden resistance, repressed feelings, excuses, denials and justifications to ignore her and what his heart spoke to him . . . love had won over.

Now, as he cruised down 15-501 Expressway, he prayed she'd have him . . . accept his proposal. He'd never dreamed that someone would come along to fill even a portion of that aching void inside him. But someone had . . . when he wasn't looking, when his guard was down, when he least expected it. Wendy of all people, he thought, "We never can tell what life's gonna bring." They'd started out as quasi-sister and brother, business associates, then grew to be friends, and finally overtime blending more into the fabric of their personal lives. He'd grown to love the twins and they him. Cedric chuckled to himself, "Boy will everybody be surprised or what?"

Beyond being emotional . . . Cedric had moved to a point of making decisions based on objective conditions and on what was rational and responsible with a potential bigger than himself. Through his new consciousness and perspective of manhood he'd developed and accurate image of himself and the world around him. Angela's murder had thrown him into the arena of life and reality. He experienced pain and confronted himself as a man, a Newsome man who'd been socialized according to the legacy of Big Tom. But through the process of self examination he'd realized the fallacy of the intergenerational passage to manhood as seen by the Newsome's. He'd experienced a paradigm shift. He loved the Newsome men and women but had to separate their good from their bad as well as their beauty from their ugliness. He'd realized the solution to the underline problem of promiscuity, poor parenting, failed relationships and marriages amongst the ancestors of Big Tom. Through a real life problem he'd learn responsibility and discovered the fullness of his potential as a man, prospective husband and family member. Cedric's planned proposal to Wendy was indicative of his jump into the waters of husband-hood. He refused to engage in irresponsible and unaccountable sex and shacking because he knew that both acts were a game and a failure to take full responsibility for one's actions. He believed that if he was ever to break the Newsome's mold of manhood, he must take full responsibility for his actions. Shacking outside of wedlock offered a trap door. Though marriage is escapable, he would not escape without learning a thorough lesson in decisions, actions, consequences and responsibility for himself and others. Shacking and co-habilitation, out of marriage, would allow him to play the husband game without a secure or legally binding commitment, therefore, continuing in the way the Newsome's in the shadows of Big Tom's Ghost.

Marriage and fidelity would be a lesson in manhood for himself and a model for a new generation of Newsome's. He knew that he'd never learn the role of husbanding until he decided to be a husband . . . not a roommate, a husband. He knew also, that others in his family needed a different example of manhood. He believed someway or how men had to learn what it meant to be with another person for better or worse and not be able to walk away on just a whim. It was clear that strong, stable and functional families come from being bound with a person and people socially, legally, spiritually and emotionally. Cedric was encouraged by responsibility and a sense of commitment. Thought his commitment to a wife, family and fathering he prayed it would stimulate his growth and create a new model of manhood for those around him.

Fines Diner was closed the day after Christmas and would be for the next two days. Wendy and the twins had invited Cedric over for a early breakfast and for him to assemble two bicycles.

Cedric parked his SUV and rang the door bell at 8:30 A.M. India open the door jumping into his arms. They smell of bacon, eggs and pancakes filled the air. Wendy worked in the kitchen, looking fresh and stylish in a red terry cloth robe, it tied at the waist.

When the last pancake and last egg, the last drop of maple syrup had disappeared, Chyna and India ran off to their room enjoying their new toys. Wendy began to tackle the kitchen saying, "Now I know what's meant when it's said a women's work is never done." Cedric smiled and ordered her to sat down, taking charge of cleaning the kitchen. When he finished he laid the tiny gift wrapped box in her lap. "Let's see," she said, weighting it, "This feels heavier than a feather, but lighter than a bread box."

Cedric smiled, "Open it" . . . she tore the paper from around the tiny box. Her mouth hung open as she saw the stone. "Oh my God, Cedric this is fantastic," she said.

He smiled, "I'm glad you like it." She looked at him in anticipation.

Cedric finally spoke, "I . . . . I would like for you to be my wife." The words sounded strangely formal and stilted to them both. Wendy shifted uncomfortable in her seat, opened her mouth to say something clever and then closed it again when she realized the seriousness of the situation.

"I don't understand," she stammered finally. "I mean, you never . . . that is, I didn't . . . I mean, you and I aren't . . . . Well, you know like that."

"Just because we haven't been doesn't mean we couldn't be," he observed.

"But we're friends," she protested, "Good friends. I can count on your friendship. I don't want to change that."

He shrugged, "I happen to think that friendship is a pretty solid foundation to build on."

"I'm really very flattered," she began gently, "but the idea of marrying you . . . well, it never entered my head . . . although the girls asked me about us getting married just the other day. I think you're wonderful, attractive, kind and dependable . . . this is such a surprise. Can I have a day or two to think?"

"Sure, take as long as you need" he replied. Look, I know I'm not exactly the knight in shining armor you probably expected to come along and rescue you. I've had some of the spunk knocked out of me, I'll admit it. I'm a workaholic, haven't been romantic and you've known me since my days of shooting marbles. Right now altogether, I'm nobody's idea of a prize package. But, I'm determined to be faithful, honest and a good provider and a good father for the twins, and the thing is, I care for you in a very special way, adore you, desire you, love you and think we could make a good life together." He stopped talking suddenly, surprised that he'd actually managed to make that whole speech without stumbling.

Wendy defended him saying, "How could you think you're not a good catch? You're terrific . . . I've thought about you on many days and nights. You're sensible, caring, stable and sincere. I can't imagine any women who wouldn't be proud to ride off with you. Let's talk about it again in two days . . . agreed?"

"Fine in two days" he replied.

Later in the day Wendy listened to the soothing sounds of Jesse Powell's "From This Day Forth" and thought of Cedric. He was so terribly nice and the last thing in the world she wanted to do was hurt him. But she'd never thought of marriage since her horrific experience with Tyrone back in D.C., some years earlier. She'd been afraid to risk involvement and chose to devote herself to Fines Diner and her girls. She'd found a comfort zone. And she believed her painful experience with Tyrone was behind her, until now. She was sure of Cedric's love, sincerity and honor as a man. She knew in her heart of hearts he'd make a good husband and father. She also realized her fear wasn't about Cedric; it was about her own suppressed fear and pain. Her mind raced "I got to find a way to let him down gently." In the next minute she though, "No, I'd like the security of being married." She was thoroughly confused.

Wendy moved from the love seat and made her way to the kitchen, filling her tea glass with scotch and drinking it down in one long shallow. The facade she'd cultivated in the recent years, the ability to enclose her emotions behind a curtain of denial crumbled as she giggled and cried and shivered all together. She suddenly begun to reconsider, "Why didn't I just say no?" She murmured out loud. "I shouldn't have left him dangling."

From the day that Tyrone Beckwith had brutally assaulted her, she had been devastated. Although, she realized it was no fault of her own . . . . only after an attempt to confront him concerning their relationship; other women and his involvement in drugs. She thought she had been able to shake the feeling of betrayal and Tyrone's debasement of her as a person. But now it was questionable. She'd sworn that she would never again put herself in that position. The risk of betrayal and pain was too great. In her heart she knew all men were not alike but she thought, "How do I know what will happen? People love you as long as things are going their way. When it's not; all the promises made earlier are forgotten." She had to admit to herself that her theory resulted entirely from her experience with Tyrone.

Since Tyrone she'd come to terms with being uninvolved and single. In many ways, she'd found she was well-suited for the role of solitude, being a single mom and enjoying her consequent, peace and privacy. Then, too, the idea of being a single woman with children no longer carried the stigma it once had. She knew women who were enjoying a whole new life and freedom as single women. They were functioning and succeeding in business as well as socially. Some lived intimately and openly with men to whom they were not married. A few were planning and having babies without having husbands.

Changing the CD to the sounds of Whitney Houston, Wendy breathed a sigh of defeat, knowing in her soul even though she'd truly made peace with her way of life, she would gladly have given it up for the security of true love, stability, and a husband like Cedric. She knew exactly that was what he'd offered. "Boy!" she murmured, "What a choice to make."

It wasn't that she didn't like Cedric; in fact she felt she loved him. Although, there had been no sex between them she had fallen for him. The thought of sharing a bed with him instantly aroused her. "What must I do?" She felt so awkward. She bit her lower lip and felt the fear which lurked inside and in the next instant felt the warm joy and expectation of love.

Two days after Christmas Wendy sat in her parent's home. As a tradition she'd shared meals with her parents on Christmas day and the two days after. There was no ritualistic reasoning for the tradition, it happened overtime mostly because of her stagnet social life. She sat at the dining room table with her mother recovering from over stuffing herself from dinner as the flipped the pages of an interior design catalogue. "Jesus," her mother breathed, "The wallpaper and curtains I'd like for the master bedroom looks so great in the catalogue, I wonder what they'll look like in real life?" Wendy replied, "Tomorrow we can ride over on Broad Street and look around . . . that's where the place is located."

"Do you think the stuff there will be as nice as the catalogue makes it look?" Her mother grasped.

"It probably does. If not, there are other interior designers who can get you what you'd like. You'll have the house looking different as planned."

But, it'll probably cost a small fortune." Her mother replied.

Wendy sighed, "Momma, stop worrying about money. You know you and daddy got the money ya'll made in the 1960's."

After considerable debate on price, they came to an agreement on ignoring cost for the project because hiring an interior designer was what Berma Dockery wanted at any cost. Wendy convinced her that she deserved to splurge a little. Berma smiled saying, "I suggest you help me keep up with the detailed cost of this."

"I'll stay close by your side, ma." Wendy replied, "Just relax."

They discussed and decided on their plans for each room in the house. They detailed the color schemes, wallpaper, carpeting, pictures and new pieces of furniture.

It was not until then, that Wendy closed the catalogues, stacking them in a pile and dropped the bombshell. "Ma, Cedric asked me to marry him." The ink pen in her mother's hand dropped from her hand and her hazel eyes almost popped out of her head. "And you waited through all these catalogues to tell me?" she cried.

Wendy shrugged, "He proposed to me on yesterday and offered me a wonderful ring."

"Yesterday?" her mother squealed, "Why didn't you speak of it yesterday?" Wendy slowly stated, "Well I wasn't sure how you'd take it. Plus I've been turning it over in my head."

"How I'd take it". Berma shouted, "I've been hoping and praying for this for a year now. Honey you need a husband and the girls need a daddy. That man loves you girl, I've seen it in his eyes for some time now."

Wendy picked up a catalogue from the table and flipped the pages nervously. "The thing is, you see, I've thought of Cedric in those terms but we never . . . you know been involved like that."

Her mother replied, "Child there is no rule to say that you have to sleep with a man to love him or marry him. That's part of the problem with young folks today . . . . they jump into bed as the first thing, not knowing a thing about each other . . . . living together and the other mess you see going on. Honey, whether you marry Cedric or not he's a good man. I can tell. Plus, don't punish him for what somebody else did to you . . . that Tyrone wasn't half the man Cedric is. Just keep that in mind. Don't let you past blind you, you hear. And Cedric was raised by two good grandparents."

Wendy starred into her mother's face with a compassionate smile and replied, "I'm set in my ways. I need my space."

Berman forcefully replied, "Stop it honey! It's really about what happened to you in D.C., isn't it?"

Wendy looked away, "It's about a lot of things," she murmured.

"But things can change," Berma insisted, "That is, if you want them too." There was a pause, neither of them knowing quite where to go next. "I believe that everyone has two sides," Wendy said finally, "The public side that they present to the world each day as they go about their business and a private side that they basically keep to themselves . . . hidden mostly from others. The public side at times serves to mask the private side. I'm afraid of what I don't know about people, the private side." Her mother considered her words. This was two women in dialogue, mother and daughter, closest friends, in great part because of their shared values, interest and because of a mother's upbringing. Berma believed in the old saying, "you must bend a tree in the direction you'd like it to grow." With Wendy she could see she'd raised a morally sound and strong woman. Berma spoke, "Don't over think honey, and trust your instincts. Don't sell yourself short. And Cedric either. He really cares about you and your babies and you know it. Don't shut the door because one man failed you." A shadow flickered across Wendy's face. "I'm just a little afraid right now."

The next evening at Fines Diner it was closing time. The last meal had been served and eaten, the last drop of tea drank, and the last paying customer politely ushered out the door. Cedric was in the office tallying receipts and as soon as Wendy finished closing the register she went in search of him, finding him in the office hunched over the desk calculator.

The light from the lamp glinting off his chocolate skin, "Are you busy?" She asked hesitantly.

"Never too busy for you," he replied, raising his eyes from the calculator and standing up to stretch his back muscles. Then he moved over and sat on the small sofa against the far wall. "Are you guys finished out front?" He asked.

Wendy nervously replied, "Yeah, Cecil's finishing up with the floor and Miss Ester is sanitizing the kitchen area."

"Come, sit down" he invited, patting the sofa. Wendy sat on the opposite end, turning in his directions. "You must have thought I've been ignoring you all day?" She began.

"Nonsense" he told her, "I know how busy we've been around here all day." How can any man be so understanding; She thought, he's nice about everything. Nice but not, a whimp. "Well, I didn't want you to think I'd forgotten you . . . . your kind offer . . . proposal." She said.

He smiled at her, his dark brown eyes dancing. "You make it sound like a business deal." He said.

"Oh, I didn't mean too," she apologized. "It's just that I . . ." Wendy faltered, she had simply meant to ask for more time and then leave as quickly as possible. "All this has been such a shock," she heard herself saying instead. "We don't know each other when it comes to being intimate and sexual, I mean, we're friends, and I really do like you. But you don't know if you love me." She looked down at her hands twisted in her lap. "It's not that so much," she whispered, "I'm so afraid Cedric, it seems as if my past experience with Tyrone still has me afraid of all men. So, it isn't you, it's me . . . . I just don't know."

He looked at her thoughtfully for a moment, while she struggled with her hands. "Honey, I understand. For a long time after Angela's death I was convinced that I never wanted to get close to anyone again. Losing her had hurt so much, and I know I couldn't risk going through anything like that again. So, I built an invisible wall around myself and closed myself off from the world. I had my work here at the Diner, my grandparents, a few friends, and I figured that was enough. But, I was wrong, because all of life is a risk . . . . this business we're sitting in right now is a risk . . . nothing has guarantees beyond your commitments and the work you put into it. So, I do understand your fear but I challenge you to move forward and take this risk with me as my wife."

Wendy forced her eyes away from her hands to glance up at Cedric. He was strong, sensitive and caring and he was trying so hard. Her glance slipped past his face. "Cedric, I've thought about it and I do love you. Plus I like you in a very special way," she said. "I trust you more than any man I've known, outside my daddy. I feel good when I'm with you. I look forward to the time I spend with you and so do the twins, and all that means more to me than I can say." Her eyes fastened on her hands once again. "I discussed your proposal with momma last night . . . she was happy and thought it was the best idea in the world." She returned her eyes to meet his, "Cedric I'll marry you . . . but I'm so afraid please don't hurt me." Cedric took a deep breath, stood and reached for her hand. He hugged her long and tight. "I will not hurt you . . . . I will take care of you, protect you and love you." He assured her. He kissed her lips lightly and turned to the desk reaching for the small box with the ring inside. He placed the ring on her finger.

Their engagement was announced the following week. The date was set for June 10th on a Saturday. Berma and Josh Dockery as well as Jack and Clara Newsome were all elated and saw it as a perfect match. Berma and Clara started immediately to take charge of the planning while Wendy over-looked their efforts and details. Every member of both families was approving and all their friends thought Cedric and Wendy were made for each other.

Jack Newsome was happy and supporting of Cedric's choice of a wife. He'd known Wendy from birth, knew she was a good girl as he would say and above all she was the daughter of his long time best friend, Josh Dockery. But that didn't stop him from discussing the issue of marriage with Cedric. Consequent to being informed of the engagement, he made it his business to wait up for Cedric until he arrived home, after closing the Diner for the night. Cedric walked in the door to fine his grandfather in the den in front of the TV, right off, he knew his grandfather was waiting for his arrival. Jack gave Cedric time to undress, shower and change into a robe and slippers. Once Cedric joined him, he spoke. "Congratulations son . . . Wendy's gonna make you a good wife. She comes from a good daddy and momma. I want ya'll to be happy and give me some more Newsome babies."

Cedric smiled, "We'll be happy, I'm sure . . . it's a little early to be thinking about having babies."

Jack chuckled, "I dunna, sometimes the babies come without planning. Now you listen yeah. Be good to that girl, provide for her well, come home each night and keep other women out your marriage. I knows you got Newsome blood in you and there'll be times you'll want a little stray tail, that's okay but keep all that away from home. If you do that and be a good provider and be kind to your wife it'll work for you."

Cedric loved his grandfather but was appalled by his advice. He knew he meant well but his grandfather's words of wisdom were out of step with his personal views of his expected behavior as a husband. His grand-dad was attempting to pass on the Newsome's approach to maintaining a wife and marriage. Cedric knew very well where the ill-advice originated. He looked, listened and stayed focused while his grand-dad finished speaking.

Cedric lowered his head and shuffled in his seat before speaking. "Grand-dad, I love you and respect you, and respect your advice and its good advice, I'm sure. But, I've thought about myself as a husband for some time now, I plan to be somewhat different than what the Newsome men have been as husbands. The Newsome men are good providers, the ones who chose to get married. You've always took good care of grandma, momma and me. But, a great many of the men in our family haven't taken care of their families like you have. Many of them have fathered children and don't even know them or given them a thing. I know that happens sometimes when men love a lot of different women. I plan to do it different once married. I will be committed to my wife totally. I'm gonna be loyal, committed and apply the self discipline to stay away from other women. Being married will be bigger than me . . . my desires. My idea of manhood and marriage is to be committed to one woman, through the good, bad, tough times and all. It will also be a show of respect toward my wife by not cheating and running around on her I know it's gonna be rough times but that's part of what marriage and commitment calls for . . . enduring the challenges of the relationship, compromising, solving problems, being able and willing to work through issues while maintaining your loyalties and commitment. So, for me this marriage to Wendy is much greater than me . . . it's about another person as well and our children and future family." Jack had kept his eyes on Cedric the entire time he'd spoke. Jack chimed in, "I hear what you're saying boy, but remember what I said. And put that under your hat with your own ideas." Cedric nodded, "Grand-dad I will do that . . . . I've always listened to you."

Wendy had driven to her parent's home to pick up Chyna and India. She had to drive across the city and get them back home and to bed before it was too late. Chyna and India being school children needed their sleep and would be called to get up early the next morning. Berma offered her a cup of coffee. Wendy knew that meant she wanted to talk. Her mom said, "We're so happy for you Wendy. Cedric is such a lovely man and he loves you." Wendy didn't reply she waited for the punch line and then it came, "What finally tipped the scale in Cedric's favor?" She asked. Wendy looked down into her coffee cup, as she stirred it. "Ma, I guess in the final analysis I realized that my career, and the Diner would not be a substitute for marriage forever and the desire to be connected to another human being, not to be alone any longer. My instincts, and in a secret place inside, I knew I'd come upon a man who cared about me and loved me as well. Cedric has been my knight in shining armor. He accepts me. My imperfections, my past and when he look, into my eyes and takes my breath away. Cedric snuck up on me, in the guise of a friend and gained my confidence and stole my heart. I trust him with laughter, my hopes and my fears. I know he won't turn away from me. A good marriage is my chance for happiness." Smiling with a tear in her eye, she asked, "Do that answer your question satisfactorily?"

"Oh, girl I just wanted to know that you were sure. You better run before it gets too late, honey."

Jumping up from her seat, Wendy cried, "I'm going, I'm going."

Saturday, June 10, 2000

Everything with creation seemed to be in harmony and synchronized. The sun had warmed the air, there wasn't a cloud that could be found in the sky, and the chirping of birds could be heard. At 1 P.M., three hours before the wedding of the decade, a half dozen workers from Duke University's Environmental Services Special Events cadre' made their final rounds in Duke's Bryon Center making sure it was in order for the Newsome and Dockery wedding reception.

By 3 P.M., Chapel Drive which circles around Duke Gardens had been officially closed to the public by the University Police. The entire street was off-limits to everyone except those bearing the silver-engraved cards from Cartier that simply stated "Wedding Guest".

Wendy selected her mother's bedroom as a dressing room and was setting still as Beverly meticulously enhanced her face while applying make-up. Beverly treated Wendy's wedding day as if it was the greatest day of her own life. Beverly, her mother, Mrs. Jackson and her cousin Lisa had fussed over her all afternoon.

By 3:15 Wendy had finished dressing. She wore a beautiful gown of creamy satin. Both the veil and train were of understated Belgian lace. A single strand of pearls encircled her throat. She couldn't have been any happier. She felt beautiful inside and out. Not only was Cedric healed, so was she.

"Elegant. Lovely, Perfection." Beverly pronounced approval, eyeing Wendy as though she was Leonardo and Wendy was the Mono Lisa. Wendy found it hard to keep from laughing at Beverly's serious and grandiosity.

"You look cool, mom," India said as she peeped through the door.

Wendy replied, "Thank you honey." Then she looked around facing everyone in the room and said, "Could ya'll give me a few minutes alone? I just need a little time to take it all in."

"Sure" Beverly said, matter-of-factly, "Go, go, everyone out," Clapping her hands like a mother toward her children.

They left but Wendy held her mother aside. She held her mother's hand saying, "Thanks for putting up with me for these few months. Now, go get pretty, only not too much prettier than the bride, okay?"

"Don't worry about that. That couldn't happen even if I wanted to, which I don't. I love you," she whispered.

"I love you even more, mom."

"Couldn't be so" Her mom replied.

"I do, get it, I do." Wendy recanted.

The wedding list was filled with a variety of guest. The Dockery's clan from Shakragg in Person County, Virginia and D.C. had arrived throughout the week and had been in and out of Josh and Berma's home in streams from morning till late night. The Newsome's from Murfreesboro, Virginia, D.C., New York and all over for the most part were in Durham since Wednesday, throwing parties in their hotels each night. Mrs. Clara's family from, Ahoskie, North Carolina were scheduled to arrive on the wedding day, as well as Mrs. Berma's family from Hillsborough. Randy Dockery had finished his drug treatment and was driving from

Greensboro with his wife. A few of Cedric's former team-mates at Virginia Union; Carlo, Dean and Bracy in addition to Fat Ralph, Goofiend, his mother, Paula and church members from Greater Saint Paul made up the more familiar guest. There were musicians; reporters for the Herald Sun News, photographers . . . . it seemed to be more strangers than family and friends.

Once in the Gardens amongst the flowers, greenery and small round ponds with hand size gold fish, Wendy was escorted to the bride's tent where she would exit at the sound of the "wedding march'. As she waited with Nicole by her side, at the entranceway, the tent suddenly swung open.

"Now who . . . . Ced, you're not suppose to be . . . ." "Getting married today, huh?" He said as he smiled. He looked gorgeous in a black Brioni tuxedo, but he also looked refined.

"I know I don't suppose to be here but with a woman as beautiful as you, how could I resist? Do you know how much I thought of you last night? I could probably show you." He took a step forward.

"Don't you dare," Wendy started to laugh. He could always make her laugh. "Out, I mean it."

He continued undaunted, and took her in his arms. His hands gently touched her breast. Nothing too provocative . . . . and thus provocative, "Ummm," He said, "You're an eyeful, and a handful too."

"Cedric!"

"Yes I am" She said.

"I love you so much. Now go."

"Enough, enough, I respect your wishes. I shall honor and obey, from this moment on."

Obediently, he left the tent, humming "Always." Wendy smiled and thought it was a perfect prelude.

The salt and peppered haired pianist, who was seated at his mounted piano on the side of the gold fish pond, sent the first notes of the wedding march crescending across the picture book lawn of Duke Gardens. The music, everything, sent shivers up Wendy's spine and caused a lump in

Cedric's throat. They loved their day even more than they thought they would.

Late comers were hurried to their seats which were placed around the entire circle of the garden wall. People whispered in awe and exultation as Wendy entered the Garden. Photographers with cameras strapped around their shoulders seemed to never stop snapping photographs of the guest, bride and groom. The bouquet of white Calla lilies that Wendy carried trembled in her arm. She wasn't use to large crowds and felt a little nervous. She spotted her mother, and brother, Randy smiling tenderly. Beverly her maid of honor, stood solemnly, near the Alter. Miss Ester sat in the front row between Chyna and India who wiggled in their seats. Cedric's mother Paula was there with cousin Bertha from Murfreesboro looking strikingly beautiful and with Aunt Ida looking matronly.

Wendy was escorted down the flower-strewn grass aisle by her father, Josh. He looked stately in his black Brioni tuxedo with a white Calla lily on his lapel. "You're so beautiful, you actually have a glow. I hate to give you away," he whispered as he let go of her arm and turned to find his seat in the front row.

She lifted her eyes to the white alter trimmed with yellow and white roses. It was a bit too much, she thought, but it was beautiful. Cedric stood beside his best man, Danny Hutchinson, a dear friend since first meeting him at Union their freshman year, who looked as if he was a professional model displaying Brioni tuxedos and fashions. Cedric smiled as his bride approached. The crowd grew quiet as Reverend William Smith began to speak. "To all the family and friends of Cedric and Wendy, I welcome you here to share with them their joy as they pledge the vows which will unit them in marriage. Let us join them in love and support of Cedric and Wendy, with our best wishes for their everlasting happiness. Marriage is one of the most important obligations that two people can commit to in their life time. Marriage offers the greatest challenge to overcome, but, in return, marriage gives love, strength, and support from one another. Your love for each other will grow with each passing day, but a genuine liking each other, the willingness to accept each other's strong and weak points with understanding and respect, is the foundation of a strong marriage. The vows which you are about to exchange serve as a verbal representation of the love you pledge to each other. For it is not the words you speak which will bond you together as one, but it is the inner sense of love and commitment that each of you feel in your heart and soul." Reverend Smith look around at the guest and took a deep breath and then continued, "Cedric, do you take Wendy to be your wife. Do you promise to love and respect her and share all life has to offer . . . . your hopes . . . . your dreams, achievements, and disappointments with her from this day forward?"

Looking in Wendy's eyes, Cedric stated, "I do."

Reverend Smith looked over at Wendy and continued, Wendy, do you take Cedric to be your husband. Do you promise to love and respect him and share all life has to offer . . . . your hopes . . . . your dreams, achievements, and disappointments with him from this day forward?'

Wendy looked into Cedric's eyes and stated, "I do."

Reverend Smith smiled and continued, "May these rings always remain a symbol of the covenant which you now make and may your love be as endless as the circle in which these rings are formed."

Cedric placed the ring on Wendy's third finger on her left hand and Wendy repeated the same, placing the ring on Cedric's third finger on his left hand. Both of them individually stated, "I take you, just as you are above all others, to share my life. I give you this ring as a symbol of our everlasting love."

In the tradition of the Mende people of Africa, Cedric and Wendy tasted the four flavors from small wine glasses that represented the different emotions within a relationship. The four flavors used were sour lemon, bitter vinegar, hot cayenne, and sweet honey. By tasting of each of the flavors, they symbolically demonstrated that they will be able to get through the hard times in life, and, in the end, enjoy the sweetness of marriage.

After the tasting of the flavors, Reverend Smith cleared his throat and continued on with the pronouncement, "By virtue of the authority given me by the State of North Carolina, and in conformity with the law, I pronounce you are husband and wife. May, you live together in blissful happiness from this forward. You may kiss the bride!"

Cedric lifted the veil and gently kissed his bride. Reverend Smith then stated, "I present to you Mr. and Mrs. Cedric and Wendy Newsome." The guest applauded. Camera flashes popped like yellow daisies all over the manicured lawn. People smiled, nodded and cried. What a beautiful time!

Once the crowd had moved to the Bryan Center on Duke's central campus, waiters burst from the kitchen area with silver trays bearing glasses of champagne. Others circulated with caviar, canapés of crabmeat, tea sandwiches, cheese, fruits and pates. A jazz band led by Yusef Salim began to play from a highly polished pinewood platform installed against the back right wall.

The guest began to mingle. The room came alive with laughter and joy. In the center floor Fat Ralph immaculately dressed in a white tuxedo danced smooth and graceful with his guest, Jackie the mother of his children. Children dotted between tables covered with white linen clothes, and graced with silver centerpieces filled with baby's breath and yellow rosebuds.

The music by Yusef Salim ranged from Count Bassie, Thelonius Monk, to George Benson and Al Jarreau. After a formal and delicious dinner and dessert, songstress Stephanie Gunn song, "The Wind Beneath, My Wings" to a standing ovation.

Then Randy spoke, his voice silencing the crowd. "The bride will cut the cake." Waiters arrived bearing two gargantuan wedding cakes. On each stood a marzipan man and woman; with chocolate faces embracing one another. Cedric and Wendy mashed cake into each other's mouth; camera flashes caught each crumb of cake which covered their mouths.

After dinner the tables were removed. The band began to cook. Cedric and Wendy danced to the first tune, and then other guest joined in.

The new Mr. and Mrs. Cedric Newsome honeymooned in Sierra Leone in the Southwestern part of West Africa, in a villa in the market district of Freetown. They spent some of their time browsing around the quaint little towns along the coast, but most of their time was spent between the sheets of the huge bamboo bed provided for their pleasure. The staff at the Villa was kept busy changing the sheets several times each day. Wendy delighted every moment of it. Right from the start, Cedric was able to generate such a feverish level of desire in her that their mutual climaxes left her laughing and crying and begging for more . . . . far more than she'd ever imagined. They were in an exotic, tropical land in the middle of Africa. Each time they returned to the Villa from a daily excursion, Wendy came out of her clothing as though out of chrysalis, transforming from classy respectable wife, mother and business-woman to accommodating nymph. She lent herself so naturally to the sensuous acts of lovemaking that she became more and more innocent in the eyes of her new husband. She'd been prepared for an adjustment, a time during which they would learn each other's bodies and each other's likes and dislikes, but there seemed to be no need for that. Somehow, Cedric knew exactly how to please her.

On their fourth day in Freetown Wendy found herself with Cedric on a guided journey to one of the oldest Mende settlements in the area. The excursion through Mende land allowed Cedric to visit the territory of his ancestors. He thought to himself, "So this is where it all began for the Newsome's." He could feel the spirit of his ancestral grandparents, Kimbo and Kali.

The man who had been hired as their guide name was named, Sali. He appeared to be thirty something, tall, slim, and very dark with curly-napped hair and a reddish color surrounding the pupils of his eyes. He spoke English well enough to communicate sufficiently as he drove the blue and white striped Land Rover along rugged, washed out single lane roads. As he described the history and traditions of the different tribes, he glanced into Cedric's face momentarily drawing his attention away from the road. Every so often he'd flash a soft smile offering sight of his pearly white teeth.

The guide rounded a curve so fast that the Rover nearly skidded off the narrow road. The skid would have carried them into the thick uninhabited brush. Wendy held tightly onto Cedric, wanting to be as close as she could. Her mind concentrated on the tiniest details; how fast his skin darkened under the direct sun returning it to correspond with the people of Sierra Leone. She wanted to know everything there was to know about his life, her husband, the man she'd spend the rest of her life with. A long and happy life, growing old together, an elderly couple holding hands as they walked around the mall.

She noticed that the further they traveled into the brush and scattering settlements, the more distracted Cedric became from her. He'd become more and more attentive and focused toward the people tending their gardens, observing the small wooden structured houses and the goings and comings of the tribes people. As they drove Sali explained, "We're entering the Mende areas." He informed, "The Mendes have occupied this particular area for as long as anyone can remember." He talked about the social and political structure of the Mende people. He expounded in his thick West African-French accent. "The Mende villages or towns are controlled by the sub-chief. He's the oldest man of the village. Each village have sections, each section have a chief. All the chiefs are controlled by the paramount chief who possesses the most power." Cedric listened intensely, taking in every word that Sali spoke. Sali continued, "The young boys are admitted into the Mende society at puberty. They are then taught the roles of men, adulthood and family."

Wendy asked, "What about the women?"

Sali gave a soft smile saying "Women have very little authority other than through their husbands. They mostly take care of the farming, household and the gardens."

Sali was well versed with the history of the Mende ethnic group. He spellbound Cedric and Wendy with his account. Speaking as they neared a large settlement of the Mendes, he explained, "The Mende people live primarily through farming. The first contact with the white man was through the Portuguese who visited Sierra Leone around 1460. European trading ships stopped at Sierra Leone around the early 1500's and began taking Mende people to America as slaves."

Cedric turned to Wendy saying that's probably around the same time that my ancestors were kidnapped according to Aunt Ida's research."

Sali listened to Cedric and then continued, "Many of the Mende people were kidnapped and taken unwillingly. The tribes suffered because large amounts of the working people were no longer available."

Cedric turned back and looked into Wendy's face with a certainty in his eyes. "Honey, this sounds exactly like the narrative Aunt Ida wrote on our family, doesn't it?"

Sali continue, "The Mende tribes were colonized by the British around 1808. About four hundred Mende who had been previously captured were returned and from their return came Freetown. Because the returning slaves had been away so long, they'd begin to adhere to British traditions which in turn changed the Mende society from within."

As the Rover neared the large settlement, Sali said, "All the Mende comes from somewhere in this area we're in now." Precipitously, Cedric could almost visualize the white slavers raiding the villages kidnapping and chaining the tribe's people. As he observed the village he could hear the cries and screams of the women and children. In his soul he knew he was home. He felt the connection between himself by way of Aunt Ida's narrative and the people who starred at him in awe and suspicion. The women looked while they grinned corn meal, and tended their children. The small children bare backed and bare foot watched with unrestrained eyes without a sign of noticeable feelings. Sali drove the Rover down a lane between the wooden structured houses, waving and greeting the Mende by standers using the Mende dialect. The Rover slowed to at stop. Sali motioned for Cedric and Wendy to exit the vehicle. The three of them walked slowly through the village. Some of the children followed them from a safe distance. The adults smiled and nodded their heads as they passed through. Cedric and Wendy both were in another time zone. Cedric thought, "This is where it all began for the Newsome's." The realization of the Newsome's roots played over and over in his head as he walked, kicking up the dust in Mende land. The idea of it all was overwhelming and too much to conceive for the moment. It would take time for Cedric to be able to put it all into perspective with his life and the Newsome's lives.

As they approached the far end of the houses by the lane, as old man who appeared weathered by time and life was seated on a block of wood counting beads on a string. He was gray and frail, he smoked some type of tobacco from what appeared to be ah homemade pipe. As Cedric with Wendy by his side approached, the old man looked at Sali speaking to him in the Mende dialect. Cedric looked at Wendy with a questionable look. She returned his look with a blank stare. The old man began to point toward Cedric saying, Mende, Mende, Mende." Afterwards the old man returned to the counting of the beads as if they no longer existed. Cedric nudged Sali's arm asking, "What was that all about?"

Sali replied, "The old man says you're Mende." The words from Sali stirred an emotion inside Cedric. He felt pride as well as a loss and hurt. He felt a lump in his throat and tears in the welt of his eyes. He knew he'd never be the same again. He'd found the land of his ancestors.

"How about let's go for a swim?" Cedric asked when they got back to the Villa. He sounded shy, and she liked the sound of his voice. "Let's throw on our suites and explore the deep blue sea."

Cedric and Wendy were gently rocking back and forth, hugging each other under a revolving teak ceiling fan.

"Maybe a little later," She murmured, "We're finally alone, and I think I want to enjoy this. In fact, I'm sure I do. Can we . . . just . . . do nothing?"

Cedric laughed, "Okay, no deep blue sea. Let's try the Jacuzzi; no suits, and an exploration of the Jacuzzi."

"That sounds better. I like that idea a lot." She recanted.

Once in the Jacuzzi, they kissed softly for a long time. Wendy thought, "Am I losing control or finding myself again?"

Cedric slide the glass door that opened onto the terrazzo and Jacuzzi. They continued to undress until they stood in front of the Jacuzzi that glittered with steaming hot water. Green, blue and yellow birds chattered in the surrounding forest. Wendy thought to herself, "This is paradise or so it seemed." With a timid sampling of the water, Wendy made her way into the Jacuzzi, pulling Cedric after her. They played and acted silly, like a couple of children.

Cedric grabbed her and drew her to him. He was already hard. She sled her hands down his muscular body and stroked his thighs. He felt warm and tender. He continued to be nothing like she'd expected.

They kissed again . . . . soft and long. Cedric raised her from the tile flooring of the Jacuzzi and turned her so she could brace himself against the Jacuzzi edge. He slowly, slowly entered her. She closed her eyes, becoming aware of new sensations, relishing the warm sun on her face, and even a greater heat building inside. She'd never been with anyone like Cedric. He made her feel special.

After another week of romance, love and mingling with the people of Sierra Leone and visiting the Mende settlements, Cedric and Wendy were headed across the Atlantic, the same route as his ancestors had traveled over four hundred years earlier. As the cruise ship made its way toward European and Western waters, Cedric held Wendy close as they looked out into the ocean. His mind slowly traveled to an imaginary time when Kali and Kimbo had traveled in the same direction in the belly of a slave-ship, not knowing their destination or fate. He could feel their spirit circulating in the atmosphere above the cruise ship. Cedric didn't speak for a long time as he and Wendy stood on the deck in the darkness of night in the moist ocean air. He drew close to Wendy in a long deep and soul searching silence.

Friday, July 19, 2000

Almost a month after they'd returned to Durham, Cedric and Wendy decided to take the twins on a week's mini vacation before school began. They visited, the Washington Monument, the Nation's Capitol, Lincoln's Memorial and ended the week on Saturday driving through Virginia for a fun day at Kings Dominion. Wendy could see that Chyna and India adored Cedric. He was attentive, patient and protective of the girls as they ran with excitement from carnival to carnival eating cotton candy and hotdogs. She felt a great joy and a sense of safety and security. As she watched her family, she contemplated when she'd inform Cedric that she was carrying his child. It had been two days since she'd realized she was pregnant. But, they'd been so busy with the tours in D.C, and nurturing the twins she hadn't found the right moment. The timing hadn't been right. For some unknown reason she was hesitate and nervous. She hadn't been able to determine the source of her feelings, other than a short reminder of her pregnancy with the twins and the horror of her experience with Tyrone at the time of their conception. It was all somehow connected.

As they drove down I-85 South in route to Durham, Wendy took hold of Cedric's hand. The twins were asleep in the back seat. The highway traffic was flowing with ease and the radio was turned to Foxy 107.5's blue light basement. D.J. Heavy D teased his listeners with oldies but goodies. Clarence Carter's "Slip Away" was ordered by request. Wendy breathed a deep sigh, before she spoke. "Ced"

"Yes honey." He responded.

"I'm pregnant." She said. Cedric raised her hand to his lips and kissed it. He was instantly filled with tremendous emotions. The news of Wendy carrying their first born filled his heart with jubilation. He looked into Wendy's eyes while trying to stay focused on the highway. "Are you sure, when did you realize, you were pregnant?' He asked.

She murmured, "Just a day or so."

He kissed her hand again saying, "Oh, honey I'm so happy . . . I love you so much." In another ten minutes Wendy had dozed off to sleep relaxed, tied from the week's activities. Cedric drove in the silence. His mind began to ramble . . . . He understood his responsibility to his unborn child as well as to Wendy and the twins. He knew that changing the social and family personality and the Newsome's thinking would start with him, through the model he'd offer in his marriage and example of fathering his children. Killing Big Tom's Ghost would be tough. Big Tom's Ghost had followed the men and women in the Newsome's family for several generations. He knew he had the unique opportunity to start a new generation of Newsome men and women, independent of sexual infidelity, promiscuity and of measuring their value as human beings through fathering and mothering of children; children who wasn't invited to heal from the scars passed on by Big Tom's frightful experience while under the charge of his captors. Cedric knew he had the fiber to meet the challenge. He could visualize himself as the head of the new generation of Newsomes. A tear squeezed out of the corner of his eye, but it wasn't a product of sadness, it was the essence of a great joy. "Big Tom had laid the foundation, left his mark, symbols, indicators, and the road map to manhood. He'd been shaped and molded into a breeder because of the place and time of his life, and his legacy which proceeded had polluted the minds of his prodigy.

Cedric had arrived. He'd reached the exodus of manhood. He knew who he was and what he stood for . . . with a set of unchanging morals and principals. Through self-sufficiency, an examination of himself and his family's socialization and with challenging himself he'd evolved, grown, matured . . . found a new way toward manhood. He'd shaped a new character as an individual, mastered his will, acquired discipline over his desires and could direct his own life and lay the foundation for his prodigy. He'd become the keeper of the garden. He wouldn't violate the covenant of his marriage nor deceive or mislead his off-spring. His choices would not be dictated by the change of season, trends, or sexual desire for women other than his wife. He'd be ruled by his belief in God, his commitment, intelligence, and rationality. He would work to build a solid moral and economic foundation for his children and their children. He knew that each generation must prepare for the coming of the next.

As he crossed into Durham County, he glanced over toward Wendy, his wife, his love that would be mother of the new generation of Newsomes. Perhaps she carried his son . . . . A son he'd train and nurture to measure his manhood through a standard of morals and principals founded in fairness, justice and a responsibility greater than himself . . . . being thoroughly cleansed of the dreadfulness grown from granddaddy Tom's life as a slave.